FATES

and

FURIES

04374008

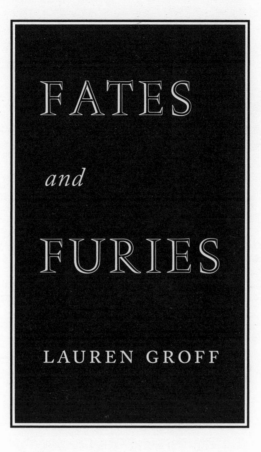

FATES

and

FURIES

LAUREN GROFF

125 YEARS

WILLIAM HEINEMANN: LONDON

1 3 5 7 9 10 8 6 4 2

William Heinemann
20 Vauxhall Bridge Road
London SW1V 2SA

William Heinemann is part of the Penguin Random House group of companies
whose addresses can be found at global.penguinrandomhouse.com.

First published in Great Britain by William Heinemann in 2015
(First published in the United States by Riverhead Books, an imprint of
Penguin Random House LLC in 2015)

www.randomhouse.co.uk

A CIP catalogue record for this book is available from the British Library.

ISBN 9781785150142 (Hardback)
ISBN 9781785150159 (Trade Paperback)

Book design by Gretchen Achilles

Printed and bound by Clays Ltd, St Ives Plc

Penguin Random House is committed to a sustainable future for our
business, our readers and our planet. This book is made from Forest
Stewardship Council® certified paper.

For Clay

[Of course]

FATES

A THICK DRIZZLE FROM THE SKY, like a curtain's sudden sweeping. The seabirds stopped their tuning, the ocean went mute. Houselights over the water dimmed to gray.

Two people were coming up the beach. She was fair and sharp in a green bikini, though it was May in Maine and cold. He was tall, vivid; a light flickered in him that caught the eye and held it. Their names were Lotto and Mathilde.

For a minute they watched a tide pool full of spiny creatures that sent up curls of sand in vanishing. Then he took her face in his hands, kissed her pale lips. He could die right now of happiness. In a vision, he saw the sea rising up to suck them in, tonguing off their flesh and rolling their bones over its coral molars in the deep. If she was beside him, he thought, he would float out singing.

Well, he was young, twenty-two, and they had been married that morning in secret. Extravagance, under the circumstances, could be forgiven.

Her fingers down the back of his trunks seared his skin. She pushed him backward, walking him up a dune covered in beach-pea stalks, down again to where the wall of sand blocked the wind, where they felt warmer. Under the bikini top, her gooseflesh had taken on a lunar blue, and her nipples in the cold turned inward. On their knees now, though the sand was rough and hurt. It didn't matter. They were reduced to mouths and hands. He swept her legs to his hips, pressed her down, blanketed her with his heat until she stopped shivering, made a dune of his back. Her raw knees were raised to the sky.

He longed for something wordless and potent: what? To wear her. He imagined living in her warmth forever. People in his life had fallen away from him one by one like dominoes; every movement pinned her further so that she could not abandon him. He imagined a lifetime of screwing on the beach until they were one of those ancient pairs speed-walking in the morning, skin like lacquered walnut meat. Even old, he would waltz her into the dunes and have his way with her sexy frail bird bones, the plastic hips, the bionic knee. Drone lifeguards looming up in the sky, flashing their lights, booming *Fornicators! Fornicators!* to roust them guiltily out. This, for eternity. He closed his eyes and wished. Her eyelashes on his cheek, her thighs on his waist, the first consummation of this terrifying thing they'd done. Marriage meant forever.

[He'd planned for a proper bed, a sense of ceremony: he'd stolen his roommate Samuel's beach house, having spent most summers there since he was fifteen, knowing that they hid the key under the hawksbill turtle carapace in the garden. A house of tartan and Liberty print and Fiestaware, thick with dust; the guest room with the light-house's triple blink in the night, the craggy beach below. This was what Lotto had imagined for the first time with this gorgeous girl he'd magicked into wife. But Mathilde was right to agitate for plein-air consummation. She was always right. He would know this soon enough.]

It was over too quickly. When she shouted, the gulls hidden by the dune buckshot the low clouds. Later, she'd show him the abrasion against her eighth vertebra from a mussel shell when he dug her in and dug her in. They were pressed so close that when they laughed, his laugh rose from her belly, hers from his throat. He kissed her cheek-bones, her clavicle, the pale of her wrist with its rootlike blue veins.

His terrible hunger he'd thought would be sated was not. The end apparent in the beginning.

"My wife," he said. "Mine." Perhaps instead of wearing her, he could swallow her whole.

"Oh?" she said. "Right. Because I'm chattel. Because my royal family traded me for three mules and a bucket of butter."

"I love your butter bucket," he said. "*My* butter bucket now. So salty. So sweet."

"Stop," she said. She'd lost her smile, so shy and constant that he was startled to see her up close without it. "Nobody belongs to anybody. We've done something bigger. It's new."

He looked at her thoughtfully, gently bit the tip of her nose. He had loved her with all his might these two weeks and, in so loving, had considered her transparent, a plate of glass. He could see through to the goodness at her quick. But glass is fragile, he would have to be careful. "You're right," he said; thinking, No, thinking how deeply they belonged. How surely.

Between his skin and hers, there was the smallest of spaces, barely enough for air, for this slick of sweat now chilling. Even still, a third person, their marriage, had slid in.

2

THEY CLIMBED ACROSS THE ROCKS toward the house they'd left bright in the dusk.

A unity, marriage, made of discrete parts. Lotto was loud and full of light; Mathilde, quiet, watchful. Easy to believe that his was the better half, the one that set the tone. It's true that everything he'd lived so far had steadily built toward Mathilde. That if his life had not prepared him for the moment she walked in, there would have been no *them*.

The drizzle thickened to drops. They hurried across the last stretch of beach.

[Suspend them there, in the mind's eye: skinny, young, coming through dark toward warmth, flying over the cold sand and stone. We will return to them. For now, he's the one we can't look away from. He is the shining one.]

LOTTO LOVED THE STORY. He'd been born, he'd always say, in the calm eye of a hurricane.

[From the first, a wicked sense of timing.]

His mother was beautiful then, and his father was still alive. Summer, late sixties. Hamlin, Florida. The plantation house so new there were tags on the furniture. The shutters hadn't been screwed down and made a terrific din in the wild first passage of the storm.

Now, briefly, sun. Rain dripped off the sour-orange trees. In the pause, the bottling plant roared five acres across his family's scrubland. In the hallway, two housemaids, the cook, a landscaper, and the plant's foreman pressed their ears to the wooden door. Inside the room, Antoinette was aswim in white sheets and enormous Gawain held his wife's hot head. Lotto's aunt Sallie crouched to catch the baby.

Lotto made his entrance: goblinesque with long limbs, huge hands and feet, lungs exceeding strong. Gawain held him to the light in the window. The wind was rising again, live oaks conducting the storm with mossy arms. Gawain wept. He'd hit his apex. "Gawain Junior," he said.

But Antoinette had done all the work, after all, and already the heat she'd felt for her husband was half diverted into her son. "No," she said. She thought of a date with Gawain, the maroon velvet in the theater and *Camelot* on screen. "Lancelot," she said. Her men would be knight-themed. She was not without humor of her own.

Before the storm hit again, the doctor arrived to sew Antoinette back together. Sallie swabbed the baby's skin with olive oil. She felt as if she were holding her own beating heart in her hands. "Lancelot," she whispered. "What a name. You'll be beat up for sure. But don't you fret. I'll make sure you're Lotto." And because she could move behind wallpaper like the mouse she resembled, Lotto is what they called him.

THE BABY WAS EXIGENT. Antoinette's body was blasted, breasts chewed up. Nursing was not a success. But as soon as Lotto began to smile and she saw he was her tiny image with her dimples and charm, she forgave him. A relief, to find her own beauty there. Her husband's family were not a lovely people, descendants of every kind of Floridian from original Timucua through Spanish and Scot and escaped slave and Seminole and carpetbagger; mostly they bore the look of over-cooked Cracker. Sallie was sharp-faced, bony. Gawain was hairy and huge and silent; it was a joke in Hamlin that he was only half human, the spawn of a bear that had waylaid his mother on her way to the out-house. Antoinette had historically gone for the smooth and pomaded, the suave steppers, the loudly moneyed, but a year married, she found herself still so stirred by her husband that when he came in at night she followed him full-clothed into the shower as if in a trance.

Antoinette had been raised in a saltbox on the New Hampshire coast: five younger sisters, a draft so dreadful in the winter that she thought she'd die before she got her clothes on in the morning. Draw-ers of saved buttons and dead batteries. Baked potatoes six meals in a row. She'd had a full ride to Smith but couldn't get off the train. A magazine on the seat beside hers had opened to Florida, trees dripping golden fruit, sun, luxe. Heat. Women in fishtails undulating in mot-tled green. It was ordained. She went to the end of the line, the end of her cash, hitched to Weeki Wachee. When she entered the man-ager's office, he took in her waist-length red-gold hair, her switchback curves, murmured, *Yes*.

The paradox of being a mermaid: the lazier she looks, the harder the mermaid works. Antoinette smiled languorously and dazzled. Manatees brushed her; bluegills nibbled at her hair. But the water was a chilly seventy-four degrees, the current strong, the calibration of air in the lungs exact to regulate buoyancy or sinking. The tunnel the mermaids swam down to reach the theater was black and long and sometimes caught their hair and held them there by the scalp. She couldn't see the audience but felt the weight of their eyes through the glass. She turned on the heat for the invisible watchers; she made them believe. But sometimes, as she grinned, she thought of sirens as she knew them: not this sappy Little Mermaid she was pretending to be, but the one who gave up her tongue and song and tail and home to be immortal. The one who'd sing a ship full of men onto the rocks and watch, ferocious, while they fell lax into the deep.

Of course, she went to the bungalows when summoned. She met television actors and comics and baseball players and even that swivel-hipped singer once, during the years he'd made himself over into a film star. They made promises, but not one made good. No jets would be sent for her. No tête-à-têtes with directors. She would not be installed in a house in Beverly Hills. She passed into her thirties. Thirty-two. Thirty-five. She could not be a starlet, she understood, blowing out the candles. All she had ahead of her was the cold water, the slow ballet.

Then Sallie walked into the theater set under the water. She was seventeen, sun-scorched. She'd run away; she wanted life! Something more than her silent brother who spent eighteen hours a day at his bottling plant and came home to sleep. But the mermaids' manager just laughed at her. So skinny, she was more eel than nixie. She crossed her arms and sat down on his floor. He offered her the hot dog concession to get her up. And then she came into the darkened amphitheater and stood dumbstruck at the glinting glass, where Antoinette was in mid-performance in a red bikini top and tail. She took up all the light.

Sallie's fervent attention dilated down to the size of the woman in the window and there it would stay, fixed, for good.

She made herself indispensable. She sewed sequined posing tails, learned to use a respirator to scrape algae from the spring side of the glass. One day a year later, when Antoinette was sitting slumped in the tube room, rolling the sodden tail off her legs, Sallie edged near. She handed Antoinette a flyer for Disney's new park in Orlando. "You're Cinderella," she whispered.

Antoinette had never felt so understood in her life. "I am," she said.

She was. She was fitted into the satin dress with hoops beneath, the zirconium tiara. She had an apartment in an orange grove, a new

9

roommate, Sallie. Antoinette was lying in the sun on the balcony in a black bikini and slash of red lipstick when Gawain came up the stairs carrying the family rocking chair.

He filled the doorway: six-foot-eight, so hairy his beard extended into his haircut, so lonely that women could taste it in his wake when he passed. He'd been thought slow, yet when his parents died in a car crash when he was twenty, leaving him with a seven-year-old sister, he was the only one to understand the value of the family's land. He used their savings as down payment to build a plant to bottle the clean, cold water from the family's source. Selling Florida's birthright back to its owners was borderline immoral, perhaps, but the American way to make money. He accumulated wealth, spent none. When his hunger for a wife got too intense, he'd built the plantation house with vast white Corinthian columns all around. Wives loved big columns, he'd heard. He waited. No wives came.

Then his sister called to demand he bring family bits and bobs up to her new apartment, and here he was, forgetting how to breathe when he saw Antoinette, curvy and pale. She could be forgiven for not understanding what she was seeing. Poor Gawain, his mat of hair, his filthy work clothes. She smiled and lay back to be adored again by the sun.

Sallie looked at her friend, her brother; felt the pieces snap together. She said, "Gawain, this is Antoinette. Antoinette, this is my brother. He's got a few million in the bank." Antoinette rose to her feet, floated across the room, set her sunglasses atop her head. Gawain was close enough to see her pupil swallow her iris, then himself reflected in the black.

The wedding was hasty. Antoinette's mermaids sat glinting in tails on the steps of the church, throwing handfuls of fish food at the newlyweds. Sour Yankees bore the heat. Sallie had sculpted a cake topper in marzipan of her brother lifting a supine Antoinette on one arm, the adagio, grand finale of the mermaid shows. Within a week, furniture for the house was ordered, help arranged for, bulldozers gouging out dirt for the pool. Her comfort secured, Antoinette had no more imagination for how she'd spend the money; everything else was catalog quality, good enough for her.

Antoinette took the comfort as her due; she hadn't expected the love. Gawain surprised her with his clarity and gentleness. She took him in hand. When she shaved away all that hair, she found a sensitive face, a kind mouth. With the horn-rimmed glasses she'd bought him, in bespoke suits, he was distinguished if not handsome. He smiled at her across the room, transformed. At that moment, the flicker in her leapt into flame.

Ten months later came the hurricane, the baby.

IT WAS TAKEN FOR GRANTED by this trio of adults that Lotto was special. Golden.

Gawain poured into him all the love he'd swallowed back for so long. Baby as a lump of flesh molded out of hope. Called dumb his whole life, Gawain held his son and felt the weight of genius in his arms.

Sallie, for her part, steadied the household. She hired the nannies and fired them for not being her. She chewed up banana and avocado when the baby began to eat food, and put them into his mouth as if he were a chick.

And as soon as Antoinette received the reciprocal smile, she turned her energies to Lotto. She played Beethoven on the hi-fi as loudly as it would go, shouting out musical terms she'd read about. She took correspondence courses on Early American furniture, Greek myth, linguistics, and read him her papers in their entirety. Perhaps this pea-smeared child in his high chair got only a twelfth of her ideas, she thought, but no one knew how much stuck in child brains. If he was going to be a great man, which he was, she was certain, she would start his greatness now.

Lotto's formidable memory revealed itself when he was two years old, and Antoinette was gratified. [Dark gift; it would make him easy in all things, but lazy.] One night Sallie read him a children's poem before bed, and in the morning, he came down to the breakfast room and stood on a chair and bellowed it out. Gawain applauded in astonishment, and Sallie wiped her eyes on a curtain. "Bravo," Antoinette said coolly, and held up her cup for more coffee, masking the tremble in her hand. Sallie read longer poems at night; the boy nailed them by morning. A certainty grew in him with each success, a sense of an invisible staircase being scaled. When watermen came to the plantation with their wives for long weekends, Lotto snuck downstairs, crawled in the dark under the guest dinner table. In the cavern there, he saw feet bulging out of the tops of the men's moccasins, the damp pastel seashells of the women's panties. He came up shouting Kipling's "If—" to a roaring ovation. The pleasure of these strangers' applause was punctured by Antoinette's thin smile, her soft "Go to bed, Lancelot," in lieu of praise. He stopped trying hard when she praised him, she had noticed. Puritans understand the value of delayed gratification.

IN THE HUMID STINK of Central Florida, wild long-legged birds and fruit plucked from the trees, Lotto grew. From the time he could walk, his mornings were with Antoinette, his afternoons spent wandering the sandy scrub, the cold springs gurgling up out of the ground, the swamps with the alligators eyeing him from the reeds. Lotto was a tiny adult, articulate, sunny. His mother kept him out of school an extra year, and until first grade, he knew no other children, as Antoinette was too good for the little town; the foreman's daughters were knobby and wild and she knew where that would lead, no thank you. There were people in the house to silently serve him: if he threw a towel on the ground, someone would pick it up; if he wanted food at two in the morning, it would arrive as if by magic. Everyone worked to please, and Lotto, having no other models, pleased as well. He brushed Antoinette's hair, let Sallie carry him even when he was almost her size, sat silently next to Gawain in his office all afternoon, soothed by his father's calm goodness, the way once in a while he'd let his humor flare like a sunburst and leave them all blinking. His father was made happy just by remembering Lotto existed.

One night when he was four, Antoinette took him from his bed. In the kitchen, she put cocoa powder in a cup but forgot to add the liquid. He ate the powder with a fork, licking and dipping. They sat in the dark. For a year, Antoinette had neglected her correspondence courses in favor of a preacher on television who looked like Styrofoam a child had carved into a bust and painted with watercolors. The preacher's wife wore permanent eyeliner, her hair in elaborate cathedrals that Antoinette copied. Antoinette sent away for proselytizing tapes and listened to them with huge earphones and an 8-track beside the pool. Afterward, she'd write giant checks that Sallie would burn in the sink. "Darling," Antoinette whispered that night to Lotto. "We are here to save your soul. Do you know what'll happen to nonbelievers like your father and your aunt when Judgment Day comes?" She didn't wait for the answer. Oh, she had tried to show Gawain and Sallie the light. She was desperate to share heaven with them, but they only smiled shyly and backed away. She and her son would watch in sorrow from their seats in the clouds as the other two burned below for eternity. Lotto was the one she *must* save. She lit a match and began to read Revelation in a hushed and tremulous voice. When the match went out, she lit another, kept reading. Lotto watched the fire eat down the slender wooden sticks. As the flame neared his mother's fingers, he felt the heat in his own as if he were the one being burned. [Darkness, trumpets, sea creatures, dragons, angels, horsemen, many-eyed monsters; these would fill his dreams for decades.] He watched his mother's beautiful lips move, her eyes lost in their sockets. He woke in the morning with the conviction that he was being watched, judged at all times. Church all day long. He made innocent faces when he thought bad thoughts. Even when he was alone, he performed.

LOTTO WOULD HAVE BEEN BRIGHT, ordinary, if his years continued so. One more privileged kid with his regular kid sorrows.

But the day came when Gawain took his daily three-thirty break from work and walked up the long green lawn toward the house. His wife was asleep by the deep end of the pool, her mouth open and palms facing the sun. He put a sheet gently over her body to keep her from burning, kissed her on the pulse of her wrist. In the kitchen, Sallie was pulling cookies from the oven. Gawain went around the house, plucked a loquat, rolled the sour fruit in his mouth, and sat on the pump beside the wild roselles, looking down the dirt lane until at last there was his boy, a gnat, housefly, mantis on his bicycle. It was the last day of seventh grade. The summer was a broad, slow river before Lotto. There would be rerun orgies, the originals he'd missed because of school: *The Dukes of Hazzard*; *Happy Days*. There would be gigging for frogs in the lakes at midnight. The boy's gladness filled the lane with light. The fact of his son moved Gawain, but the actual person was a miracle, big and funny and beautiful, better than the people who made him.

But all at once, the world contracted around his boy. Astonishing. It seemed to Gawain that everything was imbued with such searing clarity that he could see to the very atoms.

Lotto got off his bike when he saw his father on the old pump, apparently napping. Odd. Gawain never slept during the day. The boy stood still. A woodpecker clattered against a magnolia. An anole darted over his father's foot. Lotto dropped the bike and ran, and held Gawain's face and said his father's name so loudly that he looked up to see his mother running, this woman who never ran, a screaming white swiftness like a diving bird.

THE WORLD REVEALED ITSELF AS IT WAS. Threatened from below with darkness.

Lotto had once watched a sinkhole open suddenly and swallow the old family outhouse. Everywhere: sinkholes.

He would be hurrying down the sandy lanes between the pecan trees and simultaneously feel terror that the ground would break beneath his feet and he'd go tumbling into the darkness, and that it would not. The old pleasures had been sapped of color. The sixteen-foot alligator in the swamp he'd stolen whole frozen chickens from the freezer to feed was now just a lizard. The bottling plant just another big machine.

The town watched the widow retch into the azaleas, her handsome son patting her on the back. Same high cheekbones, red-gold hair. Beauty puts a fine point on grief, shoots bull's-eye into the heart. Hamlin cried for the widow and her boy, not for massive Gawain, their native son.

But it wasn't only grief that made her vomit. Antoinette was pregnant again, prescribed bed rest. For months, the town watched suitors come out in their fancy cars and black suits and briefcases, and speculated which she'd choose. Who wouldn't want to marry a widow so rich and lovely?

Lotto was sinking. He tried to torpedo school, but the teachers were used to considering him excellent and would not comply. He tried to sit with his mother and listen to her religious programs, holding her swollen hand, but God had soured in him. He retained only the rudiments: the stories, the moral rigidity, the mania for purity.

Antoinette kissed his palm and let him go, placid as a sea cow in her bed. Her emotions had gone underground. She watched every-thing from a tremendous remove. She grew plump, plumper. Finally, like a great fruit, she split. Baby Rachel, the pip, fell out.

When Rachel woke in the night, Lotto got to her first, settled in the chair, and fed her formula, rocking. She got him through that first year, his sister, who was hungry, whom he could feed.

His face had broken out in cystic acne, hot and pulsing under the skin; he was no longer a beautiful boy. It didn't matter. Girls were falling over themselves to kiss him now, in pity or because he was rich. In the soft, silty mouths of girls, grape gum and hot tongue, he concentrated and was able to dissolve the horror that had settled on him. Make-out parties in rec rooms, in parks at night. He biked home in the Florida dark, pumping his legs as fast as he could as if to outpace his sadness, but the sadness was always swifter, easily over-took him again.

A year and a day after Gawain died, fourteen-year-old Lotto came to the breakfast room in the dawn. He was going to take a handful of hard-boiled eggs to eat on his bike ride into town, where Trixie Dean was waiting, her parents away for the weekend. He had a bottle of WD-40 in his pocket. Lube, the boys at school had told him, was important.

From the dark, his mother's voice said, "Darling. I have news." He startled and turned on the light to see her in a black suit at the far end of the table, her hair upswept, crowning her head in flames.

Poor Muvva, he thought. So undone. So fat. She thought the painkillers she didn't stop taking after Rachel was born were her se-cret. They were not.

Hours later, Lotto stood on the beach, blinking. The men with the briefcases had not been suitors, but attorneys. It was all gone. The servants had vanished. Who would do the work? The plantation house, his childhood, the bottling plant, the pool, Hamlin where his ancestors had lived forever, gone. His father's ghost, gone. Traded for an obscene amount of money. The area was nice, Crescent Beach, but this house was tiny, pink, set on stilts above the dunes like a concrete Lego box on pilings. Beneath, all was palmetto tangle and pelicans canting in the hot, salted wind. This was a beach one could drive on. The pickups blaring thrash metal were hidden by the dunes, but in the house they could hear them.

"This?" he said. "You could've bought miles of beach, Muvva. Why are we in this dinky little box? Why *here*?"

"Cheap. Foreclosure. That money's not for me, darling," his mother said. "It's yours and your sister's. It's all in trust for you." A martyr's smile.

But what did he care about money? He hated it. [All his life, he'd avoid thinking of it, leaving the worry to others, assuming he'd have enough.] Money wasn't his father, his father's land.

"Betrayal," Lotto said, weeping in fury.

His mother took his face in her hands, trying not to touch the pimples. "No, darling," she said. Her smile was radiant. "Freedom."

LOTTO SULKED. He sat alone on the sand. He poked dead jellyfish with sticks. He drank slushies outside the convenience store down on A1A.

And then he went for a taco at the stand where the cool kids ate lunches, this mini-yuppie in his polo shirts and madras shorts and docksiders, although this was a place where girls wore bikini tops to stores and boys left their shirts at home to bronze their muscles. He was six feet tall already, fourteen tipping into fifteen at the end of July. [A Leo, which explains him entirely.] All raw elbows and knees, his hair tufted in the back. The poor blasted acned skin. Bewildered, blinking, half orphaned; one longed to hold him to one's body to soothe him. A few girls had been attracted, had asked his name, but he was too overwhelmed to be interesting, and they abandoned him.

He ate all by himself at a picnic table. A fleck of cilantro remained on his lips, which made a sleek-looking Asian boy laugh. Beside the Asian boy sat a wild-haired girl with slashes of eyeliner, red lipstick, a safety pin over her eyebrow, a fake emerald glittering in her nose. She was staring at him so intently Lotto felt his feet begin to tingle. She'd be good at sex, he understood, without knowing how. Beside the girl was a fat boy with glasses and a sly expression, the girl's twin. The Asian boy was Michael; the intense girl was Gwennie. The fat boy would be the most important. His name was Chollie.

That day there was another Lancelot at the taco shack, this one called Lance. What were the odds? Lance was scrawny, pale due to a lack of vegetables, feigned a hitch in his walk, wore a hat sideways and a T-shirt so long that it bagged over the backs of his knees. He went beatboxing to the bathroom, and when he came back, he brought a stench with him. The boy behind him kicked his shirt and out fell a tiny poop.

Someone yelled, "Lance shat his shirt!" And this went around for a while until someone else remembered that there was another Lancelot, this one vulnerable, new, weird-looking, and Lotto was being asked, "Rookie, did we scare you shitless?" and "What's your full name? Sir Luvsalot?" He slouched miserably. He left the food, trudged off. The twins and Michael caught up to him under a date palm. "That a real Polo?" Chollie asked, fingering the sleeve of his shirt. "Those things cost eighty bucks retail." "Choll," Gwennie said. "Stop with the consumerism." Lotto said, shrugging, "A knockoff, I think," though it clearly wasn't. They looked at him for a long moment. "Interesting," Chollie said. "He's cute," Michael said. They looked at Gwennie, who narrowed her eyes at Lotto until they were mascara-clotted slits. "Oh, fine," she sighed. "We can keep him, I guess." There was a dimple in her cheek when she smiled.

They were a little older, going into eleventh grade. They knew things he didn't. He began to live for the sand, the beer, the drugs; he stole his mother's painkillers to share. His sorrow for losing his father went vague during the day, though at night he still woke weeping. His birthday came, and he opened a card to find a weekly allowance that was stupid for a fifteen-year-old. Summer stretched long into the school year, ninth grade, a cakewalk with his memory. The beach was the constant from after school to night.

"Huff this," the friends said. "Smoke this." He huffed, he smoked, he forgot for a little while.

Gwennie was the most interesting of the three new friends. There was something broken in her, though nobody would tell him what. She'd walk through four lanes of traffic; she'd shove whipped cream cans into her backpack at the QuickieStop. She seemed feral to him, though the twins lived in a ranch house, had two parents, and Gwennie was taking three AP classes as a junior. Gwennie longed for Michael, and Michael put his hands on Lotto's knees when the others weren't looking, and Lotto dreamt at night of taking off Gwennie's clothes and making her jiggle; once, late at night, he took her cold hand and she let him hold it for a moment before he squeezed it and let it go. Lotto sometimes imagined them all as if from a bird's hover in the sky: round and round, they chased one another, only Chollie separate, gloomily watching the others' endless circles, rarely trying to edge himself in.

"You know," Chollie said to Lotto once, "I don't think I've ever had a real friend before you." They were in the arcade, playing video games and talking philosophy, Chollie from a bunch of tapes he'd gotten at the Salvation Army, Lotto from a ninth-grade textbook he could summon and quote without understanding. Lotto looked over and saw Pac-Man reflected in the grease blooms on Chollie's forehead and chin. The other boy shoved his glasses up his nose, looking away. Lotto felt tender. "I like you, too," he said, and he didn't know it was true until he'd said the words aloud: Chollie, with his uncouthness, his loneliness, his innocent money hunger, reminded him of his father.

Lotto's wild life was sustainable only into October. A small hand-ful of months, to change so much.

This would be the pivot: late afternoon, Saturday. They'd been on the beach since morning. Chollie and Gwennie and Michael asleep on the red blanket. Sunburnt, salted by ocean, beer souring their mouths. Pipers, pelicans, an angler down the beach hauling in a foot-long golden fish. Lotto watched for a long time until an image slowly gath-ered that he'd seen in a book: red sea with a stony pathway flicking out into it like a hummingbird's curled tongue. He picked up a shovel a child had left behind and began digging. Skin taut, as if coated in rubber glue; the burn was bad, but beneath, the muscles loved the movement. A strong body is a glory. The sea hissed and gurgled. Slowly, the other three awoke. Gwennie stood, *pop pop* of bikini flesh. Goodness, he would lick her crown to hallux. She looked at what he was doing. She understood. Tough girl, pierced, jailhouse-tattooed by her own pen and pins, but her eyes overflowed the liner. She knelt and bulldozed sand with her forearms. Chollie and Michael stole shovels from the beach cops' truck bed. Michael shook a bottle of speed he'd taken from his mother into his palm and they licked the pills up. They took turns digging, popping their jaws. Four troubled kids in early October, through twilight deep into dark. Moon rose blowsily, pissing white on water. Michael gathered driftwood, started a fire. Gritty sandwiches long in the past. Hands blistered to blood. They didn't care. For the most internal space, the beginning of the spiral, they flipped a lifeguard's chair on its side and buried it and packed the sand down hard on it. One by one, they guessed aloud about what Lotto had meant by this sculpture: nautilus, fiddlehead, galaxy. Thread running off its spindle. Forces of nature, perfect in beauty, perfectly ephemeral, they guessed. He was too shy to say *time*. He'd woken with a dry tongue and the urge to make the abstract concrete, to build his new understanding: that this was the way that time was, a spiral. He loved the uselessness of all the effort, the ephemerality of the work. The ocean encroached. It licked their feet. It pushed around the outside wall of the spiral, fingering its way in. When the water had scooped the sand from the lifeguard's chair, revealing white like bone beneath, something broke and the fragments spun into the future. [This day would bend back and shine itself into everything.]

THE VERY NEXT NIGHT IT ALL ENDED. Chollie, grandiose in his high, had leapt in the dark from the same lifeguard's chair, upright again. For a moment he'd been outlined against the full moon, but then he'd come down on his shin with a sickening crack. Michael had sped him to the hospital, leaving Gwennie and Lotto alone on the beach in the cold autumn wind and darkness. Gwennie took his hand. Lotto could feel the fizz in his skin—it was his moment—he was going to lose his virginity. She rode on his handlebars to a party in an abandoned house on the marsh. They drank beers, watching the older kids hook up around the enormous fire until, at last, Gwennie pulled Lotto through the house. Votives on the windowsills, mattresses with gleaming limbs, buttocks, hands. [Lust! Old story renewed in young flesh.] Gwennie opened a window and they climbed through and sat on the roof of the porch. Was she crying? Her eye shadow made scary dark jags on her cheekbones. She moved her mouth onto his, and he, who hadn't kissed a girl since he came to the beach, felt the familiar white-hot liquid move through his bones. The party was loud. She pushed him back on the sandy tar paper, and he was looking up at her face in the glow, and she lifted her skirt and moved the crotch of her underwear aside, and Lotto, who was always ready, who was ready at the most abstract imaginings of a girl—footprints of a sandpiper like a crotch, gallons of milk evoking boobs—was not ready at this oh-so-abrupt beginning. It didn't matter. Gwennie shoved him in though she was dry. He shut his eyes and thought of mangoes, split papayas, fruits tart and sweet and dripping with juice, and then it was off, and he groaned and his whole body turned sweet, and Gwennie looked down with a smile growing on her bitten lips, and she closed her eyes and went away from him, and the farther she went, the closer Lotto tried to come to her, as if he were chasing a nymph in the scrub. He remembered his furtive porn mags, rolled her over on her hands and knees, and she laughed over her shoulder at him, and he closed his eyes and pounded in and felt her arch her back like a cat, and buried his fingers in her hair, and this is when he noticed the flames licking out of the window. But he couldn't stop. Couldn't. Just hoped the house would hold until he was finished. Glorious, he was made to do this. There was cracking all around and a blistering sunlike heat, and Gwennie was shuddering beneath him, and one-two-three, he burst within her.

Then he was shouting in her ear that they had to go, go, go. He didn't tuck himself in, scooted to the edge of the roof, leapt into the sago palms below. Gwennie floated down to him, her skirt uppetaling like a tulip. They crawled out of the bushes, his ween hanging out of his fly, and were greeted by firemen sardonically applauding. "Nice work, Romeo," one said.

"Lancelot," he whispered.

"Call me Don Juan," a cop said, cranking handcuffs around Lotto's wrists, then Gwennie's. The ride was short. She wouldn't look at him. He would never see her again.

Then there was the cell with its filthy troll of a toilet in the corner, Lotto scrambling for splinters he could use as a shiv, the sputtering lightbulb that finally popped in a rain of glass at dawn.

HOME. Sallie's bleak face, Rachel resting on Lotto's chest, sucking her thumb. One year old and already clenched with anxiety. It had been decided: they had to get him away from those delinquents. Antoinette closed the door behind her, cracked her thumbs, picked up the phone.

Enough cash will grease any wheel. By afternoon, it was done. By evening, he was on a gangplank shuffling into a plane. He looked back. Sallie was holding Rachel, and both were bawling. Antoinette stood, arms akimbo. She wore a twisted look on her face. Anger, he thought. [Wrong.]

The hatch closed on Lotto, boy banished for his sins.

He would never remember the trip northward, only the shock. Waking in the morning to sun and Florida, going to bed that same day in cold New Hampshire gloom. A dormitory smelling of boys' feet. An ache of hunger in his gut.

At supper that evening in the dining hall, a wedge of pumpkin pie had smacked his forehead. He looked up to find the boys laughing at him. Someone yelled, *Aw, poor Punkin Pie.* Someone else said, *Poor Florida Pie*, and someone else said, *Bumblefuck Pie*, and this got the most laughs, so this was what they called him. He, who all his life had walked everywhere in the sultry heat as if he had owned the place [he'd owned the place], felt his shoulders press to his ears as he scuttled over the cold, hard ground. Bumblefuck Pie, a hick to these boys from Boston and New York. Zitty, the childhood loveliness vanished, too tall, too skinny. A Southerner, inferior. His wealth, which had once singled him out, unremarkable among the wealthy.

He woke before dawn and sat shivering at the edge of the bed, watching the window lighten. *DOOM-doom, DOOM-doom*, went his heart. The cafeteria with the cold pancakes and half-cooked eggs, the walk over frozen ground to the chapel.

He called every Sunday at six PM, but Sallie was not much for small talk, and Antoinette went nowhere these days and had little to report beyond her television programs, and Rachel was too tiny to put together sentences. His call was over in five minutes. A dark sea to swim until the next call. Nothing in New Hampshire was warm. Even the sky bore an amphibian chill. Lotto went to the hot tub by the pool as soon as the gym opened at five-thirty, trying to boil ice out of his bones. He'd float, imagining his friends smoking up in the sun. If he were near Gwennie, they'd already have exhausted every mode of intercourse he knew of, even the apocryphal. Only Chollie sent mail, though it was little more than jokes on pornographic postcards.

Lotto fantasized about the gym's beams, which were at least fifty feet high. A swan dive into the shallow end would put an end to it all. No, he'd climb to the top of the observatory, tie a rope around his neck, jump. No. He'd steal into the physical plant and take some of the white powders used to clean the bathrooms and eat them like ice cream until his innards frothed out. An element of the theatrical already in his imaginings. He wasn't allowed to come home for Thanksgiving, for Christmas. "Am I still being punished?" he asked. He tried to keep his voice manly, but it wobbled. "Oh, honey," Sallie said. "It's not punishment. Your mama wants you to have a better life." Better life? He was Bumblefuck Pie here; he didn't ever swear, so he couldn't even complain of his own nickname. His loneliness howled louder. All boys did sports, and he was forced to row in the novice eight and his hands grew blisters that grew calluses, their own shells.

THE DEAN SUMMONED HIM. He'd heard that Lancelot was troubled. His grades were perfect; he was no dummy. Was he unhappy? The dean's eyebrows were caterpillars that chew down apple trees overnight. Yes, Lotto said, he was unhappy. Hm, the dean said. Lotto was tall, smart, rich. [White.] Boys like him were meant to be leaders. Perhaps, the dean hazarded, if he bought facial soap, he might find a higher perch on the totem pole? He had a friend who could write a prescription; he searched for a notepad to write the number down. In the open drawer, Lotto caught a glimpse of the familiar oily gleam of a pistol. [Gawain's nightstand, leather holster.] It was all Lotto could see before him as he stumbled through his days afterward, that brief glimpse of gun, the weight he could feel in his hands.

IN FEBRUARY, the door of his English class opened and a toad in a red cape walked in. Grublike face. Pasty sheen, sparse hair. A round of snickers. The little man swirled the cape off his shoulders, wrote *Denton Thrasher* on the chalkboard. He shut his eyes, and when he opened them, his face was racked with pain, his arms extended as if holding something heavy.

> *Howl, howl, howl, howl!* he whispered. *O, you are men of stones:*
> *Had I your tongues and eyes, I'd use them so*
> *That heaven's vault should crack. She's gone for ever!*
> *I know when one is dead, and when one lives;*
> *She's dead as earth. Lend me a looking-glass;*
> *If that her breath will mist or stain the stone,*
> *Why, then she lives.*

Silence. No scoffing. The boys were still.

An unknown room in Lotto illuminated. Here, the answer to everything. You could leave yourself behind, transform into someone you weren't. You could strike the most frightening thing in the world—a roomful of boys—silent. Lotto had gone vague since his father died. In this moment, his sharpness snapped back.

The man heaved a sigh and became himself again. "Your teacher has been stricken with some disease. Pleurisy. Dropsy? I shall be taking his place. I am Denton Thrasher. Now," he said, "tell me, striplings, what are you reading?"

"*To Kill a Mockingbird*," Arnold Cabot whispered.

"Lord save us," Denton Thrasher said, and took the wastebasket and swept up and down the rows, tossing the boys' paperbacks in. "One mustn't concern oneself with lesser mortals when one has barely breached the Bard. Before I am through with you, you will be sweating Shakespeare. And they call this a fine education. The Japanese will be our imperial masters in twenty years." He sat on the edge of the desk, buttressing himself before the groin with his arms. "Firstly," he said, "tell me the difference between tragedy and comedy."

Francisco Rodríguez said, "Solemnity versus humor. Gravity versus lightness."

"False," Denton Thrasher said. "A trick. There's no difference. It's a question of perspective. Storytelling is a landscape, and tragedy is comedy is drama. It simply depends on how you frame what you're seeing. Look here," he said, and made his hands into a box, which he moved across the room until it settled on Jelly Roll, the sad boy whose neck gooped out over his collar. Denton swallowed what he was about to say, moved the box of his hands on to Samuel Harris, a quick, popular, brown boy, the cox of Lotto's boat, and said, "Tragedy." The boys laughed, Samuel loudest of all; his confidence was a wall of wind. Denton Thrasher moved the frame until it alighted with Lotto's face, and Lotto could see the man's beady eyes on him. "Comedy," he said. Lotto laughed with the others, not because he was a punch line, but because he was grateful to Denton Thrasher for revealing theater to him. The one way, Lotto had finally found, that he could live in this world.

HE WAS FALSTAFF IN THE SPRING PLAY; but out of makeup, his own miserable self slid back into him. "Bravo!" said Denton Thrasher in class when Lotto delivered a monologue from *Othello*, but Lotto only gave a half smile, returned to his seat. In rowing, his novice eight beat the varsity in practice and he was promoted to stroke, setting the rhythm. Still, all was drear, even when the buds tipped the trees and the birds returned.

In April, Sallie called, weeping. Lotto couldn't come home for the summer. "There are . . . dangers," she said, and he knew she meant his friends were still hanging around. He imagined Sallie seeing them walking up the highway, her hands of their own accord veering the car to smush them. Oh, he longed to hold his sister; she was growing, she wouldn't remember him. To taste Sallie's food. To smell his mother's perfume, to let her tell him in her dreamy voice about Moses or Job as if they were people she'd known. Please, please, he wouldn't even leave the house, he whispered, and Sallie had said, in consolation, that the three of them would come visit and they would all go to Boston in the summer. Florida had gone sun-bright in his mind. He felt he might go blind if he looked directly at it. His childhood was obscured in the blaze, impossible to see.

He hung up the phone, hopeless. Friendless. Abandoned. Hysterical with self-pity.

A plan solidified at dinner, after a food fight with mint brownies.

When it was dark, flowers on the trees like pale moths, Lotto went out.

The administrative building held the dean's office; the office held the drawer that held the gun. He pictured the dean opening the door in the morning to find the splatter, his shuddering backward step.

Sallie and his mother would explode from grief. Good! He wanted them to cry for the rest of their lives. He wanted them to die crying for what they'd done to him. He felt wobbly only when he thought of his sister. Oh, but she was so little. She wouldn't know what she'd lost.

The building was a lightless chunk. He felt for the door—unlocked—it slid open under his hand. Luck was on his side. [Someone was.] He couldn't risk turning on the lights. He felt along the wall: bulletin board, coat rack, bulletin board, door, wall, door, corner. The edge of a great black space that was the enormous hall. He saw it in his mind's eye as if it were daylit: double curved staircase at the far end. Second-floor catwalk lined with oils of fleshy white men. Antique boat hanging from the rafters. During the day, high clerestory windows shifted light one to the next. Tonight they were pits of dark.

He closed his eyes. He would walk bravely toward the end. He took one step, another. Loving the swishy feel of the carpet, the giddy blankness before him, he took three joyous running steps.

He was smacked in the face.

He'd fallen to his knees, was scrabbling on the carpet. Hit him again in the nose. He reached up but nothing was there; no, here it was again, and he fell back, felt the thing graze over him. His hands flailed, touched cloth. Cloth over wood, no, not wood, foam with a steel core, no, not foam, pudding with a tough skin? Felt down. Felt leather. Laces? Shoe? He was dabbed in the teeth.

He crabwalked backward, a high-pitched keening noise coming from somewhere, and moved wildly down the walls, and after an eternity found the light switch, and in the horrible bright found himself looking at the boat suspended from the ceiling, tipped down on one side, dangling the worst Christmas ornament ever. A boy. Dead boy. Blue-faced. Tongue out. Glasses cocked. In a moment came the recognition: oh, poor Jelly Roll, hanging from the bow ball of a sweep eight. He'd climbed up, tied the noose. Leapt. Mint brownie from dinner all over his shirt. The sound died out of Lotto's chest. He ran.

AFTER THE POLICE, the ambulance, came the dean. He brought Lotto doughnuts and a cup of cocoa. His eyebrows danced all over his face, chewing on lawsuits, copycat suicides, leaks to newspapers. He dropped Lotto at his dorm, but when the taillights winked away, Lotto came out again. He couldn't be near all the other boys, who were, just then, dreaming innocent anxiety dreams of girl bits and summer internships.

He found himself sitting in the auditorium on the stage when the chapel bell chimed three AM.

The long sweep of seats held the memory of bodies. He pulled out the joint he'd been intending to smoke just before he touched the barrel to his teeth.

Nothing made sense. There was an airy whistling off stage right. Denton Thrasher, sans glasses and in frayed plaid pajamas, crossed the stage, dopp kit in hand.

"Denton?" Lotto said.

The man peered into the shadows, clutching the bag to his chest. "Who's there?" he said.

"Nay, answer me: stand, and unfold yourself," Lotto said.

Denton padded upstage. "Oh, Lancelot. You startled the sap out of me." He gave a cough and said, "Do I scent the sultry waft of cannabis?"

Lotto put the joint into his outstretched fingers, and Denton took a drag.

"What are you doing in your pajamas?" Lotto said.

"The question is, my dear, what you are doing here." He sat next to Lotto, then said, with a sideways grin, "Or were you looking for me?"

"No," Lotto said.

"Oh," Denton said.

"But here you are," Lotto said.

When there was no more joint to smoke, Denton said, "Saving my pennies. Crashing in the costume room. I'm resigned to a destitute old age. It's not the worst. No bedbugs. And I like the constant bells."

On cue, the three-thirty bell chimed, and they laughed.

Lotto said, "Tonight I found a boy who hanged himself. Hung himself. Hanged himself."

Denton went still. "Oh, child," he said.

"I didn't really know him. They called him Jelly Roll."

"Harold," Denton said. "That boy. I tried to get him to talk to me, but he was so sad. You boys were terrible. Savages. Oh, not you, Lotto. I never meant you. I'm so sorry you had to be the one to find him."

Lotto's throat filled with something, and he saw himself swinging from the scull until the door opened, the light flicked on. It came over him that even had he crept up the stairs and found the dean's office unlocked and opened the drawer and felt the weight of the gun in his hand, something in him would have resisted. It would never have ended that way. [True. It was not his time.]

Denton Thrasher gathered Lotto in his arms and wiped his face with the hem of his pajama top, revealing a furry white belly, and Lotto was rocked on the edge of the stage, smelling witch hazel and Listerine and pajamas worn too many times between washes.

THIS LANCELOT CHILD in Denton's lap. So young, crying past the point of immediate sorrow into something deeper. It frightened Denton. Four o'clock. Sweet Lancelot, so talented, but this was a little much, even if Denton saw in him the rare spark. His looks were both promising and as if some essential promise had fled and left wreckage in its wake, which was odd, the boy being fifteen at most. Well, beauty could come back, perhaps. In ten years he might be ravishing, grow into his great goofy body, into his charm: already, there was the bigness of a real actor on the stage. Alas, Denton knew, the world was full of real actors. Christ, the bells of four-thirty, he was about to go out of his skull. Denton could not hold this sorrow. He was too weak. [Grief is for the strong, who use it as fuel for burning.] He thought, I'll be stuck here with this boy forever. He knew only one thing that could shut off this flow of tears, and in a panic, he pushed the child upright and scrabbled in his lap and took the surprised pale worm out of his jeans, and it grew impressively in his mouth, thank god, and this alone was enough to stop the sobs. Baton of youth! Youthfully swift, too. O, that this too too solid flesh was now melting, thawing, resolving itself into a spunky dew. Denton Thrasher wiped his mouth and sat up. What had he done? The boy's eyes vanished in shadow: "Going to bed," he whispered, and he ran down the aisles, through the doors, out. A shame, Denton thought. Dramatic, to be forced to flee in the night. He would miss this place. He would regret not watching Lancelot grow. He stood and took a bow. "Be blessed," he said to the great empty theater and went off to the costume room to pack.

SAMUEL HARRIS, up early for crew, was watching out the window when he saw poor Bumblefuck Pie run across the dark quad, weeping. Ever since the other boy had arrived halfway through the fall semester, he'd been so blue he was almost iridescent with sadness. Samuel was the cox of Bumblefuck's boat, practically nestled every day in his lap, and despite the fact that the other kid was kind of a pariah, Samuel worried about him, six-foot-three and only a hundred fifty pounds, frozen-looking, cheeks like slabs of beaten tenderloin. It seemed clear he was going to hurt himself. When Samuel heard Lotto rushing up the stairs, he opened his door and manhandled him into the room, fed him oatmeal cookies that his mother sent from home, and this way got the whole story. Oh god, Jelly Roll! Lotto said that after the police came, he'd sat in the theater for hours to calm down. He seemed to want to say something more, considered it, packed it away. Samuel wondered. He thought of what his father the senator would do, and drew a man's stern face over his own. He reached out a hand to Lotto's shoulder and patted him until he calmed. It felt as if they'd crossed a bridge a second before it collapsed.

For a month, Samuel watched Lotto drag himself around the campus. And when school let out, Samuel took the other boy with him to his summerhouse in Maine. There, with the senator father and Samuel's whippet mother, star debutante of Atlanta's highest black society, Lotto experienced sailboats and clambakes and friends in Lilly Pulitzer and Brooks Brothers knitwear, champagne, pies cooling on the windowsill, Labrador retrievers. Samuel's mother bought him facial soap and good clothes, made him eat and stand tall. He grew into himself. He found success with a forty-year-old cousin of Samuel's who cornered him in the boathouse; brown skin tasted the same as pinkish, Lotto learned to his delight. When they returned to school for sophomore year, Lotto had tanned so golden it was easy to overlook the zit scars on his cheeks. He was blonder, looser. He smiled, made jokes, learned to expand himself on the stage and off. By never swearing, he showed his cool. Near Christmas, Samuel's friend had become more popular than even Samuel was, he of the dust-devil confidence, of the shining great brown eyes, but it was too late to mind. Every time Samuel looked at his friend, all those many years of their friendship, he would see how he himself was a miracle worker, how he had brought Lotto back to life again.

THEN, just before Thanksgiving of sophomore year, Lotto, coming back to his room after math study one day, found Chollie, waxy and smelly, slumped in the hallway outside his door. "Gwennie," Chollie said, and groaned, folded himself in half. Lotto dragged him into the room. He got a garbled story; Gwennie had overdosed. She couldn't have died, dangerous Gwennie, vibrating with life. But she had. Chollie had found her. He'd run away. He had nowhere to go but to Lotto. The beige linoleum floor turned into the ocean, crashed and crashed against Lotto's shins. He sat down. How swiftly things spun. Two minutes ago, he'd been a kid, thinking about his Nintendo system, worried about asymptotes and sines. Now he was heavy, adult. Later, when the boys had calmed and they went for pizza in the little town,

Lotto said to Chollie what he'd wanted to say to Gwennie since the night of the fire: "I'll take care of you." He felt brave. Lotto let Chollie sleep in his bed for the rest of the term; he didn't mind the floor. [Through the rest of Lotto's high school, through college, Chollie would take the money Lotto would give him gladly, go out into the world, eventually return. He sat in on every class he could; he had no degrees, but he learned more than enough. If people didn't report Lotto, it was because they loved Lotto, not because they cared a whit about Chollie, who was a person only Lotto could stand.]

The world was precarious, Lotto had learned. People could be subtracted from it with swift bad math. If one might die at any moment, one must live!

Thus began the era of women. Trips to the city, sweating through polo shirts at the nightclubs, lines of coke on midcentury-modern coffee tables, parents out of town. *It's okay, man, don't freak, the house-keeper doesn't care.* Threeway with two girls in someone's bathroom. "Maybe you could come home this summer," Antoinette said. "Oh, *now* you want me," Lotto said sarcastically, refusing. Headmaster's daughter on the lacrosse field. Hickeys. Maine again, forty-one-year-old cousin at a seedy motel, neighbor girl in a hammock, tourist girl swimming out to the sailboat at night. Samuel rolling his eyes with envy. Volvo station wagon bought with Lotto's fat allowance. Three inches by September, six-foot-six. Othello in eponymous same, and a Desdemona from town, seventeen, shaved down there like a prepube, Lotto discovered. Spring; summer in Maine; autumn, Head of the Charles, the varsity eight placed. Thanksgiving at Samuel's New York house. Christmas, Sallie took him and Rachel to Montreal. "No Muvva?" he said, trying not to show his hurt. Sallie blushed. "She's ashamed of the way she looks," she said gently. "She's fat now, hush-puppy. She never leaves the house." Early admission to Vassar, the only school he applied to, overconfident; an excellent party there, a party to end all parties, no reason for his choice but that. Celebration with

Samuel's fifteen-year-old sister up for the weekend, in a handicapped bathroom. Never, never tell Samuel. Searing glare. What am I, an idiot? Surprise! Samuel was going to Vassar, too, had gotten in everywhere but would have died before he missed Lotto's fun. Only skinny Sallie and four-year-old Rachel, who wouldn't let him put her down, came up for his graduation. No Muvva. To offset the sadness, Lotto imagined his mother as the mermaid she'd once been, not the obese woman who'd swallowed her. In Maine, Samuel's forty-three-year-old cousin in Switzerland, alas. Samuel's sister in an orange bikini, with a mop-haired boyfriend mooning behind her, thank god. Only one girl that whole summer, adder-tongued ballerina: what she could do with her legs! Games of croquet. Fireworks. Keg on the beach. Sailing regatta.

Then it was the last week of the summer. Samuel's parents getting misty, untangling the new Labrador puppy from the table. "Our boys," the mother said at the lobster restaurant. "They're growing up." Boys, considering themselves grown-up lo! these four years, were kind to her and kept straight faces.

From the airless campus of the boys' prep school to the wonderland of college. Coed bathrooms: soapy breasts. Dining hall: girls tonguing soft-serve ice creams. Within two months, Lotto was called Master of the Hogs. Hoagmeister. It's not true that he had no standards, it's simply that he saw the stun in every woman. Earlobes like drupes. Soft golden down edging the temples. Such things outshone the less savory rest. Lotto imagined his life as an antipriest, devoting his soul to sex. He'd die an ancient satyr, a houseful of sleek nymphs gamboling him to the grave. What if his greatest gifts were the ones he employed in bed? [Delusion! Tall men have such miles of limbs that it strains the heart to pump blood to the nether bits. He charmed others into believing him better than he was.]

His roommates couldn't believe the parade of girls. Fleabitten women's studies major with nip rings; townie with a roll cresting out of her acid-washed jeans; neuroscience major, prim part, thick glasses, who specialized in the reverse cowgirl. The roommates would watch the trek through the common room, and when Lotto and the girl disappeared into his room, they would fetch the book they kept with taxonomies.

Australianopithecus: floppy-haired Aussie, later a famous jazz violinist.

Virago stridentica: ambiguously gendered punkette Lotto had picked up downtown.

Sirena ungulatica: valedictorian, velvety face atop a three-hundred-pound body.

The girls would never know. The roommates didn't think they were cruel. But when, two months in, they showed the book to Lotto, he was furious. He bellowed, called them misogynists. They shrugged. Women who screwed deserved the scorn they got. Lotto was doing what men do. They didn't make up the rules.

Lotto never brought home the men. They didn't get put in any book. They remained unseen, these ghosts of hungers in his bed, out of it.

IT WAS THE LAST NIGHT of Lotto's college play. *Hamlet.* The theatergoers who came in after the circuit of the cowbell were soaked; clouds that had oppressed the valley all day had split. Ophelia was played naked, her tremendous boobs blue-veined like Stilton cheeses. Hamlet was Lotto and vice versa. Every performance, he'd gotten a standing ovation.

In the dark wings, he cracked his neck and took a breath into his stomach. Someone was sobbing, someone lit a cigarette. Shuffling of a barn at dusk. Whispers. *Yeah, I got a job in banking . . . She stood upon the balcony, inimically mimicking him hiccupping while amicably welcoming him in . . . Break a leg. Break both!*

35

Reverberating hush. Curtain opened. Watchmen clomped out. "Who's there?" Inside Lotto the switch flipped on, and his life receded. Relief.

Husk of Lotto watched in the wings as he, Hamlet, sauntered on.

He came to himself again when his doublet was sweat-soaked and he was bowing, and the noise of the audience rose until his final standing ovation. Professor Murgatroyd in the front row, supported between his lover and his lover's lover, shouting in his Victorian bluestocking's voice, "Bravo, bravo." Armful of flowers. Girls he'd slept with, one after the other, hugging him, oily slicks of lip gloss on his tongue. Who's this? Bridget with the spaniel's face, oh dear, clutching him. They'd hooked up, what, two times? [Eight.] He'd heard she was calling herself his girlfriend, poor thing. "See you at the party, Bridge," he said gently, extricating himself. The audience faded into the rain. Ophelia squeezed his arm. See him later? He'd enjoyed the two times they'd met up in the handicapped bathroom during rehearsals. Indeed, he *would* be seeing her, he murmured, and she carried her mad-girl's body away.

He closed himself into a bathroom stall. The building emptied out, front doors locked. When he emerged, the dressing rooms were swept. All was dark. He took his greasepaint off slowly, watching himself in the low wattage. He reapplied foundation, smoothing the pits in his face, and left the eyeliner on, liking how vivid it made his blue. It was good to be the last person in this sacred place. Anywhere else, he hated being left with himself. But tonight, the last glory of his youth, everything he'd lived so far filled him up: his steaming lost Florida, the ache where his father had been, his mother's fervent belief in him, God who watched, the gorgeous bodies he'd temporarily forgotten himself inside. He let it all wash over him in waves. He took the blaze of feeling through the dark rain toward the cast party, which he could hear from a half mile away, and walked in to applause, someone putting a beer in his hand. Minutes or aeons later, he stood on a window ledge while the world behind him flashed with lightning.

Trees turned to sparked neurons in silhouette. The campus quick ember, slow ash.

At his feet the party roiled with cutting-edge early nineties fashions, midriffs and piercings and ball caps to hide receding hairlines, teeth empurpled by the black light, brown lipstick with brown liner and cartilage cuffs and biker boots and exposed boxers and bump and grind and Salt-N-Pepa and green-glowing dandruff and deodorant streaks and cheekbones highlighted to shine.

Somehow he'd acquired an empty jug of water that someone had Ace-bandaged to his head. There was shouting: "All Hail the Water Princeling." Oy: this was bad. His friends had found out where his money came from. He had hidden it, drove a beat-up Volvo for goodness sakes. He was shirtless, he found, better to show off his muscles. He was aware of how he appeared at every angle in the room, and what the jug stole in dignity, it returned in militaristic jauntiness. He puffed his chest. Now he had a bottle of gin in his hand and his friends were shouting, "Lotto! Lotto! Lotto!" as he tilted it to his lips and took in a long draught, which would turn to soldering flux in his brain by morning and make his thoughts impenetrable, impossible to part.

"The world is ending," he bellowed. "Why not hump?"

A cheer from the dancers at his feet.

He raised his arms. [The fatal look up.]

In the doorway, suddenly, her.

Tall, in silhouette, wet hair casting the hall light into a halo, stream of bodies on the stairs behind her. She was looking at him, though he couldn't see her face.

She moved her head and there was half of it, strong and bright. High cheekbones, plush lips. Tiny ears. She was dripping from walking through the rain. He loved her first for the stun of her across this thump and dance.

He had seen her before, he knew who she was. Mathilde, whatsername. Beauty like hers cast glimmers on the walls even across campus, phosphorescence on the things she touched. She'd been so far above Lotto—so far above every person at the school—she had become mythological. Friendless. Icy. She went weekends to the city; she was a model, hence the fancy clothes. She never partied. Olympian, elegant on her mount. Yes—Mathilde Yoder. But his victory had made him ready for her tonight. Here she was for him.

Behind him in the crashing storm, or maybe within him, a sizzle. He leapt into the grind of bodies, kneeing Samuel in the eye, crushing some poor small girl to the ground.

Lotto swam up out of the crowd and crossed the floor to Mathilde. She was six feet tall in bobby socks. In heels, her eyes were at his lip line. She looked up at him coolly. Already he loved the laugh she held in her, which nobody else would see.

He felt the drama of the scene. Also, how many people were watching them, how beautiful he and Mathilde looked together.

In a moment, he'd been made new. His past was gone. He fell to his knees and took Mathilde's hands to press them on his heart. He shouted up at her, "Marry me!"

She threw back her head, baring her white snaky neck, and laughed and said something, her voice drowned. Lotto read those gorgeous lips as saying, "Yes." He'd tell this story dozens of times, invoking the black light, the instant love. All the friends over all the years, leaning in, secret romantics, grinning. Mathilde watching him from across the table, unreadable. Every time he told the story, he would say that she'd said, "Sure."

Sure. Yes. One door closed behind him. Another, better, flung open.

3

A QUESTION OF VISION. From the sun's seat, after all, humanity is an abstraction. Earth a mere spinning blip. Closer, the city a knot of light between other knots; even closer, and buildings gleamed, slowly separating. Dawn in the windows revealed bodies, all the same. Only with focus came specifics, mole by nostril, tooth stuck to a dry bottom lip in sleep, the papery skin of an armpit.

Lotto poured cream into coffee and woke his wife. A song played on the tape deck, eggs were fried, dishes washed, floors swept. Beer and ice carried in, snacks prepared. By midafternoon, all was shining, ready.

"Nobody's here yet. We could—" Lotto said into Mathilde's ear. He pulled her long hair away from her nape, kissed the knob of bone there. The neck was his, belonging to the wife who was his, shining, under his hands.

Love that had begun so powerfully in the body had spread luxuriantly into everything. They had been together for five weeks. The first, there had been no sex, Mathilde a tease. Then came the weekend camping trip and the besotted first time and the morning piss where he found his junk bloodied stem to stern and he knew she'd been a virgin, that she hadn't wanted to sleep with him because of it. He turned to her in the new light, dipping her face in the frigid stream to wash it, coming up cheeks flushed and glazed with water, and he knew her to be the purest person he'd ever met, he, who had been primed for purity. He knew then they would elope, they would graduate, they would go to live in the city and be happy together there. And they were happy, if still strange to each other. Yesterday, he'd found she was allergic to sushi. This morning, when he was talking to his aunt on the telephone, he'd watched Mathilde toweling off out of the shower and it struck him hard that she had no family at all. The little she spoke of childhood was shadowed with abuse. He'd imagined it vividly: poverty, beat-up trailer, spiteful—she implied worse—uncle. Her most vivid memories of her childhood were of the television that was never turned off. Salvation of school, scholarship, modeling for spare change. They had begun to accrete stories between them. How, when she was small, isolated in the country, she'd been so lonely that she let a leech live on her inner thigh for a week. How she'd been discovered for modeling by a gargoyle of a man on a train. It must have taken an immense force of will for Mathilde to turn her past, so sad and dark, blank behind her. Now she had only him. It moved him to know that for her he was everything. He wouldn't ask for more than she'd willingly give.

Outside, a New York June day steamed. Soon there'd be the party, dozens of college friends descending on them for the housewarming, though the house was already sizzling with summer. For now they were safe, inside.

"It's six. We invited them for five-thirty. We can't," Mathilde said. But he wasn't listening, he put his hands up her peacock skirt and under the band of her cotton panties, sweated through at the crotch. They were married. He was entitled. She tilted her hips back into him and put her palms on either side of the cheap long mirror that was, with the mattress and a ziggurat of suitcases where they kept their clothes, all their bedroom held. A tiger of light from the transoms prowled the clean pine floor.

He slid her underwear to her knees and said, "We'll be quick." Point: mooted. He watched in the mirror as she closed her eyes and the flush crept over her cheeks, lips, the hollow of her neck. The backs of her legs were humid and trembling against his knees.

Lotto felt lush. With what? Everything. The apartment in the West Village with its perfect garden, tended by that British harridan from upstairs, whose fat thighs, even now, were among the tiger lilies in the window. One-bedroom but enormous, underground but rent-controlled. From the kitchen or bathroom, one saw pedestrian feet passing, bunions and ankle tattoos; but it was safe down here, buried against calamity, insulated from hurricanes and bombs by earth and layers of street. After being so long a nomad, he was rooted in this place, rooted in this wife, with her fine features and sad, cattish eyes and freckles and gangly tall body with its tang of the forbidden. Such terrible things his mother had said when he'd called to tell her he was married. Horrible things. It made him misty to remember them. But today even the city was laid out like a tasting menu; it was the newly shining nineties; girls wore glitter on their cheekbones; clothes were shot with silver thread; everything held a promise of sex, of wealth. Lotto would gobble it all up. All was beauty, all abundance. He was Lancelot Satterwhite. He had a sun blazing in him. This splendid *everything* was what he was screwing now.

His own face looked back at him behind Mathilde's flushed and gasping one. His wife, a caught rabbit. The pulse and throb of her. Her arms buckled, her face went pale, and she fell into the mirror, and it gave a snap, and a crack crazed their heads in uneven halves.

The doorbell gave a long slow trill.

"Minute!" Lotto shouted.

In the hallway, Chollie shifted the enormous brass Buddha he'd found in a dumpster on the way over, and said, "Bet you a hundred bucks they're fucking."

"Pig," Danica said. Since graduation, she'd lost sandbags of weight. She was a bundle of sticks wrapped in gauze. She was planning to tell

Lotto and Mathilde as soon as they opened the door—if they ever god-damned did—that Chollie and she hadn't come together, that they'd met on the sidewalk outside the building, that she would *literally* never be caught dead alone in the same place as Chollie, this little troll man. His glasses taped at the bridge. His nasty mouth, like a crow's beak, cawing its constant bitter song. She'd hated him when he visited Lotto at school and the visits extended for months until people assumed he was a Vassar student, though he wasn't, barely a high school grad, whom Lotto had known as a kid. She hated him more now. Fattish pretender. "You smell like garbage," she said.

"Dumpster diving," he said, and hefted the Buddha in victory. "I'd be sexing it up all the time if I were them. Mathilde's weird-looking, but I'd do her. And Lotto's fucked around enough. He's got to be an expert by now."

"Right? He's the sluttiest," Danica said. "He gets away with it because of the way he looks at you. Like, if he were actually good-looking, he'd never be as deadly, but five minutes in a room with him, all you want to do is get naked. Also the fact that he's a guy. A girl screws around like Lotto and she's, like, diseased. Untouchable. But a guy can stick it a million places and everyone just thinks he's doing what boys do." Danica pushed the doorbell rapidly, over and over. She lowered her voice. "Anyway, I give this marriage a year. I mean, who gets married at twenty-two? Like coal miners. Like farmers. Not *us*. Lotto will be screwing the scary lady upstairs in about eight months. And some angry menopausal director who will make him Lear. And anyone else who catches his eye. And Mathilde will get a quickie di-vorce and marry some prince of Transylvania or something."

They laughed. Danica rang the doorbell in Morse code: SOS. "I'd take that bet," Chollie said. "Lotto won't cheat. I've known him since he was fourteen. He's arrogant as shit but loyal."

"A million bucks," Danica said. Chollie put the Buddha down and they shook.

The door swung open and there was glossy Lotto with sweat beads at his temples. Through the empty living room, they could see a slice of Mathilde as she shut the bathroom door on herself, a blue morpho folding its wings. Danica had to restrain herself from licking Lotto's cheek when she kissed him. Salty, oh my god, delicious, like a hot soft pretzel. She always went a little weak around him.

"A hundred thousand welcomes. I could weep and I could laugh, I am light and heavy. Welcome," Lotto said. Oh dear. They had so little. Bookshelves made of cinder blocks and plywood, couch from the college common room, rickety table and chairs meant for a patio. Still, how happy the place felt. In Danica, a pulse of envy.

"Spartan," Chollie said, and hefted the giant Buddha to the mantelpiece, where it beamed over the white room. Chollie rubbed the statue's belly, then went into the kitchen and had a bird bath of dish soap and handfuls of water to wash all the dumpster stink off his person. From there, he watched the arriving flood of the poseurs, phonies, and jolly prepsters with whom he'd had to contend since Lotto had been sent off to boarding school, then college; his friend had taken him in when Chollie had no one else. That awful Samuel kid who pretended he was Lotto's best friend. False. No matter how much Chollie insulted him, Samuel was unperturbed: Chollie knew he was too low, too much of a slug, for Samuel to care about. Lotto was taller than all, shooting off laser beams of joy and warmth, and everyone coming in blinked, dazzled by his grin. They handed over spider plants in terra-cotta, six-packs, books, bottles of wine. Yuppies in embryo, miming their parents' manners. In twenty years, they'd have country houses and children with pretentious literary names and tennis lessons and ugly cars and liaisons with hot young interns. Hurricanes of entitlement, all swirl and noise and destruction, nothing at their centers.

In twenty years, Chollie announced silently, I will own you all. He snorted. Smoldered.

Mathilde was standing at the refrigerator, frowning at the puddle around Chollie's feet, the water stains on his khaki shorts. On her chin there was a raspberry abrasion shining through her cover-up.

"Hey, there, Sourpuss," he said.

"Hi, Sour Pussy," she said.

"You kiss my friend with that dirty mouth of yours?" he said, but she only opened the fridge and took out a bowl of hummus and two beers and gave him one. He could smell her, the rosemary of her silky blond hair, the Ivory soap, the unmistakable starch of sex. Ah, so. He'd been right.

"Mingle," she said, moving off. "And don't make anyone punch you, Chollie."

"Risk destroying this perfection?" he said, and gestured at his face. "Never."

Like fish in an aquarium, bodies moved through the hot space. In the bedroom, a ring of girls was forming. They were looking at the bank of irises in the window above their heads.

"How can they afford this?" Natalie murmured. She'd been so nervous to come—Lotto and Mathilde so glamorous—that she'd had a few shots before leaving her house. She was actually pretty drunk now.

"Rent-controlled," a girl in a leather miniskirt said, looking around for somebody to save her. The others had melted away when Natalie joined them; she was one of those people it was nice to see when you're tipsy at some college party, but now they were in the real world, all she did was complain about money. It was exhausting. They were all poor, they were *supposed* to be poor out of college, get over it. Miniskirt snagged a freckled girl passing by. All three had at one time slept with Lotto. Each of them secretly believed he liked her best.

"Yeah," Natalie said. "But Mathilde doesn't even have a job. I'd get how they could pay if she was still modeling, but she already caught a husband, so she stopped, yadda yadda who knows. *I* wouldn't stop modeling if anyone wanted me. And Lotto's an *actor*, and though we all think he's amazing, it's not like he's going to star in the next Tom Cruise movie or anything. I mean, that awful skin of his. No offense! I mean, he's totally *brilliant*, but it'd be hard to make ends meet even as an Equity actor, and he's not even that."

The other two looked at Natalie as if from a great distance, saw the bulging eyes, the unplucked moustache, sighed. "You don't know?" Miniskirt said. "Lotto's an heir to a fucking fortune. Water bottling. You know Hamlin Springs water? That's them. His mom, like, owns all of Florida. She's a bazillionaire. They could have bought a three-bedroom with a doorman on the Upper East Side with the change in their pockets."

"It's actually kind of humble that they live like this," Freckles said. "He's the best."

"She, on the other hand," Natalie said, lowering her voice. The others took a step in, bowed their heads to listen. Holy Communion of scuttlebutt. "Mathilde's a conundrum wrapped in a mystery wrapped in bacon. She didn't even have any friends in college. I mean, *everybody* has friends in college. Where did she come from? Nobody has any idea."

"I know," Miniskirt said. "She's so calm and quiet. Ice queen. And Lotto's the loudest. Warm, sexy. Opposites."

"I don't get it, honestly," Freckles said.

"Eh. First marriage," Miniskirt said.

"And guess who'll be there with casseroles when it all comes apart!" Freckles said. They laughed.

Well, Natalie thought. It was clear now. The apartment, the way Lotto and Mathilde floated on their own current. The balls it took to proclaim a creative profession, the narcissism. Natalie had once wanted to be a sculptor and was pretty damn good at it. She'd welded a nine-foot stainless-steel DNA helix that sat in the science wing of her high school. She'd dreamt of building gigantic moving structures like gyroscopes and pinwheels, spun only by the wind. But her parents were right about getting a job. She studied economics and Spanish at Vassar, which was only logical, and yet she had to rent someone's mothball-smelling closet in Queens until her internship ended. She had a hole in her one pair of high-heeled shoes, which she had to fix every night with superglue. Grinding, this life. Not what she had been promised. It was explicit in the brochures she'd looked at like porn in her suburban bed when she was applying: you get to Vassar, those laughing, beautiful kids promised, you live a gilded life. Instead, this dingy apartment with its bad beer was as high a life as she was going to live anytime soon.

Through the door to the living room, she saw Lotto laughing down at some joke made by Samuel Harris, son of the shadiest senator in D.C. The senator was the kind of man who, having expended all his empathetic capital on marrying someone surprising, wanted to make sure no other people had the ability to make their own choices for themselves. He was anti-immigration, antiwoman, antigay, and that was just for starters. To his credit, Samuel started up the Campus Liberals, but Lotto and Samuel had both picked up the aristocrat's inbred sense of condescension from Samuel's snotty mom. She'd made Natalie feel like shit once for blowing her nose in her dinner napkin when she and Samuel briefly dated. Lotto, at least, had enough charm to make you feel that you were interesting. Samuel just made you feel inferior. Natalie had an urge to put her Doc Marten through both of their stupid richy-rich faces. She heaved a sigh. "Bottled water is terrible for the environment," she said, but the others had vanished, comforting that chick Bridget who was crying in the corner, still in love with Lotto. She was just embarrassing to look at next to Mathilde's tall bony blond. Natalie frowned at herself in the cracked mirror, seeing only a fractured girl with a bitter mouth.

Lotto was floating. Someone had put En Vogue on the CD player, ironically, for sure, but he *loved* those girls' voices. The apartment was hot as hell, the late-afternoon sun shining in like a voyeur. Nothing mattered: all his college friends were together again. He took a moment to watch, standing with a beer in the doorway.

Natalie was doing a keg stand, held up by the ankles by the guys from the coffee shop down the block, her shirt lapping over her mealy belly. Samuel, blue bags under his eyes, was talking loudly about having worked ninety hours at his investment bank last week. Beautiful Susannah was putting her face in the freezer to cool it off, radiant with the shampoo commercial she'd landed. He swallowed his envy. The girl couldn't act, but she was dewy, doelike. They'd hooked up once junior year. She'd tasted like fresh cream. His co-captain on the crew team, Arnie, flush from mixology school, was shaking up Pink Squirrels, his skin streaked apricot from tanning lotion.

Behind him, a voice Lotto didn't know said, "What's the one forbidden word in a riddle about chess?"

And some other person paused, then said, "Chess?"

And the first person said, "You remember our freshman Borges seminar!" and Lotto laughed out loud with love for these pretentious sperm wads.

They would have this party year after year, he decided. It would be their annual June fête, the friends gathering, building until they had to rent out an airplane hangar to hold everyone, to drink and shout and dance into the night. Paper lanterns, shrimp boil, someone's kid's bluegrass band. When your family dismisses you, like Lotto's did, you create your own family. This crowded and sweaty lurch was all he wanted of life; this was the summit. Jeez, he was happy.

What's this? A spray of wet coming through the open garden windows, the old lady screaming down at them with the hose trained into the roil, her voice barely audible over the music and shouting. The girls shrieked, their summer dresses clinging to their beautiful skin. Tender. Moist. He could eat them all. He had a vision of himself in a pile of limbs and breasts, a red mouth open, sliding over his—but oh, that's right, he couldn't. He was married. He grinned at his wife, who was hurrying across the floor to the fat woman screaming down through the window, "Savages! Control yourselves! Keep the noise down! Savages!"

Mathilde spoke mollifyingly, and the cranks were turned and the garden windows shut, and those to the street thrust open, which was cooler anyway, being in the shade. Already, the lip-locks, the grinding, though the sun still shined in. They turned the noise up a notch, the voices louder.

". . . cusp of a revolution. East and West Germany reunifying, there's going to be a huge backlash to capitalism."

"Hélène Cixous is sexy. Simone de Beauvoir. Susan Sontag."

"Feminazis, ipso facto, cannot be sexy."

". . . like, the fundamental human condition to be lonely."

"Cynic! Only you would say that in the middle of an orgy."

Lotto's heart kicked froglike in his chest; sweeping toward him in her brilliant blue skirt, Mathilde. His azure lion rampant. Her long hair plaited down her left breast, she, the nexus of all the good of this world. He was reaching toward her when she shifted him over to the front door. It was open. A very small person stood there. Surprise! His baby sister Rachel in pigtails and overalls, gazing at the scene of drink and grind and cigarette with baby Baptist horror, shaking with nerves. She was only eight years old. She had an unaccompanied-minor tag hanging around her neck. There was a middle-aged couple with matching hiking boots frowning into the room behind her.

"Rachel!" he shouted, and picked her up by the loop of her back-pack and carried her in. The friends shuffled away. Kissing ceased, in this room at least; there was no telling what was happening in the bedroom. Mathilde unhooked Rachel. They had met only once before, when Lotto's aunt had brought the girl up for graduation a few weeks earlier. Rachel now touched the emerald necklace that Mathilde had impulsively given her from her own neck at that dinner. "What are you doing here?" Lotto and Mathilde shouted over the noise.

Rachel shied a little away from Mathilde, who had a reek to her. Antiperspirant, Mathilde said, gave you Alzheimer's; perfume gave her hives. There were tears in Rachel's eyes when she said, "Lotto? You invited me?"

She said nothing about waiting in the airport for three hours or the kind but stern hikers who'd seen her weeping and offered her a ride. And Lotto remembered at last that she was supposed to come, and the day dimmed because he'd forgotten his baby sister was visiting for the weekend, forgotten it as soon as he'd agreed to it on the phone with his aunt Sallie, hadn't even made it to the other room to tell Mathilde before it slipped his mind. A wave of shame rose in his chest and he imagined his sister's fear, her distress, as she waited alone for him at baggage claim. Oh, jeepers. What if some bad man had gotten hold of her. What if she'd trusted someone terrible, not these homely people by the keg with their bandannas and carabiners, laughing because they remembered the wild parties of their youth. What if she'd trusted a perv. Flashes of white slavery, Rachel scrubbing a kitchen floor on her knees, kept in a box under someone's bed. She looked as if she'd been crying, her little eyes red. It must have been terrifying to ride all the way from the airport with strangers. He hoped she wouldn't tell Muvva, that his mother wouldn't be even more disappointed in him than she already was. The things she'd said to him just after they'd eloped were molten in him still. He was such a codpiece.

But Rachel was hugging him fiercely around the waist. The storm on Mathilde's face had also cleared. He didn't deserve these women who surrounded him, who made things right. [Perhaps not.] A whispered conference, and it was decided: the party could go on in their absence but they'd take Rachel out to the diner on the corner for dinner. They'd get her to bed and lock the bedroom door by nine and turn the music down; they'd make their breach up to her all weekend.

Brunch, a movie and popcorn, a trip to FAO Schwarz to dance on the floor piano.

Rachel put her things in the closet with the camping stuff and raincoats in it. When she turned, she was immediately accosted by a short dark man—Samuel?—who looked profoundly tired, who was talking about his *extremely* important job in a bank or something. As if it's *so* hard to cash checks and make change. Rachel could do it herself, and she was only in third grade.

She stole away and slipped an envelope with her housewarming gift in it into her brother's back pocket. She savored the thought of his face when he opened it: six months of her allowance saved up, nearly two thousand dollars. It was an insane allowance for an eight-year-old. What did she have to spend it on? Muvva would freak, but Rachel had *burned* for poor Lotto and Mathilde, she couldn't *believe* they'd been cut off when they were married. As if money would ever have stopped them: Mathilde and Lotto had been born to nestle into each other like spoons in a drawer. Also, they needed the cash. Look at this tiny dark hole with no furniture to speak of. She'd never seen a place so bare. They didn't even have a television, they didn't even have a kettle or a rug. They were *impoverished*. She stole back again between Mathilde and her big brother, her nose against Lotto because he smelled like warm lotion and, well, Mathilde smelled like the high school wrestling room where her Girl Scout troop met. Hard to breathe. At last, the fear that had overwhelmed Rachel in the airport fell away, overpowered by a wash of love. The people here were so sexy, so drunk. She was shocked at all the *fuck*s and *shit*s falling out of their mouths: Antoinette had seared into her children that cusses were for the verbally moronic. Lotto would never swear; he and Mathilde were the right kind of adult. She would be like them, living morally, cleanly, living in love. She looked out at the swirl of bodies in the late sun, in the June stifle of the apartment, the booze and music. All she wanted in life was this: beauty, friendship, happiness.

THE SUN SHIFTED TO RECLINING. It was eight at night.

Calm. Mild. End of autumn. Chill in the air like a premonition.

Susannah came through the door that led up into the garden. The apartment with its new jute rug was still. She found Mathilde alone, tossing vinaigrette into Bibb lettuce in the galley kitchen.

"Did you hear?" Susannah murmured, but was struck silent when Mathilde turned her face toward her. Earlier, Susannah had thought that walking into the apartment with its new coat of bright yellow paint had been like walking into the sun, blinding. But now the color played with the cinnamon freckles on Mathilde's face. She'd gotten an asymmetrical haircut, her blond lopped at the right jawbone, at the left collar, and it set off her high cheekbones. Susannah felt a pulse of attraction. Odd. All this time, Mathilde had seemed plain, shadowed by her husband's light, but now the pairing clicked. Mathilde was, in fact, ravishing.

"Did I hear what?" Mathilde said.

"Oh, Mathilde. Your hair," Susannah said. "It's wonderful."

Mathilde put a hand up to it, and said, "Thanks. What did I hear?"

"Right," Susannah said, and picked up the two bottles of wine Mathilde indicated with her chin. She said, as she followed Mathilde out the entryway, up the back stairs, "You know Kristina from our class? In that a cappella group the Zaftones? Inky hair and, well, zaftig. I think Lotto and she—" Susannah made a face to herself, Oh, you dummy, and Mathilde paused on the step, then waved a hand as if to say, Oh, yes, Lotto and everybody screwed like bonobos, which Susannah had to admit was true, and they came up into the garden. They stopped, autumn-struck. Lotto and Mathilde had spread out thrift-store sheets on the grass and the friends had arranged the potluck in the middle, and everyone was lounging quietly, eyes closed in the last morsel of chill fall sun, drinking the cold white wine and Belgian beer, waiting for the first person to reach in and take food.

Mathilde put her salad bowl down, and said, "Eat, kiddos." Lotto smiled up at her and took a mini-spanakopita from a warm pile. The rest of them, a dozen or so, huddled into the food and began talking again.

Susannah stood on her toes and whispered up into Mathilde's ear, "Kristina. She killed herself. Hanged herself in the bathroom. Out of the blue, only yesterday. Nobody knew she was miserable. She had a boyfriend and everything and a job with the Sierra Club and an apartment in the nice part of Harlem. Makes no sense."

Mathilde had gone very still and had lost her constant small smile. Susannah knelt and served herself watermelon, cutting the big pieces into slivers: she wasn't eating real food anymore because she had a new TV role she was too embarrassed to talk about in front of Lotto. For one thing, it wasn't *Hamlet*, in which he'd shined so brilliantly their last semester in college. It was just a job as a teenager on a soap opera, she knew she was selling out. And yet it was more than anything Lotto had gotten since they graduated. He'd been the understudy in a few off-off-Broadway things; he'd had a tiny role at the Actors Theatre in Louisville. That was it for a year and a half. Lotto returned to her again as he'd looked at the end of *Hamlet*, bowing, having sweated through his costume, and she'd felt awe, had shouted "Bravo!" from the audience, having lost the role of Ophelia to a girl with huge boobs bared naked in the pond scene. Ho-bag slut. Susannah bit into her watermelon and swallowed a pulse of victory. She loved Lotto more, in pitying.

Above the scrum, Mathilde shivered and pulled her cardigan closer. A burgundy leaf fell from the Japanese maple and landed upright in a spinach-artichoke dip. It was chilly in the shadow under the tree. Soon, there would be the long winter, cold and white. An erasure of this night, the garden. She plugged in the strand of Christmas lights that they had twined through the branches above, and the tree sparked into a dendrite. She sat behind her husband because she wanted to hide, and his back was so beautiful, broad and muscled, that she rested her face there and felt comforted. She listened to his voice muffled through his chest, the smooth edge of his Southern accent.

". . . two old men sitting on a porch, shooting the sea breeze," Lotto was saying; so, a joke. "This old hound dog comes out and circles around in the dust and sits down and starts licking at his junk. Slurping and gulping and loving the heck out of his pink little stump. A tube of lipstick all the way extended. So one of the old guys winks at his friend and says, *Man, I sure wish I could do that.* And the other old guy says, *Pshaw! That dog would* BITE *you.*"

They all laughed, not so much at the joke, but at the way Lotto delivered it, the pleasure he took. Mathilde knew it had been his father's favorite, that it had made Gawain guffaw into his hand and turn red every time Lotto told it. The warmth of her husband through his emerald polo shirt began to break up the clod of dread in Mathilde. Kristina had lived on her freshman floor. Mathilde had walked in on her once crying in the coed showers, had recognized her beautiful alto voice, and had walked out again, choosing to give the gift of privacy over that of comfort. Only in retrospect was that the worse choice. Mathilde felt a slow welling of anger at Kristina in her gut and breathed into Lotto to quell it.

Lotto reached behind him for Mathilde and scooped her sideways into his lap with his paw. His stomach rumbled but he couldn't eat more than a bite or two: he'd been waiting for a callback for a week now, unwilling to leave the apartment for fear of missing it. Mathilde had proposed the potluck to get his mind off it all. The role was for Claudio in *Measure for Measure*, Shakespeare in the Park next summer. He could *see* himself in a doublet in front of thousands. Bats darting. Dusk shooting pink flares overhead. Since graduation, he had worked steadily, if in small roles. He had gotten Equity. This was the next step skyward.

He looked through the window inside the apartment, where the phone persisted unringing on the mantel. Behind it stood the painting Mathilde had brought home a few months earlier from the gallery where she'd worked for the past year. After its artist had stormed out, flinging the canvas against the wall and breaking the stretcher, the gallery owner, Ariel, told her to toss it in the dumpster. Instead, Mathilde took the broken painting, restretched it, framed it, hung it behind the brass Buddha. It was a blue abstract and reminded Lotto of the moment every morning before dawn, a misty dim world between worlds. What's the word? *Eldritch*. Like Mathilde, herself. He would come home some days after auditions to find her sitting in the dark, staring up at the painting with a glass of red wine cradled between both hands, a vague look on her face.

"Should I be worried?" he'd said once, after an audition for a show he didn't even want, when he came home to find her sitting there in the darkening room. He kissed her behind the ear.

"No. I'm just so happy," she had said.

He didn't say that it had been a long day, that he'd had to wait in the drizzle on the street for two hours, that after he finally went in and read his lines and went out the door, he'd heard the director say, "Stellar. Too bad he's a giant." That his agent wasn't returning his calls. That he would have relished a nice dinner for once. Because, in truth, he didn't mind. If she was happy, it meant she wouldn't leave him; and it had become painfully apparent over their short marriage that he was not worth the salt she sweated. The woman was a saint. She saved, fretted, somehow paid their bills when he brought in nothing. He had sat beside her until it was fully dark, and she turned with a rustling of silk and kissed him suddenly, and he carried her to bed without eating.

Now Mathilde lifted a piece of salmon burger to Lotto's lips, and though he didn't want it, she was looking at him and the gold specks in her eyes glittered, and he took the bite off the fork. He kissed her on the freckled bridge of her nose.

"Disgusting," Arnie called from his distant sheet. His arm was around some tattooed chick he was dating from his bar. "You've been married for a year. Honeymoon's over."

"Never," Mathilde and Lotto said, at once. They did jinx pinkies, kissed again.

"What's it like?" Natalie said quietly. "Marriage, I mean."

Lotto said, "A never-ending banquet, and you eat and eat and never get full."

Mathilde said, "Kipling called it a very long conversation."

Lotto looked at his wife, touched her cheek. "Yes," he said.

Chollie leaned toward Danica, who leaned away. He whispered, "You owe me a million bucks."

"What?" she snapped. She was dying for a chicken leg, but had to plow through a heap of salad before she allowed herself anything fatty.

"Last year, at their housewarming," Chollie said. "We bet a million bucks they'd be divorced by now. You lose."

They looked at Lotto and Mathilde, so handsome, the still axis of the garden, of the spinning world. "I don't know. How much of it's an act?" Danica said. "There's some sort of darkness there. Probably that he's pretending to be faithful and she's pretending not to care."

"You're mean," Chollie said with admiration. "What's your beef with Lotto? Were you one of his vanquished millions? They all still love him. I ran into that girl Bridget who was calling herself his girlfriend in college, and she burst into tears when she asked about him. He was the love of her life."

Danica's eyes and mouth tightened. Chollie laughed, revealing a roil of lasagna. "Naw, it's the opposite," he said. "He never went for you."

"If you don't shut up, you're getting salad in the kisser," she said.

They sat for a long moment, eating, pretending to eat. Then Danica said, "Fine. Double or nothing. But I get longer. Six years. Until

1998. And they'll be divorced and you'll pay me two million bucks and I'll get an apartment in Paris. *Enfin*."

Chollie blinked, bulged. "You're assuming that I'll be able to pay."

"Of course you will. You're the kind of slimy little man who makes a hundred million dollars by your thirties," Danica said.

Chollie said, "That's the nicest thing anyone ever said about me."

When the shadows thickened just enough for the gesture to be hidden, Susannah gave Natalie a pinch on the rear. They laughed into their cups. It had been tacitly agreed upon: another night they would end up at Susannah's. Only Natalie knew about Susannah's new role as the bratty daughter of a soap opera villain; only Natalie knew about the new rising sea of feeling between them. "My career would die before it was born if everyone knew I was a big fat lesbo," Susannah had said. Something sat wrong with Natalie, but she kept it in, let Susannah blaze inside her all day while she stood at her sad, gray desk trading commodities, her bank account spinning richer second by second.

Natalie was looking better, Lotto thought, watching her brush her hand over the last mint. She had bleached the moustache, lost weight, was dressing with flair. She had found the beauty he'd known was there all along. He smiled at her, and she blushed, smiled back.

Their eating slowed. The group fell silent. Caramel brownies went around. Some of the friends watched the creamy unfurl of a contrail in the darkling sky, and there was a poignancy in the way it disappeared, and this made most of them think about the dead black-haired girl, that they'd never again feel her arms around their necks in a hug. She had smelled like oranges.

"I found a boy who'd hung himself in prep school," Lotto said suddenly. "Hanged himself." They looked at his face with interest. He was pale, grim. They waited for the story because there was always a story with Lotto, but he didn't say anything more. Mathilde took his hand.

"You never said," she whispered.

"Tell you later," he said. Poor pustuled Jelly Roll dangled ghostly in the garden for a breath; and Lotto passed his hand over his face, and the boy was gone.

Someone said, "Look! The moon!" and there it was, hove up like a ship in the navy edge of sky, and it filled them all with longing.

Rachel sat down beside her brother, leaned into his warmth. She was up for fall break, had pierced her ears all the way around, and wore her hair long in front, shaved in the rear. Radical for a ten-year-old, but she needed to do *something*, otherwise she looked a slight six with jittery hands, and from her studies of her cohort, she understood that it was better to be weird than twee. [Smart girl. Yes.] She had just gone in and put the envelope with her last year's allowance in Mathilde's underwear drawer, dabbling her hands among the silks; it had not escaped Rachel that her brother's cabinets were bare, that Mathilde had called Sallie last month, that Sallie had sent cash. Now she was watching the window on the first floor where she had seen a fluttering edge of curtain, half a fist, one eye. Rachel pictured an interior with wallpapered ceilings. Cats with infirmities, Cyclops cats and cats with nubs for tails and gouty, swollen-pawed cats. Stink of joint rub. Bowl of minestrone heated in the microwave. Sad old woman inside. Muvva was heading fast toward that same future; the tiny pink beach house a tomb of figurines and chintz. Muvva loved the sound of the sea, she told Rachel, but Rachel had never even seen her go out into the sand. She just stayed in her little pink aquarium of a house like a sucker fish, gobblemouthing the glass. Poor Muvva.

I will never be old, Rachel promised herself. I will never be sad. I'd scarf a cyanide capsule first, kill myself like that friend of Lotto's everyone is crying about. Life isn't worth living unless you are young and surrounded by other young people in a beautiful cold garden perfumed by dirt and flowers and fallen leaves, gleaming in the string of lights, listening to the quiet city on the last fine night of the year.

Under the dying angel's trumpet plant, the old lady's tabby watched.

Confusing, these people lounging around their food like enormous cats sated from the kill. She longed to pad in and investigate, but there were too many of them, and they were so sudden, so unpredictable. Just so: at once the people rose, shrieking, gathering things up in their arms, rushing about. The cat was startled that they were startled, because she had smelled the rain long before she heard it. A spoon fell from a bowl of tabbouleh and spun into the dirt and was abandoned, spattered by the mud kicked up by the first raindrops. The people were gone. A hand came out of a ground-level window and unplugged the tree lights. In the plunge of darkness, the yellow cord writhed into the window like a snake and the cat hungered to chase it, but it disappeared and the window closed. The cat dabbed her paw delicately at one fat drop on the edge of a leaf, then galloped across the yard and came inside.

THE DOOR TO THE APARTMENT OPENED; in leapt the goblin. It was nine at night, unseasonably cold. Behind the goblin came Miss Piggy, a skeleton, a ghost. Albert Einstein, moonwalking. Samuel came in wearing a lampshade for a hat, a cardboard box painted to resemble a bedside table, with a magazine and two condom wrappers glued on top.

Lotto in a toga, crowned by gilded bay leaves, put his beer down on Samuel's tabletop and said, "Hello! You're a nightstand. A one-night stand. Ha ha."

A murdered prom queen froufroued by, muttering, "Wishful thinking." Samuel said, "I think that was my ex-girlfriend," grinned, went to the fridge for a beer.

"Since when does it snow on Halloween? Global warming, schmobal schwarming," Luanne said, stomping her boots on the rattan mat. She was Mathilde's friend from the gallery where they worked and was painted up cleverly as Picasso's Dora Maar, the one with the bitten apple for a cheek. She kissed Lotto lingeringly, saying, "Oh, *hail* yes, Caesar." He laughed too loudly, pulling away. Luanne was trouble. Mathilde came home most days with stories about how she tried to seduce their boss, some gross bulgy-eyed man with vaudeville eyebrows named Ariel. "Why?" said Lotto. "She's pretty. She's young. She could do way better." And Mathilde shot him a look, and said, "Babe. He's *rich*," and, of course, that explained it. Together Lotto and Luanne went toward Mathilde, who was resplendent in full Cleopatra, eating a cupcake beside the huge brass Buddha on the mantel adorned with sunglasses and lei. Lotto dipped his wife and licked the crumbs from her lips as she laughed.

"Yuck," Luanne said. "You guys can't be freaking real." She went to the kitchen, took a Zima from the fridge, moodily sipped, made a face. She'd gauged the low state of Lotto's mind by the size of his belly and how crowded the apartment was with used books; in his low moments, reading was all Lotto could do. Funny, because he seemed like such a huge goofball, and then he opened his mouth and quoted paragraphs of Wittgenstein or something. It unnerved her, the gap between who he appeared to be and the person he held inside him.

Someone put on a Nirvana CD and girls got up from the leather couch Lotto had rescued from the sidewalk. They attempted to dance but gave up, put *Thriller* on again.

Chollie, green goblin, sidled up to Lotto and Mathilde, slurringly drunk. "I never noticed how close-set your eyes are, Mathilde, and how wide yours are, Lotto." He made a stabbing motion with two fingers at Mathilde and said, "Predator," then stabbed at Lotto and said, "Prey."

"I'm the prey and Mathilde's the predator?" Lotto said. "Please. I'm *her* predator. Her *sexual* predator," he said, and everyone groaned.

Luanne was gazing at Arnie across the room. She made an impatient motion with her hand. "Shut up, you guys," she said. "I'm ogling."

Mathilde sighed, backed away.

"Wait. Who? Oh, Arnie," Chollie said, spiteful. Disappointed? "Please. He's so stupid."

"Dumb as a dead bulb," Luanne said. "Exactly my point."

"Arnie?" said Lotto. "Arnie was a neuroscience major in college. He's no dumbo. Just because he didn't go to Harvard like you doesn't make him dumb."

"I don't know. Maybe he's pickled his brains with booze," Luanne said. "At your last party I overheard him say that Sting is his spirit animal."

Lotto gave a whistle across the room; Arnie-as-the-Hulk looked up from the sea of girls for whom he was making chocolate martinis. He made his way over to Lotto, clapping him on the shoulder. Chollie and Arnie were both painted green. Side by side, Arnie was the pneumatic before and Chollie the punctured after.

Lotto told Arnie, "Luanne said she'd jump your bones if you can define 'hermeneutics' in a satisfactory manner," and he steered the two into the bedroom, closed the door.

"God," Chollie said. "I'd die."

"They haven't come out of the room yet," said Lotto. "Some Cupid kills with arrows, some with traps."

"Shakespeare again?" Chollie said.

"Forever," Lotto said.

Chollie stalked away. Lotto was alone. When he looked up, he saw only himself reflected in the night-blackened windows, the belly that had developed during his blue summer this year, the shine at the temples where his hair was going. Three and a half years out of college, and Mathilde was still paying the bills. Lotto rubbed the Buddha's head sadly and walked past a covey of witches huddled over someone's Polaroid paper, faces summoned out of the murk.

Mathilde's back was turned, and she was speaking low to Susannah. Lotto crept forward and knew she was talking about him. "—better. Coffee commercial in September. Father and toddler out on a fishing boat at dawn. Apparently the kid fell in and Lotto fished him out with an oar and saved his life. Our hero!"

They laughed together, and Susannah said, "I know! Folgers. I've seen it. Dawn, a cabin in the woods, the kid waking up on a rowboat. He's so striking, Lotto. Especially with a beard."

"Tell all the directors you know, get him a job," Mathilde said, and Susannah said, "For what?" and Mathilde said, "Anything at all," and Susannah gave a half-mouthed smile and said, "I'll see what I can do."

Lotto, stung, hurried away without letting them see him.

Mathilde was never unkind, but she wore her passive aggression like a second skin. If she didn't like her food at a restaurant, she wouldn't touch it, keeping her eyes low and saying nothing until Lotto was forced to tell the waiter the food was too salty or under-cooked and could they please have something else, thanks so much, buddy. She once maneuvered an invitation to a wedding in Martha's Vineyard by standing next to the bride all night, a big-time Broadway actress, smiling gently but not speaking a word until the bride impulsively asked them to come. They attended, danced; he charmed a producer and got a callback for a revival of *My Fair Lady*, though his voice was not great, and he didn't get the role; they sent the actress a very nice set of antique silver grapefruit spoons they'd bought in a thrift store and polished to appear expensive.

Up before Lotto rose a vision of himself as if attached to a hundred shining strings by his fingers, eyelids, toes, the muscles of his mouth. All the strings led to Mathilde's pointer finger, and she moved it with the subtlest of twitches and made him dance.

The Chollie goblin came to a stop next to Mathilde, and together they watched Lotto across the room in a ring of boys: a bottle of bourbon hung between the hook of two fingers, the gold circlet of leaves flapped off the back of his head.

"What's eating your ass?" Chollie said. "You seem off."

Mathilde sighed, said, "There's something wrong with him."

"I think he's fine," Chollie said. "We only have to worry if he's way up or way down. He's coming out of the dip from the summer." He paused, watched Lotto. "At least he's losing his potbelly."

"Thank god," she said. "All summer I thought he was about to jump in front of a train. He needs to get a role. Some days he never leaves the apartment." She shook herself resolutely. "Anyway. How's the used-car business?"

"Quit," Chollie said. "I'm in real estate now. In fifteen years, I'll own half of Manhattan."

"Right," Mathilde said. Then, suddenly, "I'm leaving the gallery." They both looked startled.

"Okay," Chollie said. "Who'll support the genius?"

"I'll work. I got a job in some Internet start-up. A dating site. Begin in a week. I haven't told anyone yet, not Luanne or Ariel or Lotto. It's just. I needed a change. I thought my future would be in art. It's not."

"Is it in the Internet?"

"All of our futures," she said, "exist in the Internet." They smiled together into their drinks.

"Why are you telling me?" said Chollie, after some time. "I mean, I'm a weird choice of a confidant. You know?"

"Don't know," Mathilde said. "I can't tell if you're benign or malignant. But I feel like I could tell you all my secrets right now and you'd keep them to yourself, waiting for when best to deploy them."

Chollie went very still, watchful. "Tell me all your secrets," he said.

"Fat chance," she said. She left Chollie and went across to her husband and whispered in his ear. Lotto's eyes widened, and he bit down on a grin and didn't watch his wife as she went around the party and out the apartment's front door, turning down the dimmer switch on her way so that the only illumination in the room was from the flicker of the jack-o'-lanterns.

In a minute, Lotto went out the door with ostentatious nonchalance.

He went up a flight of stairs, found Mathilde outside the old lady's door. His party churned below; from within he hadn't been aware it was so loud. He wondered why the old lady hadn't called the cops yet, as she usually did. Still before ten, perhaps. There was a flush of cold as the front door opened and a clump of clowns clattered down the stairs to their apartment, and Lotto's exposed buttocks prickled with goose bumps. But the front door closed; the door to their apartment opened and swallowed the clowns. He loosed Mathilde's left breast from her bustier, his mouth on the curve of her throat.

He turned her around to press her cheek against the door, but she struggled back, her eyes flashing, and he submitted to the standing missionary. Not as exciting, perhaps, but still a prayer to the gods of love.

Inside the second-floor apartment, Bette was eating a runny egg sandwich alone in the dark, kept up by the festivities below. Now, unmistakable, a creak on the stairway, and Bette thrilled to the thought of a burglar, the tiny gun she kept in the fern stand. She put the sandwich down and pressed her ear to the door. But here was another creaking, a murmur. Some preparatory thumps. Indeed! This was happening. It had been so very long since her Hugh; but what had passed between them still felt fresh to her, a peach bitten into. Felt like yesterday, all that bodily joy. Begun so young they didn't even know what they were doing and they wouldn't give it up, so when they were old enough, they married. Not the worst thing to build a marriage around, such juice. The first years had been delirious, the latter ones merely happy.

The girl on the landing moaned in her chest. The boy was muttering but not so distinctly that Bette could understand the words, and the girl's moans became louder, then were muffled as if she were biting something—his shoulder? The rattling of the door was strenuous. Bette pushed herself against the heaving wood [so long since anyone had touched her; she offered up her change on her palm at the grocery store so that the clerk would brush her hand with his fingers]. Such athletes. Put Bette in mind of the monkey house on a Sunday visit to the zoo, the capuchins' gleeful whoring.

A mingled half shout and Bette whispered to her tabby figure-eighting her ankles, "Trick or treat, old girl. Indeed."

Out on the landing was hoarse breathing and rustling and those silly creatures. Oh, she knew who it was, the strange-looking giant from downstairs and his tall, plain wife, though she would pretend that she didn't to save embarrassment when they met in the foyer. Then the footsteps down, away, the music intensifying, quieting as their door closed, and Bette was alone again. Now for a stiff scotch and a toddle off to bed, dovey, like the good girl you've become.

TEN O'CLOCK and Mathilde was on her knees picking up the pieces of their millionth shattered wineglass since they moved into this dismal apartment five years ago. After all this time, still Goodwill crap. Someday, when Lotto got a gig, they'd afford better. Oh, she was tired. She hadn't even bothered to put in her contacts tonight, and her glasses lenses were smeared with fingerprints. She longed for everyone to go home.

She heard Lotto say from the couch, "An attempt to shake things up. At least it's not as bright as a mouthful of Lemonheads anymore."

Rachel stroked the freshly painted wall. She muttered, "What's this color? Suicide at Dusk? Church on a Winter Afternoon? It's the darkest blue I've ever seen." She seemed even more nervy than normal; a car had just backfired on the street, and she'd dropped the glass. "*Please* let me do that," she said sheepishly to Mathilde. "I'm such a klutz," she said.

"I've got it. And I can hear you about the new paint, you know. I love it," Mathilde called out, letting the pieces of glass rain into the garbage. But a drop of blood fell onto the mess—she had sliced her index without feeling it. "Fuck," she whispered.

"I love it, too," Luanne said. She had plumpened in the past year like dough before the second punch-down. "I mean, at least as a background for that stolen painting it's nice."

"Stop *saying* that," Mathilde said. "Pitney smashed it, Ariel told me to throw it out. And I did. If I picked it up out of the dumpster later, it was fair game."

Luanne shrugged, but her smile was tight.

"With all due respect," Chollie said. "This is the worst party in the history of parties. We're talking about *walls*. Susannah and Natalie are making out, and Danica's asleep on the rug. What possessed you to have a wine-tasting party? What twentysomething knows balls about wine? We went to better parties in high school."

Lotto smiled, an effect like dawn. The others perked up. "We *were* wild," Lotto said. He turned to the others, and said, "I only lived in Crescent Beach for a few months before Chollie debauched me and my mom sent me away to prep school. But it was the best. We stayed up all night pretty much every night. I can't even tell you how many drugs we did. Choll, remember that party up in the old abandoned house by the marsh? I was screwing a girl on the roof when I realized the house was on fire and hurried things up and rolled off her and fell two stories into a bush, and when I crawled out, my peen was out of my fly. The firemen gave me a round of applause." The others laughed, and Lotto said, "That was the very last night I ever spent in Florida. My mom shipped me off the next day. She'd promised an enormous gift to the school, screw admissions criteria. Haven't been back home since."

Chollie gave a choked noise. They looked at him. "My twin sister," he said. "It was. You were screwing."

"Shoot," Lotto said. "I'm so sorry, Choll. I'm such a jerk."

Chollie took a deep breath, let it out. "That was the night I broke my leg in a spiral fracture when we were prepartying on the beach. I was in surgery when all the other stuff happened."

Long silence.

"I'm so embarrassed," Lotto said.

"Don't worry," Chollie said. "She'd already fucked the whole soccer team by then." Chollie's date made a stricken sound. She was a downy model from some USSR country whose beauty, Lotto had to admit, cast even Mathilde's into the shade. [Not difficult, these days.] Lotto looked across to his wife standing in the kitchen. How bedraggled she was, her hair unwashed, in her glasses and sweatshirt. He shouldn't have insisted on the get-together. But he had been worried about her; for weeks she had been quiet, remote. Something was wrong. Nothing he said was right, none of the jokes. Was it her job? he'd finally asked. If she was so unhappy, she should quit and they should start a family. If he gave Antoinette a grandbaby, they'd be reinstated for sure. They'd have plenty of money then, jeez, enough for Mathilde to relax a little, figure out what it was she really wanted to do with her life. She struck him as an artist who'd never found her medium, restlessly testing this and that but unable to find a way to articulate her urgency. Maybe she'd find it in children. But, *Oh my god, Lotto, stop, please, stop talking, stop your endless talking, stop about having babies,* she'd hissed; and it was true they were still too young, too few of their friends had spawned, at least intentionally, and so he'd tabled the discussion and distracted her with videos and booze. He'd had the idea that a wine-tasting party would cheer her, but it was clear that all she wanted to do was go to their new mattress, the bedroom with the embroidered curtains, the antique etchings of nests, and bury herself there. He had forced tonight on her.

The panic deepened. What if she was getting ready to leave him, what if her dark span wasn't about her, but rather about *him*? He knew he'd disappointed her; what if she knew she could do better? He opened his arms to her, more to console himself, but she only brought over a paper towel so he could fashion a bow around her bleeding finger.

"I don't know. I think this is fun," said Rachel. Loyal Rachel with the sharp little face, hungry eyes. She was down in the city from her prep school for the weekend. Barely fourteen years old, but she looked weary. Her nails were bitten beyond the quick, Lotto noticed. He'd have to ask Sallie if there was anything going on with her that he should know about. "I'm learning a lot. Beats Friday night's all-dorm slumber party for sure."

"I can imagine. Bottle of peppermint schnapps. *The Breakfast Club* on the VCR. Someone would be crying in the bathroom all night long. Midnight streaking across the quad. A game of all-girls' spin the bottle. My Rachel reading a book in the corner in her lobster-print pajamas, judging them all like a mini-queen," Lotto said. "The review in her journal would be devastating."

Rachel said, "Disappointing, trite, and vapid. Two thumbs down." They chuckled, the knot of desperation in the room gently loosed. This gentling would be Rachel's effect, not a flashy gift, but good.

In the silence afterward, Luanne said, "Of course, there were professional ethics that should have precluded you taking the canvas, Mathilde."

"For fuck's sake," Mathilde said. "It'd have been all right had someone else dug it from the dumpster? You? What is it, Luanne? You're jealous?"

Luanne made a face. Of course she was jealous. It must have been so hard for Luanne, Lotto thought, back when Mathilde worked at the gallery. Mathilde was always the second in charge. Knowledgeable, clever, gracious. Surely Ariel had favored Mathilde. Everyone favored Mathilde.

"Ha," Luanne said. "That's hilarious. Jealous of *you*?"

"Please stop," said Chollie. "If it had been a Picasso, everyone would have praised Mathilde for her foresight. You're being a total vagina."

"You're calling me a vagina? I don't even know who you are," Luanne said.

"We've met a million times. You say that every time," Chollie said.

Danica was watching the argument as if it were a game of Ping-Pong. She'd lost even more weight; her arms and cheeks were downy with strange fur. She was laughing.

"Please stop fighting," Rachel said quietly.

"I don't know why I come to your stupid freaking parties anyway," Luanne said, standing. She started to cry with anger. "You're a total fake, Mathilde, and you know what I'm talking about." She turned toward Lotto, and said, venomously, "Not you, Lotto, you're just a freaking Bambi. Anybody but you would understand by this point you don't have enough talent for the stage. But nobody wants to hurt you by saying it. Least of all your wife, who thrives on making you a freaking infant in your own life."

Lotto was out of his chair so fast the blood fled from his head. "Shut your pig face, Luanne. My wife is the best human being on the planet and you know it."

Rachel said, "Lotto!" and Mathilde said, low, "Lotto, stop," and Natalie and Susannah said, "Hey!"

Only Chollie burst into high-pitched laughter. Olga, whom they had all forgotten, whipped around and socked him hard on the shoulder, then stood and clattered across the floor in her high heels, threw open the apartment door, shouted, "You are monsters!" and stormed up to the street. The frigid wind blew down the stairs from the front door and spangled them with snowflakes.

For a long moment, nothing. Then Mathilde said, "Go after her, Chollie."

"Nah," he said. "She won't get far without her jacket."

"It's ten below, you fuck," said Danica, and threw Olga's synthetic fur at Chollie's face. He got up grumbling and went out, slamming both doors. Mathilde rose and lifted the painting off the wall, over the shining pate of the brass Buddha, and handed it to Luanne.

Luanne looked at the painting in her hands. She said, "I can't take this." The others in the room had the sense of a ferocious battle being fought in the silence.

Mathilde sat, folded her arms, closed her eyes. Luanne put the painting against Mathilde's knees. She went out and the door closed on her forever. In her absence, the room seemed brighter, even the overhead lights mellowed.

The friends left, one by one. Rachel shut herself into the bathroom, and they could hear the bath running.

When they were alone, Mathilde knelt in front of Lotto and took off her glasses and buried her face in his chest. He held her helplessly, making soothing sounds. Conflict nauseated him. He couldn't bear it. His wife's thin shoulders shook. But when at last she lifted her head, he was startled; her face was flushed and swollen, but she was laughing. Laughing? Lotto kissed the plum presses under her eyes, the freckles on her pale skin. He felt a vertiginous awe.

"You called Luanne a pig face," she said. "You! Mr. Genial. Leaping in to save the day. Ha!"

Marvelous girl. He saw, with a warm rush, that she would come through this period of stringiness and woe so terrible she couldn't share it with him. She would return. She would love him again. She wouldn't leave. And in every place where they lived from then on, that painting would blue the air. It would be a testament. Their marriage picked itself up off the ground, stretched, looked at them with its hands on its hips. Mathilde was coming back to Lotto. Hallelujah.

"HALLELUJAH," Chollie said, knocking back an eggnog, mostly brandy. It was eleven o'clock. "Christ is born." He and Lotto were silently competing to see who could be drunker. Lotto hid it better, seemed normal, but the room spun if he didn't blink it straight.

Outside, a thickness of night. Streetlights were lollipops of bright snow.

Aunt Sallie hadn't stopped talking for hours, and now she was saying, ". . . course, I don't know nothing, being not sophisticated as all y'all bachelor artists, and I sure as heck can't tell you what to do, Lotto my boy, but if it was me, which it isn't, I know, but if it was, I'd say I done gave it my all, be mighty proud of the three-four plays I done these past years and say, well, not everybody can be Richard Burton, and maybe I got something else I can do with my life. Like maybe, oh, take over the trust or something. Get back in Antoinette's graces. Get undisinherited. You know she's faring poorly, that sick heart of hers. Rachel and you both stand to gain a lot when she passes, god forbid it be soon." She looked at Lotto cannily over her canary's beak.

The Buddha laughed in silence from the mantelpiece. Around him, a lushness of poinsettias. Below, a fire Lotto had dared to make out of sticks collected from the park. Later, there would be a chimney fire, a sound of wind like a rushing freight train, and the trucks arriving in the night.

"I'm struggling," Lotto said. "Maybe. But come on, I was born wealthy, white, and male. I'd have nothing to work with if I don't have a little struggle. I'm doing what I love. That's not nothing." It sounded mechanical even to his own ears. Bad acting, Lotto. [But acting has slipped away from him a little, hasn't it.] His heart wasn't in the fight anymore.

"What's success, anyway?" said Rachel. "I say it's being able to work as much as you want at whatever lights you up. Lotto's had steady work all these years."

"I love you," Lotto said to his sister. She was in high school, as skinny as Sallie. She took after the Satterwhite side, dark and hairy and ill-favored; her friends couldn't believe that Lotto and she were related. Only Lotto thought her stunning, planar. Her thin face reminded him of Giacometti sculptures. She never smiled anymore. He pulled her close and kissed her, feeling how tightly she was coiled inside.

"Success is money," Chollie said. "Duh."

"Success," Sallie said, "is finding your greatness, hushpuppies. Lotto, you were born with it. I saw it the moment you came screaming out of Antoinette. Middle of a hurricane. You're simply not *listening* to what your greatness is. Gawain told me he always thought you'd be the president of the USA or an astronaut. Something bigger than big. It's in your stars."

"Sorry to disappoint you," Lotto said. "And my stars."

"Well. You also disappointed our dead father," Rachel said, laughing.

"To our disappointed dead father," Lotto said. He raised his glass at his sister and swallowed the bitterness. It wasn't her fault; she'd never known Gawain, didn't know what pain she'd summoned.

Mathilde came back in the door, carrying a tray. Glorious in her silver dress, her hair platinum, in a Hitchcock twist: she'd gotten fancy since she'd been promoted six months earlier. Lotto wanted to take her into the bedroom and engage in some vigorous frustration abatement.

Save me, he mouthed, but his wife wasn't paying attention.

"I'm worried." Mathilde put the tray down on the counter in the kitchen, turned to them. "I left this up there for Bette this morning, and it's eleven, and she hasn't touched it. Has anyone seen her the last few days?"

Silence, the clicking of the heirloom clock Sallie had brought as a carry-on in her duffel. They all looked ceilingward, as if to see beyond the layers of plaster and floorboard and carpet into the cold, dark apartment [silent save for the refrigerator hum, a large cold lump on the bed, the only thing breathing the hungry tabby rubbing against the window].

"M.," Lotto said. "It's Christmas. She probably left yesterday for some relative's place, forgot to tell us. Nobody's alone on Christmas."

"Muvva is," Rachel said. "Muvva's alone in her dank little beach house, watching the whales with her binocs."

"Bullhonkey. Your mother had her choice and she chose her agoraphobia over spending Christ's birthday with her children. Believe me, I know it's a disease. I live with it every dang day. I don't know why every year I buy her a ticket. This year she even packed. Put on her jacket, her perfume. Then just sat on the couch. She said she'd rather organize the photo boxes in the spare bathroom. She made her own choice, and she's a grown woman. We can't feel bad," Aunt Sallie said, but her pinched lips belied her words. Lotto felt a rush of relief. Her scratching at him tonight, her picking and prodding, arose from her own guilt.

"I don't feel bad," said Rachel, but her face was also drawn.

"I do," Lotto said quietly. "I haven't seen my mother for a long time. I feel very bad."

Chollie heaved a sarcastic sigh. Sallie glared at him. "Well, it's not like you kids can't go see her," Sallie said. "I know she cut you off, but all you have to do is spend five minutes with her and she'll love you both. And that's a promise. I can make it happen."

Lotto opened his mouth, but there was too much to say, and it was all sour toward his mother, un-Christmassy, and so he shut it and swallowed the words back.

Mathilde put a bottle of red wine down hard. "Listen. Antoinette's never been inside this apartment. She has never met me. She chose to be angry and stay angry. We can't be sorry for her choices." Lotto saw her hands trembling; rage, he realized. He loved the rare times she showed how thin her calm surface was; how, beneath, she boiled. A perverse part of Lotto, it's true, wanted to lock Mathilde and his mother in a room and let them claw it all out. But he wouldn't do it to Mathilde; she was far too sweet to spend even a minute in his mother's company without coming out maimed. She turned off the chandelier so the Christmas tree with its lights and glass icicles overcame the room, and he pulled her onto his lap.

"Breathe," Lotto said softly into his wife's hair. Rachel blinked in the tree's gleam.

Sallie had been speaking hard truths, he knew. It had become evident over the past year that he could no longer count on his charm, which had faded; he tested it again and again on coffee baristas and audition gauntlets and people reading in the subway, but beyond the leeway given to any moderately attractive young man, he didn't have it anymore. People could look away from him these days. For so long, he had thought it was just a switch he could flick. But he had lost it, his mojo, his juju, his radiance. Gone, the easy words. He could not remember a night when he didn't fall asleep drunk.

And so he opened his mouth and began to sing. "Jingle Bells," a song he hated, and he was never the world's best tenor anyway. But what else was there to do but sing in the face of dismay, the image of his fat mother sitting up alone by a potted majestic palm strung in colored bulbs? The others now were joining in, miraculous, all of them save Mathilde, still rigid with anger, though even she was softening, a smile cracking her lips. At last, even she sang.

Sallie watched Lotto, cleaving. Her boy. Heart of her heart. She was clear-eyed, knew that Rachel, being of finer moral stock, kinder, humbler, deserved her affection more than Lotto. But it was for Lotto that Sallie woke praying. These years of distance were hard on her. [. . . *in a one-horse open sleigh* . . .] It came back to her now, the Christmas before he'd finished college, before Mathilde, when he had met Sallie and Rachel in Boston, where they stayed at a redoubtable ancient hotel and were snowed in under three feet of powder, like being

73

stuck in a dream. Lotto had maneuvered a rendezvous with a girl at another table at dinner, his smoothness so like his mother's when she was young and lovely that it took Sallie's breath away. Antoinette, undulating, had for a moment been superimposed on her son. Later, Sallie waited in ambush until midnight, standing at the diamond window at the end of the hallway where their rooms were, the endless snow falling into the Common at her back. [. . . *o'er the fields we go . . .*] At the other end, in minuscule, three housemaids with their trolleys were laughing, shushing one another. At last, her boy's door opened and he emerged, bare but for a pair of running shorts. Such a beauti- ful long back he had, his mother's, at least when she was thin. There was a towel around his neck; he was going up to the pool. The sin he intended to enact so painfully obvious that Sallie's cheeks burned in imagining the girl's buttocks gridded with tile marks, Lotto's knees scabby in the morning. Where did he learn such confidence, she thought, as he became smaller, going toward the housemaids. He said something and all three pealed, and one gave him a little flick with a cloth, and another sent a slow glitter, chocolates, at his chest. [. . . *laughing all the way, ha ha ha!*] He caught them. His laugh rumbled back to Sallie. How ordinary he was becoming, she'd thought. He was turning banal. If he wasn't careful, some sweet girl would glue herself to him, Sallie saw, and Lotto would drift into marriage, a job as some high-paid menial, a family, Christmas cards, a beach house, middle-aged flab, grandchildren, too much money, boredom, death. He'd be faithful and conservative in old age, blind to his privilege. When Sallie stopped crying, she found herself alone, the cold draft of the window at her neck, and on both sides the rows of doors went on and on, diminishing to nothing at the end. [. . . *what fun it is to ride and sing a sleighing song tonight, oh!*] But glories! Mathilde came; and though she appeared to be the selfsame sweet girl Sallie had been afraid of, she was not. Sallie saw the flint in her. Mathilde could save

Lotto from his own laziness, Sallie had thought, but here they were, years later, and he was still ordinary. The chorus caught in her throat.

A stranger hurrying as fast as he could over the icy sidewalks looked in. He saw a circle of singing people bathed in the clean white light from a tree, and his heart did a somersault, and the image stayed with him; it merged with him even as he came home to his own children, who were already sleeping in their beds, to his wife crossly putting together the tricycle without the screwdriver that he'd run out to borrow. It remained long after his children ripped open their gifts and abandoned their toys in puddles of paper and grew too old for them and left their house and parents and childhoods, so that he and his wife gaped at each other in bewilderment as to how it had happened so terribly swiftly. All those years, the singers in the soft light in the basement apartment crystallized in his mind, became the very idea of what happiness should look like.

ALMOST MIDNIGHT and Rachel couldn't get over the ceiling. What chutzpah had made Mathilde gild it! Their bodies echoed, globs in the brightness above. It did transform the room, shining elegantly against the dark walls. On this frigid last day of the year, it seemed a hand had peeled back the roof like the lid of a sardine can and they were standing beneath an August sun.

It was unbelievable that this was the same empty white space that she had walked into on the day of their housewarming party more than seven years earlier, with its wild roil of bodies and beer stink, the glorious sweaty heat and the garden radiant with early-summer light out the windows. Now there were icicles shining in the streetlights. There were orchids around the Buddha, overgrown money plants in the corners, Louis XIV chairs covered in French flour sacking. It was elegant, overstuffed, too beautiful. A gilded cage, Rachel thought. Mathilde had been short with Lotto all evening. She no longer smiled when she looked at him. Well, she barely looked at him. Rachel was afraid that Mathilde, whom Rachel loved as dearly as anyone, was about to bust out of it all in a commotion of wings. Poor Lotto. Poor all of them if Mathilde left him.

Rachel's new girlfriend, Elizabeth, a girl so pale of hair and skin she seemed made of paper, felt Rachel's nerves ratcheting up and squeezed her shoulder. The tension went out of Rachel. She took a wobbly breath and kissed Elizabeth shyly on the neck.

Outside, the swift passing of a cat body on the sidewalk. It couldn't be the tabby owned by the old lady from upstairs. That cat had been ancient when Lotto and Mathilde had moved in; last Christmas it starved for three days, until Lotto and Mathilde got ahold of the landlord vacationing in the British Virgin Islands and had someone investigate. Poor rotted dead Bette. Lotto had to take a hysterical Mathilde to Samuel's apartment for a week just to get her to calm down while the fumigators were in. Strange to witness composed Mathilde lose it; it made Rachel see her as the thin, big-eyed little girl she must have been, made Rachel love her even more. Now there was a couple with a new baby up there, which was why this New Year's Eve party tonight was so small. Newborns, apparently, dislike noise.

"Breeders," said Mathilde, out of nowhere, Mathilde, who could read minds. She laughed at the astonished face Rachel made, then returned to the kitchen, pouring champagne into glasses on the silver tray. Lotto thought of the baby upstairs, then the way Mathilde would look when pregnant, svelte as a girl from behind, but in silhouette as if she'd swallowed a calabash. He laughed at the thought. Her strap down, breast lolling out, fat enough for even his hungry mouth. Days expanding outward from clean, warm skin and milk; that was what he wanted, exactly that.

Chollie and Danica and Susannah and Samuel sat quietly, pale, serious-ish. They had come alone to the party, this year bad for breakups. Samuel was skinny, his skin cracked around his mouth. This was the first he'd been out since having surgery for testicular cancer. He seemed, for the first time, diminished. "Speaking of breeders, last week I saw that girl you dated in college, Lotto. What was her name? Bridget," Susannah said. "Pediatric oncology fellow. Hugely pregnant. Swollen like a tick. She seems happy."

"I didn't date in college," Lotto said.. "Except for Mathilde. For two weeks. Then we eloped."

"Didn't date. Just fucked every girl in the Hudson Valley." Samuel laughed. Chemo had suddenly balded him; without his curls he looked newly ferretlike. "Sorry, Rachel, but your brother was a slut."

"Yeah, yeah, I've heard," Rachel said. "I think that Bridget girl used to come to your parties when you first moved in here. She was so boring. You always packed about a million people in this room. I miss those days."

Up there rose the ghosts of parties, of themselves when they were younger, too dumb to understand that they were ecstatic.

Whatever happened to all of those friends of ours? Lotto wondered. The ones who had seemed so essential had faded away. Nerd princes with their twins in strollers, Park Slope and craft beers. Arnie, who owned a bar empire, still doing girls with plates in their ears and jailhouse tattoos. Natalie now a CFO of some Internet start-up in San Francisco, a hundred others faded off. The friends had been whittled down. The ones who remained were heartwood, marrow.

"I don't know," Susannah was saying softly. "I guess I like living alone." She was still a teenager in the soap opera. She'd be a teenager until they killed her off and then she'd play mothers and wives. Women in narratives were always defined by their relations.

"I get so sad sleeping alone," Danica said. "I want to buy a sex doll just to wake up next to someone in the morning."

"Date a model. Same thing," Chollie said.

"I hate your face, Chollie," Danica said, trying not to laugh.

"Yadda yadda," Chollie said. "Keep singing that same old song. We both know the truth."

"Less than a minute until the ball drops," called Mathilde, carrying in the tray of champagne.

Everyone looked at Samuel, who shrugged. Even cancer couldn't dent him.

"Poor One Ball Samuel," Lotto said. He'd gotten into the bourbon after dinner and hadn't recovered yet.

"Old Single Dingle?" Chollie suggested, but not unkindly, for once.

"Half-sack Sam," Mathilde said, and kicked lightly at Lotto, who was stretched out on the couch. He sat up, yawned. He'd unbuttoned his pants. Thirty, at the end of his youth. He felt the darkness settle on him again, and said, "This is it, you guys. The last year of humanity. Next New Year's, it'll be Y2K and all the planes will fall out of the sky and the computers will explode and the nuclear power plants will go off-line and we'll all see a flash and then the great blank whiteness will come over all of us. Done. Finito, the human experiment. So live it up! It's the last year we get!"

He was joking; he believed what he was saying. He thought of how the world without humans would be more brilliant, greener, teeming with strange life, rats with opposable thumbs, monkeys in spectacles, mutant fish building palaces below the sea. How, in the grand scheme of things, it would be better without human witness anyway. He thought of his mother's young face flickering in candlelight, in revelation. "And I saw the woman drunken with the blood of the saints, and with the blood of the martyrs of Jesus; and when I saw her, I wondered with great admiration," Lotto whispered, and his friends looked at him, saw something terrible, looked away.

He broke Rachel's fucking heart. Her whole family broke her fucking heart. Muvva burying herself in solitude, in unhappiness. Doglike Sallie slaving away. Lotto, whose pride she couldn't understand; only a child could stay so angry so long, only a child wouldn't forgive in order to make things right. Mathilde saw Rachel's eyes fill with pity and shook her head slightly: No. He'll see it.

"Thirty seconds," Mathilde said. Prince was playing from the computer, of course.

Chollie leaned toward Danica, angling for the midnight kiss. Horrible little man. Such a mistake to let him feel her up in the taxi one night coming back from the Hamptons this past summer. What was she thinking? She'd been between boyfriends, but still. "Not a fucking chance," she said, but he was speaking.

". . . owe me two million dollars," he said.

"What?" she said.

He grinned, said, "Twenty-something seconds until 1999. You bet me they'd be divorced by 1998."

"Fuck you," she said.

"Fuck you, welsher," he said.

"We have until the end of the year," she said.

"Twenty seconds," Mathilde said. "Good-bye, 1998, you slow and muddy year."

"There is nothing good or bad, but thinking makes it so," Lotto said drunkenly.

"You speak an infinite deal of nothing," Mathilde said. Lotto recoiled, opened his mouth, closed it.

"See?" Danica muttered. "They're fighting. If one of them storms out, I'm calling it a win."

Mathilde snatched a glass from the tray, and said, "Ten." She licked at the champagne she spilled on her hand.

"I'll absolve your debt if you go on a date with me," Chollie said, his hot breath in Danica's ear.

"What?" Danica said.

"I'm rich. You're mean," Chollie said. "Why the hell not."

"Eight," Mathilde said.

"Because I loathe you," Danica said.

"Six. Five. Four," the others said. Chollie raised an eyebrow.

"Okay, fine," Danica sighed.

"One! Happy New Year!" they shouted, and someone gave three stomps from the apartment above, and the baby wailed, and outside they could hear the very faint noise of voices shouting all the way over the crystalline night from Times Square, then a blast of fireworks in the street.

"Happy 1999, my love," Lotto said to Mathilde; and it had been so very long since they had kissed like this. A month at least. He had forgotten about the freckles on her pretty nose. How had he forgotten such a thing? Nothing like having a wife who worked herself to death to stifle the mood for love. Nothing like dying dreams, he thought, and disappointment.

Mathilde's irises shifted smaller when she pulled her head back. "This will be your breakthrough year," she said. "You'll be Hamlet on Broadway. You'll find your groove."

"I love your optimism," he said, but felt sick. Elizabeth and Rachel were both kissing Susannah's cheeks because she looked so lonely. Samuel kissed her also, blushing, but she laughed him off.

"I'm trashed," Danica said, pulling away from her kiss with Chollie. She looked startled.

They left, two by two, and Mathilde turned off the lights, yawned, piled the food and glasses on the counters to clean them up in the morning. Lotto watched as she shimmied off her dress in the bedroom and climbed under the duvet in her thong.

"You remember when we used to have sex before we even went to bed on New Year's Day? A bodily blessing for the new year," he called to her through the doorway. He considered saying more; that this year, maybe, they could have a kid. Lotto could be the stay-at-home parent. For sure, if he was the one who had the relevant anatomy, a mistake would already have been made with the birth control and a little Lotto would be even now kicking its heels in his gut. It was unfair that women could have such primordial joy and men could not.

"Baby, we used to have sex on garbage day and grocery-shopping day, too," she said.

"What changed?" he said.

"We're old," she said. "We still do it more than most of our married friends. Twice a week's not bad."

"Not enough," he muttered.

"I heard that," she said. "As if I've ever made myself unavailable to you."

He heaved a sigh, prepared to stand.

"Fine," she said. "If you come to bed now, I'll let you do me. But don't be mad if I fall asleep."

"Glory. How tempting," Lotto said, and sat back down with his bottle in the dark.

He listened to his wife's breath even into snores and wondered how he had arrived here. Drunk, lonely, stewing in his failure. Triumph had been assured. Somehow, he'd frittered his potential away. A sin. Thirty and still a nothing. Kills you slowly, failure. As Sallie would have said, he done been bled out.

[Perhaps we love him more like this; humbled.]

Tonight, he understood his mother, burying herself alive in her beach house. No more risking the hurt that came from contact with others. He listened to the dark beat under his thoughts, which he had had forever, since his father had died. Release. A fuselage could fall from a plane and pin him into the earth. One flick of a switch in his brain would power him down. Blessed relief at last, it would be. Aneurysms ran in the family. His father's had been so sudden, forty-six, too young; and all Lotto wanted was to close his eyes and find his father there, to put his head on his father's chest and smell him and hear the warm thumpings of his heart. Was that so much to ask? He'd had one parent who'd loved him. Mathilde had given him enough but he'd ground her down. Her hot faith had cooled. She'd averted her face. She was disappointed in him. Oh, man, he was losing her, and if he lost her, if she left him—the leather valise in her hand, her thin back unturning—he might as well be dead.

Lotto was weeping; he could tell from the cold on his face. He tried to keep quiet. Mathilde needed sleep. She had been working sixteen-hour days, six days a week, kept them fed and housed. He brought nothing to their marriage, only disappointment and dirty laundry. He fished out the laptop he'd stored under the couch when Mathilde had ordered him to clean up before everyone had come over tonight. He just wanted the Internet, the other sad souls of the world, but instead, he opened a blank document, shut his eyes, thought of what he'd lost. Home state, mother, that light he'd once lit in strangers, in his wife. His father. Everyone had underestimated Gawain because he was quiet and unlettered, but only he had understood the value of the water under the scrubby family land, had captured and sold it. Lotto thought of the photos of his mother when she was young, once a mermaid, the tail rolled like a stocking over her legs, undulating in the cold springs. He remembered his own small hand immersed in the source, the bones freezing past the point of numbness, how he'd loved that pain.

Pain! Swords of morning light in his eyes.

Mathilde was haloed blindingly in the icicles in the window. She was in her slattern's robe. Her feet were red at the knuckles with cold. And her face—what was it? There was something wrong. Eyes puffed and red. What had Lotto done? Surely something awful. Maybe he'd left porn on his laptop and she'd seen it when she had woken up. Maybe a terrible kind of porn, the worst, maybe he'd been led into it by wild curiosity, clicking through wormholes so progressively more evil that he ended up at the unforgivable. She would leave him. He'd be finished. Fat and alone and a failure, not even worth the air he'd breathe. "Don't leave me," he said. "I'll be better."

She looked up, then stood and came across the rug to the couch and put the computer down on the coffee table and took his cheeks in her cold hands.

Her robe parted, revealing her thighs, like sweet pink putti. Practically bearing wings.

"Oh, Lotto," Mathilde said, and her coffee breath mingled with his own dead muskrat breath, and he felt the swoop of her eyelashes on his temple. "Baby, you've done it," she said.

"What?" he said.

"It's so good. I don't know why I was so surprised, of course you're brilliant. It's just been a struggle for so long."

"Thank you," he said. "I'm sorry. What's happening?"

"I don't know! A play, I think. Called *The Springs*. You started it at 1:47 last night. I can't freaking believe you wrote all that in five hours. It needs a third act. Some editing. I've already started. You can't spell, but we knew that."

It snapped back to him, his writing last night. Some deep-buried acorn of emotion, something about his father. Oh.

"All along," she said, "hiding here in plain sight. Your true talent."

She had straddled him, was easing his jeans down his hips.

"My true talent," he said slowly. "Was hiding."

"Your genius. Your new life," she said. "You were meant to be a playwright, my love. Thank fucking god we figured that out."

"We figured that out," he said. As if stepping out of a fog: a little boy, a grown man. Characters who were him but also not, Lotto transformed by the omniscient view. A shock of energy as he looked on them in the morning. There was life in these figures. He was suddenly hungry to return to that world, to live in it for a while longer.

But his wife was saying, "Hello there, Sir Lancelot, you doughty fellow. Come out and joust." And what a beautiful way to fully awaken, his wife astraddle, whispering to his newly knighted peen, warming him with her breath, telling him he's a what? A genius. Lotto had long known it in his bones. Since he was a tiny boy, shouting on a chair, making grown men grow pink and weep. But how nice to get such confirmation, and in such a format, too. Under the golden ceiling, under the golden wife. All right, then. He could be a playwright.

He watched as the Lotto he thought he had been stood up in his greasepaint and jerkin, his doublet sweated through, panting, the roar inside him going external as the audience rose in ovation. Ghostly out of his body he went, giving an elaborate bow, passing for good through the closed door of the apartment.

There should have been nothing left. And yet, some kind of Lotto remained. A separate him, a new one, below his wife, who was sliding her face up his stomach, pushing the string of her thong to one side, enveloping him. His hands were opening her robe to show her breasts like nestlings, her chin tipped up toward their vaguely reflected bodies. She was saying, "Oh god," her fists coming down hard on his chest, saying, "Now you're Lancelot. No more Lotto. Lotto's a child's name, and you're no child. You're a genius fucking playwright, Lancelot Satterwhite. We will make this happen."

If it meant his wife smiling through her blond lashes at him again, his wife posting atop him like a prize equestrienne, he could change. He could become what she wanted. No longer failed actor. Potential playwright. There rose a feeling in him as if he'd discovered a window in a lightless closet locked behind him. And still a sort of pain, a loss. He closed his eyes against it and moved in the dark toward what, just now, only Mathilde could see so clearly.

4

He was still drunk. "Best night of my life," he said. "A million curtain calls. All my friends. And look at you, gorgeous. Ovations. Off-Broadway. Bar! Walk home, stars in the sky!"

"Words are failing you, my love," Mathilde said.

[Wrong. Words, tonight, had not failed. Unseen in the corners of the theaters, the forces of judgment had gathered. They watched, considered, found it good.]

"Body taking over now," he said, and she was game for what he had in mind, but when she returned from the bathroom, he was asleep, naked atop the duvet, and she covered him, kissed his eyelids, tasted his glory there. Savored it. Slept.

ONE-EYED KING, 2000

"Baby, this play is about Erasmus. You can't name it *The Oneiroi*."

"Why?" Lotto said. "It's a good name."

"Nobody's going to remember it. Nobody knows what it means. I don't know what it means."

"The Oneiroi are the sons of Nyx. Night. They're dreams. Brothers of Hypnos, Thanatos, Geras: Sleep, Death, Old Age. This is a play about Erasmus's dreams, baby. Prince of the Humanists! The bastard of a Catholic priest, orphaned by the plague in 1483. Desperately in love with another man—"

"I read the play, I know this already—"

"And the word *Oneiroi* makes me laugh. Erasmus was the man who said, *In the land of the blind, the one-eyed man is king.* One-eyed king. *Roi d'un oeil.* Oneiroi."

"Oh," she said. She'd frowned when he'd spoken French; she'd been a French, art history, and classics triple major in college. Dark purple dahlia in the garden-side window, gleam of autumn light beyond. She came over to him, rested her chin on his shoulder, put her hands down his pants. "Well. It's a sexy play," she said.

"Yes," he said. "Your hands are very soft, my wife."

"I'm just shaking hands with your one-eyed king."

"Oh, love," he said. "You're brilliant. That *is* a better title."

"I know," she said. "You may have it."

"Generous," he said.

"Except that I don't like the way your king there is looking at me. He's giving me the evil one-eye."

"Off with his head," he said, and carried her into the bedroom.

ISLANDS, 2001

"It's not that I *agree* with them," she said. "But it *was* pretty ballsy of you to write about three Caribbean hotel maids in the middle of a Boston snowstorm."

He didn't pick his head up from the crook of his elbow. Newspapers were strewn around the living room of the new second-floor apartment they'd bought. They were still too house-poor to afford a rug. The austere way the oak floors gleamed reminded him of her.

"Phoebe Delmar, I get," he said. "She hates everything I have done and will ever do. Cultural appropriation, whatever, strident, shrill. But why did the *Times* reviewer have to bring up my mother's money? What does that have to do with anything? I sure as stinkers can't afford the heat now, so why do they care? And why can't I write about poor people if I was raised with money? Don't they understand what *fiction* is?"

"We can afford heat," she said. "Cable, maybe not. But other than that, it's a good review."

"It's mixed," he groaned. "I feel like dying."

[In a week planes would crash a mile away, and Mathilde at work would drop her cup on the floor, shattering it; and Lotto at home would put on his running shoes and run forty-three blocks north to her office and into the revolving door, only to see her leaving in the parallel glass compartment. They would gaze at each other palely through the glass as she was now outside and he in, and he'd feel a confused shame within his panic, though its source—this very moment with the intensity of his tiny despair—would already have been forgotten.]

"You're such a drama whore," she said. "Phoebe Delmar would win if you died. Just write a new one."

"About what?" he said. "I'm dried up. Done at the age of thirty-three."

"Go back to what you know," she said.

"I don't know anything," he said.

"You know me," she said.

He looked at her, his face smeary with newsprint, and began to smile. "I do," he said.

THE HOUSE IN THE GROVE, 2003

ACT II, SCENE I

[*The porch of the plantation house, Olivia in tennis whites, waiting for Joseph to come out. Joseph's mother is in a rocking chair with a glass of white wine spritzer in her hand.*]

LADYBIRD: Now come on over here and set yourself down. I'm glad we get a minute to chat. Rare Joseph brings a girlfriend home, you know. Most Thanksgivings, it's just us. Family. But why don't you tell me about *you*, darling. Where do you come from? What do your parents do?

OLIVIA: Nowhere. And nothing. I don't have any parents, Mrs. Dutton.

LADYBIRD: Nonsense. Everybody's got parents. You sprung out of somebody's head? I am sorry, but Minerva you are not. Now, you may not like your parents, the Good Lord knows I do not like mine, but you have them, for sure.

OLIVIA: I'm an orphan.

LADYBIRD: Orphan. Nobody wanted to adopt you? Beauty like you? I do not believe this. Of course, you must've been a sullen girl. Oh, yes. I can see you were quite a sullen girl. Difficult. Too smart for your own good.

OLIVIA [*After a long pause.*]: Joseph's taking a really long time.

LADYBIRD: Boy's vain. Staring in the mirror making faces, looking at his pretty hairdo. [*They both laugh.*] In any event, you clearly do not want to talk about it, which I do not blame you for. Sore wound, I'm sure it is, darling. Family being the most important thing in the world. The most important.

Why, it's your family that tells you who you are. Without a family, you're a nobody.

[*Olivia, startled, raises her eyes. Ladybird is looking at her, smiling broadly.*]

OLIVIA: I'm not a nobody.

LADYBIRD: Darling, I don't wish to offend, but I have come to doubt that very much. You're pretty, sure, but you don't have much to offer a boy like Joey. And yes, he's in love, but he's a lover. You don't have to worry about him having a broken heart. He'll have a new girl in minutes. You can just skedaddle. Save us both some time. Let him find someone a little more apropos.

OLIVIA [*Slowly*.]: Apropos. You mean a girl with a rich family? That's funny because, Mrs. Dutton, I have a family. They're rich as kings.

LADYBIRD: You a liar? Because you are either lying now or you were lying when you said you were an orphan. Either way, I haven't believed a word out of your mouth since you got here.

JOSEPH [*Comes out, smiling brightly, whistling*.]: Hello, beauties.

OLIVIA: I never lie, Mrs. Dutton. I'm a pathological truth-teller. Now, if you'll excuse me, I'm off to play some tennis with my little hubby here. [*Grins*.]

JOSEPH: Olivia!

LADYBIRD [*Standing*.]: Your. Your what, your hubby? Hubby? Husband? Joseph!

"Cuts a little close to the quick," Mathilde said, looking up. She wore sadness at the corners of her mouth.

"You'll meet my mother someday," Lotto said. "Just want you

to be prepared. She still asks when I'm going to settle down with a nice girl."

"Ouch," Mathilde said. She looked at him over the table, coffee and bagel, half eaten. "Pathological truth-teller?"

He looked at her. Waited.

"Okay," she conceded.

GACY, 2003

"'What would possess the young playwright Lancelot Satterwhite, whose only real talents, thus far, have shown themselves to be a kind of wild reimagining of the Southern experience, to write a play glorifying John Wayne Gacy, the pedophile serial-murdering clown? As if the wooden dialogue, the awful a cappella songs Gacy sings, and the graphic scenes of murder and mayhem weren't bad enough, the audience leaves after three hours with an overwhelming question: Why? Not only extremely bad, this play is in extremely bad taste. Perhaps this is a nod to Satterwhite's betters, or some sort of homage to *Sweeney Todd*, but, sad to say, Lancelot Satterwhite is no Stephen Sondheim and he never will be,'" Mathilde read.

She tossed the newspaper down.

"You guessed it. Phoebe fucking Delmar," she said.

"All the rest of them loved it," he said. "Normally, I feel some sort of shame with a bad review. But this chick is so off base I don't even care."

"I think the play is funny," Mathilde said.

"It *is* funny," Lotto said. "The whole audience was cracking up."

"Phoebe Delmar. Five plays, five pans. The woman knows nothing," Mathilde said.

They looked at each other, started to smile.

"Write another," he said. "I know."

GRIMOIRE, 2005

"You're a genius," she said, putting the manuscript down.

"So do me," he said.

"Gladly," she said.

HAMLIN IN WINTER, 2006

Sallie, Rachel, and Rachel's new husband came up for the opening night. Husband? A man? Where was Elizabeth? Mathilde and Lotto held hands in the taxi going to brunch, communicating, not speaking.

The husband chitter-chattered like a squirrel. "Affable dimwit" was Mathilde's assessment later.

"Illiterate snake" was Lotto's. "What is she doing? I thought she was a lesbian. I loved Elizabeth. Elizabeth had gorgeous breasts. Where did she pick this meth-head up?"

"Just because he has a tattoo on his neck doesn't mean he's a meth-head," Mathilde said. She thought for a moment. "I think."

They had the story over eggs Benedict. Rachel had had a bad year after college. She had so much energy her hands darted like humming-birds from plate to utensil to glass to hair to lap, without cease.

"You don't get *married* at twenty-three because you had a bad year," Lotto said.

"Why *do* you get married at twenty-three, Lotto?" Rachel said. "Pray tell."

"Touché," Mathilde murmured. Lotto looked at her. "Actually, we were twenty-two," she said.

Anyway, as she had said, Rachel had had a bad year. Elizabeth broke up with her because of something Rachel had done. Whatever it was, it was bad enough that Rachel flushed a brighter red and the husband squeezed her knee under the table. She came home to the beach so Sallie could take care of her. Pete here worked at Marineland.

"Are you a scientist, Pete?" Mathilde said.

"No, but I feed the dolphins," he said.

Pete was exactly right at exactly the right time, Rachel said. Oh, and she was going to law school, and if Lotto didn't mind, she'd take over the trust when she was done.

"Did Muvva cut you off, too?" Lotto said. "Poor lady. Denied the huge, frothy celebration she'd so longed for. She wouldn't have known who to invite and wouldn't have attended anyway, but she would have delighted in planning. Muttonchop sleeves for you, Rachel. A cake like Chichén Itzá. Flower girls in hoopskirts. Her whole Yankee family getting sunburnt and internally combusting with envy. I wouldn't be surprised if she changed the beneficiary of the trust to a schizoid pit-bull rescue or something."

There was a pause. Sallie winced and busied herself with her napkin. "She didn't cut me off," Rachel said quietly.

A long silence. Lotto blinked the sting away.

"But I had to sign a prenup. I only get two mil," Pete said, making a comically sad face, and they all looked down into their Bloody Marys, and he blushed and said, "I meant if something bad happens. Nothing's happening, baby," and Rachel gave a tiny nod.

He would prove a temporary embarrassment; in six months, Elizabeth, of the great, soft boobs, the cat's-eye glasses, the pale hair and skin, would be back for good.

At the theater, Lotto watched his aunt and sister. Ten minutes in, when their mascara started running, he sighed and relaxed and passed a hand over his face.

After all the curtain calls and congratulations and hugs and the speech he gave to his actors, who loved him, *loved* him, it was plain from the way they looked at him, Mathilde at last snuck Lotto out the back door to the bar where she'd had the assistant take his family.

Sallie leapt up, burst into tears, hung on his neck. Rachel hugged him fiercely around the waist. Pete darted in here and there to pat Lotto on his arms. Sallie said in his ear, "I had no idea, my sweet, how much you wanted babies."

He looked at her surprised. "*That* is what you got from this? That I want kids?"

"Well. Yeah," Rachel said. "The play is all about family, how you pass things down from one generation to another, how when you're born, you belong to a certain patch of family land. It was just obvious. Plus, Dorothy is pregnant. And Julie has a baby upstairs. And even Hoover carries his baby around on his chest. That's not what you meant?"

"Nope," Mathilde said, laughing.

Lotto shrugged. "Maybe," he said.

ELEANOR OF AQUITAINE, 2006

A small man came rushing into the black box at the VIP reception. His sparse hair was white. He wore a faded green cloak and looked, flapping up, like a luna moth. "Oh, my dear boy, oh, my dear, dear Lotto, you have done it, you've done what I always knew you would do. You have it in your blood, the theater. Tonight, Thalia kisses your cheeks."

Lancelot smiled at the little man aping Thalia, kissing his cheeks. He took a glass of champagne from a passing tray. "Thank you so very much. I love Eleanor of Aquitaine. She was a genius, the mother of modern poetry. Now, forgive me, I know that we know each other, but tell me how, exactly?"

Lotto smiled, never taking his eyes off the little man, who drew his head back quickly and blinked. "Oh. Dear boy. I apologize. I have followed your career, you see, with such delight and knew you so well through your plays that I thought, of course, you knew me in return. The old authorial fallacy. I'm mortified. I'm your old teacher at prep school. Denton Thrasher. Does that ring a"—he took a breath, let it out theatrically—"does that ring a bell?"

"I'm so sorry, Mr. Thrasher," Lancelot said. "I don't recall. Losing my memory. But thank you ever so much for coming back here and reminding me."

He smiled down at the little man.

"You don't," the man said, his voice faltering; then he blushed and seemed to fade where he stood.

Mathilde, who had been at her husband's side this whole time, wondered. His memory was as sharp as a diamondcutter. He never forgot a face. He could act out a play verbatim, having seen it only twice. She watched him turn and meet a legendary musical star with a kiss on her hand and saw, past the charm and the easy laughter, a prickly energy. Denton Thrasher walked away. She put a hand on her husband's arm. When the musical star moved on, Lotto turned to her and silently docked his head on her shoulder for two moments. Recharged, he turned to face the others.

WALLS, CEILING, FLOOR, 2008

"*Walls, Ceiling, Floor?*" the producer said. He was a gentle, sleepy-eyed man who hid a ferocious heart in the flesh of his chest.

"First part of a trilogy of the dispossessed," Lotto said. "Same family, different main characters. They lose the family house. It's where they store everything. History, furniture, ghosts. A tragedy. All three would, we hope, play concurrently."

"Concurrently. Christ. Ambitious," the producer said. "Which part of the trilogy is this?"

"The mental-health part," Lotto said.

LAST SIP, 2008

"*Last Sip*, let me guess," the producer said. "Alcoholism."

"Foreclosure," Lotto said. "And the last, *Grace*, is the story of an Afghanistan veteran who comes home."

GRACE, 2008

"A war story called *Grace*?" the producer said.

"I embedded with the Marine Corps in Afghanistan," Lotto said. "Two weeks, but every moment I thought I was about to die. And every moment I didn't, I felt blessed. Even if I left religion as a kid. Believe it or not, the title fits."

"You're killing me." The producer closed his eyes. When he opened them, he said, "Fine. If I read them and love them, we'll do it. I'm bats for *The Springs*. And *Grimoire*. I think you have something interesting in your brain."

"Deal," Mathilde said from the kitchen, arranging fresh-baked speculoos on a plate.

"But only off-off-Broadway," he said. "Maybe in New Jersey somewhere."

"For the first run," Mathilde said, setting the tray of cookies and tea on the table. The producer laughed, but nobody else did.

"You're serious," he said.

"Read it. You'll see," Mathilde said.

ONE WEEK LATER, the producer called. Mathilde answered the phone.

"I see," the producer said.

"I thought you would," Mathilde said. "Most people eventually do."

"Did you?" the producer said. "He's so clownish on the surface. All joke and dazzle. How in the world could you have seen it?"

"But I did. The moment I met him," she said. "A fucking supernova. Every day since." She thought but did not say *almost*.

AFTER SHE HUNG UP with the producer, she came to Lotto over the veranda of their new house in the country [still a disaster of siding and drywall; but she had known there was something beautiful— fieldstone, ancient beams—under the mess]. There was a cherry orchard in the front, a perfect flat space for a pool in the back. She had quit her job months ago, had taken over the business side of his. They kept the one-bedroom as a pied-à-terre in the city; she would make this house perfect for them. Life was rich with possibility. Or life was possibly rich; soon, perhaps, she wouldn't have to worry about phone bills, juggling this credit card to pay off the next. She felt incandescent with the news.

Cold sun, jack-in-the-pulpits nosing out of the still-frozen mud. Lotto lay watching the world incrementally wake up. They had been married for seventeen years; she lived in the deepest room in his heart. And sometimes that meant that *wife* occurred to him before *Mathilde*, helpmeet before herself. Abstraction of her before the visceral being. But not now. When she came across the veranda, he *saw* Mathilde all of a sudden. The dark whip at the center of her. How, so gently, she flicked it and kept him spinning.

She put her cold hand on his stomach, which he was sunning to banish the winter's white.

"Vain," she said.

"An actor in a playwright's hide," he said sadly. "I'll never not be vain."

"Oh, well. It's you," she said. "You're desperate for the love of strangers. To be seen."

"You see me," he said, and he heard the echo with his thoughts a minute before and was pleased.

"I do," she said.

"Now. Please. Talk," he said.

She stretched her long arms over her head, and there were little nests of winter hair in the pits. She could hatch baby robins in those things. She looked at him, savoring her own knowing, his unknowing. She put her arms down with a sigh, and said, "Do you want to hear?" And he said, "Oh my goodness, M., you are absolutely killing me." And she said, "It's a go. All three." And he laughed and took her hand, callused from house demolition, and kissed it, bitten fingernail to bitten finger, up the arm, the neck. Hefted her over his shoulder and pinwheeled her until the ground heaved, and then, because the air was bright and the birds were watching, he kissed a long trail down her stomach, and he shucked her right there.

5

AFTER THE INCOMPREHENSION and the raw fish came the long flight, then the short. At last, home. He sat, watching through the window as the staircase approached the plane over the sun-shot asphalt. Spring rain had blown through as they taxied in and just as swiftly was gone. He wanted his face in Mathilde's neck, the soothe of her hair. Two weeks as playwright-in-residence in Osaka and as long as he'd ever been away from his wife. Too much. He'd woken up to the absence of Mathilde in his bed and felt grief in the coolness where her heat should have been.

The rolling staircase fumbled and missed the door three times before it clicked in. Eager as a virgin. How lovely to stretch this long body of his, to stand and breathe for a few moments at the top of the stairs, savoring the oil and manure and ozone smell of the little Albany airport, sun on his cheeks, wife inside the building waiting to take him to the pretty house in the country, his early dinner. The luxuriant fatigue in his bones chased by cold prosecco then hot shower then smooth Mathilde-skin then sleep.

His happiness stretched out its wings and gave a few flaps.

He hadn't accounted for the other passengers' impatience. It wasn't until he was already midair that he felt the hand hard in the middle of his back.

How outrageous, he thought. Pushed.

Now the pavement was billowing up toward him like a flicked

tablecloth, one distant wind sock tonguing eastward, the crenellated roof of the airport building, a shine of the sandpapery steps in the sunlight, the plane's nose somehow peeling into his vision and the pilot stretching his arms in the window; and Lancelot had twisted entirely around by the time his right shoulder hit the edge of a stair and he was looking at his ostensible pusher looming out of the dark cave mouth at the top, a man with tomato-colored hair and face, lines embossed on his forehead, wearing madras shorts, of all ugly things. Lancelot's head hit the tread at the moment his rear and legs did, if somewhat lower, and things got a bit swimmy now; and behind the man was the flight attendant who'd snuck Lancelot two minibottles of bourbon after he'd spent a few minutes exercising his old actor's charm on her—brief fantasy of her with skirt up, legs around his waist in the plastic bathroom, before he banished the image; he was married! and faithful!—and she was in the process of putting her hands slowly up to her mouth as his body made a satisfying *thunkata-thunkata* rhythm in sliding downward; and he kicked out toward the rail with the instinct to stop his fall, but felt a curious sharp clicking in the shin region and all in that general direction went numb. With delicious slowness, he came to rest in a shallow puddle, his shoulder and ear seeping up the sun-warmed water, his legs still extended up the stairs, though his foot, it appeared, canted outward in a manner unbefitting its owner's dignity.

Down, now, the tomato-headed man was coming. A moving stop sign. His footsteps rocked some locus of pain in Lancelot. When the man was close, Lancelot held up the hand that wasn't numb, but the man stepped over him. Lancelot got a flash up the tube of his shorts; hairy white thigh, dark genital tangle. Then the man was running over the shining asphalt, swallowed up by the slab of a terminal door. Pushed? Fled? Who would do such a thing? Why? Why to *him*? What had he done?

[There'd be no answers. The man was gone.]

The flight attendant's face came into view, soft cheeks and horse nostrils blowing, and he closed his eyes as she touched his neck and someone somewhere began to shout.

BACKLIT, the fracture was tectonic, the plates of him overlapping. He was given two casts, a sling, a crown of gauze, pills that made his body feel as if it were encased in three inches of rubber. As if, had he been on the same drugs when he fell, he would have hit asphalt only to bounce delightedly high, startling pigeons midair and coming to rest on the airport roof.

He sang falsetto to Earth, Wind & Fire all the way to the city. Mathilde let him eat two doughnuts, and his eyes filled with tears because they were the most amazing doughnuts in the history of glazed doughnuts, food of the gods. He was full of joy.

They would have to spend the summer in the country. Alas! His *Walls, Ceiling, Floor* was in rehearsal, and he should be there for it, but really, there was so little he could do. He couldn't climb the stairs to the rehearsal space, and it would be an abuse of power to make his dramaturge carry him; he couldn't even climb the stairs to their tiny apartment. He sat on the building's staircase, looking at the pretty black-and-white tiles. Back and forth Mathilde went, gathering the food, the clothes, everything they needed from the apartment on the second floor down to the car double-parked in the street.

The building manager's child stuck her shy brown head out the door and looked at him.

"What, ho, spratling!" he said to the kid.

She stuck a finger in her mouth and took it out all wet. "What is that nutty bo-bo doing out there on the stairs?" she said, tiny echo of some adult.

Lancelot brayed, and the building manager peered out, a bit more ruddy than normal, and took a look at the casts, sling, crown. He nodded at Lancelot, then pulled his kid and head inside and shut the door fast.

In the car, Lancelot marveled at Mathilde: what a smooth face she had, lickable, like a vanilla ice cream cone. If only the left side of his body hadn't suddenly become buried in concrete, he would leap over the emergency brake and treat her the way a cow treats a block of salt.

"Kids are jerks," he said. "Bless their hearts. We should have some, M. Maybe now that you're my nurse for the rest of the summer, you can have free license with my body, and in all the lust and frenzy, we'll beget a sweet wee thing." They weren't using birth control, and there was no question that either one of them was defective. It was clearly a matter of luck and time. When he wasn't high, he was more careful, kept quiet, sensitive to the stoic longing he'd felt in her whenever he brought it up.

"Those drugs of yours spectacular?" she said. "They seem pretty spectacular."

"It's time," he said. "It's more than time. We've got some cash now, a house, you're ripe still. Your eggs may be getting a little wrinkly, I don't know. Forty. We're risking some springs going sproing in the kid's head. Though it may not be so bad to have a dumb kid. Smart ones are off as soon as they're able to escape. Dumbos stick around longer. On the other hand, if we wait too long, we'll be cutting his pizza for him until we're ninety-three. No, we got to do this thing ASAP. As soon as we get home, I'm going to impregnate the heck out of you."

"Most romantic thing you've ever said to me," she said.

Down the dirt road, up the gravel drive. Graceful dripping limbs of cherry trees, oh, gosh, they lived in *The Cherry Orchard*. He stood at the back door, watching Mathilde open the French door to the veranda, go down the grass to the new and sparkling pool. There were two tanned and muscled men gleaming in the last sun, unrolling a strip of sod. Mathilde in her white dress, her cropped platinum hair, her slim body, the sunburst sky, the shining muscle men. It was unbearable. *Tableau vivant.*

He sat suddenly. A hot dampness overcame his eyes: all this beauty, the stun of his luck. Also, the pain that had just surfaced, a nuclear submarine out of the deep.

HE WOKE AT HIS USUAL TIME, 5:26, drifting from a dream in which he was in a bathtub barely bigger than his body, and it was full of tapioca pudding. Scrabble as he might, he couldn't get out of it. The pain made him nauseated and his groaning woke Mathilde. She hovered over him with her terrible breath, her hair tickling his cheek.

When she came back with a tray of scrambled eggs and a bagel with cream cheese and scallions and black coffee and a rose in a vase with dew all over it, he saw the excitement in her face.

"You prefer me as an invalid," he said.

"For the first time in our lives together," she said, "you're neither a black suck of depression nor a swirl of manic energy. It's nice. Maybe we can even watch an entire movie together now that you're stuck with me. Maybe," she said breathlessly, reddening [poor Mathilde!], "we could collaborate on a novel or something."

He tried to smile, but overnight the world had turned, and her translucence today seemed anemic, no longer confected of sugar and clarified butter. The eggs were greasy, the coffee overstrong, and even the rose from his wife's garden emitted an odor that cloyed and put him off.

"Or not," she said. "It was just an idea."

"Sorry, my love," he said. "I seem to have lost my appetite."

She kissed him on the forehead, then rested her cool cheek on it. "You're hot. I'll get you one of your magical pills," she said, and he had to hold his impatience in as she fumbled for the water, the cap of the bottle, the cotton, the tablet that gloriously dissolved on his tongue.

SHE CAME OUT TO THE HAMMOCK where he was contemplating darkly, though the sun shimmied and played in the bright leaves and the pool suckled at its gutters. Three glasses into a bottle of bourbon; it was past four, who cared? He had nowhere to be; he had nothing to do; he was deeply depressed, fracking depressed, deep-shale shat-tered. He had put on Pergolesi's *Stabat Mater* and it was blasting out of his special speakers in the dining room all the way out to him in the hammock.

He wanted to call his mother, to let her sweet voice swathe him, but instead he watched a documentary about Krakatoa on his laptop. He was imagining what the world would look like under volcanic ash. As if some mad child had come along and scribbled black and gray over the landscape: the streams gone greasy, the trees powder puffs of ash, greensward a slick of gleaming oil. An image of Hades. Fields of punishment, screams in the night, the Asphodel Meadows. The dead clacketing their bones.

Luxuriating in the horror, he was. In the unhappiness of being broken. There was not *not* a kind of wallowing joy in this.

"Love," his wife said gently. "I've brought you some iced tea."

"No iced tea," he said, and, surprise, his tongue wasn't working as well as it ought. It was thick. He made as if to look cross-eyed at it, then said, "Whether the weather be cold, whether the weather be hot, we'll be together whatever the weather whether we like it or not."

"Too true," Mathilde said. And now he saw she was wearing her ancient blue skirt, her hippie gear from a million years ago when they were new to each other and he jumped her bones four times a day. She was alluring, still, his wifey. She crawled on the hammock carefully, but the motion still sent a million fangs deep into his broken bones, and he groaned but bit back his shout and could still barely see when she hiked her skirt to her waist and took off her tank top. A fillip of interest down in his always interested fillip. But the pain ground it down again. She cajoled, but to no avail.

She gave up. "You must've broken your peenbone, too," she joked.

It was all he could do to keep himself from flipping her out of the hammock.

A FASCINATING PBS SPECIAL on black holes: the suck and draw so strong it can gulp down light. Light! He drank deeply, watching; he kept his own council. There were problems at the rehearsal; they *needed* him, they said; there was a difficult performance of *The Springs* in Boston and a reportedly great series of *Walls, Ceiling, Floor* in Saint Louis. He generally went to all that invited him, and yet he couldn't move from this cottage in the middle of cornfields and cows. Lancelot Satterwhite was *needed*. And Lancelot Satterwhite was not there. He had *never* not been there. He might as well already be dead.

A *clip-clop* in the library. There was a horse in the house? But no, it was Mathilde in her cycling shoes coming in, in her silly padded trou. She shined with health and sweat. She stank of armpit and garlic.

"Baby," Mathilde said, taking his glass away, turning off the show. "It's been two weeks and you've drunk four bottles of Blanton's. No more documentaries on disaster. You need to do something to fill up your time."

He sighed, rubbed his face with his good hand.

"Write something," she commanded.

"Not inspired," he said.

"Write an essay," she said.

"Essays are for chumps," he said.

"Write a play about how you hate the world," she said.

"I don't hate the world. The world hates me," he said.

"Boo-hoo," she laughed.

She couldn't know, he thought. Don't punish her. Plays don't just get ground out. You need to be filled with a hot kind of urgency to make it right. He gave her a pained smile and took a sip from the bottle.

"Are you drinking because you're sad, or are you drinking to show me how sad you are?" she said.

Direct hit. He laughed. "Viper," he said.

"Falstaff," she said. "You're even getting fat. All that running for nothing. And I thought we'd banished it for good. Come on, kid, buck up, stop drinking, get right in the head."

"Easy for you to say," he said. "You are in robust good health. You exercise two hours a day! I get winded going out to the hammock. So until my benighted bones knit themselves to a semblance of solidity, I shall exercise my right to intoxication and bile and mooning."

"How about a Fourth of July party," she said.

"No," he said.

"It wasn't a question," she said.

And then, as if magic, here he was three days later among shish kebabs and multicolored sparklers going off in those gorgeous, paw-like children's hands as they ran across the acres that Mathilde had cropped herself on her roaring mower. There was nothing that miracle woman couldn't do, he thought, then thought about how this fresh-cut-grass smell was the olfactory scream of the plants.

There was a whole keg and corn on the cob and veggie bratwurst and watermelon and Mathilde in a pale low-cut dress, looking beyond beautiful, nestling her head beneath his chin and kissing him on the neck so that all night he carried around a red lipstick mark on his throat like a wound.

All of his friends swirling around in the dusk, in the night. Chollie with Danica. Susannah like a Roman candle herself in a red dress, and her new girlfriend, Zora, young and black with a tremendously beautiful Afro, kissing under the weeping willow. Samuel with his wife and their triplets wobbling around with watermelon rinds in their hands, and Arnie with his newest bar-back teenager, Xanthippe, almost as stunning as Mathilde had been in her heyday, black bob and a yellow dress so short the toddlers could certainly see her thong and dewy loins. Lotto imagined sprawling on the grass to get his own eyeful, but inversion meant tremendous pain and he remained upright.

The fireworks blister-popping in the sky, the party sounds. [Doomed people celebrate peace with sky bombs.] Lotto watched himself as if from a distance, playing his own stiffly acted role of jocular clown. He had a terrible headache.

He went into the bathroom, and the bright lights, the sight of his flushed cheeks and his air splints made him woozy, and he let the smile out of his face, looked at the drooping mask that remained. Midway on life's journey. He said in a low voice, *"Nel mezzo del cammin di nostra vita, mi ritrovai per una selva oscura, ché la diritta via era smarrita."* He was ridiculous. Lugubrious and pretentious at the same time. Lugentious. Pretubrious. He poked at the belly the size of a six-month-old baby glued to his midsection. When Chollie had seen him, he'd said, "You okay there, fella? You're looking kind of fat."

"Hello, Pot," Lancelot had said. "You're looking black," which was true, Chollie's girth strained the buttons of his four-hundred-dollar shirt. But then again, Chollie had never been a beautiful boy; Lancelot had had much farther to fall. Danica, chic in the one-shoulder designer dress that Chollie's money had bought her, said, "Leave him be, Choll. The man's body is broken head to toe. If there's any time in a man's life that he gets to get fat, this is it."

He couldn't bear to go back out there, Lancelot decided, to see those people he was pretty sure at times he hated. He went into their room and undressed as well as he could and climbed into bed.

He was in a murky anteroom of sleep when the door opened, the hall light blasting him awake, then closed, and there was a body in the room that wasn't his. He waited, panicky. He could barely move! If someone crawled into bed with him to ravish him, he couldn't flee! But whoever it was was two whoevers and they had no interest in the bed, because there were some low laughs and some whispers and the shush of fabric, and they began to pound out a rhythm against the bathroom door. A kind of syncopated slap-thump with some surprising percussive ughs.

That door was really rattling away, Lancelot thought. He should tighten the knob tomorrow.

And then came the thought, a knife of grief in his heart, that once he would have been the one to bring some girl in to do her, and it would have been far, far better than this girl was being done, poor thing, though she seemed to be having a good time. Still, there was something a little fakey about her moaning. Once, even, he would have gotten up and made an orgy out of the event, joining so smoothly it would have been as if he had been invited. Now he lay puddled in his broke-bone carapace, critiquing the performance, soft as a hermit crab. Sure of the dark, he made a hermit crab's frowning whiskered face, snapping claws with his good hand.

The girl said, *"Aaaaaaah!"* and the guy said, *"Urrrgh!"* and there was more hushed laughing.

"Oh my god, I needed that," the guy whispered. "These parties are such shitshows when people bring their kids."

"I know," she said. "Poor Lotto watching those babies with that longing on his face. And Mathilde so skinny these days she's getting ugly. She keeps letting it go, she's going to be some kind of witchy old hag. Like, I don't know, but Botox exists for a reason."

"I was always confused why anyone thought she was hot. She's just tall and blond and skinny, never pretty," he said. "I'm a connoisseur." The sound of flesh slapped. Buttocks? Lotto thought. [Thigh.]

"She's interesting-looking. Remember how that was a thing in the early nineties? We were all so jealous. Remember when Lotto and Mathilde had the grandest love story ever? And their parties! Christ! I kind of feel bad for them now."

The door opened. A pumpkin-colored head, balding. Aha, Arnie. Followed out by a bare shoulder, jagged with bones. Danica. Old affair revisited. Poor Chollie. Lotto felt sick that matrimony could seem so cheap to some people.

Weary, weary, sick to death, Lancelot stood and dressed again. Those people could rabbit themselves until they died of exhaustion, but he wouldn't let them mealymouth Mathilde and him. How appalling, to be pitied by such gnats. Adulterer gnats. Worse.

He came downstairs again and stood in the door with his wife and said cheery good-byes to the friends, the children passed out in the parents' arms, the drunk adults being driven, the merely tipsy driving themselves. He spackled so much extra charm onto Arnie and Danica that they both blushed and began flirting shyly back, Danica hooking her fingers through his belt loop when she kissed him good night.

"Alone again," Mathilde said, watching the last taillights wink away. "For a while, I thought we lost you. And then I would have known we were really in trouble. Lotto Satterwhite intentionally missing a party equals Lotto Satterwhite hacking off a leg."

"In truth, I just grinned," he said, "and bore it."

She turned to him, narrow-eyed. She let her dress fall off her shoulders, pool on the floor. She wore nothing underneath. "I just bared it," she said.

"Not boring," he said.

"Darling, bore me," she said. "As in drill."

"Like a wild boar," he said. But he was more, to her dismay, like a tired piglet snoozing mid-suckle.

———

AND THEN THE SWIFTER DOWNWARD SWOOP. All things had lost their savor. He had his casts taken off, but the left side of his body was limp and tender pink and the texture of an overcooked egg noodle. Mathilde looked at him standing before her naked; she closed one eye. "Demigod," she said. She closed the other. "Dweeb." He laughed but was smacked right in the vanity. He was too weak yet to go home to the city. He longed for pollution, noise, light.

The things he'd discovered online had lost their luster. There were only so many cute baby videos one could take, after all, or cats falling off high places. The sun's very shine had been besmirched! And his wife's beauty, which had been so unimpeachable, was irritable, weakened. Such thighs she had, like *jamones serranos*, salty and overly firm. In morning light, her facial lines had been etched by too strong a hand. Her lips thinning, her eyeteeth surprisingly long, catching on the rims of mugs, on soup spoons, it made him cringe. And always hovering! Blowing on him her breath of impatience! He took to staying in bed past wake-up time, waiting for Mathilde to go off on her run or to her yoga class, off on her bike rides out into the countryside, so that he could go back to sleep.

It was almost noon. He held his body still, hearing Mathilde creep in the bedroom door. Then the coverlet lifted, and something soft and furry clambered up his body and licked him, chin to schnozz.

He was laughing when he saw the sweet face, like an earmuff with eyeballs and triangular felted ears.

"Oh, you," he said to the puppy. And then he looked at Mathilde, and he couldn't help it, there were hot tears in his eyes. "Thank you," he said.

"She's a Shiba Inu," Mathilde said, and crawled to his side. "What's her name?"

Dog, he wanted to say. He'd always wanted to call a dog Dog. It was meta. It was funny.

Oddly, thrillingly, the word came out as *God*.

"God. Nice to meet you, God," she said. She picked the puppy up and looked in her face. "Most sensible epistemology I've ever heard."

THERE IS LITTLE that a puppy won't fix, even if the fix is for a short time. For a week, he was practically happy again. Such delight he took in the snarfle of God's hunger, the way she took each piece of kibble out of her bowl to eat off the top of his foot. The pained way she pinched her back legs to her front and flagged her tail, and her little arsehole apertured and bulged, and then she squinted like a philosopher when she eliminated. How she sat quietly with him, chewing on the cuffs of his pants, as he lay on his back and dreamt on a blanket spread in the grass. How he always had something soft under his palm as soon as he called out "God!" which sounded like the first curse he'd ever said in his life, but was not, as it was a proper noun. How he was rewarded with joy, tiny needle teeth in the meat of his thumb. Even her shrill scream when she was tangled in her leash or kept in her crate for the night made him laugh.

He did not fall out of love with the dog, per se; it was merely that luster dulled under the grind of the daily. God could not bridge the distance between his hermit life as a broken man and the life he longed to live again in the city, all interviews and dinners out and being recognized on the subway. She couldn't knit his bones together faster. Her small quick tongue could not stanch all wounds. Dogs, being wordless, can only be mirrors of their humans. It's not their fault that their people are fatally flawed.

Within a week, he felt himself riding the dip again. The thoughts were not serious when he imagined baking a soufflé out of the rat poison Mathilde kept in the garden house or grabbing the wheel out of Mathilde's hands when she let him come with her to the grocery store, veering over this cliffside, into that stand of maples. They weren't serious, but they surfaced more and more frequently until he felt carbonated with dark ideas. He was sinking again.

AND THEN IT WAS HIS BIRTHDAY, the big forty, and he would rather have slept through the day, but woke to God shuffling off his chest where she slept and clattering down the stairs to Mathilde, who'd been up before dawn trying not to make a sound in the kitchen. Back door opened, closed. Soon enough, she was in the room, pulling his nicest summer suit out of the closet.

"Shower," Mathilde said. "Put this on. Don't complain. I have a surprise."

He did, but it felt bad, waistband so tight it might have been a girdle. She bundled him into the car and they set off through the still-faint dew, illuminated by dawn. She handed him a hot egg muffin with excellent goat cheese, and tomatoes and basil from her garden.

"Where's God?" he said.

She said, beatifically, with a great swoop of her arms, "All around us."

"Hardeehar," he said.

"Your puppy is with the neighbor's girl and will return to us bathed and coddled and wearing tiny pink bows above her ears. Relax."

He settled in, let the landscape pour all over him. This country-side, bled of humans, was entirely right for his mood. He dozed off and awoke to the car parking, a fine bright morning, a smooth lake, something that seemed like an excessive brown barn in the distance. His wife carried their picnic basket to the edge of the lake under a willow so old it no longer wept, just sort of bore its fate with thickened equanimity. Deviled eggs and champagne, vegetable terrine and Mathilde's own focaccia, Manchego cheese and bright red cherries from their orchard. Two tiny black-bottom cupcakes, chocolate and cream cheese, his with a candle she lit.

He blew it out, hoping for something inexpressible. For something finer, more worthy of him.

Someone came around the building ringing a cowbell and Mathilde packed up slowly. He used his wife as his crutch as they crossed the meadow, all stubble and field mice, to the opera house.

It was cool inside, and around them there was a sea of whitehairs. "Beware," Mathilde whispered in his ear. "Geriatrism. Contagious, mortal. Don't breathe too deeply."

He laughed for the first time, it felt like, in weeks.

The long, tender, non-chords of the strings tuning. He could listen to such anticipatory non-music for hours and leave this place feeling replenished, he thought.

The sides of the opera house began to slide shut against the day, the murmuring hushed, and the conductor came out and raised her arms. She shot them down to an upwelling of what? Not quite music. Sound. Astringent, strange, wild; and yet it slowly resolved itself out of cacophony into a sort of melody. He leaned forward and closed his eyes and felt the mildew that had grown itself over his being these weeks slowly wiped away by the sound.

The opera was called *Nero*. It was a story of Rome burning, but the fire was offstage, and this was not Nero the emperor, but a doppelgänger Nero, Nero the keeper of the wine cellars, who could have been the emperor's twin brother, who lived in the palace below the king. It was less a story than a great creature surfacing from the deep; it was more sudden audible wave than narrative. It made Lancelot's head spin. True recognition does this. Dizzies.

At intermission, he turned to his wife and she smiled as if trying to see him from a very high place. Watchful, waiting. He whispered, "Oh, M., I can barely breathe."

OUT IN THE COURTYARD, stunned by sunlight, the soft, cool wind among the poplars. Mathilde fetched them sparkling water. Alone at a café table, a woman recognized him: this was happening more and more. He held a general taxonomy of faces in his mind and could usually place people within a second; not this woman. She laughed, assured him she didn't know him; she had seen the profile in *Esquire.* "How nice," Mathilde said, when the woman went off to the restrooms. "A little bug-zap of fame." Of course, these were his people, theater people. It was to be expected that some of them might have known something about him, but still the woman's starstruck blush had fed something hungry in him.

Contrails in the blue sky. Something beginning to break in him. A good breaking; not, this time, bone.

In the second act, the story was even more incidental, a tone poem; dancers emerged with rope to become the fire embodied. By the hot-iron gush on his tongue, he understood he'd bit his lip.

Curtain. *Fin.*

Mathilde put her cold hands on his face. "Oh," she said. "You're weeping."

FOR MOST OF THE WAY HOME he kept his eyes closed, not because he didn't want to see his wife or the green-blue-gold of the day, but because he couldn't bear losing the opera.

When he opened them, Mathilde's face was drooping. He couldn't remember the last time he saw her without her smile. The light was such he could see the crazing in her skin by her eyes and nose, fine gray hairs in an electric fizz around her head.

"Medieval Madonna," he said. "In gouache. Haloed in gold leaf. Thank you."

"Happy birthday, friend of my heart," she said.

"It was happy. It is. That opera changed me."

"I thought it would," she said. "I'm glad it did. You were getting to be kind of a drag."

Spectacular burst of grapefruit as the sun burned itself out. They watched it on their veranda with another bottle of champagne. He picked God up and kissed her on the crown. He wanted to dance, and so he went in and put on Radiohead and swept Mathilde out of her chair with his strong side and pulled her to him.

"Let me guess," Mathilde said, her cheek on his shoulder. "Now you want to write an opera."

"Yes," he said, breathing her in.

"You've never lacked for ambition," she said, and laughed, and it was a sad sound, echoing against the flagstone and the flit of bats above.

Now the hours that he would have spent moping, watching voice-overed destruction or pinkish naked people working up a sweat, were passed in a frenzy of research. He spent an entire night reading what he could find about the composer.

One Leo Sen. Sen, surname South Asian, derived from the Sanskrit for *army*, bestowed upon those who did an honorable deed. Lived in Nova Scotia. Fairly new artist, having compositions performed for only about six years, fairly young. Hard to tell, because there were no images of Leo Sen online, only one CV from two years earlier and a smattering of praise for his work. *The New York Times* listed him as an exciting foreign composer; *Opera News* had a two-paragraph description of a work titled *Paracelsus*. There were a few audio clips of a work in progress on someone's amateurish website, but it was from 2004, so long ago as to have possibly been student work. Inasmuch as a person can be a ghost on the Internet, Leo Sen had made himself into one.

Genius hermit, Lancelot pictured. Monomaniacal, wild-eyed, made mad by his own brilliance or, no, semiautistic. Burly beard. Loincloth. Socially incompetent. Savage at heart.

Lancelot e-mailed nearly everyone he knew to find out if anybody knew him. Not a soul did.

He e-mailed the festival director up at the opera house in the cow fields to see if she would give him contact information.

Distillation of her response: What's in it for us?

Distillation of his: First pass on a possible collaboration?

Distillation of hers: You have my blessing, here you go.

SEPTEMBER? ALREADY? Leaves flaked off the trees. God grew a fluffy underlayer of down. Lancelot still had a hitch in his walk from his weakling leg. His narcissism so vast that it seemed the world itself had gone tentative and wobbly to mimic his body.

They'd gone to the city for the week, come home to the country for the weekend. At night, every night, he wrote a short e-mail to Leo Sen. No response yet.

Mathilde was wary, watchful. When he finally came to bed, she turned to him in her sleep, clinging, she who never wanted to be touched while she slept. He woke with her hair in his mouth, an arm somehow gone missing until he sat upright and felt the blood coming painfully back.

At last, a day in early October, a new chill in the air, he got Leo Sen on the telephone. The voice was not what he was expecting. It was soft and hesitant, British accent, which surprised him at first; and on second thought, well, India had been colonized; the educated class certainly would have fine-grained BBC inflections. Was this racist? He wasn't sure.

"You said Lancelot Satterwhite?" Leo Sen said. "This is a thrill."

"A thrill for me," Lancelot said too loudly in his discomfort. He had imagined this so often it was strange, now, to hear the soft voice, to be told, first, that he was admired. He was expecting Leo Sen to be isolated in his genius, to be irritated by contact. Leo Sen explained: There was no Internet on the island where he lived, and the phone worked only when someone was around to answer it. It was an intentional community. Dedicated to humble daily work and contemplation.

"Sounds like a monastery," Lancelot said.

"Or a nunnery," Leo said. "Feels like it sometimes, too."

Lancelot laughed. Oh! Leo had a sense of humor, what a relief. In his gladness, Lancelot found himself describing his reaction to Leo's work at the opera house in the summer, how it rocked something in him. He used the word *great*, he used the phrases *sea change* and *sui generis*.

"I'm so glad," Leo Sen said.

"I would do almost anything to collaborate on an opera with you," Lancelot said.

The silence was so long he almost hung up, defeated. Well, good effort, Lancelot, it wasn't in the stars, sometimes things don't work out, back up on that horse, head down and into the wind, onward, pardner.

"Sure," said Leo Sen. "Yes, of course."

Before they hung up, they agreed on a three-week residency at an artists' colony for them both in November. Lancelot was owed a favor and he thought he could get them in. The first day or so, Leo had to finish a commission for a string quartet, but they could start thinking, talking things over. Then they would have endless, relentless work for the next three weeks until they had some ideas, maybe even a stab at the book.

"What do you think?" said Leo's voice on the line. "The concept part is actually the most difficult for me."

Lancelot looked at the bulletin board in his office, where he'd pinned at least a hundred ideas, a thousand ideas. "I think the concept part won't be a problem for us," he said.

IN THE MORNING, Mathilde went whirring off on an eighty-mile bike ride. Lancelot undressed and looked at himself in the mirror. Oh, middle age, how awful. He was used to having to look for his lost beauty in his face, but not in his body that had been so tall and strong all his life. Now, though, the wrinkles in the skin of his scrotum, the swirl of gray in the chest hair, the fetal neck wattle. One chink in the armor and death seeps in. He turned this way and that until he found the angle that made him look the way he'd been before his impromptu flight down the stairs in the spring.

Over his shoulder, he saw God on the bed, watching him, her chin on her paws.

He blinked. He gave a brilliant grin at the Lancelot he saw in the mirror, winking and nodding and whistling through his teeth as he put his clothes back on, even brushing imaginary dust off the shoulders of his sweater, picking the pills, making a satisfied grunt before hurrying off as if remembering an urgent chore.

AND THEN IT WAS NOVEMBER and they were spinning past the thwarted graying fields, over the Hudson, into Vermont, New Hampshire. A hush in the air, a gathering of energy.

In his feverish preparations, Lancelot had lost ten pounds. He'd spent hours on the stationary bicycle, because only movement made him think. Now his knees jerked to some music inaudible to Mathilde, who drove.

"I've narrowed the ideas down to five, M.," he said. "Listen to this. Retelling of Maupassant's 'The Necklace.' Or 'The Little Mermaid,' the opposite of Disney. Andersen, but extended to even more extreme weirdness. Or the trials of Job, but kooky, funny-dark. Or interlocking stories of soldiers in Afghanistan that together tell a kind of longer story, like *Chronicle of a Death Foretold.* Or *The Sound and the Fury* in opera form."

Mathilde bit her bottom lip with her long incisors and looked only at the road.

"Kooky?" she said. "Funny-dark? People don't really think opera and funny. You think fat ladies, solemnity, Rhinemaidens, women killing themselves for the love of a good man."

"Opera has a long tradition of humor. Opera buffa. It used to be the primary entertainment for the masses. It'd be nice to democratize it again, make it popular entertainment. Make the mailman sing it on his rounds. He looks as if he's hiding a beautiful voice under that little blue uniform."

"Yes," she said. "But you're known for your lyricism. You're serious, Lotto. Exuberant, sometimes, but not funny."

"You don't think I'm funny?"

"*I* think you're hilarious. I think your work isn't really funny, though."

"Not even *Gacy*?" he said.

"*Gacy* was dark. Wry. Humorous in a bleak way. Not funny, per se."

"You think I can't be funny?" he said.

"I think you can be dark, wry, and humorous in a bleak way," she said. "For sure."

"Splendid. I will prove you wrong. Now, what do you think of my ideas?"

She made a face and shrugged.

"Oh," he said. "None of those."

"Lots of retellings," she said.

"I mean, not the Afghanistan one."

"No," Mathilde said. "True. That's the only great idea. Maybe too on-the-nose, though. Too obvious. Make it more allegorical."

"Brank your tongue, witchy-wife," he said.

Mathilde laughed. "Maybe this is something that both of you will have to agree on anyway. You and this Leo Sen of yours."

"Leo. I feel like a teenager all dressed up in cummerbund and bow tie, heading off to the winter dance," he said.

"Well, my love, this is how people sometimes feel when they meet you," Mathilde said gently, gently.

His cabin was small, stone, with a fireplace, not so far from the main house where dinner and breakfast would be, and he worried for the first time about ice, about falling with his still-flimsy leg. There was a desk, a chair, and a bed that was normal size, which meant his legs would hang off up to the shins.

Mathilde sat at the edge of it and bounced. The frame squeaked like a mouse. Lancelot sat next to her and bounced to her offbeat. He put his hand on her leg and moved it, bounce by bounce, up her thigh until his finger was pushing against her groin, and then he hooked it under her elastic and found an anticipatory lushness there. She stood, and he stopped bouncing, and without pulling the curtains, she pushed the crotch of her panties to the side and straddled him. He put his head up her shirt, loving the companionable darkness there.

"Hello, Private," she said, teasing the tip of him. "Atten-hut."

"Three weeks," he said, as she escorted him in. She moved her hips like a cowgirl. He said, "Long time without release."

"Not for me. I bought a vibrator," she said breathlessly. "I named him Lancelittle."

But this wasn't the right thing to say, perhaps, because he felt pressured and had to turn her around on her hands and knees to complete things, and the punctuation was a pallid little orgasm that left him discontented.

She called from the bathroom, where she was soaping herself with sink water, "I'm feeling queasy about leaving you here. Last time I let you go away from me for a little while, you came back broken." She returned to him, pressed his cheeks in her hands. "My eccentric old man, thinking you could fly."

"This time, only my words will fly," he said solemnly. They both cracked up. Almost twenty years together and if blazing heat had turned to warmth, humor, it was less wild but easier to sustain.

She said tentatively, "There will be brilliant women here, Lotto. And I know how much you love women. Or did. Once. I mean, before me."

He frowned. Never in their lives together had she been jealous. It was undignified of her. Of him. Of their marriage. He withdrew a little. "Oh, please," he said, and she shook it off and kissed him deeply, and said, "If you need me, I'll come. I'm four hours away, but I'll be here in three." And then she went out the door; she was gone.

ALONE! The twilit forest watched him through the windows. He did push-ups out of exuberance because it wasn't yet dinnertime. He unpacked his notebooks, his pens. He went out to the circular drive around his cottage and pulled a fern out by the roots and planted it in a white-speckled navy mug and put it on the mantel, even though it was already curling at the corners with the unexpected indoor heat. When the dinner bell rang, he limped up the dusky dirt road, past the meadow with its statue of a deer. Or no, a real and rather springy deer. Past the hayrick turned to chicken house in the raspberry canes, past the garden replete with pumpkins glowing in the dim, the overgrown stalks of Brussels sprouts, to the old farmhouse from which delicious food smells were emanating.

The two tables were already filled and he stood in the French doors until someone waved him over, touching an empty seat. He sat and the whole table turned, blinking, as if a sudden bright light had clicked on.

These people were so beautiful! He didn't know why he had been nervous. This frizzled and famous poet who was showing everybody the perfect cicada husk on her palm. This German couple who could be twins, with their identical rimless eyeglasses and hair as if it had been cropped with a sling blade in their sleep. This gingerheaded boy barely out of college, with the sudden pink wash of debilitating shyness: poet, clearly. This novelist, blond, athletic, not bad despite the breeder's gut and purple bags under her eyes. Nowhere near Mathilde, but young enough to be the kind of person who might give Mathilde pause. She did have lovely white forearms, as if cut from polished spruce wood. Once upon a time, when every woman dazzled with particular beauty, her forearms would have been plenty for him, and young Lotto returned for a moment, sexy hound dog, in sucking orgy, the novelist's round belly with the silvery stretch marks on it. Lovely. He passed her the pitcher of water and shook the image away.

A very young African-American filmmaker studied Lancelot, said, "Satterwhite? I just graduated from Vassar. There was a Satterwhite Hall there," and Lancelot winced a little, sighed. It had been an unpleasant shock when, this past spring, he'd visited his alma mater for a lecture, and the dean had stood and, among other encomiums in his introduction, mentioned that Lancelot's family had donated the dormitory to the school. Lotto did the math, and remembered finding Sallie, graduation weekend, standing before a vast pit in the ground where bulldozers were moving, her face set and skirt blowing against her skinny legs. She'd hooked her arm through his and led him away. It was true he'd applied to only one school and that the acceptance letter had apparently been mailed home to Florida; he'd never seen it.

If there was perfidy, it had the stamp of Antoinette all over it. "Oh," he said to the filmmaker, who was looking at him strangely. Lancelot's face must have betrayed him. "No relation."

Lights came on over the porch outside: a raccoon triggering the sensor. When they went off, the sky was doubled navy velvet. They passed the whole shining salmon in its bed of kale and lemons, the bowl of quinoa salad.

Lancelot found he could not stop talking. He was simply thrilled to be here. Someone had poured him wine after wine. Some artists had disappeared by dessert, but most had pulled their chairs over to his table. He told the story of his failed flight down the plane's staircase; he told the story of the disastrous audition when he was an actor, when he was asked to strip to the waist and had forgotten that Mathilde had that morning in the shower shaved a smiley face into his chest hair.

"I had heard you were a character," the poet said, over the crème brûlée, laying her hand on his arm. She had laughed so hard that her eyes were dewy. "I had no idea *what* a character."

At the other table, there had been a vaguely Indianish woman in a tunic, and Lancelot felt a flutter in his gut: could Leo be short for Leona? There were women with male voices. She had a white streak in her black hair that seemed appropriately eccentric for the maker of that opera he had seen this summer. She had gorgeous hands, like owlets. But she stood abruptly, carried her plate and utensils to the kitchen, and left; and he swallowed a bitter mouthful. She hadn't wanted to meet him.

Now they were in the main room, with its pool and Ping-Pong tables, and he was playing. Even with the alcohol, his reactions were swift: he was still a bit of an athlete, he was pleased to see, even after his summer encased in plaster. Someone brought out the whiskey. When he stopped, panting, his noodled left arm a little pangy, a tiny circlet of artists formed around him. Lancelot fell into his automatic charm. "What's your name? What do you do?" he asked them, one by one.

Artists! Narcissists! Some better than others at concealing, but like children standing at the edge of the playground, fingers in mouths, watching the others wide-eyed as they were one by one induced to play. Each, when invited to talk, was secretly relieved that *someone* saw them as important as they were. That the most important person in the room had recognized them as equally the most important in the room. If only potentially so. If only in the future.

Because, Lancelot knew, beaming so kindly upon all the others, that he was the only real artist at the place.

When it was his turn, the bright, blushing redheaded boy said his name so softly that Lancelot had to lean forward and ask him to say it again and the boy looked at him with a flash of something— stubbornness, amusement—and said, "Leo."

Lancelot moved his mouth until words at last came out. "You're Leo? Leo Sen? Leo Sen the composer?"

"In the flesh," said Leo. "Glad to meet you."

And when Lancelot still couldn't speak, the ginger boy said drily, "Expecting an Indian, weren't we. I get that often. My father's half Indian and looks it. His genes were steamrolled by my mother's. On the other hand, my sister looks like she should be in a Bollywood film and nobody can believe we are related one iota."

"All this time, and you were just *standing* there?" Lancelot said. "Letting me make a fool of myself?"

Leo shrugged, and said, "I was amused. I wanted to see what my librettist was like as a person."

"But excuse me, you can't be a composer. You're in kindergarten," Lancelot said.

"Twenty-six," Leo said. "Hardly in nappies." For such a blusher, there was an edge to his words.

"You are nothing like what I expected," Lancelot said.

Leo blinked hard. His hue had deepened to angry lobster. "And that, I think, is a marvelous thing. Who wants what's expected?"

"Not I," said Lancelot.

"Nor I," said Leo. He regarded Lancelot for a caesura and finally relaxed into an off-kilter smile.

HE HAD HANDS that could palm a basketball, Leo Sen, though his frame was a slight and stooping six feet. This was their first intoxicating talk on the couch, everyone else faded back to Ping-Pong or pool or home over the dark ground to work some more, dim headlamps to light their paths.

The opera this past summer came out of his struggles with a foundering kind of sadness, the feeling of panic as the outside world came roaring in. "I work my way out of it usually," Leo said. "I fight my music until we're both too exhausted to feel much of anything."

"I know exactly what you mean. It's like Jacob wrestling with God," Lancelot said. "Or Jesus with the devil."

"I'm an atheist. But they sound like nice myths," Leo said, and laughed.

He said his house on the Nova Scotia commune island was made of hay bales and mud, and that his job there was to teach music to anyone who wanted to learn. He owned few things: ten white button-down shirts, three pairs of jeans, socks, underwear, pair of boots, pair of moccasins, a jacket, musical instruments, and that was about it. Stuff had never interested him, beyond the music he could make from it. Books were necessary but borrowed. His only extravagance was soccer, though he called it football, of course, rooted for Tottenham. His mother, you see, was Jewish; she loved how Tottenham fought back against anti-Semitic slurs and called themselves the Yid Army. The Yiddos. For Leo, he said, it had also been the name, so meaty, so metrical. Tottenham Hotspur, its own tiny song. In the common house on the island there was a television, satellite dish like a cocked ear on the roof, mostly for emergencies, but they made an exception for Leo Sen's passionate love of the game.

"I *hated* my violin as a boy," he said, "until my father made me compose a score as a match was happening on the telly. Tottenham, Manchester, our boys losing. And suddenly, as I was playing, everything that I had felt so deeply without music deepened even more. The dread, the joy. And that was it for me, re-creating that moment was all I wanted to do. I called the composition *Audere Est Facere*." He laughed.

"To dare is to do?" Lotto said.

"Tottenham's motto. Not a bad way to be an artist, in fact."

"Your life seems simple," Lancelot said.

Leo Sen said, "My life is beautiful."

Lancelot saw that it was. He was enough of a lover of forms to understand the allure of such a strict life, how much internal wildness it could release. Leo waking to dawn over the cold seabird ocean, the fresh berries and goat-milk yogurt for breakfast, the tisanes of his own herbs, blue crabs in the black tide pools, going to bed with the whipping winds and rhythm of waves against hard rock. Lettuce shoots glowing in the south-facing windows. The celibacy, the temperate, moderate life that Leo lived, at least on the outside, in his state of constant cold. And the feverish musical life within.

"I knew you'd be an ascetic," Lancelot said. "I just thought you'd be a wild-bearded one who speared fish and wore a loincloth. In a saffron-colored turban." He smiled.

"On the other hand, you," Leo said, "were always dissolute. It's clear in your work. Privilege is what lets you take risks. Life of oysters and champagne and houses on the beach. Coddled. Like the precious egg you are."

Lancelot felt stung, but said, "True. If I had my druthers, I'd be three hundred fifty pounds of jollity and fun. But my wife keeps me to heel. Makes me exercise every day. Keeps me from drinking in the morning."

"Ah," said Leo, gazing at his own enormous hands. "So, there's a wife."

The way he said it. Well. It made the ideas Lancelot had about Leo reshuffle themselves once more in his head.

"There's a wife," Lancelot said. "Mathilde. She's a saint. One of the purest people I've ever met. Just morally upright, never lies, can't bear a fool. I'd never met someone who stayed a virgin until just before she got married, but Mathilde was. She thinks it's unfair that other people clean up your dirt, so she cleans our house even though we can afford a housekeeper. She does it all. Everything. And everything I write I write for her first."

"The grand love story, then," Leo said lightly. "But it's exhausting to live with a saint."

Lancelot thought of his tall wife with her blaze of white-blond hair. "It is," he said.

And then Leo said, "Oof, look at the time. I need to go to work. Nocturnal beastie, I'm afraid. Shall I see you in the afternoon?" and Lancelot saw they were alone, most lights turned out, and it was three hours past any bedtime he usually had. Also, he was drunk. He couldn't locate the words that would tell Leo how profoundly familiar he had found him. He wanted to say how he, too, had had a good dad who understood him, and he, too, longed for a simple, clean life, and how he, too, found his fullest joy in the midst of work. But Leo's studio was across the field and through the forest, and when they came out of the main house, the boy said good-bye quickly, invisible, though his breath plumed white into the darkness. Lancelot on his own slow shuffle through the pitch-black had to be satisfied with the thought of tomorrow. The revelations falling off in layers, like the separate skins of an onion. He would find a true friend all the way on the inside.

He fell asleep watching the lick of flames in his fireplace, a long, slow submergence and smoky contentment that led into a sleep the depth of which he could not remember having had for years.

HOT MILK OF A WORLD, with its skin of morning fog in the window. Lunch on the porch, in a plaited basket, vegetable soup and focaccia and good cheddar and celery and carrot sticks and an apple and cookie. Glorious blue-gray day, and he couldn't stay inside. He wanted to be working. In late afternoon, he pulled on his boots and his Barbour jacket and went out for a walk in the woods. The chill on his face turned itself inside out and he grew warm. Heat begat lustiness and lustiness carried him to a moss-covered rock, a deep cold beneath the warm green velvety nap. With his pants to his knees, engaged in heavy self-fondle. Thoughts of Mathilde had become amagnetic, rebounding off her, spinning outward, ending up hopelessly tangled in thoughts of an Asian nymphet cooing at him in a schoolgirl's kilt, as fantasies tended to. Tree branches gray slats above and moving polka dots of crows. Frantic motions in the groinal area until the inevitable upward spin and the slick in the palm.

The lake at his heels so still. Poxed by the touch of scattered rain.

By the time he stood, anxiety was thickening in his chest: he hated putting off work when he was in the mood. It was as if the muses were singing [rather, humming] and he'd stuffed up his ears. He walked in the general direction of Leo's cabin, the silence of the woods so eerie the ancient poems of his babyhood returned to him. He sang them to himself as if they were songs. When he arrived at Leo's—pinkish stucco, pseudo Tudor, flanked with ferns that gleamed in the dim gray light—he understood that he'd been hoping he'd find his collaborator noodling around on his porch. But there was no movement anywhere, and inside, the curtains were unstirred. Lancelot sat behind a birch tree, wondering what to do. When it grew dark enough, he crept near and looked in the window. No lights had been turned on, but the curtains had been opened and someone was moving in the room.

It was Leo, and he was standing, his skinny white chest bare, and he had his eyes closed, his freckled face young, almost teenaged-looking, and his hair in little sandy tufts all over his head. He was waggling his arms. Once in a while, he would move over to the sheets set on the piano and make notations and hurry back to where he had been, closing his eyes again. His bare feet were as enormous as his hands and, like the hands, red at the knuckles with cold.

How strange it felt to Lancelot to see someone else being lifted on a creative crest.

He thought of the hours and hours *he'd* spent carried along and how utterly silly he might have looked had anyone at all peeped in and seen him. First in the windowless closet they'd converted to his study in the city, and then, in the country house, in his glossy attic study, with the Shakespeare compendium on its prayer stand and the gardens in the window, Mathilde moving among them. For many months up there he had looked down and considered how the lifespan of a sunflower reflected the lifespan of man: hopeful, beautiful, brightly shooting out of the ground; broad and strong, with a face turned full and dutiful toward the sun; head so heavy with ripe thoughts it bowed toward the ground, turned brown, lost its bright hair, grew weak on its stalk; mowed down for the long winter. He'd spoken in voices, strutted, cringed, marched, minced up there. Eleven major plays, two additional probably not so major, in retrospect, and he'd performed all of them as he wrote them, to blank walls, then the audience of sunflowers and Mathilde's slim back bending toward the weeds below.

He came to when he saw Leo buttoning up one of his shirts, putting on his sweater, then his jacket, sliding moccasins over his feet. He walked around to the road and headed toward the boy's front door, calling out to him as Leo came out and fiddled with the lock.

"Oh, hullo," Leo said. "Have you come to find me? I'm so glad. I'm feeling rather guilty about you. I had planned to wrap up early and talk over our project, but the composition I was working on rudely insisted that I stick with it to the bitter end. We're off to supper, then? We can talk as we walk, perhaps."

"Let's go," Lancelot said. "I have a million ideas. I'm boiling over with them. I had to go for a walk to get away from them, but the problem with ideas is that the more you walk, the more you get. They breed in the brainpan."

"Brilliant," Leo said. "Glad to hear it. Go ahead and spin."

By the time they sat at supper, Lancelot had gone over his top five. Leo was frowning, pink from the cold. He passed the roasted vegetable torte, then said, "No. None of those, I think. I wait for the spark, you see. And those ideas don't have the spark, I'm afraid."

"All right," said Lancelot, and he was about to launch into the next five when he felt a hand on his shoulder and a voice hot in his ear saying, "Lotto!" and he looked up at first uncomprehendingly at Natalie. Natalie! Of all people! Natalie of the potato nose over the thin black moustache. She had done well in the Internet boom, but apparently had cashed out her stock and was so rich she could return to what she loved most. Which was—how very unexpected—*sculpture*, of all things. She was white with plaster dust and heavier; well, they all were heavier. Fine etchings around her eyes, which were still so strangely resentful. There was lots of hugging, lots of celebration, Natalie sitting beside Lancelot and filling him in on life. But when Lancelot turned to introduce Natalie to Leo, Leo had already bussed his plate and utensils, and had vanished, leaving an apologetic note in Lancelot's mailbox: he was under pressure to get this commission done, could concentrate fully on the opera when he was finished. *So very, very sorry.* His handwriting as tiny and precise as typescript.

AND THEN THE ENDLESS APOLOGIES. Four days in a row: "I know, I know, it's terrible, Lancelot, I'm so horribly sorry, but I really must get this commission done. It's killing me, in fact." Leo's face flaming as soon as he saw Lancelot, a new nervousness borne out of shame. Whenever Lancelot staked him out, watching in the woods through the windows, the boy was working, feverish and writing; and because he wasn't faffing about or napping or scratching himself like a sloth, Lancelot couldn't resent him, which only made the wait more difficult.

Down in the cubby in the basement laundry room of the colony house, where he had to telephone Mathilde—no cell service here, they were truly removed from the world—he vented his frustration in a whisper. She made cooing sounds, husky noises of support, but it was five in the morning, she wasn't at her best. "How about some telephonic kink?" she said at last. "A little sultry-sultry across the wires? Calm you down a bit."

"No, thank you," he said. "I'm too distressed."

A long, long pause, her breath at the other end. "This *is* bad, isn't it," she said. "This new crisis. I've never known you to pass up a little phone sex." She sounded sad.

He missed her, his wife. It felt strange to wake up without needing to bring her milky coffee every morning. He felt the lack of the tiny cares she took for him, the way she laundered his clothes, the way she trimmed his eyebrows. Part of him, here, was lacking.

"I want to be home with you," he said.

"Me too, my love. So come home," she said.

"I'll give it a few more days," he said. "Then the booty call in the dark of the night."

"I'll be beside the phone," she said. "Breathlessly waiting. I'll keep the keys in the ignition."

After dinner that night, he went with a clump of artists through the woods, flashlights spearing the black, to the German sculptors' studio. A three-story building with a removable side and a hydraulic lift for the heaviest art. There was vodka chilled in the stream in back and a sort of seething music, all electric spikes. The lights had been turned off. In the front room, a two-story flutter, love notes from the German *Frau*'s first marriage barely tethered to a structure so it shifted in the wind, one tiny home movie projected on each. A sculpture of marriage, marriage come alive.

Lancelot felt tears start to his eyes. It was so exactly right. The Germans saw the gleam, and both of them—like budgerigars on their perch—sidled up and hugged Lancelot around the waist.

ON THE FIFTH DAY of artistic stymie, Lancelot woke to a miserable drizzly dawn and took a bike and coasted down the hill to the town gym's pool.

The water made everything better. He was not a good swimmer, but the thrashing helped, and he spent longer and longer with each lap just gliding underwater. It washed over him, calmed him, brought him back to where he had been in the car, coming to the residency. Perhaps it was the oxygen depletion. Perhaps his rangy body had finally gotten the exercise it needed, especially in light of his enforced celibacy. Perhaps, only, he had exhausted himself to the point where his anxieties had fallen away. [False. He should have known a gift when he saw one.] But when he came to the end of the pool, touched the wall, pulled himself up, he knew what the opera would be. It rose before him, gleaming, more real than the water it overlay.

He sat so long at the end of the pool, having forgotten himself, that his skin was dry when he looked up to see Leo standing beside him, still in his jeans and white button-down and moccasins. "They'd told me you were down here splashing about. I've come to fetch you in a little car I've borrowed. So sorry to keep you waiting for so very, very long, but you know it means that we're both keen to begin. If it is convenient for you, I'm ready," Leo said. He moved, and at last his face, which had been silhouetted by the sun coming directly through the window, was visible.

"Antigone," Lancelot said, and smiled up at him.

"Sorry?" Leo said.

"Antigone," Lancelot said. "Spark."

"Antigone?" Leo said.

"Antigone, underground. Our opera. Antigone who hadn't hanged herself, or she had tried, but before she succeeded, the gods had cursed her with immortality. First they gave it as a gift, for hewing to their laws against those of men. And then, when she railed against the gods, it turned into a taunt. She's in her cave still, even today. I was thinking of the Cumaean Sybil, who lived for a thousand years, so long that she shrank and was put in an urn. Eliot quoted it as epigraph for 'The Waste Land,' from Petronius Arbiter's *Satyricon*, 'For once I saw with my own eyes the Cumaean Sibyl hanging in a jar. When the boys asked her, "Sibyl, what do you want?" she said, "I want to die."'"

Long silence, pool lapping at the gutters. A woman hummed to herself as she did a slow froglike kick on her back.

"Oh my god," Leo said.

"Yeah," Lancelot said. "Also, Antigone in the original was on the side of the gods and against men, as in the order of men, as in Creon's dictates against her brother's being honored by burial, but I think we can extend this to a sense of—"

"Misandry."

"No, not misandry, but perhaps misanthropy. She scorns the gods for leaving her, humans for their flaws. She has shrunk so small she is beneath humans, literally beneath their feet, and yet she's above them. Time has purified her. She has become the spirit of humanity. We should change the title. What about *Anti-gone*? Play with the fact that she's still here? No?"

He had led Leo into the locker room and was toweling himself off exuberantly. He took off his trunks. When he looked up, Leo's eyes were enormous, and he was sitting on his bench, his hands folded in his lap as he watched naked Lancelot. He was pinkish in the face.

"Antigonist," Leo said, looking down.

"Wait. *The Antigonad*," Lancelot said, first as a joke because, well, he was just then pulling up his boxer briefs. All right, it was true, he had lingered a little in the buff: there had been an internal hot flash of vanity and gratitude for being looked at. It had been so long since a stranger had seen him naked. Well, there had been that run of *Equus* in the mid-nineties, but it had played for only twelve nights and the theater had only two hundred seats. But when he said the joke, he found he liked it. *"The Antigonad,"* he said again. "Maybe it's a love story. A love story and she's stuck in a cave. The lovers can't touch."

"For now," said Leo. "We can always change if we find ourselves to be pro-gonad, I suppose." Was that suggestive? It was hard to tell with this boy.

"Leo, Leo," Lancelot said. "You are as dry as vermouth."

AND THEN CAME THE PROLIX PERIOD, when they did not stop talking. For four days, now five, now seven. Without really writing anything yet. They worked in strange twilit limbo. Lancelot always an early riser, Leo up all night, sleeping until two in the afternoon, they compromised by meeting at Lancelot's when Leo was awake. They worked until Lancelot fell asleep, full-clothed, waking briefly only when the door blasted cold into the cabin as Leo left.

Lancelot read the original Sophocles play aloud while Leo lay on his hearth before the cheery fire and dreamt, listening. And then, for context, Lancelot read aloud the other two parts of the triumvirate, *Oedipus Rex* and *Oedipus at Colonus*. He read aloud the fragments of Euripides. He read the Séamus Heaney adaptation aloud; they read Anne Carson, their heads together. They listened in silence to the Orff opera, the Honegger–Cocteau opera, the Theodorakis opera, the Traetta opera. At supper, they sat engaged, tight and thick, and they spoke of their Antigone, whom they called Go, as if she were a friend.

Leo hadn't yet written any music, but he had made drawings on butcher paper stolen from the kitchen. They curled around his walls, intricate doodles, extensions of the boy's own lean, slight body. The shape of Leo's jaw in profile, devastating; the way he gnawed his fingernails to the crescents, the fine shining hairs down the center of his nape. The smell of him, up close, pure and clean, bleachy. [The ones made for music are the most beloved of all. Their bodies a container for the spirit within; the best of them is music, the rest only instrument of flesh and bone.]

THE WEATHER CONSPIRED. Snow fell softly in the windows. It was too cold to be out for long. The world colorless, a dreamscape, a blank page. The linger of wood smoke on the back of the tongue.

The collaborators were in so deep that when Natalie tried to sit with them for dinner, Lancelot barely smiled at her before turning back to sketch out what he was saying to Leo on a piece of scrap paper. And Natalie sat back in her chair, tearing up—their friendship mostly in the past, but oh! he still had the power to hurt her with his disregard—until she smiled it away. She watched Lotto. She was listening. There was an electricity here; both men were flushed, shoulders close. If Lotto had been paying attention to Natalie, he would have understand that there would be talk later, the old friend network sparked by what she'd say she'd seen between the two men. At last she nodded and bussed her tray and left; and as this was her last night at the residency, he wouldn't see her again. [Her death would be soon and sudden. Ski tumble; embolism.]

The German sculptors had returned to Nuremberg without Lancelot's noticing it, and a pale young woman had taken their place. She painted one-story-tall oils of the shadows of objects, not the objects themselves. The blond novelist went home to her house full of boys. The colony contracted in winter: now there was only one table of artists at dinner. The frizzled poet wore a face of disappointment when she came in night after night to see the collaborators together. "Lancelot, my dear. Won't you talk anymore to anyone but that boy?" she said once, leaning close, when Leo went in to fetch the dessert tray for the group.

"I'm sorry," he said. "I'll come back to you soon, Emmylinn. It's just the initial stages. The head-over-heels phase."

She rested her papery cheek on his upper arm, and said, "I understand. But dovey, it is not healthy to be so immersed for so long. You need to come up for air."

AND THEN THERE WAS THE NOTE in the office from his wife, hurtfully terse, and Lancelot felt a dip in him, and he hurried down to the laundry room to call Mathilde.

"M.," he said, when she picked up, "I'm so sorry. I've lost track of everything but this project. It's all-consuming."

"No sign of you for a week, my love," she said. "No call. You've forgotten me."

"No," he said. "No. Of course not. I'm just in deep."

"In deep," she repeated slowly. "You are in deep something. The question is: In deep what?"

"I'm sorry," he said.

She sighed and said, "Thanksgiving's tomorrow."

"Oh," he said.

"We had planned for you to come back for the night so we can host. Our first in the country. I was going to pick you up at eight tomorrow morning. Rachel and Elizabeth and the twins are coming. Sallie's flying up. Chollie and Danica. Samuel, his triplets, but not Fiona—did you know she'd filed for divorce? Shocker, out of nowhere. You should call him. He misses you. Anyway, I've made pies."

The silence moved from interrogative to accusatory.

At last, he said, "I believe just this once that my beloveds can celebrate Thanksgiving without me. I will be giving thanks for you by working. Thereby being able to buy many more decades of Tofurky that you will all insert into your gobbets."

"How mean. And sad," she said.

"I didn't mean to be mean. And not sad for me," he said. "After the summer I had, M., I'm bloody delighted to be working."

"Bloody," she said. "I didn't know they used Anglicisms in New Hampshire."

"Leo," he said.

"Leo," she said. "Leo. Leo. Leo. Leo. Listen. I can cancel on them all and drive up there and find a bed-and-breakfast," she said. "We can gorge on pies. And watch terrible movies. And fuck."

And then a long silence and she said, "I guess not."

He sighed. "You can't hate me, Mathilde, when I say no. This is my work."

She said nothing, eloquently.

"This is probably the wrong time to bring it up," he said.

"Probably," she said.

"But Leo and I were able to extend our residency for two additional weeks. I'll be back right before Christmas. And that's a promise."

"Nifty," she said, and hung up, and when he called again and again and again for the third time, she wouldn't answer.

———————

IT IS NOT THAT HE FORGOT about the tiff with Mathilde, it was simply that when he went outside the sun had come out and the brightness against the snow and ice made the world seem as if carved of stone, marble, and mica, and the raw minerality of what had been so soft and fresh returned him to Go's cave, as everything he saw and heard and felt now seemed urgently dovetailed to the world of Go. Two nights earlier, after dinner when it came time to share work, a video artist's time-lapse hand-drawn movie of a village being built, being razed by fire, being rebuilt, seemed utterly right for their project, and necessary. Just as the puppeteer who was working with a fragment of fabric, who was able to make the piece of flaming silk into something movingly human, had a deep impression upon *The Antigonad*.

Lotto couldn't forget his wife, but she existed on a constant, unchanging plane, her rhythms in his bones. At all moments, he could predict where she was. [Now, whipping eggs for an omelet; now, hiking over the crispy fields to the pond for an illicit smoke as she always did in her angry moments.] And Lancelot existed, right now, on a plane where everything he knew and was had been turned inside out, predictability had exploded.

He took a nap and woke to Leo sitting beside him on the bed. Last light of day flaring through the window, illuminating the pellucid skin, the fair eyelashes. The boy's huge hand was warm on his shoulder, and Lancelot blinked sleepily, smiling, and there came the urge from the loyal doggish heart of him to press his cheek against it. So he did.

Leo flushed, and the hand twitched a little before he withdrew it.

Lancelot stretched to his full length, arms against the wall, feet dangling, and sat up. There was a smooth blue static in the room.

"I'm ready," Leo said. "I want to write Go's aria first. The love aria. Just the music for now. It'll dictate the rest of the score. I'm going to disappear for a few days if that's all right with you."

"Don't disappear," Lancelot said. He felt a heaviness in him. "Can't I sit quietly in the corner while you work? I'll work on the sketch of the book a little more. And do a grammar and dictionary for Go's language. I won't bother you for a second. You won't know I'm there."

"Please. As if you could be silent for even an hour," Leo said. He stood and went to the window, his back turned to Lancelot, who was fully awake now. "It would be good for us to be apart for a span," Leo said. "For me, at least. To know you are here and not be able to see you. All of that would show up in the music."

Lancelot looked at him with some wonder. He was so slight in the window, framed against the steely forest. "But Leo," he said. "I'll be lonely without you."

Leo turned around and gave Lancelot a quick look and went wordlessly out the door, through the forest, up the path. Lancelot wrapped his blanket around his shoulders and came out to the porch to watch him disappear.

Later he took himself through the dark trees to the colony house for supper; but only a single light was illuminated in the kitchen, and of the eight artists still in residence, most were in warmer places, being loved and fed and touched on the shoulders, on the cheeks, by family and friends. Being loved. And Lancelot had chosen separateness. He would have acted differently had he known that Leo would turn hermit. It gnawed at him, the old discomfort of being left with only himself.

Lancelot heated his plate of gravied tofu and potato mash and green beans. Halfway through, he was joined by a smelly, half-deaf composer with a Walt Whitman beard that sopped up his dribbles. He had eyes pink with burst veins and mostly grunted, glaring at

Lancelot like a ferocious goat. Lancelot made a game out of having a lopsided conversation with him.

"Cranberry sauce?" Lancelot said, ladling some out on his own plate, to a grunt.

"You don't say? Best you ever had, at the Ritz on Thanksgiving day in 1932?" to a grunt.

"With whom?" Grunt. "Really? Marvelous. Royalty, did you say?" Grunt. "You did *what* with Princess Margaret during the war? I had no idea, man, that that was even invented back then." Grunty-grunty-grunt.

For dessert there was pumpkin pie. Bumblefuck Pie. An entire one that they split, Lancelot shoving more sweet in to clog up his sadness, the composer matching him bite for bite as if in thrall to a ferocious sense of justice. Lancelot took an intentionally enormous bite to watch the composer mirror him. The man looked like a snake with a rat in its gob. When Lancelot swallowed, he said, "I like you, Walt Whitman."

And the composer, who had heard this at least, spat, "Oh, you think you're so funny," and stood and left the dishes and the crumby floor to Lancelot to clean.

"You contain multitudes," Lancelot said to his beetled back.

The composer turned, glared. "I'm giving thanks for you," Lancelot said solemnly.

Oh, lonely, lonely. Mathilde didn't answer at the house or at the apartment or on her cell, but of course she wouldn't; she was hosting company. His family, his friends. They were all certainly talking about him. [Indeed.] He brushed his teeth terribly slowly and went to bed with a doorstop novel. Don't be paranoid, Lotto, you're fine, he told himself. And if they were talking about you, surely they'd be saying kind things. Yet he imagined them laughing at him, their faces contorted into grotesque animal forms, Rachel a rat, Elizabeth an elephant with her long, sensitive proboscis, Mathilde an albino hawk. Fraudster, ignoramus, space cadet, they were saying of him. Former male whore. Narcissist!

Now they were having a grand time without him, deep into their drinks. Throwing their heads back, pointy teeth and wine-stained gums, laughing and laughing. He tossed his book across the room so hard it cracked its spine on landing.

HE CARRIED HIS MOROSENESS with him through the night into the morning. By noon, he was actively longing for home. For God with her hot nose, for his own pillow, his own sweet Mathilde.

On the afternoon of the fourth day of Leo's solitary confinement, Lancelot couldn't help himself: he went the long way through the woods to have plausible deniability, gathering a dandruffy birch stick on his walk, and ended up outside Leo's cabin again.

It took a moment to locate Leo in the dim inside. The boy had made a concessionary fire, too cold outside these days even for him. In the dull glow, his head was pressed against the piano's forehead, and he could have been sleeping if not for the hand rising from his lap once in a while to strike a note or a chord. The noise after a long period of silence startled, even all the way out to Lancelot behind his tree.

It was calming, this slow noisemaking. Lancelot went into a very small trance each time he waited for the next note. When it came, it was muted by the walls and windows and pockets of air, and it arrived at Lancelot's ear unexpectedly. It was like believing yourself alone in a room, beginning to fall into sleep, only to hear a sneeze muffled in the darkest corner.

He left when his shivering got uncontrollable. There was new bad darkness, a stormy one, fast descending out of the western sky. He skipped dinner for ramen noodles sucked from the styrofoam cup and hot chocolate, and finished off half a bottle of bourbon, dancing naked to a fire that blazed and popped and gave the room a mid-August Florida broil. He opened the window and watched the snow fall slantwise in and hit the floorboards as water, rebounding into mist.

He felt much better and fell asleep atop his bed, sweating and drunk. His body seemed lifted, as if he'd been tied to a kite and set afloat thirty feet above the ground, watching lesser mortals moving in their small and slow ways below.

He woke at his usual time, shivering, and when he went to boil water for coffee, there was no electricity, no heat. Behind the curtains the forest could have been made of glass, the way it dazzled in the last moonlight. In the deep night, the ice had descended, coating the fields and trees as if in epoxy. He had been so drunk he hadn't awoken, although great tree branches had cracked and fallen all around and lay in the darkness, as stunned as soldiers after an ambush. Lancelot could hardly open the screen door to his cabin. He took one confident step out onto the ice, and for a long moment, he slid gracefully, his weak foot extended back in an arabesque, but though his right toe stubbed up against a rock and stopped the slide of the foot, his body kept going forward and he spun around and cracked his tailbone so hard he had to roll to his side and gnash his teeth. He moaned for a long time in pain. When he went to stand, the skin of his cheek stuck to the ice, and he pulled the top layer off and there was a little blood on his fingertips when he touched it.

Like a mountaineer, he grimped his way hand over hand back onto the porch, into the house, and lay exhausted on the floor, breathing heavily.

Good old Robby Frost, he thought. The ones who said the world would end in ice were right. [Wrong. Fire.]

He would starve here. On the shelf he had one apple kept back from a lunch, a box of skinny-person granola bars that Mathilde had packed, one last ramen cup. He would bleed to death from his cheek. The tailbone fracture would go septic inside him. No electricity and he'd burned up all his firewood in his gluttonous frenzy last night: he would freeze. No coffee either, caffeine withdrawal the real tragedy here. He bundled himself in every article of clothing he could find, making a cloak of the lap blanket. He made a secondary hat out of his laptop case. Big as a rugby prop now, he put his legs up on the bed and ate the entire box of granola bars. When he finished, he knew it was a mistake, because they tasted like tennis balls that had been lost in the bushes for three seasons. Also, they each contained 83 percent of one's daily fiber, and therefore he'd just ingested 498 percent of his daily fiber and would die from the intestinal roughage before the bleeding or cold would do him in.

Also, he had run his laptop battery down to death the evening before and hadn't worried about plugging it in because there would always be electricity in the morning; and he had long ago gotten away from writing anything by hand. Why did he not write anything by hand? Why had he gotten away from this most essential art?

He was composing in his head, like Milton, when he heard a motor and opened the curtains and here was blessed Blaine. His pickup truck was in chains. It was pausing at the door, and Blaine was tossing sand out his window, then getting out and crunching up in ice-mountaineering cleats to knock.

"My savior," Lancelot said, opening the door, forgetting his getup. Blaine took him in head to toe, and his sweet face cracked wide open.

There were camp beds made up in the colony house, and generators, and the stoves were gas and there was plenty of food. The telephones would be back, they said, in a day or so. All was comfortable. The artists had the laughing camaraderie of disaster survivors, and when composer Walt Whitman poured out shots of slivovitz for all and sundry, Lancelot clinked glasses with him and nodded, and the men smiled at each other, letting bygones be bygones. A friendly kindliness settled over them, Lancelot fetching more gingerbread out of the refrigerator for Walt Whitman, the composer lending Lancelot thick cashmere socks.

All afternoon, Lancelot waited and waited, but Leo never came. At last, he cornered Blaine, who had just brought in enough wood to last a month and was getting ready to return home to chip his own house out of the ice.

"Oh," Blaine said. "Leo said no, thanks, he had enough wood, and he showed me the peanut butter and loaf of bread and jug of water and said he'd prefer to just keep on working. I didn't think there was harm in it. Oh, dear. Was I wrong?"

No, no, no, Lancelot assured him. But he thought, Yes, horrible, you never leave a man to fend alone with the cold, haven't you ever read about Shackleton and HMS *Endurance*? Glaciers and cannibalism. Or fairy tales, the ice goblins coming out of the woods to knock. In the deep night, working, Leo would hear someone moving at the door and go over in his bare feet to investigate, and there would be an eerie soft singing out beyond the circle of trees, and intrigued, Leo would step out briefly into the cold, and the door would close behind him. It would be locked with the ice goblins having stolen inside, and try as he might, there would be no getting back in to the devilishly hot fire, the naked dancing beasties inside, while he did a Little Match Girl huddle against the door and faded off into visions of distant happiness as his breathing slowed to nothing. Frozen. Dead! Poor Leo, stiff corpse blue of hue. Lancelot shivered, even though the colony house was tropical in the good glow of the artists' relief and the heat from the fireplaces.

Even after the kerosene lamps were blown out and the novelist had put away his guitar and the slivovitz had warmed everyone's bellies and they had fallen asleep in the communal area, feeling warm and safe, Lancelot worried about the poor boy alone in the forest, deep freeze all around. He tried not to toss and turn on his camp bed for fear of his squeaking springs and blanket rustle keeping the other artists awake, but he gave up on sleep in the wee hours and went down to the frigid telephone booth to see if the wires were up and he could call Mathilde. But the phones were still dead, and the basement was frigid. He came back up to the library and sat in the window overlooking the back fields and watched the night wash itself away.

Sitting there, thinking of Leo's quick hot flushing, the shock of his hair, Lotto fell into a fitful sleep in the armchair though he dreamt he was awake.

He came to and saw a small figure making its slow and stuttering way out of the forest. In the gleam off the ice and the moonlit dark, it could have been a messenger from a grim story. He watched as the white face under the watch cap came clear, and he felt a slow sun begin to dawn in him when he knew for certain it was Leo.

He met the boy at the kitchen door, silently opening it to him, and though there was an unspoken interdiction against their touching, Lancelot couldn't help himself; he took Leo's slight, strong shoulders in his arms and hugged him fiercely, breathing in the persimmon smell of the skin behind the ear, the hair baby fine against his face.

"I was so worried about you," he said low to keep the others from waking. He let go reluctantly.

Leo held his eyes closed, and when he opened them, it was with some effort. He seemed weary to death. "I've finished Go's aria," he said. "Of course, I haven't slept in three nights. I'm ragged with fatigue. I'm going to go home and sleep. But, well. If Blaine can drop you off with a packed supper before he leaves for the night, I will play what I have for you."

"Yes," Lancelot said. "Of course. I'll get up a little picnic and we can talk into the wee hours. But stay now and have some breakfast with me."

Leo shook his head. "If I don't get home, I'll shatter. I just wanted to invite you to my studio. Then, oh, blessed oblivion of sleep for as long as I can remain under." He smiled. "Or until you come in and wake me."

He moved to the door, but Lancelot, trying to find a way to keep him, said, "How did you know I'd be awake?"

Lancelot could feel the heat of Leo's blush from where he was standing. "I know you," he said. And then, recklessly: "I can't tell you how many mornings I've stood on the road and watched your light go on at five twenty-two before I could go home to sleep." And then the door opened, closed, and Leo was a scribble disappearing on the dark path and then the blank page of snow.

LANCELOT APPLIED DEODORANT TWICE, shaved twice. All parts of him had been scrubbed in the hot shower. He watched himself closely in the mirror, unsmiling. It was nothing, his collaborator playing the first music for their project; it was business, routine; he was nauseated, hadn't eaten a thing all day; his limbs were wrong, as if his bones had melted and been reconstituted at random. The last time he'd felt this way, he had been so young he was a stranger to himself, and there had been a girl with a moon face and self-pierced nose, a night on the beach, a house they were in going up in flames. His first completed act of love. So nervous, he forgot her name for a minute. [Gwennie.] Oh, yes, Gwennie, his memory fraying at the edges, so unlike the old him with the steel-trap brain. Though what her ghost had to say to him could not be pertinent here.

Something was happening inside him. As if inside there were

a blast furnace that would sear him if opened. Some secret so un-acknowledged not even Mathilde knew.

He hadn't wanted to put his visit to Leo's into words that Blaine could hear, so he'd made the soup himself and the sandwiches, packed them in the basket. He set out totteringly over the melting ice without telling anyone where he was going. In the twilight, the ice had retracted enough from the banks to resemble gums with exposed tooth roots. The trees were skinny bodies stripped bare in the wind. It was far more difficult to move than he'd thought it would be: he had to go crabwise, arms extended, basket dangling, and he was breathing heavily by the time he came to Leo's little Tudor, with firelight reddening the windows.

He went inside for the first time and was startled by the small evidence of habitation. All had been swept clean, and the only markers of Leo were the black shoes, shiny as beetles, in a neat pair under the bed, and the music standing on the piano.

Then the sound of water from a faucet in the bathroom, and there was Leo in the doorway, drying his hands on a towel.

"You came," he said.

"You doubted?" Lancelot said.

Leo moved toward Lancelot, then stopped in the middle of the floor. He touched his throat, then his legs, then touched his hands together at the palms. He hemmed. "I had planned that we eat first, but I don't think I can," Leo said. "I want so much to play for you, and at the same time I'm far too anxious to play for you. This is absurd."

Lancelot took a screw-top malbec that he'd scavenged from the dining area out of the basket, and said, "So, we drink. Scored a *Wine Advocate* ninety-three. Complex, fruit-forward, with notes of bravery and wit. Whenever you feel ready, we'll play." He'd meant *you'll* play, as in piano, and coughed to cover his mistake.

He poured into the same speckled blue mugs that, in his own cabin, he had planted a dead fern in. Leo took a gulp and choked, laughing, and dabbed at his face with a tissue. And then he handed the mug back to Lancelot, grazing his hand. He crossed over to the piano. It felt a violation for Lancelot to sit on the side of Leo's bed, but still he sat gingerly, aware of the mattress's coolness, the white sheets, the firmness of it beneath him.

Leo flexed his monstrous hands and, as if for the first time, Lancelot saw their unbelievable beauty. They could span a thirteenth, those hands, they were Rachmaninoff hands. Leo let them float above the keys, and they came down, and Go's aria had already begun.

After a bar, Lancelot closed his eyes. It was easier this way, to disembody the music. Like this, he heard the sound resolve into a soft song. Soaring and harmonious. So sweet it ached his teeth. Heat began in his stomach and radiated outward, up and down, into the throat, into the thighbones, an emotion so strange Lancelot had a hard time identifying what it was; but within a minute of Leo's playing, Lancelot had put a name to it. Dread. He was feeling dread, pale and thick. This music was wrong, so utterly and entirely wrong for their project. Lancelot felt as if he were choking. He had wanted the ethereal, the strange. Something a little ugly. Music with humor in it, for gadfly's sake! A biting sort of music! An undermining and deepening music, one that layered with the original myth of Antigone, which had always been a ferocious and strange story. If only Leo had replicated the music from the opera this summer. This, though. No. This was treacle; this had no humor in it. It was achy; it was trembling. This was so wrong it changed everything.

Everything had been changed.

He had to make sure that his face, turned so attentively toward Leo, his eyes closed, was composed into a mask.

He wanted to escape to the bathroom to weep. He wanted to

punch Leo in the nose to get him to stop. He did neither. He sat there, a Mathilde smile on his face, and listened. On his internal dock, a great ship that he had wanted to climb and sail away on gave a low blast. The ropes were tossed. It moved silently out into the bay, and Lancelot was left alone onshore, watching it dip low over the horizon, watching it vanish.

The music ended. Lancelot opened his eyes, smiling. But Leo had seen something in his face and was looking at him now, horror-struck.

When Lancelot opened his mouth but no words came out, Leo stood and opened his door and walked outside in his bare feet, without even a jacket, and vanished into the dark woods.

"Leo?" Lancelot said. He ran to the door and shouted, "Leo? Leo?" But Leo made no sound. He was gone.

They hadn't been paying attention. On the softest of cat feet, the winter afternoon had passed into twilight.

In the cabin, Lancelot considered. He could run after Leo, with his weak left side—and say what if he found him? Say what if he missed him? He could stay inside here and wait for Leo to come back. But the boy's pride was badly wounded, and he would very soon be physically hurt by the cold, his feet cut up, frostbite setting in before he consented to return to a cabin where Lancelot was. The only good thing, the only humane thing, was for Lancelot to leave. Allow the boy to creep back inside, lick his wounds in private. Come back tomorrow and straighten things out after they'd both had a moment to cool off.

He scribbled a note. He paid no attention to what he'd said and was too distraught to understand or remember beyond the moment the pencil lifted from the paper. It could have been a poem; it could have been a grocery list. He went out into the lonely cold and tottered painfully up the icy dirt road, feeling every day of his forty years, to the colony house. He was soaked with sweat when he reached it. When he climbed inside, the others had started to eat dinner without him.

———

LONG BEFORE THE SUN ROSE, weak tea, over the clotted fields, Lancelot was pacing in the colony house's library. The world had gone sideways; all was badly amiss. He hurried out. It was easier to move than it had been the day before, the ice having receded even further so that there was a slushy mud track all the way to Leo's. Lancelot knocked hard on the door, but it was locked. He moved around to the windows, but the curtains were pulled so tightly no crack was available for his eye. In his mind all night there had been a terrible echo of the time in prep school when he'd discovered the hanged boy. The blue face, the terrible smell. The brush of denim on his face in the dark, his hands reaching up to touch cold dead leg.

He found one window unlatched and wedged his shoulders through, his body snaking after him, and fell so hard on his bad clavicle that the ceiling swam with sparks. "Leo," he called out in a choked voice, but he knew before he hefted himself to his feet that Leo wasn't in the cabin. The shoes under the bed were gone, and the closet was empty. It smelled, still, like Leo. He looked vainly for a note, anything, and found only a clean copy of Go's aria in the piano bench, with Leo's precise penciled notation. Framable, art even without the music. Only the word *acciaccato* in black ink.

Lancelot ran as well as he could back to the colony house, catching Blaine driving in, and waved him down.

"Oh," Blaine said. "Oh, yes. Leo had some terrible news from home and had to fly off in the middle of the night. I'm just coming back from Hartford now. He seemed drawn. He's a sweet kid, isn't he? Poor boy."

Lotto smiled. His eyes filled with tears. He was absurd.

Blaine looked uncomfortable and laid a hand on Lotto's shoulder. "Are you all right?" he said.

Lancelot nodded. "I need to go home today, too, I'm afraid," he said. "Please tell them in the office when they come in. I'll hire a driver. Don't worry about me."

"All right, son," Blaine said quietly. "I won't."

LANCELOT STOOD IN THE DOORWAY of the country house's kitchen, the limo shushing off through the slush. Home.

God was clicking swiftly down the stairs, Mathilde at the table in a slant of light, her eyes closed, a cup of tea steaming before her. There was a whiff of garbage in the house's chilly air. Lancelot's heart gave a somersault: it was his job in the family to take the garbage out. In his absence, Mathilde had been letting it build.

He didn't know if she would look at him. He had never known her to be so angry that she would not look at him. Her face was so terribly closed. She looked older. Sad. Skinny. Her hair greasy. She was browned, as if she'd been pickled in her own loneliness. Something in him was breaking.

And then God was leaping at his knees, peeing with happiness to see him, and barking in her high-pitched semi-scream. Mathilde opened her eyes. He watched the great pupils narrowing in her irises, watched her see him, and by the look on her face, he understood that she hadn't known he was there until now. And that she was so very, very glad to see him. Here she was. His only love.

She stood so fast her chair tumbled backward and she came to him with her hands outspread, her face bursting open, and then he pressed his face into her hair to smell it. The earth was stuck, rotating, in his throat. And then her strong and bony body was against his, her scent in his nose, the taste of her earlobe in his mouth. She pulled back a span and looked at him ferociously and kicked the kitchen door shut with her foot. When he tried to speak, she pressed her hand hard over his mouth so he couldn't and she led him upstairs in absolute silence and had her way with him so roughly that when he woke the next day he had plum-colored bruises on the bones of his hips and fingernail cuts on his sides, which he pressed in the bathroom, hungry for the pain.

AND THEN IT WAS CHRISTMAS. Mistletoe hanging from the hallway chandelier, blue spruce wrapped up the banister, a smell of cinnamon, baking apples. Lancelot stood at the bottom of the stairs, smiling at his cragged face in the mirror, fixing his tie. Looking at him, he thought, you'd never tell that he had been so broken this year. He had suffered, had come through it all stronger. Even, he thought, possibly more attractive. Men can do that, become more handsome as they grow older. Women just age. Poor Mathilde, with her corrugated forehead. In twenty years, she'd be silver-gray, her face full of wrinkles. Oh, but she'd still be beautiful, he thought, loyal to the marrow.

The sound of a motor broke in and he looked out to find the dark green Jaguar turning off the road onto the gravel among the bare cherry trees.

"They're here," he called up the stairs to Mathilde.

He was smiling: it had been months since he'd seen his sister and Elizabeth and their adopted twins, and how they would love the rocking turtle and the rocking owl he'd had carved for them by an eccentric hermit woodworker out in the deep upstate wilds. The owl bore a startled scholarly look and the turtle seemed to be chewing a bitter root. Oh, for the kids' spritelike bodies in his arms. The soothe of his sister beside him. He came up on his toes in excitement.

But he saw, under the bowl of peppermint bark on the cherry hall stand, the corner of a newspaper peeking out. Unusual. Mathilde so neat, usually. Everything in the house in its proper place. He pushed the bowl aside to see. His legs went liquid under him.

A grainy photo of Leo Sen, smiling shyly. A small article beneath his face.

Promising British composer drowned off an island in Nova Scotia. Tragedy. Such potential. Eton and Oxford. Early prodigy on the violin. Known for his aharmonic, deeply emotional compositions. No partner. Will be missed by parents, community. Quotes by famous composers; Leo had been better known than Lancelot had believed.

What remained unsaid was almost too heavy to bear. Another sinkhole. Someone there, suddenly gone. Leo swimming in such cold water. December, rip currents, spray above the wild waves instantly freezing to bullets of ice. He imagined the shock of cold black water on the body, shuddered. Everything about it was wrong.

He had to breathe to keep on two feet. He gripped the table and opened his eyes to see his own face gone white in the mirror.

And above his left shoulder, he saw Mathilde at the top of the stairs. She was watching him. She was unsmiling, intent, bladelike in her red dress. The weak December daylight poured through the window above her and touched her around the shoulders.

The door opened in the kitchen and the children's voices were in the back of the house, shouting for Uncle Lotto, and Rachel yelled out, "Hello?" and the dog barked joyfully and Elizabeth honked out a laugh, and Rachel and Elizabeth began to softly bicker, and still, Lancelot and his wife looked at each other in the mirror. And then Mathilde took one step down and then another, and her old small smile returned to her face. "Merry Christmas!" she called out gaily in her deep, clear voice. He flinched back as if he'd put his hand down on a hot stove, and she fixed him in the mirror as she slowly, slowly, descended.

6

"MAY I AT LEAST READ what you wrote with Leo?" Mathilde asked, one night in bed.

"Maybe," Lancelot said, and rolled over on top of her and put his hands up her shirt.

Later, after she submarined below the sheets, she came up, flushed with his heat. "Maybe, as in I can read it?"

"M.," he said softly. "I hate my own failure."

"That's a no?" she said.

"That's a no," he said.

"Okay," she said.

But he had to go to the city the next day to meet with his agent, and she went to his aerie at the top of the house, all scattered papers and coffee cups growing fur, and sat and read what was in the file folder.

She stood and went to the window. She thought of the boy who had drowned in the icy black water, of a mermaid, of herself. "Shame," she said to the dog. "It could have been so great."

THE ANTIGONAD
[*First sketch, with notes for music*]

CAST OF CHARACTERS

GO: countertenor, offstage; onstage, a puppet in water or a hologram that remains the entire opera in a glass tank

ROS: tenor, Go's lover

CHORUS OF TWELVE: gods and tunnelers and commuters

FOUR DANCERS

ACT I: SOLIP

No curtains. Stage black. In the center, a cylindrical tank of water lit or composed to look like a cave. Go: inside. It is difficult after all these aeons to tell she is human. She is whittled to the necessary.

[Leo: The music begins so quietly it is mistaken for ambient sounds. Drips, rumbles from far off. Hissing, a windlike whistling. Shuffling. Heartbeat. Leathery wings. Fragments of music so filtered it is no longer music. Static of voices, as if through rock. One hopes for the audience talking, the sounds of people settling in deep into the score. The sounds gather a rhythm, a harmony, as they grow louder.]

In imperceptible increments, the lights brighten on the cave, darken on the house. The audience eventually quiets.

Go wakes, sits. She begins to sing her first aria, a lament, as she moves around her cave.

Surtitles in English projected above the proscenium arch. Go's language is her own. Ancient Greek, stripped down, no verb tenses, no cases, no genders. Also warped by millennia of solitude, changed by the fragments of words that have filtered down to her from the world above, German and French and English. She is mad in both senses: angry and insane.

Go narrates how she lives as she moves: garden of moss and mushrooms to tend, worms to milk, garments of hair and spider silk to weave more of every day. Slow showers from the water that drips off the stalactites. Terrible loneliness. Bats with baby faces that she'd bred, unable to speak more than ten words, unsatisfying conversationalists. Go is not resigned to her fate. She speaks against the gods who cursed her with immortality; she had tried to hang herself but couldn't. Woke up in shrouds with a rope burn on her neck and Haemon dead beside her. His bones she turned into the spoons and bowls she eats with. She holds her bowl, his skull, and becomes furious again, shouts imprecations against the gods.

Lights cut away from Go's cave, up to the chorus, in god garb, small lights embedded in their garments so they're almost painfully bright. They first appear to be six pillars in a half circle around her tank until we see the symbols that make them who they are: wings on the heels for Hermes, Mars's gun, Minerva's owl, et cetera.

They sing in English. They wanted to give Go immortality, a gift, but they put her in the cave until she showed gratitude. She has yet to show gratitude. Furious Go. Arrogant Go.

Flashback: the story of Antigone, in dance. The dancers are behind the tank so that the water magnifies their bodies and makes them wild and strange. They act out in a short mime how Antigone's brothers, Polynices and Eteocles, fight on opposite sides, how both die, how Antigone buries Polynices twice, against Creon's diktat, then Creon versus the gods, Antigone led away, hanging herself. Haemon killing himself, Eurydice killing herself, Creon dying. Bloodbath galore.

But one of the gods, Minerva, cuts Antigone down, revives her. Seals her into the cave.

The gods sing that they meant to let her, last root of a rotten house, daughter of incest, survive. All she had to do was to humble herself to them. But millennium upon millennium, she wouldn't. Bow, Go, and you will be set free. For the gods are nothing if not kind.

Go: HA!

Lights return to Go, and she sings a new, swifter aria in her language: The gods forgot Go. Go would kill them with her hands. Chaos would be better than they. Curse the gods; Go curses them. The humans, Go knows, are growing hot, like a volcano; they will explode, sink to nothing. The end is upon them and they celebrate themselves. Who is worse: the gods or men? Go doesn't care. Go doesn't know.

[Entr'acte: ten-minute video overlying the stage. A sparse brown field with a single olive tree, time passing with radical swiftness. The tree grows, withers, dies, the field is covered with new trees that grow, wither, die, a house is built. An earthquake, house collapses, and Go's cave is dislodged, begins to travel underground. Now the video pans. Cities are built, armies swarm, burn them to the ground. Under the Mediterranean for a few beats, sharks passing. Go's cave travels under Italy as we see the earth changing from Roman empire, aqueducts and agriculture, Rome rebuilt, under the Alps, wolves, into France in the Dark Ages—quick scroll of time—and land through Eleanor of Aquitaine, Paris, under the Channel, into London burning in 1666, where the cave's trajectory halts. We see the city's organ-like growth up to 1979.]

ACT II: DÉMO

[*Video narrows until it's a thin band above Go's cave, under the surtitles. Passionflower unfurling in real time. Forty-five minutes, bud to bloom.*]

Go does pull-ups inside her cave. Planks. She runs on a treadmill made of spider silk and stalagmites, to a ghostly, echoing, atonal music. Applause from the upside-down baby-faced bats.

She slowly strips naked and stands in a slow shower from a stalactite.

She hears something. Offstage, voices growing louder. Go presses her ear to the side of the cave, and the lights illumine a chorus of diggers in hard hats who have emerged. Their voices provide the rhythm and noises of digging, and a singing saw provides the melody. Out of the mass of working men, one, Ros, stands, taking a break: he is young, very handsome, dressed more neatly in his late-seventies clothes than the others. He is extremely tall with a full beard. The men sing about the Jubilee underground line and how the glory of mankind has killed the gods.

The gods are dead, they sing, in English. We have killed them. Humans have overcome them.

Go laughs with pleasure to hear voices so close, so clear.

But Ros breaks in with a counterpoint song, We, moles. Unthinking and blind. Stunted in the darkness. One can't be good if one can't see the sun. And what does it mean to be human if you can't end your life better than how it began.

Go presses her whole body against the wall. There is something erotic in the way she moves.

Break time: a soprano offstage sings a lunch whistle. The men's song ends. They huddle around, eating their lunch, except Ros, who sits with a book and a sandwich, apart from the others on the other side of the rock from Go.

She quietly tries to sing the song he sang. He hears and eagerly presses his ear up against the rock. He looks astounded, then afraid. Slowly, he begins to sing back to her. She modifies his song so that it becomes her own, as he and she sing quietly back and forth, in strange off harmony, Go transliterating into her own honed language, making entirely new meanings. [Surtitles are split in the middle, her translations in English, his actual words.] Their faces press at the same level, Go very shrunken, Ros on his knees. He introduces himself; she says, softly, that her name is Go.

The other men get up and work silently as Go and Ros sing louder, harder, the soprano singing a day's-end whistle, breaking off the duet, and though Ros tries to stay, the foreman won't let him. As they leave, the men modify their song to make fun of Ros: Ros is a dreamer, they sing. Dumb as the rocks around us. Useless book reader. Not a real man, Ros.

Go sings a love song, an aria, almost beautiful, and the cave music is less cacophonous behind her and seems to sing with her.

Ros returns and frantically tries to dig at the wall, not understanding that the rock has a curse on it and can't be broken. Days pass, symbolized by the workers moving down the track, the soprano singing the end-of-day tone, and still Ros tries. The eroticism of their movements has turned to downright fornication with the walls. [Leo: the music aches with longing.] Ros sings over the days going by, more and more frantically, I won't leave you, Go. I will get you out. He stops hiding what he's doing and starts doing it openly, and the others surround him and put him in a straitjacket to drag him off. He tries to make them understand, but they become vicious. He sings his love song to Go as he is dragged away to the asylum, and she sings back. It seems as if only one other person might hear Go—there's a flash of recognition—but he shrugs and helps drag Ros away.

Go sings, alone, her love song. She begins to slowly weave her wedding dress. Red.

Outside, the underground station is finished, people start getting on, getting off. They are the gods, in street clothes. You know they're gods by the shine they emit compared with the other passengers. We have been diminished, they sing. Gods are only stories now. Immortal still, but powerless.

They get on and off the underground train as they sing.

Ros returns in ratty clothes, looking urgent and hairy and homeless. He presses his face against Go's wall and sings the love song. In relief, they sing a bit of their duet, but Go's version has changed again. She takes the song darker, getting more and more frantic and fervent, fighting against her wall, punching and kicking it as Ros constructs a small cardboard house, pads it with newspaper, rolls out a sleeping bag, settles in.

I won't leave you, Ros sings. You'll never be alone again.

[Entr'acte: a five-minute video overlay like before. London swells and grows above them, the Gherkin, the Olympic Village, forward into massing overwhelming overcrowding, riots, fires, darkness, disaster.]

ACT III: ESCHAT

Opens to find Ros lying where he was at the end of the previous act, but he is ancient, the underground station filthy, graffiti-tagged, nightmarish. The apocalypse is upon them. Go is exactly the same, but more beautiful in her great floating red wedding dress, the bats even more uncanny; bald pink babies with wings, hanging upside down. Muzak, or the most soulless music on the planet. [Apologies, Leo.] It is interrupted with static and strange distant rumblings growing closer.

Ros sings to Go about the people going by, he has learned her language, but we begin to understand that he's turning the ugly world to beauty.

There's a fight on the platform, and the audience slowly realizes that one of the fighters is a god, his light diminished, looking as bedraggled and ancient as Ros; it's Hermes; one knows by the wings of dirty light on his sneakers. Ros gapes.

Tell me about the sun, Go says. You're my eyes, my skin, my tongue.

But Ros is disturbed by what he has witnessed. The gods have forgotten themselves, Ros sings, as if to himself. He presses both hands on his heart, suddenly stricken with pain. Something is wrong, Go. Something has gone wrong inside me.

She says no. She says he is her young and beautiful husband. He has made her love mankind again. He is only good, inside.

I am old, Go. I am sick. I am sorry, he sings.

The gods gather around, sing, complaining about their woe and the woes of the world. Where in the beginning there was grandeur, brilliant light, great seriousness, there is now unutterable, almost comic, diminishment. Go is overwhelmed, presses her hands over her ears.

Ros crumbles. The world is not what you . . . he begins, but doesn't finish.

Go sings a love song to him. A video projects on Ros's body, his soul rising, young, with coins on his eyes; it walks off on a slant of light; on the singer's prone body, a video is projected of deflation, a whittling to bones.

Ros? Go sings. The single word, over and over and over, no music. Shouting.

At last, she screams to the gods to help her. In English, now, Help me, gods. Help me.

But the gods are preoccupied, the blasting sounds so very loud and close now, their columns of light empty, and they are fighting, all hoboes, dirty slapstick fighting; yet it's deadly stuff. Minerva garrotes Aphrodite with a laptop charger; Saturn, a filthy, naked giant of an old man, reaches blindly for his son Jupiter, but gobbles a rat à la Goya; Hephaestus comes in with great steel robots; Prometheus throws a Molotov cocktail at him. It's all terrible, bloody, until Jupiter wheels out a great red button.

Hades summons his shades, who bring out another red button.

A standoff song, each faking the other out.

[Go has been swirling around her cave, first slowly, then with increasing speed.]

In the silence, one can hear Go moaning, *Ros, Ros, Ros.*

Suddenly, both gods press their buttons. Huge light flash, cacophony. Then silence, darkness.

Go begins, slowly, to glow. [All other light in the theater—aisle lights, exit lights—extinguished. A darkness to inspire panic.]

Please, she shouts, once, in English.

Nobody answers.

Silence.

[Leo, hold the silence until it is unbearable; one minute, at least.]

Go is alone, she sings. Deathless Go in a dead world. There is no fate worse than this. Go is alone. Alive, alone. The only one. She holds her last note until her voice breaks, and then beyond.

She folds in half on herself until she is in the position we have found her in.

The only sounds are wind, water. A slow and ancient heartbeat increases until it overcomes the wind and water noise, and becomes the only thing we can hear. There can be no applause in the intensity of this noise. There is no curtain closing. Go stays folded in her position until the audience files out.

END

7

THERE WERE FOUR PLAYWRIGHTS for the symposium on the future of theater, the university so rich it could bring them in all at once: the girl prodigy in her twenties, the Native American dynamo in his thirties, the antique voice of theater whose best work was forty years deep in the last century, and Lotto, forty-four, representative of middle age, he supposed. And because the morning was glorious, brimming with chill wind and neon-pink bougainvillea light, and because all admired one another's work to various degrees, the four playwrights and the moderator fully partook of the bourbon and gossip in the green room while waiting for the event and they were soused by the time they took the stage. The auditorium held five thousand seats and all were full, as was the overflow room with an LED screen, and there were people sitting in the aisles, and the lights were so bright those onstage could barely see beyond the front row, where the wives sat together. Mathilde was on the outside edge, elegant platinum head on fist, smiling up at him.

Lancelot soared along on the applause and the lengthy introductions, replete with short scenes from each playwright's work acted out by theater majors. He was having difficulty following along. He must have had more bourbon than he thought. His own play he could understand; the Miriam from *The Springs* was perfect, sex in a dress, all chesty growl and hips and shining copper hair. She would have a life on film, he knew it. [Yes, small roles, hers a small spark.]

Now the discussion. Future of theater! First thoughts? The codger began his grouse in a pseudo-British accent. Well, radio didn't kill the theater, then films didn't kill the theater, then television didn't kill the theater, and so it was a bit daft to believe that the Internet, as seductive as it was, would kill the theater, wasn't it? The warrior went next: marginalized voices, voices of color, voices traditionally repressed will be heard as loudly as anyone's, drowning out the voices of the boring old white men of the patriarchy. Well, Lancelot responded mildly, even boring old white men of the patriarchy had stories to tell, and the future of theater was like the past of theater: creating innovation in storytelling, inverting narrative expectations. He smiled; so far, only he had had applause. They all looked at the girl, who shrugged, bit her fingernails. "Don't know. Not a fortune-teller," she said.

Impact of technological age? We are in Silicon Valley, after all. Audience laughed. Warrior leapt in, kicking his dead horse: with YouTube and MOOCs, and all the other innovations, knowledge has been democratized. Looked at the girl, seeking alliance. With feminism equalizing home work, women are given the freedom from childbearing and drudgery. A farmer's wife in Kansas, who once had to be only a housekeeper, who had to put up the fruit and wipe the bottoms and churn the butter, et cetera, could have half her workload shared and could go from wifey to creator. She could listen to the newest innovations on her computer; she could watch new plays from the comfort of her home; she could learn how to compose music all by herself; she could be the creator of a new Broadway show without ever having to live in the soulless third circle of hell that is New York City.

Irritation bristled in Lancelot. Who was this one-note show-off, and what gave him the right to spit at the way other people chose to live their lives? Lancelot loved his circle of hell!

"Let's not patronize the wives of the world, shall we?" he said. Laughter. "Sometimes people who create are so narcissistic we assume that our way of living is the jewel in the crown of humanity. But most playwrights I know are asinine codpieces"—assenting roar from the codger—"and the wives are far better human beings. They are kinder, more generous, more worthy all around. There's a nobility in making life smooth and clean and comfortable. It's a choice at least equal to the choice of navel-gazing for a living. The wife is the dramaturge of the marriage, the one whose work is essential to what is produced, even if her contributions are never directly recognized. There is glory in this role. My wife, Mathilde, for instance, gave up her job years ago to make mine run more smoothly. She loves to cook and clean and edit my work, it makes her happy to do these things. And what piece of jerk chicken would condescend to say that she was lesser for not being the creator in the family?"

He was pleased with how smoothly the words seemed to exit his mouth. He thanked the powers that be for his glibness. [Nothing to do with it.]

Tartly, from the girl playwright: "I have a wife and I am a wife. I'm not comfortable with the gender essentialism I'm hearing here."

"I mean, of course, wife in the genderless sense of helpmeet," Lancelot said. "There are male wives. When I was an actor, I was so underemployed that I basically did all the housework myself while Mathilde earned the dough. [He did the dishes; that part was true.] Anyway, there *is* an essential difference in genders that isn't politically correct to mention these days. Women *are* the ones to bear the children, after all, they are the ones to nurse, they are the ones, traditionally, who care for the infants. That takes a huge amount of time."

He smiled, waiting for the applause, but something had gone wrong. There was a cold silence from the crowd. Someone was talking in a loud voice at the back of the auditorium. What had he done? He looked down in panic at Mathilde, who was staring at her shoes.

The girl playwright scowled at Lancelot and said, enunciating very crisply, "Did you just say that women aren't creative geniuses because they have babies?"

"No," he said. "Goodness, no. Not *because*. I wouldn't say that. I love women. And not all women have babies. My wife, for one. At least not yet. But listen, we're all given a finite amount of creativity, just like we're given a finite amount of life, and if a woman chooses to spend hers on creating actual life and not imaginary life, that's a glorious choice. When a woman has a baby, she's creating so much more than just a made-up world on the page! She's creating life itself, not just a simulacrum. No matter what Shakespeare did, it's so much less than your average illiterate woman of his age who had babies. Those babies were our ancestors, necessary to make everyone here today. And nobody could seriously argue that any play is worth a single human life. I mean, the history of the stage supports me here. If women have historically demonstrated less creative genius than men, it's because they're making their creations internal, spending the energies on *life* itself. It's a kind of bodily genius. You can't tell me that that isn't at least as worthy as genius of imagination. I think we can all agree that women are just as good as men—better, in many ways— but the reason for the disparity in creation is because women have turned their creative energies inward, not outward." The murmurs had turned angrier. He listened, astonished, and heard only a very small smattering of applause. "What?" he said.

The codger jumped in to agree, giving such a long, convoluted, self-regarding story that name-dropped Liam Neeson and Paul Newman and the Isle of Wight that Lancelot's cold sweat dried and the pulse in his gut calmed down. He looked again for Mathilde, hoping to catch her eye and comfort himself in her, but where she had been sitting was an empty seat.

There was an enormous crack in the world. Lancelot was teetering. Mathilde had left. Mathilde had stood and walked out of the auditorium publicly. Mathilde was so angry she'd had enough. Enough what? Forever enough? Maybe, when she emerged into the astringent light of Palo Alto, she felt the sun on her face and realized the truth: that she was far better off without him, that she, a saint, was only being dragged down for the dog *crotte* of a husband he was. His hands itched to call her. For the rest of the discussion, the younger two panelists and the moderator declined to look at Lancelot, which was for the best anyway, because it took all his concentration to stay in his chair. He sat in his discomfort until the end, and when there was the meet-and-greet afterward, he said to the moderator, "I may skip the cheese and crackers just now. Don't want to get my head handed to me," and the moderator winced and said, "Might be a good call." Lancelot sped to the green room to look for Mathilde, but she wasn't there. And there was such a tsunami of people pouring out now into the hallway that he darted into a private handicapped bathroom to call her, but though her phone rang and rang, she didn't answer. He listened to the crowd noise outside intensify, then gradually diminish.

He spent a long time looking at himself in the mirror: the forehead so huge he was wearing his own billboard, the strange nose that seemed to be growing as he aged, the fine hairs on the lobes of his ears an inch long when uncurled. All this time and he'd been carrying around his ugliness as confidently as if it were beauty. How strange. He played a game of solitaire on his phone. Then about fifteen more games of solitaire, calling Mathilde between each. The phone made an ignominious bleep and died. His gut spoke to him, and he remembered he hadn't eaten since breakfast in the hotel in San Francisco and that there was supposed to have been a lunch, and he thought of the usual bitter iced tea and chocolate torte for dessert, but his heart quailed, and as it was somewhere near three o'clock already, the lunch was long over. He poked his head out into the corridor, where there had been crowds milling when he went into the bathroom, but it was empty. He slid along the wall and poked his head around the corner to look, but the way to the front door was clear as well.

He walked out and stood looking at the piazza where students with giant backpacks beetled on their way to world dominance. The wind felt lovely on his face.

"For shame," said a voice to his right, and he slid his eyes toward a woman: desiccated head covered thinly with dyed black hair. "To think I've always loved your work, too. I wouldn't have paid for a single ticket if I knew you were such a misogynist."

"I'm not a misogynist! I love women," Lotto said, and she snorted and said, "That's what all misogynists say. You just love to pork women."

It was no use. He did love to pork women, even if he'd porked only one since matrimony. He sped away along the stucco wall, darting under the shadows and through the copses of eucalyptus, berries crunching underfoot, stepping out confusedly on a street called El Camino Real. He was feeling the opposite of royal. He took the road in the vague direction of San Francisco. He sweated through his shirt, the sun far hotter than he'd thought. The street was endless and he was light-headed. He wandered through a neighborhood with odd little split-levels behind palatial gates, pink oleander, cactus gardens. He came to another great road and crossed the street to a cafeteria-style Mexican restaurant, where, surely, he could buy some sustenance and get his druthers back, and he ate half of his chile relleno burrito while waiting in the line to pay. He was still chewing when he dug in his pocket for his wallet. With a leap of fear, he remembered he'd left it in the hotel room. He never had to pay for a thing on these jaunts, and if he did, Mathilde was there with her purse, and frankly, he hated the way wallets made his buttocks look as if they were sporting a huge canker. He preferred the sleek profile of the walletless rear.

He shrugged at the cashier, whose eyes narrowed, who said something menacing in Spanish. He put the plate down, and said, "I'm sorry, *lo siento*," until he backed all the way to the door.

At last, he found himself in a horseshoe-shaped strip mall, where, out of the corner of his eye, he saw something that made a flutter of astonishment in his chest: a telephone booth, the first he'd seen in, what, decades? He found himself dialing collect the only number he still knew by heart in this age of cell phones. Such a relief, the weight of the receiver in the hand, the reek of others' breath and grease. His mother's voice rose on the other end. Collect? Oh dear, oh dear, yes, she'd take it, and then she said, "Lancelot? Darling? What's wrong? Is it that wife of yours? Gracious, has she left you?"

He swallowed. He felt a strange echo of having lived this moment before. When? College, just after the Saturday marriage ceremony, when he ran up to his dorm, how small it had suddenly seemed, skim-coated with childhood. After he'd stuffed his clothes into a duffel for the stolen honeymoon on the Maine coast, he picked up the phone with suppressed glee and called his mother to tell her he was married. "No, you're not," she'd said. "I am. It's done," he'd said. "Undo it. Quickie divorce," she'd said, and he'd said, "No." She'd said, "What kind of girl would marry you, Lancelot? Think. An immigrant? A gold digger?" "Neither," he'd said. "A Mathilde Yoder. The best person on the planet. You'll love her." "Won't," she'd said. "I'll never meet her. You get it annulled or you're disinherited. No more allow-ance. And how are you going to survive in the big bad city without money? How are you going to survive as an *actor*," she'd said, and he'd smarted at the sneer. He'd thought of a life empty of Mathilde. He'd said, "I'd rather die," and she'd said, "My darling, you will eat your words." And he'd sighed and said, "I hope you and your tiny heart have a great life together, Muvva," and hung up. The wedge had been driven all the way in.

He felt sharp now in the California sunlight. Nauseated. "What did you say?" he said.

"I'm truly sorry," his mother was saying. "I am. All those years I've bitten my tongue, darling. All the pain between us, all the distance, all of it unnecessary. That horrible creature. I knew she'd end up hurting you. Just come on home. Rachel and Elizabeth and the kids are here for a visit. Sallie would leap the moon to baby you again. Come on home and your women will take care of you."

"Oh," he said. "Thank you. But no."

"Sorry?" she said.

"I called because I lost my cell," he said. "I wanted to let Sallie know in case Mathilde was frantically calling around for me. Tell her I'll be home soon with the champagne and cheese for the party," he said.

"Listen, darling—" Antoinette began, but Lancelot said, "Bye," and she said, "I love you," into the dead phone.

Antoinette put down the receiver. No, she thought. He hadn't chosen that wife over his mother again. Not when Antoinette had given him everything. Without her, he would never have become what he was; he never would have written her into immortality the way she'd groomed him to do. Boys belong to their mothers. Cord cut decades ago, but they'll always share the warm, dark swim.

The ocean out the window cast its net of waves onto the white sand, withdrew it, catching nothing. Antoinette knew the little pink house on the dunes was listening, her sister-in-law rolling peanut butter cookies in the kitchen, her daughter and grandchildren just coming in from the beach, the outdoor shower spitting on below where she sat. Lord give her strength, but she was sick of these dark, small, fearful people. Surely it was natural she'd love them less than she loved her son, who was big and golden like her. Mice are nice but lions roar.

In the kitchen, Sallie rolled dough in greasy palms, fretting. The phone had rung and Antoinette's voice had risen in her bedroom sharply. "Is it that wife of yours?" she'd said. Sallie considered her sister-in-law; though she appeared confected of sugar and air, there was a bitter black walnut at her core. Sallie worried for Lancelot, poor child, whose sweetness went all the way through. She considered calling Mathilde to see what was going on but refrained. Nothing is gained in the immediate; her work was slow and at a distance.

After some time, Antoinette stood, and with the movement, she caught sight of her own face in the vanity mirror. Wrinkled at the corners, exhausted, swollen. Well, no wonder. Such a force of effort it cost her to keep her son safe. The world more perilous by the moment, liable to disintegrate if she wasn't constantly vigilant. The things she had done for Lancelot, the sacrifices she'd made! She thought of the grand reveal when she was dead, the strings he'd never know she'd pulled until she was gone, the horrors she'd endured for his sake. Did she choose to plant herself here in this shabby pink house? She did not. With the money Gawain left, she could have been bathing in luxury. Top floor of the Mandarin Oriental in Miami, room service and steel bands summoned at whim. Marble bathrooms the size of this shack. Sunlight like diamonds on the water below. But she wouldn't touch more of Gawain's money than she must to survive. It was all for her children, their shocked faces when they knew the extent of what she'd done. She brought the old comforting image before her again, so real that it was like a scene she'd watched in rerun on television: her son in a black suit—she hadn't seen him in decades; in her mind he was still the gawky, pustuled child she'd let the North swallow up—his shirt threadbare, his wife all drab in cheap black, tartishly made up. Blue eye shadow, brown lip liner, feathered hair, she imagined. Sallie would hand him the envelope with the letter in which Antoinette had explained it all, everything she had done for him. He would turn away, choking, open it, read. "No!" he'd shout. And when his wife would touch his shoulder tentatively, he'd shake her off, bury his face in his hands, mourning all the years he neglected to be grateful to his mother.

Rachel came down the hallway and saw Antoinette standing in her room. When Antoinette looked up into the mirror, she saw her daughter and slipped her smiling face over the stern one like a mask. Her teeth were still beautiful. "I believe Sallie made cookies for the little ones, Rachel," Antoinette said. She moved her huge body through the door and down the hallway with painful slowness and sank into her chair. "I don't think it will do much harm for me to taste one or two," she said, smiling coquettishly. And Rachel found herself bowing with a plate of cookies in the same old subservient position. Only her brother could wind their mother up like so. God, Lotto! Now Rachel would have to spend the rest of the break appeasing the old beast; and the ancient resentment toward her brother came swiftly up out of the deep. [The noble feel the same strong feelings as the rest of us; the difference is in how they choose to act.] The urge to utter a few destructive words that would have let pandemonium into Lotto's world was quelled, locked in. She heard her children coming loudly up the stairs, took a breath, bent lower. "Take a few more, Muvva," she said, and her mother said, "Well, thank you, darling, don't mind if I do."

It took Lancelot twenty minutes of standing in the shade under a bus stop, listening to the nervous young people chittering around him, to calm down after his call with his mother. Only when the bus sighed and knelt the passengers off like a carnival elephant did he remember that, without money, he couldn't even catch the BART. He imagined Mathilde, feeling sickly. His words redoubled to him, sounding venomous now. If he'd said a woman's creative genius went into her babies, what did it mean about Mathilde, a woman who had none? That she was lesser? Lesser than other women who did? Lesser than he was, who created? But he didn't think so, not at all! He knew she was better than everyone. He didn't deserve her. She had made it back to the Nob Hill hotel, was packing, was stepping into a yellow taxi, was boarding a plane to fly away from him. The day had at last come. She was leaving him, and he would be left with nothing, bereft.

How would he live without her? He had cooked but had never scrubbed a toilet; he had never paid a bill. How would he write without her? [The buried awareness of how completely her hands reached into his work; don't look, Lotto. It'd be like looking at the sun.]

The sweat had dried on his shirt. He had to do *something*; he had to expend his energy somehow. It couldn't be more than thirty miles to the city. There was only one way there, straight north. It was a beautiful day. He had long legs and great endurance: he could walk fast, five miles an hour. He'd get to the hotel at about midnight. Perhaps she wouldn't have left yet. Maybe she wasn't so angry anymore; maybe she had just gone to the spa for a massage and facial and would order room service and watch a naughty movie and take her vengeance this way. Passive-aggressively. Her style.

He set off, keeping the sun at his left, and drank water at a succession of dog parks. Not enough. He was thirsty. In the twilight, he passed the airport and smelled the salt marsh on the wind. The traffic was terrible and he was nearly hit by a peloton of cyclists, three semitrailers, and a man driving a Segway in the dark.

As he walked, he chewed over what had happened at the panel. He saw it over and over and over again. After a few hours, it became a story, as if he were telling it at a bar to a band of friends. A few times through, and the imaginary friends at the bar had become tipsy and laughed at the story. With repetition, what had happened lost its power to wound him. It had become comical, no longer shameful. He was no misogynist. He could summon hundreds of women from the time before Mathilde to attest to his lack of misogyny. He was simply misunderstood! His fears of Mathilde's leaving him dulled under the friction of the story. An overreaction, and she would be ashamed of herself. She would be the one to apologize to him. She had proved her point; he'd give that to her. He didn't blame her. She loved him. He was an optimist at heart. All would be well.

He came into the city and nearly wept with gratitude for the tighter blocks, for the sidewalks, for the streetlights gently leading him one to the next.

His feet were bleeding, he could feel it. He was sunburnt, mouth dry, stomach knotted with hunger. He stank as if he'd taken a dip in a pond of sweat. He made a very halting way up the hill to the hotel and went in, and the desk clerk, who'd blessedly checked them in the day before, went, "Oop! Mr. Satterwhite, what happened?" And Lotto rasped, "I was mugged," because in a way he was, the audience robbing him of his dignity; and the man summoned the bellhop who brought the hotel's wheelchair and Lotto was escorted up to his room in the elevator, and the key was produced, and he was pushed inside, and Mathilde sat up in bed, naked under the sheet, and smiled at him.

"Oh, there you are, love," she said. Such magnificent self-possession. Really, she was a wonder of the world.

The bellhop bowed his way out, murmuring something about complimentary room service in a moment.

"Water," Lotto croaked. "Please."

Mathilde stood, put on her robe, and went to the bathroom and poured out a glass and brought it with extreme slowness to him. He drank it down in a single draught. "Thank you. More, please," he said.

"I'm happy to serve," she said, smiling broadly. She didn't move.

"M.," he said.

"Yes, my creative genius?" she said.

"No more punishment. I'm a dope unfit for human society. I wear my privilege like an invisible cloak and imagine it gives me super-powers. I deserve at least a day in the stocks and probably some rotten eggs heaved at my head. I'm sorry."

She sat on the edge of the bed and looked at him calmly. "That would have been nicer if it had been sincere. You're arrogant."

"I know," he said.

"Your words have more weight than most people's. You swing them wildly and you can hurt a lot of people," she said.

"I only care that I hurt you," he said.

"You assume so much about me. You don't get to speak for me. I don't belong to you," she said.

"I'll stop doing anything that displeases you. Would you please, please, please bring me more water?"

She sighed and brought him more, and there was a knock at the door, and she opened it, and there was the bellhop with a rolling table, and on the table there was a bucket of champagne and a plate of salmon and asparagus and a basket of soft hot rolls and a chocolate cake for dessert, compliments of the hotel, with apologies for the mugging. San Francisco was a genial town, mostly, and this rarely happened. Should he need medical attention, they had a doctor on retainer, et cetera. Please tell us if there is anything more we can do.

Lotto fell to and she watched. He could manage only a few bites before queasiness set in; then he stood, although his feet felt as if they had been lopped off by an ax, and he tottered to the bathroom and put his clothes and shoes directly in the trashcan and took a long hot bath, watching the tendrils of blood eke out of his wounds. He'd lost or was in the process of losing all ten toenails. He put cold water on his face and arms, which were blistered with sun. He stood up, feeling new in his body, and with his wife's tweezers, he plucked the long fine hairs on his earlobes and massaged his wife's expensive lotion deep into the skin of his forehead, willing the lines away.

When he came out, Mathilde was still awake, staring at the book in her hands. She put it down, tucked her glasses atop her head, frowned at him.

"If it helps, I won't be able to walk tomorrow," he said.

"Then you get to spend the day in bed with me," she said. "So you win. No matter what, you win. It all works out for you in the end.

Always. Someone or something's looking out for you. It's maddening."

"Were you hoping it wouldn't work out for me? That I'd get hit by a truck?" he said, crawling under the sheets and resting his head on her stomach. It gurgled gently. The rest of the cake was gone from the tray.

She sighed. "No, idiot. I just wanted to scare you for a few hours. The moderator stayed in his office all night because we were sure someone would bring you to him. Which is what a sane person would have done, Lotto. Not walk all the way back to San Francisco, you crazed maniac. I just called him to tell him you'd showed up. He was still there. He'd freaked his shit completely. He thought you'd been abducted by a band of wild feminists for a videotaped scapegoating. He'd been going over castration scenarios in his head." Lancelot imagined a machete swinging, shuddered.

"Eh," she said. "It all fizzed out by the time the lunch rolled around. Apparently, last year's Nobel laureate was found today to have plagiarized half of his speech, and there was a huge free-for-all on social media. I looked up and saw full tables gaping at their smart phones. You, my love, were today's small-fry."

He felt cheated; he should have been even more inflammatory. [Glutton!]

He stewed until he slept, and she watched him for a while, turning things over in her head, and when she fell asleep, she did so without switching off the light.

8

ICE IN THE BONES, 2013

*Dean of students' office of an all boys' boarding school. On the wall
a poster of a waterfall at sunset with* ENDURANCE, *sans serif,
underneath.*

DEAN OF STUDENTS: man with eyebrows that take up half his
   face

OLLIE: skinny boy, recently fatherless, exiled from home for
   juvenile delinquency. Southern accent he tries to swallow;
   face full of pustules. Still, sharp-eyed, notices everything

FROM ACT I

DEAN: It has been reported that you, Oliver, do not seem to be
   fitting in. You have no friends. Your nickname [*Peers at an
   index card, blinks.*] is Bumblefuck Pie?

OLLIE: Apparently, sir.

DEAN: Oliver, you're making a difficult transition.

OLLIE: Yes, sir.

DEAN: Your grades couldn't be better, but you don't speak
   in class. Don't call me sir. Our boys here are intellectually
   curious, vital citizens of the world. Are you an intellectually
   curious, vital citizen of the world?

OLLIE: Nope.

DEAN: Why not?

OLLIE: I'm unhappy.

DEAN: Who could be unhappy here? That's nuts.

OLLIE: I'm cold.

DEAN: Physically? Or spiritually?

OLLIE: Both, sir.

DEAN: Why are you crying?

OLLIE: [*Struggles. Says nothing.*]

DEAN: [*Opens his drawer. Under a spill of papers is something that Ollie sees, and he sits up as if goosed. The dean shuts the drawer, lifting out a rubber band, tenting it back with his thumb. He aims it at Ollie's nose and lets fly. Ollie blinks. The dean sits back in his chair.*]

DEAN: An undepressed person would have avoided that.

OLLIE: Probably.

DEAN: You, my friend, are a whiner.

OLLIE: [. . .]

DEAN: Ha! You look like Rudolph the Red-Nosed La-di-da.

OLLIE: [. . .]

DEAN: Ha ha!

OLLIE: Dean. If I may ask a question. Why do you have a gun in your desk?

DEAN: Gun? No gun. That's crazy. You don't know what you're talking about. [*Sits back, puts his arms behind his head.*] Anyway, listen to me, Oliver. I've been doing this for a billion years. I was a boy like you once at this school. Even I was picked on, believe it or not. And I don't see why you're being shat on. You seem to have everything. Wealthy, tall, you'd be good-looking if you washed your face once or twice, Christ. Little acne cream and you'd be strapping. You seem nice. Smart. You don't stink, not like one of those hopeless loser kids. You know Jelly Roll? Just irredeemable.

He smells bad and cries all the time. Foul to look at. Even his little friends, all the Dungeons & Dragons kids, even they only barely tolerate Jelly Roll to make up their bridge parties or something. You? You could be the king of this school. But you're not, because, one, you're new, which will burn off in time. *Numero dos*, you're scared, which you have to change. Fast! Because kids who go to schools like this one are sharks, my friend. They're baby sharks bred out of a long line of sharks, every one of 'em. And sharks can smell the blood in the water from miles away, and the blood in the water to these particular sharks? Fear. They smell that blood in the water, they're going to hunt the bleeder down. Not their fault. They can't help it! What kind of shark is a shark that doesn't attack? A dolphin. Who needs dolphins? Dolphins are delicious. They make great snacks. So, you listen carefully to what I'm about to say. You need to learn to be a shark. Punch someone in the schnozz, just don't break it, don't want to be sued by these kids' daddies. Play a prank. Cellophane the toilet so when they piss, the piss bounces on their jeans. Ha! If someone throws a hard-boiled egg in your face, throw a steak in his. Because this is like prison. Only the strong survive. You gotta earn your respect. Gotta do what you gotta do. You hearing me? *Capiche?*

OLLIE: *Capiche.*

DEAN: All right, Oliver. What kind of a name is Oliver anyway? Kind of a dolphin kind of name if you ask me. Pussy name. You a pussy?

OLLIE: No. But I like them.

DEAN: Ha! You're getting it. What did they call you at home?

OLLIE: Ollie.

DEAN: Ollie. You see. There we go. Ollie's a shark name. King shark. Next time someone calls you Bumblefuck Pie, you get all up in their *faccia*, make them call you Ollie. You hear me?

OLLIE: Loud and clear.

DEAN: Do you feel your teeth sharpening? Smell the blood in the water? Do you feel like a shark?

OLLIE: Maybe. Or like a dolphin with a razor blade on his fin.

DEAN: It's a start. Go slay them, slayer.

OLLIE: Slay. Check.

DEAN: Not literally, of course, god, could you imagine? *The dean told me to kill them all!* I meant figuratively. Don't slay anyone. You didn't hear that from me.

OLLIE: Of course. Good-bye, sir. [*Exits.*]

DEAN: [*Alone, takes the gun hurriedly from his drawer, inserts it under the couch.*]

TELEGONY, 2013

"Masks. Magic. Circe and Penelope and Odysseus and patricide and incest. Music and film and dance. You crazy-ass man," Mathilde said.

"*Gesamtkunstwerk,*" Lotto said. "Melding all the forms of art as theater. Now we just have to find someone nuts enough to put it on," he said.

"Don't worry," Mathilde said. "Everyone we know is nuts."

SHIP OF FOOLS, 2014

ACT I, SCENE I

Postnuclear wasteland, whale belly-up in the red tide, two women among the rubble.

PETE: wiry, small, skinny, furry, a chimp woman

MIRANDA: enormously fat, three vertical feet of red hair with a scorched bluebird's nest atop it à la Madame du Barry. Swinging in a hammock between two blackened and skeletal palms

PETE [*Dragging a dead gator into camp.*]: Gator tail for supper this evening, Miranda.

MIRANDA [*Vaguely.*]: Lovely. It's just that. Well. I was hoping. Well, for some whale steaks? If it were only possible to get whale steaks? I mean, don't worry too much about it, but it's the only thing in the world I could possibly digest tonight, but I can get down a little gator. If I must.

PETE [*Picks up hacksaw, sets off, returns wet, chunk of meat in her arms.*]: Gator tail and whale steaks for supper, Miranda.

MIRANDA: What a surprise! Pete! You can do anything! Speaking of which, while you're up, mind pouring me another cocktail? It's five o'clock somewhere!

PETE: Reckon not. No such thing as time anymore. [*Pours kerosene out of a drum, stirs it with a peppermint stick kept for the purpose, hands it over.*]

MIRANDA: Wonderful! Now. I think it must be time for my soap? *The Starrs in Your Eyes?*

PETE: Time's dead, Miranda mine. Television's dead. Electricity's dead. Actors dead, too, I warrant, in that H-bomb blast over L.A. Or the black-tongue plague after. Or the earthquake. The human experiment done bust.

MIRANDA: Then just kill me, Petey. Just kill me dead. No use in living. Just take that hacksaw and chop off my head. [*Weeps into her great pale hands.*]

PETE [*Sighs. Picks up kelp, places it on her head. Sucks in cheeks like Silvia Starr, heroine of the eponymous soap* The Starrs in Your Eyes, *and speaks in a gravelly voice.*]: Oh, whatever are we going to do with that dastardly dastard, Burton Bailey . . .

MIRANDA [*Sinks back, gaping. They are both so entranced, they don't hear the mechanical whirring that grows until, stage right, a battered boat hull looms into view, and survivors peer at the women from above.*]

Rachel was agitatedly pacing the black-box theater, empty save for her brother, as the opening night reception thudded behind the door. "Cripes, Lotto. I didn't even know how to watch that," she said, digging her palms into her eyes.

He went still. "I'm sorry," he said.

"Don't get me wrong, there's part of me that kind of savagely delighted in watching Muvva and Sallie duke it out at the end of the world. Sallie scraping and bowing until she finally snaps, you know?" Rachel laughed, then pivoted toward him. "You're so good at fooling us, aren't you. You're so charming you make us forget that you have to be a serial killer on the inside to do what you do to us. Put us in your plays, warts and all, showing us off like we're some sort of sideshow freaks. The audience out there just kind of laps it up."

He was shocked cold. Rachel, of all people, turning on him. But no. She wasn't. She wouldn't. Now she was standing on her tiptoes to touch his cheek. In such light, his baby sister's eyes were framed in fine wrinkles. Oh, for the god of love, where did time go? [Clockwise swirl going nowhere.] "At least you wrote a better version of Antoinette. At least by the end she puts herself in front of the beast for her kids. Praise the lord," she said, in Sallie's voice, making twinkle fingers in the air. They laughed.

[But in a drawer in Florida, half written, a note. *Darling. I have never seen a play of yours in the flesh, as you know. A great sorrow of my life. But I read them all, I've seen the ones on DVDs and online. It goes without saying how proud of you I am. Of course, I'm not surprised. I took such great care from the day you were born to mold you into the artist you are! But how, Lancelot, how dare you*]

THE BATS, 2014

"It's great," Mathilde said.

But Lotto detected something in her voice that he wasn't ready for, and he said, "It hurt my feelings at that symposium when they all implied I was a misogynist. You know I love women."

"I know," she said. "You love them almost too much." Still, the coolness in her voice, the way she was avoiding looking at him. Something was wrong.

"I think Livvie came off pretty well. I hope you don't mind that I used you as a model for her character."

"Well. Livvie *is* a murderer," Mathilde said flatly.

"M., I meant that I just used your personality."

"A murderer's personality," she said. "My husband of more than twenty years says I have a murderer's personality. Okay!"

"My love," he said. "Don't get hysterical."

"Hysterical. Lotto, please. Do you know the root of that word?

Hystera. Womb. You basically just called me a sissy, crying because of her pink parts."

"What is wrong with you? You're freaking out."

She spoke to the dog. "He gave my personality to a murderer and he's asking why I'm freaking out."

"Hey. Look at me. You're being ridiculous, and not because you have woman parts. Livvie found herself cornered by two bad dudes and she killed one. If some big mean dog bit God in half, you'd kick its brains out. Who knows you better than I know you? You're a saint, but even saints have their breaking points. Do I think that you'd ever kill someone? I do not. But if we hypothetically had a kid and some man was hypothetically putting his Mr. Winky somewhere near our hypothetical kid with bad intent, you would, without hesitation, rip his throat out with your fingernails. I would too. It doesn't mean you're any less than good."

"Oh my god. We are discussing the fact you wrote me into a murderer, and out of nowhere, here you are again with the kid nonsense."

"Nonsense?"

". . ."

"Mathilde? Why are you breathing like that?"

". . ."

"Mathilde? Where are you going? Okay, fine, lock yourself in the bathroom. I'm sorry I hurt your feelings. Can you please talk to me? I'm just going to sit right here. I'm going to wear you down with my devotion. I'm sorry that we got sidetracked. Can we talk about the play? Other than the fact that I gave your personality to a murderer, what did you think? It feels a little wonky in the fourth act. Like a table with one wobbly leg. Needs some rethinking. Maybe you can try your hand? Oh. A bath? In the middle of the day? Okay. Do whatever you need to do. That feels nice, I bet. All warm. Lavender. Wow, you're going for it. Can we talk through the door? Overall, the piece is really solid, I think. Yes? Mathilde, don't be like this. This is really important to me. Oh, fine. Be that way. I'm going downstairs to watch a movie, and you are welcome to join me if you like."

ESCHATOLOGY, 2014

Only when they came to a stop in the drive, the bourbon-pickled guests already leaping out, and Lotto saw the skateboard broken on a stump, the clumps of wet kid bathing suits on the grass, God so exhausted she couldn't pick up her head, did Lotto realize that perhaps he had not thought this through. Oh, dear. Mathilde had been left alone to take care of Rachel's three children since before breakfast when Lotto went out to fetch milk at the grocery store but then got a call in the aisle that he was wanted immediately in the city for a last-minute hour-long interview on a radio program—the end of his victory lap for *Eschatology*, which even Phoebe Delmar loved, though as he said to Mathilde, "Eh, praise from a hack is worse than a pan." It was important, so he drove swiftly into the city, sat in his pajama pants being personable for the airwaves, and then set out to drive home with the morning still bright in his eyes, but he ran into Samuel and Arnie laughing together on the sidewalk, and, jeez, it had been so long! Of course, they had lunch together. Of course, lunch extended into drinks, and Samuel saw a man from his club at the bar, who joined them, some radiologist or oncologist or something, and when they grew hungry at dinnertime, Lotto suggested they come home because, as everyone knew, Mathilde cooked like a goddess and he was drunk, but not so drunk he couldn't drive.

He sniffed the milk that had been rolling around on the floor since morning. Maybe it would still do. He came in to find Samuel Pepé Le Pewing kisses up Mathilde's arms, Arnie searching through the liquor cabinet for the grand old Armagnac he'd given them for

Christmas, the doctor doing a spoon airplane to deliver peas into Lotto's younger niece's mouth, who was wary of airplane spoons. He kissed Mathilde, rescuing her; she smiled tightly. "Where are the twins?" he said. She said, "Passed out in the only place in the house they agreed to sleep. Your studio." Her smile maybe had some spite in it. And he said, "Mathilde! Nobody's allowed to go up there but me. It's my work space!" And she shot him a look so sharp it went all the way through him, and he nodded, contrite, picked the little girl up, helped her with bedtime necessaries in double time, and came back down.

The guests were sitting on the terrace, getting blotto. The moon had risen sharp against the velvety blue. Mathilde was pulsing herbs in the Cuisinart, pasta on boil. "Sorry," he said into her ear, then he took her lobe between his teeth, oh, delicious, maybe they had time, maybe she'd? But she bumped him back, and he went outside, and presently the four men were in their skivvies, in the pool, floating on their backs, laughing, and Mathilde was coming out to the table, a huge white bowl between her hands, trailing steam.

"This is," Samuel said through a mouthful of pasta, dripping all over the flagstones, "the most fun I've had since I got divorced." He looked glossy, a little fat at the waist, like an otter. So did Arnie, for that matter, but of course he would now that he was a big-time restaurateur. His sun-ravaged back was spotted darkly; Lotto wanted to warn him about skin cancer, but Arnie had so many girlfriends, surely one of them already had.

"Poor Alicia. What is this, your third divorce?" Mathilde said. "Third Strike Sam. You're out."

The other men laughed, and Lotto said, "Better nickname than the one he had in his early twenties. Remember? One Ball Sam."

Samuel shrugged, imperturbable. That same old self-confidence still spun in him. The doctor looked at him with interest. "One Ball Sam?" he said.

"Testicular cancer," Samuel said. "Didn't matter in the end. One ball made four kids."

"I have two beautiful balls," Lotto said, "that have made zero."

Mathilde sat silently while the others gabbed on, then gathered up her plate and went inside. Lotto told a story about the overdose of a very famous actress, all the while smelling some kind of berry cobbler baking; and he waited and waited, but Mathilde didn't come out. At last he went in to check on his wife.

She was in the kitchen, back turned toward the veranda door, not doing the dishes, listening. Oh, that tiny cocked ear, the white-blond hair brushing her shoulder. The radio was on, comfortingly low. He listened also and heard with a little pulse in the gut a familiar voice, something with the drawn-out vowels of a storyteller, and the pulse turned into a flap of dismay when he understood that the voice was his. It was the radio show from this morning. Which part? He could barely remember. Oh, yes, a story from his lonely Florida childhood. His own broadcast voice went uncomfortably intimate. There'd been a swamp he'd go down to in the middle of a sinkhole. One day, a leech stuck to his leg. And he'd been a boy so terribly hungry for companionship that he left it there to suck his blood, walked home and ate supper, and the whole time took comfort in his companion against his skin. When he turned over in the night and exploded the thing, there was so much blood that he felt as guilty as if he'd murdered a person.

The hostess laughed, but it was a half-shocked laugh. Mathilde's hand went out and clicked the radio off hard.

"M.?" he said.

She took a breath, and he watched her rib cage compress as she let it out. "Not your story," she said. She turned around. She was not smiling.

"Of course it was," he said. "I remember it vividly." He did. He could feel the hot mud on his legs, the horror dissolving to a kind of tenderness when he found the small black leech on his skin.

"Nope," she said, and took the ice cream out of the freezer, the cobbler out of the oven, the bowls and spoons outside.

As he ate, a slow bad feeling spread up from his gut. He called for a car to take the other men back. By the time it drove off, he knew Mathilde was right.

He came into the bathroom in the middle of Mathilde's ablutions and sat on the side of the tub. "I'm so sorry," he said.

She shrugged, spat foam into the sink.

"To be fair, it was a leech," he said. "A story about a leech."

She rubbed lotion on her hands, one, the other, looking at him in the mirror, and said, "My loneliness. Not yours. You've always had friends. It's not that you stole my story, it's that you stole my *friend*." And she laughed at herself, but when he came into bed, her light was out, and she was on her side, and though he put his hand on her hip, then between her legs, and kissed her neck, and whispered, "What's yours is mine and what's mine is yours," she was already sleeping or, worse, she was pretending to be asleep.

THE SIRENS *(unfinished)*

Too much pain. It would kill her.

Mathilde put the manuscript in the archival box without reading it, and the movers carried it away.

9

Scene: A gallery. Cavernous, shadowy, gilded birch trees foresting the walls. *Tristan und Isolde* on the sound system. Piratical crowd drinking from the bars in all four corners of the room, all bloodlust and hunger. Sculptures on plinths uplit in blue: large, amorphous, molded-steel forms that resolve into terrified faces, titled *The End*. The gallery, the art, brings to mind Dürer's woodcuts of the apocalypse. The artist was Natalie. She was posthumously celebrated; a photo of her was blown up, pale, buzz-cut, triumphant over the scene.

Two bartenders during a lull. One young, one middle-aged, both handsome.

MIDDLE-AGED: . . . telling you, these days I swear by juice. Kale, carrot, and ginger—

YOUNG: Who's that? Tall man, just came in, with the scarf. Oh my stars.

MIDDLE-AGED [*Smiling*]: That? Lancelot Satterwhite. You know who he is.

YOUNG: The *playwright*? Oh my god. I *have* to meet him. Maybe he'll give me a role. Never know. Oh, man. He kind of sucks up all the light in the room, am I right?

MIDDLE-AGED: You should've seen him when he was young. Demigod. At least he thought so.

YOUNG: You know him? Let me touch your arm.

MIDDLE-AGED: He was my understudy one summer. Years ago. Shakespeare in the Park. We were Ferdinand. *My language! Heavens! I am the best of them that speak this speech,* et cetera. Though I always thought of him more as a Falstaff than anything. So gabby. Arrogant as hell. He never made a go of the acting thing, though. There was something just, I don't know, unconvincing about him. Also, he was far too tall and then he got fat and then skinny again, apparently. It was kind of pitiful. Though, I mean, he did fine in the end. Sometimes I wonder if I should have taken a separate path, you know? If I got stuck, my moderate success propelling me moderately, all that. Better to flame out, try something new. I don't know. You're not listening.

YOUNG: Sorry. I'm just. Look at his wife. She's stunning.

MIDDLE-AGED: Her? She's bloodless, all bones. I think she's hideous. But if you want to meet Lotto, you got to go through her.

YOUNG: Huh. I think she's unbelievably beautiful. Is he . . . faithful?

MIDDLE-AGED: Two camps on that one. Hard to tell. He'll flirt until you're a blob of goo and make you fall in love, then look all befuddled when you come on to him. Happened to all of us.

YOUNG: To you?

MIDDLE-AGED: Sure.

[*They look at the froglike man who has sidled up, who is now listening, the ice in his glass clicking.*]

CHOLLIE: You, boy. Need you to do a piece of work. Easy hundred bucks. What do you say?

YOUNG: Depends on what it is, sir.

CHOLLIE: You need to accidentally spill a glass of red wine on

Satterwhite's wife. All over that white dress, really get it in there. Bonus is, while you're at it, you'll get close enough to Satterwhite to slip a note in his pocket. See where it takes you. Maybe he'll call you for an audition or something. You in?

YOUNG: Five hundred.

CHOLLIE: Two. There are seven other bartenders in the room.

YOUNG: Done. Let me borrow your pen. [*He takes Chollie's fountain pen, scribbles on a napkin, tucks it into his pocket. Looks at the pen, tucks it in, too.*] This is *so* awful. [*He laughs, puts wine on a tray, speeds off.*]

MIDDLE-AGED: What are that kid's chances of scoring with Lancelot, I wonder.

CHOLLIE: Less than zero. Lotto's as straight as a stick and sickeningly monogamous, too. But it's fun to watch. [*Laughs.*]

MIDDLE-AGED: What are you up to, Chollie?

CHOLLIE: Why are you talking to me? You don't know me.

MIDDLE-AGED: I do, actually. I used to go to the Satterwhites' parties in the nineties. We've had some conversations in our time.

CHOLLIE: Oh. Well, everybody went to those.

[*There is a shattering of glass, and the crowd sound hushes briefly.*]

MIDDLE-AGED: Mathilde took that gracefully. Of course she did. Ice queen. Off to the bathroom with salt and seltzer. And you're right, everybody went to those parties. And everybody wondered why you were Lancelot's best friend. Brought nothing to the table, really, did you. So unpleasant.

CHOLLIE: Well, I've known Lotto the longest, you know, all the way from when he was this skinny Florida Cracker with a serious zit problem. Who would have thought? These days he's famous and I own a helicopter. But I can see that you've really come into your own with this mixology pursuit of yours. So, you know. Congratulations.

MIDDLE-AGED: I—

CHOLLIE: *Any*way, glad we got all caught up, blah blah. I have something to do. [*Moves off toward the center of the room, where Young is dabbing at Lancelot's pants with a paper napkin.*]

LANCELOT: No, buddy, I'm serious, I don't believe you got any wine on my pants. But thank you. No. Please stop. Please. Stop. Stop.

YOUNG: Tell your wife how sorry I am, Mr. Satterwhite. Please send me the bill.

ARIEL: Nonsense, nonsense. I will replace the dress. Back to your station. [*Young exits.*]

LANCELOT: Thank you, Ariel. Don't worry about Mathilde. It's an old dress, I think. By the way, this is spectacular, all of this. As if you made an exact replica of the inside of my brain. Actually, I saw it was Natalie and dragged Mathilde here, though she wasn't feeling well. Natalie was a friend from college, we had to come. So tragic, her accident. I'm glad you're doing her honor. To tell you the truth, I think Mathilde may still feel a little strange about quitting the gallery so suddenly when she got the dating-website job all those years ago.

ARIEL: I understood that she'd leave me one day. All my best girls do.

LANCELOT: I think she misses art, though. She makes me go to museums wherever we are in the world. It'll be good for you two to reconnect.

ARIEL: One can never have too many old friends. In any event, I've heard something about you. Someone told me you've come into a shocking inheritance. Is this true?

LANCELOT [*Sucking in his breath sharply*]: My mother died four months ago. No, five. True.

ARIEL: I'm so sorry. I didn't mean to be flip, Lotto. I knew you were estranged and didn't think through what I was saying. Please forgive me.

LANCELOT: We were estranged, yes. I hadn't seen her for decades. Sorry. I'm not sure, really, why I'm getting all misty. It's been five months. Long enough to have gotten over grieving for a mother who never loved me.

CHOLLIE [*Stepping near*]: If your mother never loved you, it was because your mother was a loveless cunt.

LANCELOT: Chollie, hello! He is deformed, crooked, old and sere; ill-faced, worse bodied, shapeless everywhere; vicious, ungentle, foolish, blunt, unkind; stigmatical in making, worse in mind. My best friend.

CHOLLIE: You can shove your Shakespeare up your ass, Lotto. God, I'm sick of it.

LANCELOT: Charles, I thank thee for thy love to me.

ARIEL: Wouldn't be much use up there. Shakespeare in the dark.

CHOLLIE: Oh, Ariel. Good effort, man. You've always been so almost funny.

ARIEL: Funny thing to say, Charles, when we hardly know each other. You've bought a few paintings from me in the last year, but that's not enough for you to explain to me how I've always been.

CHOLLIE: You and me? Oh, no, we're ancient friends. I've known you for so long. You don't remember, but I met you in the city long ago. All the way back when Mathilde and you were an item.

LANCELOT: [*Long pause.*] An item? Mathilde and Ariel? What?

CHOLLIE: Was I not supposed to say that? Sorry. Oh, well, ancient history. You've been married a million years, doesn't matter. Those canapés are breaking my willpower. Excuse me. [*Chases off after a waiter with a tray.*]

LANCELOT: An item?

ARIEL: Well. Yes. I thought you knew Mathilde and I . . . were involved.

LANCELOT: Involved?

ARIEL: If it helps, it was purely business. At least for her.

LANCELOT: Business? You were a, I guess, a patron? Oh, I see! You mean at the gallery. When I was trying to act. Failing mostly. Yes, it's true. You supported us financially then for years, thank god. Did I ever thank you? [*Laughs with relief.*]

ARIEL: No, well. I'd been her, ah, well, lover. Boyfriend. We'd had an arrangement. I'm sorry. This is awkward. I thought you and Mathilde had no secrets. Otherwise I wouldn't have said a word.

LANCELOT: We don't. Have secrets.

ARIEL: Of course. Oh, dear. If it helps, nothing has happened since. And she broke my heart. But I'm a million years beyond that. It doesn't matter.

LANCELOT: Wait. Wait, wait, wait, wait, wait, wait.

ARIEL [*Pausing for a very long time, getting more and more agitated.*]: I should get back to—

LANCELOT [*Booming.*]: Stay where you are. You have seen Mathilde naked? You have made love to my wife? Sex? There has been sex?

ARIEL: It's so long ago. It doesn't matter.

LANCELOT: Answer me.

ARIEL: Yes. We were involved for four years. Listen, Lotto, I'm sorry this was such a surprise. But it's between you and Mathilde now. You won, you got her, I lost. I have to get back to my guests. I can't tell you how little this matters in the long run. You know where to find me if you need to talk. [*Exits.*]

[*Lancelot stands alone in a pocket of his fame, the crowd circling respectfully but nobody nearing. His face is blue in the light.*]

MATHILDE [*Breathless, transparent circle on her dress where the wine had stained her.*]: Here you are. Ready to go yet? I can't believe you somehow maneuvered me into stepping into this gallery again. Christ, talk about a sign we should never have come. Lucky this is silk, and the wine just sort of beaded off— Lotto? Lotto Satterwhite. Lotto! Are you okay? Hello? My love? [*Touches his face.*]

[*He looks at her as if from a very great height.*]

MATHILDE [*Voice trailing off.*]: Love?

IO

SUNSET. House on the dunes like a sea-tossed conch. Pelicans thumb-tacked in the wind. Gopher tortoise under the palmetto.

Lotto stood in the window.

He was in Florida. Florida? In his mother's house. He had no idea how he had found himself here.

"Muvva?" he called out. But his mother had been dead for six months.

The place smelled of her, talcum and roses. Dust a soft gray skin over the chintz and Lladró. Also mildew, the sea's armpit stink.

Think, Lotto. Last thing remembered. Home, moonlight planing the surface of the desk, bone fingers of winter trees plucking stars from the sky. Papers strewn. Dog wheezing on his feet. One floor below, his wife sleeping, hair in a white-blond plume on the pillow. He'd touched her shoulder and climbed to his study, the residue of her warmth in his palm.

A slow dark bubble rising and it returned to him, the badness between them, their great love gone sour. How furious he'd been. How his anger had shrouded all he saw.

For the past month he had been standing on a thin wire between staying with her and leaving her. It had been exhausting to clench his feet, to wonder where he'd fall.

He was in the business of narrative; he knew how one loose word could make the whole edifice crumble. [A fine woman! A fair woman! A sweet woman!] For twenty-three years, he'd thought he'd met a girl who was as pure as snow, a sad, lonely girl. He had saved her. Two weeks later, they were married. But, like a squid from the deep, the story had turned itself inside out. His wife had not been pure. She'd been a mistress. Kept for money. By Ariel. It made no sense. Either she'd been a whore or Lancelot was a cuckold; he, who had been faithful from the first.

[Tragedy, comedy. It's all a matter of vision.]

HE FELT THE COLD OF DECEMBER through the window. How long would this sunset take? Time was not behaving the way he had come to expect. The beach was absent of souls. Where were the marching old folks, the dog walkers, the boozy strollers, where were the sunset lovers, the lotus eaters? Gone. The sand was inexplicably smooth as skin. He felt his fear building. He reached inside the house and flicked the light switch.

The lights were as dead as, well. As dead as his mother.

No electricity; no phone. He looked down. He was wearing a pajama top. He was, however, not wearing pants. This lit the fuse. He heard the sizzle. The panic in him went off.

He saw himself running through the little house as if from above. He peered in the cupboards. He went into Sallie's room, vacated after Antoinette died.

All the while, outside, the sun was setting, shadows creeping out of the sea on swift amphibian feet and moving toward the Gulf, over the Intracoastal Waterway, the St. Johns River, the cold springs and gatored swamps, the fountains dyed turquoise in the sad, cheap developments, half foreclosed upon. Over the mangroves, over the manatees, over the clams in their beds, one by one closing their hard little lips like a choir at the end of a song. There the shadows dove deeper into the Gulf, rolled in their underwater doubled darkness toward Texas.

"What in the fuck is happening?" he said to the darkening house. The first time in his life he'd ever uttered a swear; he'd earned the word, he felt. The house did not answer him.

He stood before his mother's door, brandishing a flashlight. No telling what he would find. Sallie and Rachel had spoken of hoarding. Late-night binges, Antoinette buying everything that flashed up on the shopping network. Lotto's old room stuffed with foot spas still in their boxes, watches with interchangeable straps. "Open the door to your old room, you die in an American-style consumerist avalanche," Rachel had said. The little money Antoinette allowed herself wasted on junk.

"Do you want us to clean out the house?" he'd asked on the phone the morning his mother had died. They'd hung in there past the sobbing and the story: Sallie getting up for water in the night to find huge Antoinette felled in the middle of the floor.

"Naw. Leave it be. House'll burn down eventually," Aunt Sallie had said darkly. She had announced her intention to travel the world. Her brother had left her money. She had no reason to stay put.

"At least Muvva was allergic to animals," Lotto said. "There could've been cats. Eye-watering cat stink all the way down to the beach."

"Cats smushed flat by falling boxes," Sallie said.

"Ha! Herbarium of flat cats. A bouquet. Mount them in a frame, put them on a wall. Memento meowi," he said.

He took a breath and opened his mother's door.

It was neat. Floral coverlet, some kind of leak from the water bed hooping the floor in brown. Above the headboard hung a green-hued Jesus on the cross. Oh, her sad life. Oh, his poor mother. Like something out of Beckett. A woman growing like a goldfish to the size of her bowl, the only escape the final leap.

A cold hand passed through Lotto's chest. Rising through the nightstand, half of his mother's head: one eye huge behind glasses, one cheek, a half mouth.

He shrieked and threw the flashlight, and the light swirled twice, and there was a clatter of broken glass, and the beam came to rest crosswise on the bed, shining in Lotto's eyes. He found a journal with a white cover. Pennies scattered. His mother's glasses. A glass cup. They all must have been placed in such a way to make for an optical illusion. But it had been so clear, so purely Antoinette, unmistakable, even one-eyed. He shivered, ransacked her drawers for money to get himself home [only empty pill bottles, hundreds], escaped to the kitchen again.

HE STOOD IN THE WINDOW. He was unable to move.

Something rustled through the room at his back. It came, swift and sure. He held still. He felt a face press itself up against his nape. The face breathed coldly. In the coil of time, it remained there for decades. At last, the face withdrew.

"Who's there?" he called out, to nothing.

He wrestled open the glass door, and the house filled with a whipping cold wind. Sound revived. He came out onto the balcony and leaned up against the rail and put his head into the rush of air. When he looked up, he understood why the world had seemed so off.

The sky was all a strange boil, purplish black. Costume designers would stab their competitors to get their mitts on such a hue. Wearing it, one would walk onstage already great with authority, Lear or Othello before a syllable was spoken.

It was the sea, though, that was most wrong.

It was frozen. The waves were cresting so slowly that it was hard to see when they broke.

This Florida was not Florida. More strange than true.

He thought, he was pretty sure by now, that this was a nightmare and he couldn't wake up.

How swift, the slippage from keeping it together to losing it. He found himself midstride on the boardwalk, barefoot, terror swooping at his shoulders. Down into the dark, through the tiny frogs hovering inches from the ground midhop, above the dunes ragged with vines and palmetto and snake holes. The slide of sand on his feet settled him. He fell into a walk, stopped. He breathed in. As if he'd conjured it, there the moon was, glowering. Fickle, inconstant, that monthly changes in her circle orb.

The banks of condominiums and huge houses that should have been alight were not. He looked closer. No, they were gone, as if swept from shore by a huge hand.

"Help!" he shouted into the blasting wind.

"Mathilde!" he shouted.

The Mathilde he called for was the one from the first days of love, the last of college, the first sexless week in her bed on Hooker Avenue above the antique shop. Rasp of unshaved legs, cold feet, coppery taste to her skin. In daylight, she walked in her slips of clothing and left men staring like beasts in her wake. Her loneliness an island he'd shipwrecked on. The second night Lotto slept in her bed, he woke to find a room that was elongated in places, contracted in others, odd bursts of shimmering gray light on the walls, a stranger beside him. Dread poured into him. A handful of times over the years to come, he would awaken to a bedroom that was his but profoundly not, a woman sleeping beside him about whom he knew nothing. That first night of terror, he rose and went for a run as if the dread were chasing him, at dawn trotting back to Mathilde's apartment above the antique shop with hot coffee in his hands, rousing her with the steam. Only when she smiled at him was he finally able to relax. Mathilde was there in the dawn, this perfect girl as if made to his specifications. [A different life, had Lotto listened to the terror: no glory, no plays; peace, ease, and money. No glamour; children. Which life was better? Not for us to say.]

HE HAD BEEN SITTING on a dune for ages. So cold the wind. So strange the sea. Far out, there were icebergs of garbage the size of Texas. Spin of bottles and flip-flops and zip ties and packing peanuts and boas and baby-doll heads and false eyelashes and inflatable taxidermy and bicycle tires and keys and mud flaps and remaindered books and insulin syringes and doggie bags and backpacks and antibiotic bottles and wigs and fishing line and police tape and dead fish and dead turtles and dead dolphins and dead seabirds and dead whales and dead polar bears and a whole teeming knot of death.

Shell-torn feet. He lost his pajama top. He wore only underwear against the elements.

He'd give his fortune to appease what angry god had brought him here. [Joke! Money's for fools.] Then he'd give the work, he thought. The fame. The plays, well, not *The Sirens*. Yes, even this latest, newest, and favorite, a story of women's buried selves, his best yet, he could sense it. Even *The Sirens*. Take the plays and he'd live a humble life, an ordinary one. Take it all but let him come home to Mathilde.

Light sparked at the edge of his eyesight, which usually augured migraines. The sparks came near, resolved themselves into sunlight, into the kumquat tree in the backyard in Hamlin. Sun slanted through the Spanish moss; at the edge of the lawn, a thicket of Virginia creeper, and under the thicket, the house of his ancestors returning to the Florida dirt, menaced by termites' million chewing mouths or the great gob of a hurricane. In the shadows of the vines, the last windows gleamed.

Behind Lotto was the plantation house that his father had built, that his mother had sold one year and a day after Gawain died, moving them all to the sad little beach house. In this confused childhood world, his father stood on the other side of the pool. He was looking at Lotto tenderly.

"Dad," Lotto whispered.

"Son," Gawain said. Oh, his father's love. The gentlest Lotto had known.

"Help," Lotto said.

"Caint," Gawain said. "Sorry, son. Maybe your mama can. She was the clever one."

"My mother was many things, but not clever."

"Bite your tongue," Gawain said. "You got no idea the things she done for you."

"She did nothing. Loved nobody but herself. I haven't seen her since the eighties."

"Son, you see things awry. She loved you too much."

There was a rippling in the pool; Lotto looked in. The water was green-brown with murk, oak leaves coated the surface. A whiteness like an egg emerging, his mother's forehead. She smiled up. She was young, beautiful. Her red hair licked the surface, golden leaves knitted in. She spat dark water from her mouth.

"Muvva," he said. When he looked up, his father was gone. The old ache at his center, again.

"Darling," she said. "What are you doing here?"

"You tell me," he said. "I just want to go home."

"To that wife of yours," she said. "Mathilde. I never liked her. I was wrong. You never understand these things until you're dead."

"No. You were right," he said. "She's a liar."

"Who cares. She loved you. A good wife. Made your life beautiful, calm. Did the bills. You never worried about a thing."

"We were married for twenty-three years, and she never told me she'd been a whore. Or an adulteress. Or both. Hard to tell. Pretty huge lie of omission."

"Huge thing's your ego. Awful that you weren't the only man for her. Girl scrubs your toilets for twenty-three years, you begrudge her the life she had when you weren't around."

"But she lied," he said.

"Please. Marriage is made of lies. Kind ones, mostly. Omissions. If you give voice to the things you think every day about your spouse, you'd crush them to paste. She never lied. Just never said."

A rumble; thunder over Hamlin. Sun went dull, sky gray felt. His mother sank so her chin was obscured by the murk.

"Don't go," he said.

"It's time," she said.

"How do I come home?"

She touched his face. "Poor darling," she said, and sank down.

HE TRIED TO RETURN to his wife by imagining her deeply. By now, Mathilde would be alone in the house with God. Her hair would be darkened with grease, face drawn. She would have begun to smell. Bourbon for dinner. She'd have fallen asleep in her favorite chair by the fireplace with its cold ashes, veranda doors open to the night so that Lotto could wander back. In sleep her eyelids were so translucent that he always thought if he looked hard, he could see her dreams pulsing like jellyfish across her brain.

He would have liked to go deeper into her, to seat himself on the seat of her lacrimal bone and ride there, tiny homunculus like a rodeo cowboy, understand what it was she thought. Oh, but it would be redundant. Quiet daily intimacy had taught him. Paradox of marriage: you can never know someone entirely; you do know someone entirely. He could sense the phrasing of the jokes she was about to tell, feel the goose bumps on her upper arms when she felt chilled.

She'd wake soon with a startle. His wife, who never cried, would cry. Masked with her own fingers, she'd wait in the dark for Lotto to return.

MOON A NAVEL, light on the water a trail of fine hair leading straight to Lotto.

Coming toward him on it, all the girls he'd had before Mathilde. So many. Naked. Shining. Chollie's sister, Gwennie, his first at fifteen, hair wild. Glossy private-school girls, dean's daughter, townies, college girls: breasts of bread *boules* and fists and squash balls in athletic socks and bull's-eyes and buckeyes and teacups and mouse snouts and tick bites, bellies and rumps, glorious, all beautiful to Lotto. A few slender boys, his theater teacher. [Look away.] So many bodies! Hundreds! He would bury himself in them. Twenty-three years faithful to Mathilde. Without compunction, he could roll his body on the sea of theirs like a dog rolls on fresh new grass.

It would serve his wife right. It would make them equal. He could return to her afterward, avenged.

But he couldn't. He shut his eyes and put his fingers in his ears. The sand pressed against his tailbone. He felt them passing by, fingers flicking like feathers over his skin. He counted a slow thousand after the last and looked to see the trail from the moon extruded out of the stopped water, the sand torn up in one long line.

THE WATER WAS THE ONLY WAY, he decided, to return to Mathilde. He would swim back into time.

He took off his boxer briefs and walked into the ocean. His feet, touching the water, set off bolts of electricity like lightning. He watched, thrilled, as the light branched into the deep and slowly faded. Saltatory conduction. Each time it was gone, he made it shoot outward again. He took a breath and plunged into the water and began to swim, loving the phosphorescence as his arms struck the surface. The moon drew him along. It was not difficult, swimming in stilled water, though he had to climb the crests of the waves as if they were bumps on the land. Lobes of warmth, of cold, always the dazzle. He thrashed away, feeling a good tiredness come over him. He swam until his arms burned and his lungs were salted, and he swam some more.

He imagined passing schools of unmoving fish. He thought of galleons below, foundered in mud spangled with bullion. Stone trenches as deep as the Grand Canyon, which he flew over as if he were an eagle in a sky of water. At the bottom of these canyons were rivers of mud, creatures all goop and sudden gleam of teeth. He imagined a vast sea creature below, unfurling its arms to grasp him, but he was slippery and strong and escaped.

He'd been swimming for hours, if not days. If not weeks.

He couldn't anymore. He stopped. He turned onto his back and went down. He saw the soft cotton of dawn wipe over the face of the night. He opened his mouth as if to eat the day. He was drowning, and in his drowning there came a glorious, vivid vision.

He was tiny, polyp of his mother, still attached by milk and warmth. Beach vacation. A window was open, waves sizzling beyond. [Antoinette, forever connected to the ocean, grasping what it reached, pulling it in, spitting up shells and bones.] She hummed. The slatted shades were down, casting streaks of light onto her. Hair glorious to her hips. She'd been a mermaid only recently, still a mermaid in her soft, pale, damp skin. She took one strap down slowly. Over a shoulder, the arm. The other. Now over her breasts, pop, out they came, soft pink like chicken cutlets, over her pale stomach with its breading of sand. Over her pubis with its luxuriant curls, down the white columns of her legs. She'd been so thin. Beautiful. From his nest of towels, Lotto, tiny, watched his gold-banded mother and had an inkling. She was over there; he was here. They were not, in fact, connected. They were two, which meant that they were not one. Before this moment, there had been a long warm sleep, first in darkness and then in gradual light. Now he had awoken. It came out of him in a squawk, this awful separateness. She startled out of her daydream. *Hush, my little,* she said, coming over, putting him against her chilly skin.

She, at some point, had stopped loving him. [He couldn't know.] It was a sorrow of his life. But perhaps, right then she did.

He floated down until he shipwrecked on the bottom of the ocean. Poofs of sand. He opened his eyes. His nose was barely below the surface, where the last of the moon rode the tip of a stilled wave. He put his feet down and pushed, and his body rose out of the water to his thighs.

Like a dog that had followed him, the shore was ten feet behind.

THE DAY DAWNED FIRST ON THE CLOUDS. Golden cattle of sun. At least he'd have this comfort. The beach stretched perfect, the dunes black with foliage. Untouched by man. History, during the night, had been peeled to the beginning.

He had read once that sleep does to the cerebellum what waves do to the ocean. Sleep sparks a series of pulses across the webs of neurons, pulses like waves; it washes out what is unnecessary and leaves only what's important behind.

[It was clear now, what this was. His family inheritance. The final blinding salvo in the brain.]

He longed to go home. To Mathilde. He wanted to tell her he'd forgive her anything. Who cared anymore what she'd done, with whom? But all that was gone. He, too, would be gone soon.

He wished he could have known her old. He thought of how magnificent she would be then.

No sun but a dim gold. Tide tight to shore. His mother's pink house. Three black birds huddled on the roof. He'd always loved the ocean's scent of fresh sex. He climbed out of the water and went naked up the beach, the boardwalk, into the house of his mother, outside onto the balcony.

For years, it seemed, he stood in the dawn.

[THE THREAD OF SONG has been measured to its bare spool, Lotto. We'll sing the last of it to you.]

Look, now. In the distance, a person.

Closer, it's two people, hand in hand, ankle deep in the froth. Sunrise in hair. Blond, green bikini; tall, shining. They kiss, handsy things happening under his trunks, her top. Who wouldn't envy such youth, who wouldn't grieve what has been lost, in watching. They come up the dune, she pushing him backward, up. Study them from the balcony, holding your breath, while the couple stops in a smooth bowl of sand, protected by dunes. She pushes down his trunks; he takes off her bathing suit, top and bottom. Oh, yes, you'd return to your wife on hands and knees, crawl the distance of the Eastern Seaboard to feel her fingers once more in your hair. You're unworthy of her. [Yes. [No.]] Even as you think of flight, you're transfixed by the lovers, wouldn't dare move for fear of making them flap like birds into the blistered sky. They step into each other and it's hard to tell where one begins and one ends: hands in hair and warmth on warmth, into the sand, her red knees raised, his body moving. It is time. Something odd happening though you are not ready for it; there is an overlap; you have seen this before, felt her breath on your nape, the heat of her beneath and the cold damp of day on your back, the helpless overwhelm, a sense of crossing, the sex reaching its culmination [come!]. Lip bitten to blood and finish with a roar and birds shoot up and crumbles in the pink folds of an ear. Serrated coin of sun on water. Face turned skyward: is this drizzle? [It is.] Sound of small shears closing. Barely time to register the staggering beauty, and here it is. The separation.

FURIES

ONE DAY, WHEN MATHILDE was walking in the village where they'd been so happy, she heard a carful of boys drive up behind her. They were yelling lewd things. Anatomy they suggested she suck. What they'd like to do to her ass.

The shock became a flush of warmth, as if she'd drunk a tumbler of whiskey down.

It's true, she thought. I still have a perfect ass.

But when the car drew level to her face, the boys went dumb. She saw them, pale, in passing. They gunned the engine and were gone.

This moment returned to her a month later when she crossed a Boston street and heard someone calling her name. A small woman darted up. Mathilde couldn't place her. She had damp eyes and reddish hair hanging around her ears. Soft at the midsection, a breeder. From the looks of things, four little girls in matching Lilly Pulitzer were at home with the au pair.

The woman stopped five feet from Mathilde with a little cry. Mathilde brought her hands to her cheeks. "I know," she said. "I've looked so old ever since my husband—"

She couldn't finish the sentence.

"No," the woman said. "You're still elegant. It's just. You look so *angry*, Mathilde."

Later, Mathilde would remember the woman: Bridget, from her class in college. With the recollection came some small pang of guilt. Time, however, had obscured why.

For a breath, she studied the sidewalk waltz of chickadee and sun through windblown leaves. When she looked up again, the other woman took a step back. Then another.

Slowly, Mathilde said: "Angry. Sure. Well, what's the point in hiding it anymore?"

And then she lowered her head, pressed on.

IT WOULD COME to her decades later, when she was old, in a porcelain bathtub held aloft on lion claws and her own body mercifully submerged, that her life could be drawn in the shape of an X. Her feet duck-splayed and reflected in the water.

From a terrifying expanse in childhood, life had focused to a single red-hot point in middle age. From there it had exploded outward again.

She slid her heels apart so they were no longer touching. The reflection moved with them.

Now her life showed itself to have been in a different shape, equal and opposite to the first. [Complex, our Mathilde; she can bear contradictions.]

Now the shape of her life appeared to be: greater than, white space, less than.

WHEN THEY WERE BOTH forty-six years old, Mathilde's husband, the famous playwright Lancelot Satterwhite, left her.

He went away in an ambulance without sirens. Well, not him. The cold meat of him.

She called his sister, Rachel. Rachel screamed and screamed, and when she stopped, she said, ferociously, "Mathilde, we're coming. Hang tight, we're coming." His aunt Sallie was traveling and hadn't left a number, so she called Sallie's lawyer. Within a minute after

Mathilde hung up, Sallie called from Burma. "Mathilde," she said. "You wait, darling, I'm coming."

She called her husband's best friend. "I'm taking the helicopter," Chollie said. "I'm coming."

They were soon to descend upon her. For now, she was alone. She stood on a boulder in the meadow, wearing one of her husband's shirts, and watched the dawn hit the frost, prismatic. There was an ache in her feet from the cold stone. For a month or so, something had been eating at her husband. He'd gloomed around the house and hardly looked at her. It was as if the tide of him had been ebbing from her, but she knew, like a real tide, time would bring him back. A beating came near, and the wind started up, and she didn't turn to watch the helicopter land, but she leaned against the freezing force of the wind. When the blades slowed, she heard Chollie's voice at her elbow.

She looked down at him. Grotesque Chollie, gone bad with money, overrich like a pear ripened to ooze. He wore a sweatshirt and sweatpants. She'd woken him, she saw. He had to fold his hand into a visor to peer up at her.

"Insane," he said. "He exercised every day. It should have been fatass me to go first."

"Yes," she said. He moved as if to hug her. She thought of the last warmth of her husband that she'd soaked into her skin, and said, "Don't."

"I won't," he said.

The meadow sharpened. "When we landed, I saw you standing there," he said. "You looked the same age as when I first met you. You were so brittle. So full of light back then."

"I feel ancient now," she said. She was only forty-six.

"I know," he said.

"You can't," she said. "You loved him, too. But you weren't his wife."

"I wasn't. But I had a twin sister who died. Gwennie." He looked away, then said with cold in his voice, "She killed herself when she was seventeen."

Chollie's mouth was twisting in and out. Mathilde touched his shoulder.

"Not you," he said quickly, and by this she understood him to mean that her fresh sorrow outblazed his own, that she should be the one to be comforted now. She could feel the grief coming on fast, shaking the ground like a hurtling train, but she hadn't been hit by it yet. She had a little time still. She could soothe; it was what she was best at, after all. Being a wife.

"I'm so sorry," she said. "Lotto never told me that Gwennie had killed herself."

"He never knew. He thought it was an accident," Chollie said, and this didn't sound strange to her in the meadow full of winter light. It wouldn't ring strange for some months, because here the horror was, plowing through her, and she could feel nothing for a very long time but its wild and whistling force.

It comes over us that we shall never again hear the laughter of our friend, that this garden is forever locked against us. And at that moment begins our true grief.

Antoine de Saint-Exupéry said this. He, too, had found himself crashed into the desert when, just moments before, all had been open blue sky.

Where are the people? said Saint-Exupéry's Little Prince. *It's a little lonely in the desert . . .*

It's lonely when you're among people, too, said the snake.

LIKE CARP, the loved ones surfaced, mouthing the air around her face before sinking deep again.

They put her in a chair, put a blanket on her. God the dog sat trembling beneath.

These loved ones all day were lowering their faces at her, moving away. Lotto's nieces and nephew creeping up to put their cheeks on her knees. Food on her lap, taken away. The children sat there through the long afternoon. They understood at an animal level, new enough to the world to be uneasy in language. Sudden night in the window. She sat and sat. She thought of what her husband might have been thinking the moment he died. A flash of light, perhaps. The ocean. He had always loved the ocean. She hoped he'd seen her own younger face coming near his. Samuel put his shoulder under one arm, Lotto's sister put hers under the other, they deposited her in the bed that still smelled like him. She put her face in his pillow. She lay.

She could do nothing. Her whole body had turned inward. Mathilde had become a fist.

2

MATHILDE WAS NOT UNFAMILIAR with grief. That old wolf had come sniffing around her house before.

She had one picture of herself from when she was tiny.

Her name had been Aurélie. Fat cheeks, gold hair. The only child in a large Breton family. Her bangs clipped from her face in a barrette, scarves on her neck, lacy socks to her ankles. Her grandparents fed her galettes, cider, caramels with sea salt. The kitchen had rounds of Camembert ripening in the cabinet. It could knock you down to open the door, unsuspecting.

Her mother was a fishwife at the market in Nantes. She'd rise in the blue night and drive to the city and come home midmorning with her hands chapped and glittering with scales, cold to the bone from contact with ice. Her face was delicate, but she had no education. Her husband had wooed her with his leather jacket, his pompadour, his motorcycle. Small things to trade for a life, but at the time they had seemed powerful. Aurélie's father was a stonemason, and his family had lived in the same house in Notre-Dame-des-Landes for twelve generations. Aurélie was conceived during the revolution of May 1968; though her parents were far from radical, there was so much excitement in the air that they didn't know how to express themselves except animally. When it was impossible for the girl's mother to hide her pregnancy, they were married with orange blossoms in her hair, a slice of coconut cake in the freezer.

Aurélie's father was quiet, loved few things. Putting stone on stone, the wine he made in his garage, his hunting dog he called Bibiche, his mother who'd survived World War II by black-marketing blood sausages, and his daughter. She was spoiled, a happy and singing girl.

But when Aurélie was three, the new baby came. He was a fretful and screaming creature. Still, he was cooed over, that wizened turnip in blankets. Aurélie watched from under a chair, burning.

Colic arrived in the baby, and the house went piebald with vomit. Aurélie's mother walked around as if shattered. Four aunts, smelling of butter, came to help. They gossiped viciously and their brother showed them his grapes and the aunts chased Bibiche from the house with a broom.

When the baby at last began to crawl, he got into everything, and the father had to build a gate at the top of the stairs. Aurélie's mother cried during the day in her bed when the children were supposed to be asleep. She was so tired. She smelled of fish.

The baby liked best to crawl into Aurélie's bed and suck his thumb and twirl her hair, the snot in his nose catching so it sounded as if he were purring. During the night, she would slowly move both of their bodies toward the edge of the bed so that when he finally fell asleep and rolled onto his back he'd tumble out and wake shrieking from the floor. She'd open her eyes in time to watch her mother rush in and pick the baby up with her swollen red hands and, scolding in whispers, carry him back to his own crib.

WHEN THE GIRL was four years old and the baby brother one, the family went for supper to the grandmother's house one afternoon.

The house had been the grandmother's ancestors' for centuries, and she'd brought it to her marriage with the neighbor boy. The fields, still conjoined, were all hers. The house was far finer than the little girl's family's, the bedrooms larger, a stone creamery from the eighteenth century still attached to the main building. The manure had been spread that morning and could be tasted in the milk. The grandmother was like her son, square, strong-featured, taller than most men. Her mouth was carved down into a sharp *n* shape. She had a granite lap and a way of puncturing the jokes of others by sighing loudly at the punch line.

The baby was put down for a nap in the grandmother's bed and everyone else was outside under the oak, eating. Aurélie was on the downstairs potty, trying to go. She was listening to her brother upstairs thumping around in the grandmother's room, crowing to himself. She pulled up her panties and slowly went up the stairs, collecting a gray fur on her finger from the dust between banisters. She stood in the honey-bright hallway listening to him through the door: he was singing to himself, thumping his feet on the headboard. She thought of him inside the room and smiled. She opened the door to him, and he climbed off the bed and toddled into the grandmother's hallway, grabbing at her, but she stepped backward, away from his sticky hands.

She sucked a finger and watched him move beyond her, toward the top of the stairs. He looked at her, beamish, teetering. He reached out his daisy of a hand, and she watched as her baby brother fell.

WHEN AURÉLIE'S PARENTS returned from the hospital, they were silent, gray-faced. The baby's neck had broken. There was nothing they could have done.

Her mother wanted to take Aurélie home. It was late and the girl's face was swollen with crying, but her father had said no. He couldn't look at her, though she clung to his knees, smelling his jeans stiff with sweat and stone dust. After the baby fell, someone had dragged Aurélie down the stairs and her arm was black with a bruise. She showed it to them, but they didn't look.

The parents were holding up something invisible but terribly heavy between them. There was no power in them to lift anything else, certainly not their daughter.

"We'll leave her for tonight," the mother said. The sad face with the apple cheeks, the glorious eyebrows, came near, kissed the girl, went away. Her father slammed the door to the hatchback three times. They drove off, Bibiche gazing out the back window. The taillights winked in the dark, were gone.

In the morning, Aurélie woke to her grandparents' house, the grandmother downstairs making crêpes, and she washed herself neatly. All morning, her parents didn't come. They didn't come and they didn't come.

The kiss on the forehead was the last she'd smell of her mother [Arpège by Lanvin, undermusk of cod]. The brush of her father's stiff jeans on her hand when she held it out to touch him as he walked by, the last she'd feel of him.

After the fifth time she begged her grandparents for her mother and father, her grandmother stopped answering her.

That night, when she waited by the door and they still didn't come, a terrible rage rose in Aurélie. To get it out of her, she kicked and screamed, broke the mirror in the bathroom, the glasses one by one in the kitchen; she punched the cat in the throat; she ran into the dark and tore her grandmother's tomato plants out of the ground with her fists. The grandmother first tried to embrace her for hours to calm her, but lost patience and had to tie her to the bed with the curtain tassels, which, being ancient, snapped.

Three scratches beading blood on her grandmother's cheek. *Quelle conne. Diablesse,* she hissed.

Hard to say how long this went on. Time, to a four-year-old, is flood or eddy. Months, perhaps. Years, it's not impossible. The darkness in her circled, landed. In her mind's eye, her parents' faces turned to twin smears. Was there a moustache atop her father's lip? Was her mother bright blond or dark? She forgot the smell of the farmhouse where she'd been born, the crunch of gravel under her shoes, the perpetual twilight in the kitchen even when the lights were on. The wolf spun, settled in her chest, snored there.

3

THERE WERE THOUSANDS of people at Lotto's funeral. She knew he'd been loved, and by strangers, too. But not this excess. All these people she didn't know were lining the sidewalk, keening. O! great man. O! playwright of the bougie. She rode at the head of a shining line of black limos like the head raven in a convocation of blackbirds. Her husband had moved people and, in so moving, had become their Lancelot Satterwhite, too. Something of him lived in them. Was not hers. Was now theirs.

It felt unhygienic, this flood of snot and tears. Too much coffee breath in her face. All that assaultive perfume. She hated perfume. It was a cover for poor hygiene or for body shame. Clean people never aspired to the floral.

After the interment, she drove to the country alone. There may have been a reception planned, she didn't know. Or if she did know, she blocked the knowledge; she never would have gone. She'd had enough of people.

The house was hot. The pool winked sunlight. Her black clothes on the kitchen floor. The dog made herself tiny on her cushion, her eyes beading out from the corner, feral.

[God licking at Lotto's bare bluing feet below his desk, licking and licking as if she could lick the life back into him, dumb thing.]

And then there was the strange separation of self from body so that she watched her own nakedness from very far away.

The light slid across the room and extinguished itself, and the night stole in. This impassive self watched the friends come to the back window, recoil at seeing her nude body at the kitchen table, turn their eyes away, and call through glass: "Let us in, Mathilde. Let us in." The nude body outsat them until they eked on home.

Naked in the bed, she wrote *Thank you, Thank you* to all of the e-mails until she remembered control-C, control-V, and then she copied and pasted *Thank you*. She found hot tea in her hand and thanked naked Mathilde for her thoughtfulness and found herself in the pool under the moonlight and worried about naked Mathilde's mental state. Naked Mathilde neglected to answer the doorbell, woke on the wrong side of the bed seeking heat that wasn't there, let the food rot on the porch, let the flowers rot on the porch, watched the dog piddle in the middle of the kitchen, made scrambled eggs for the animal when she ran out of kibble, gave her the last of the vegetable chili that Lotto had made, and watched the dog lick her own bum, sore from the spices, until it was red. Naked Mathilde locked the doors and ignored the loved ones peering in, calling, "Mathilde, come on! Mathilde, let us in, Mathilde, I'm not going anywhere, I'm camping in the yard." The last was her husband's aunt Sallie, who actually did camp in the yard until naked Mathilde left the door open for her so she could come in. Aunt Sallie had lost the two loves of her life in a few short months, but she chose to peacock her grief, wearing Thai silk dresses in jewel colors, dyeing her hair blueblack. Naked Mathilde put the covers over her head when a tray appeared on the mattress, and shivered until she slept again. Tray, sleep, bathroom, tray, sleep, bad thoughts, terrible memories, God whining, tray, sleep; on and on it went, forever.

I REMAIN HERE, *cold, a widow in your halls.* Andromache, the perfect wife, railed while holding dead Hector's head in her white arms. *You have left me only bitterness and anguish. You didn't die in bed, stretching your arms toward me. You didn't give me one last sweet word that I might remember in all my sorrow.*

Andromaque, je pense à vous!

ON AND ON IT WENT, forever, except that during the first week she was a widow, somewhere inside the tent of covers, in the bed that held her naked body, a lust rose so powerfully she felt choked by it. What she needed was a fuck. A series of fucks. She saw a parade of thrusting men all in silent black-and-white, like talkie movies. Jangling over it all, organ music. Organ music. Ha!

There had been a few times before when lust was just this powerful. The first year with Lotto. Also, her first year of sex, long before Lotto. He'd always believed he'd deflowered her, but she'd just gotten her period, that was all. She indulged his belief. She hadn't been a virgin, but there had been only one man before him. This was a secret that Lotto would never know. He would never have understood; his egotism would not admit a precursor. She winced to remember herself at seventeen, in high school, how, after the first illuminating weekend, everything spoke sex to her. The way the light pulsed the leaves of the ragweed in the ditches, the way clothes teased her skin as she moved. The words leaving a person's mouth, how they were tongued, rolled, lipped before they emerged. It was as if the man had suddenly reached into her and pulled out an earthquake and set it loose on her skin. She walked the last weeks of high school wanting to eat every one of these delicious boys. If she had only been allowed, she would have swallowed them whole. She smiled at them hugely; they scurried away. She'd laughed, but felt it was a shame.

None of this mattered. Since they were married, it had only ever been Lotto. She had been faithful. She was nearly certain he had been, too.

In her little house in the cherry orchard, the house of bleakest widowhood, Mathilde remembered and got up out of her dirty bed and showered. She dressed in the dark bathroom and crept past the room where Aunt Sallie was whistle-snoring. Past the next room, door open, where her husband's sister Rachel looked at her passing from the pillow. In the dark, a face like a ferret's: triangular, alert, quivering. Mathilde got into the Mercedes.

Her hair was in a wet bun, she was wearing no makeup, but it didn't matter. Three towns north there was a yuppie bar, and in the yuppie bar was a sad-faced man in a Red Sox cap, and a mile away in a little copse of trees where the road split, where they would have been pinned like moths on a board by headlights had any passed, she stood on her right leg, the left around the sad-faced Red Sox's jerky hips, and shouted, "Harder!" And the man's face, which had been first set in concentration, began taking on a look of alarm, and he kept on valiantly for some time while she shouted at him, "Harder! Faster, you fucker!" until it was clear that he was spooked, and he faked an orgasm and pulled out and mumbled something about taking a whiz, and she heard his feet in the crunchy leaves as he hurried away.

Rachel's face was still looking at Mathilde from the dark when she went back upstairs. The marital suite, the bed obscene in its empty enormity. In her absence, the sheets had been changed. When she climbed in again, they were cool and smelled like lavender and brushed her skin like accusations.

THERE HAD BEEN A TIME when she'd sat beside Lotto in the dark on the opening night of one of his wild earlier plays and was so overcome by what he'd done, the grandness of his vision being transmuted before her eyes, that she leaned across the space between them and licked his face from ear to lip. She couldn't help it.

Just as, holding Rachel and Elizabeth's newborn daughter, she so longed to have the baby's innocence for herself that she put the tiny clenched fist in her mouth and held it there until the baby screamed.

This widow's lust was the opposite of that.

WIDOW. *The word consumes itself,* said Sylvia Plath, who consumed herself.

4

SHE HAD BEEN OVERCOME by fear over the apple crisp in the dining hall; she had fled to the bathroom and had been sitting, frozen, on the paper ring atop the toilet for a very long time. This was during the final days of college. For the previous month, she'd been frightened at the gulf the future opened before her. She who had been in one cage or another since birth was free to fly soon, but she was petrified at the thought of all that air.

The door opened and two girls came in, talking about how rich Lancelot Satterwhite was. "Bottled Water Princeling, you know," one said. "His mom's, like, a billionaire."

"Lotto? Really?" said the other. "Shit! I hooked up with him freshman year. If only I'd known."

The girls laughed, and then the first said, "Yeah, right. He's such a bro-ho. I think I'm the only girl in the Hudson Valley who hasn't seen his junk. They say he never sleeps with a girl twice."

"Except Bridget. Which I don't get. She's so blah. I heard her saying they're dating, and I was, like, *Really?* I mean, she looks like a children's librarian. Like one who is caught in a perpetual rainstorm or something."

"Yeah, well, Bridget is to dating Lotto the way a remora is to dating a shark."

The girls laughed, left.

Mathilde thought, Huh. She flushed, came out, washed her hands. She looked at herself critically in the mirror. She smiled. "Hallelujah," she said aloud to the Mathilde in the mirror, and the Mathilde in the mirror said it back with her lovely lips, her pale and angular face.

She claimed finals and eschewed the weekend trip to the city. She dressed carefully. She saw her quarry onstage that night and was impressed: he was very good, a manic Hamlet, puppyish in his energy even if so very tall. From afar, the pits in his cheeks were not discernible, and he threw off a kind of golden light that cast even the audience in its glow. He made the shopworn monologue sexy and showed it to them anew. *"Tis a consummation devoutly to be wished,"* he said, with a pirate's smile; and she imagined in seats all throughout the audience a tingly heat rising. Promising. By the aisle lights, she read his full name in the program, Lancelot "Lotto" Satterwhite, and frowned. Lancelot. Well. She could make it work.

The cast party was in a Brutalist dorm where she'd never been. For four years, she had not allowed herself parties, friends. She couldn't risk them. She went early and stood out of the rain under a portico, smoking a cigarette. She was watching for Bridget. When the girl and her three dour friends came trotting up under umbrellas, Mathilde followed them inside.

It was easy to separate Bridget from her friends. Mathilde only had to ask a question about serotonin reuptake inhibitors for their neurobiology class final in a few days, and the other girls faded away as Bridget earnestly explained. And then Mathilde refilled Bridget's cup with mostly vodka and a splash of Kool-Aid.

Bridget was flattered to be talking to Mathilde, "I mean, my god!" she said. "You never, ever, ever go out! Everyone has heard about you but nobody ever talks to you. You're like the white whale of Vassar." Then she flushed, and said, "Like the skinniest, prettiest white whale ever," and then said, "Aargh! You know what I mean." She drank nervously. Mathilde refilled and Bridget drank, Mathilde refilled, Bridget drank, and then Bridget was throwing up on the common stairway and people who were trying to pass were saying, "Sick!"

And, "Oh my god, Bridget." And, "Nasty, ho-bag, take it outside." The friends had been summoned. Mathilde was watching through the banister from a higher landing when they took her home.

Bridget went down the stairs and Lotto passed her coming up. He said, "Yikes!" and patted her on the shoulder, and leapt the last few steps and went into the party.

From her perch above, Mathilde had watched it all.

The first problem dispatched. What ease.

She stood outside in the chill rain, smoking two more cigarettes, listening to the party. She gave it ten songs. When Salt-N-Pepa was playing, she went back inside, up the stairs. She looked across the room.

There he was on the windowsill, drunk, bellowing, and it took her by surprise, how very muscular that body of his was. He was wearing some girl's gel eye-mask as a loincloth. He had an empty water jug Ace-bandaged to his head. No dignity, but Christ there was beauty. His face was strange, as if it had once been handsome, and still was from afar; but she had seen him only clothed before now and would not have guessed at how perfect his body was. She had made so many calculations, but none involved her legs melting from under her with the instant desire to screw.

She willed him to look up, to see her.

He looked up. He saw her. His face went still. He stopped danc-ing. She felt the hair of her neck stand. He leapt into the crowd and crushed some poor tiny girl in falling and swam his way out and over to Mathilde. He was taller than she was. She measured six feet, six-three in these heels; men taller than she was were rare. She liked the unexpected feeling of being smaller, more delicate. He touched her hand. He went down on one knee and shouted up, "Marry me!" And she didn't know what to do; she laughed and looked down at him, and said, "No!"

In the story he told of this—spun at so many parties, so many dinners, she listening with her smile, her head cocked, laughing slightly—she said, "Sure." She never corrected him, not once. Why not let him live with his illusion? It made him happy. She loved making him happy. Sure! It wasn't true, not for another two weeks when she would marry him, but it did no harm.

Lotto had made the story of their meeting a *coup de foudre*, but he was a born storyteller. He recast reality into a different kind of truth. It was, as she knew, actually a *coup de foutre*. Their marriage had always been about the sex. It had been about other things at first and would be about other things later, of course, but within days it was about the sex. She'd held out until she'd settled her previous commitments, and the wait had inflamed both. For a long time after, the genital had taken primacy over other concerns.

Even then, she knew that there is no such thing as *sure*. There is no absolute anything. The gods love to fuck with us.

YET IT'S TRUE THERE WAS, for a brief spell, a happiness that was absolute, it was *sure*, it swallowed her whole. Dim day, rocky beach. She felt the joy even through the tiny irritations, the sand flies that bit and the cold that soaked to her bones and the sharp stones on the Maine beach that split her hallux open like a sliced grape and made her limp back to the house they'd borrowed for their wedding day. They were twenty-two. The world drenched with potential. As fine as they'd ever be. She kept her hands warm on her new husband's back and felt the muscles moving under his skin. A shell dug into her spine. She felt herself engulf him. First consummation as husband and wife. She thought of a boa swallowing a fawn.

If he'd had flaws then, she couldn't see them; and perhaps it was true, perhaps she had found the only faultless person in the world.

Even if she had dreamt of him, she couldn't have come up with him. Innocent, charming, funny, loyal. Rich. Lancelot Satterwhite; Lotto. They had been married that morning. She was grateful to the sand that eked its way into the naughty bits and stung; she couldn't trust pleasure in its pure form.

But their first married consummation was over so fast. He laughed into her ear; she into his throat. It didn't matter. Their separate selves had elided. She was no longer alone. She was crushed with gratitude. He helped her up and they bowed to gather their clothing and the ocean over the dune applauded. All weekend she rang with joy.

One weekend should have been enough. She was given so much more than she deserved. But she was greedy.

Brilliant May sun on the drive back from their stolen honeymoon. Lotto, who would always be labile as a preteen, drove and, hearing a sweet song, burst into tears. She did the only thing she could think of and put her head in his lap and disinterred Little Lotto to make Big Lotto stop. A semi, in passing, honked its approval.

Back in Poughkeepsie, in front of her apartment, she said, "I want to know everything about you. I want to meet your mother and aunt and sister immediately. Let's fly to Florida after graduation. I want to *eat* your life." She laughed, a little, at her own earnestness. Oh, to have a mother, a family! She'd been alone for so long. She'd let herself daydream of a kind mother-in-law who took her away for spa days, who had in-jokes, who sent small presents with notes saying, "Saw this, thought of you."

But there was something wrong. After a moment, Lotto put her knuckles to his mouth and said, "M. My love. We'll have the rest of our lives for that."

A vein of cold shot through her. What was this? Hesitation? Perhaps he was already ashamed of her. Before her rose the Cranach diptych, Adam and Eve with the long thighs, tiny heads, huge feet cold at the knuckles. It's true that even in Eden there were snakes.

"I have to write my sociology final," he said apologetically. "I have six hours till it's due, but I'll bring us dinner tonight after I hand it in. I love you beyond love."

"Me, too," she said, closing the car door and trying to stifle the panic.

She came into her apartment, which had contracted, filled as it was with her small and gray previous life. She took a hot bath and climbed under her down comforter for a nap. She was deep in a dream when her phone rang. It had to be bad. Nothing but badness would be calling so insistently.

She braced herself. "Yes," she said.

"Well. Hello," said a soft, sweet voice. "Come to find out you're my daughter and I don't even know you from Cain."

It took Mathilde a moment, and then she said, "Mrs. Satterwhite. It's so lovely to finally speak with you."

But the voice didn't stop. "I must confess that I did what any doting mother would do and I made inquiries as to who you are and where you're from. My inquiries ended up in some strange places. You *are* lovely, just as I was told. I've seen your photographs, those bra catalog ones particularly, even though your bosoms seem rather smallish and I wonder at the person who hired you to show them off. To speak honestly, if I may, I didn't love the spread in the teenybopper's magazine where you looked like a half-drowned rat terrier, bless your heart. Funny that people would pay you to look like that in public. But some of your photos are very fine. You're a pretty girl. Good match for my Lancelot, at least in looks."

"Thank you," Mathilde said, wary.

"But you're not a churchgoing girl and, frankly, that gives me pause. A heathen in the family," she said. "Not sure I like it. Much worse is what I come to find out about your uncle, the people he's mixed up with. Shady beyond all measure. You only really know about a person when you know about their kin. I must say I do not like what

I have come to find out. Add this to my fear of the kind of person who seduces such a kindhearted boy as mine and marries him in such a short courtship. Only a very dangerous or a very calculating person could do such a thing. All these things put together make me believe that you and I would have a hard time seeing eye to eye. Not in this lifetime, at least."

"Well," Mathilde said. "Seems that ours will be your standard mother-in-law, daughter-in-law relationship, Antoinette." They both laughed.

"You may call me Mrs. Satterwhite," Lotto's mother said.

"I may. Probably won't," Mathilde said. "How's *Mother* sound to you?"

"You're a tough little cookie, aren't you," said Antoinette. "Well, my Lancelot is so tenderhearted that the woman he marries has got to be a little hard. I am, however, afraid that someone won't be you."

"Already is," Mathilde said. "How can I help you? What do you want?"

"The question, my girl, is what *you* want. I assume you know that Lancelot comes from money. Oh, of course you know! That's why you married him. Going together for two weeks, no way you actually love the dear boy, lovable as he may be. Knowing my son as I do, he hasn't told you yet how you aren't going to see a penny of my money while I've got breath to breathe and he's married to you. We discussed it all yesterday morning after you did the deed and he called me up to gloat. Impetuous, both of you. Acting like the children you still are. And now you're penniless. I do wonder how you feel at this moment. I'm so sorry that all your plans are coming to naught."

Despite herself, Mathilde caught her breath.

Antoinette continued: "Of course, that means you'd do far better for yourself to get it all annulled. Take a hundred thousand dollars and call it a day."

"Ha!" Mathilde said.

"Darling, you name your price, I don't mind. Not the time to be cheap, I suppose. Say the word and it'll be done. Just ask what you require to start up your life after graduation and you'll have it all wired this afternoon and you can sign some papers and just walk away. Leave my poor child in peace, let him sow his wild oats, eventually find himself some good, sweet girl and come home to Florida to me."

"Interesting," Mathilde said. "You're possessive for a woman who couldn't bother to visit her son for a whole year."

"Well, darling, you grow a baby in your belly for near on a year, you see your husband and yourself in his face, of course you'll be possessive. He's my blood. I made him. You'll see someday."

"I won't," Mathilde said.

"Five hundred? No? Would a million do?" said Antoinette. "All you have to do is abandon ship. Take your money and run. You could do what you like with a million dollars. Travel, see foreign cultures. Open up your own business. Run your hustle on richer men. The world is your oyster, Mathilde Yoder. Consider this that first grain of sand to make your pearl."

"You sure have the gift of the mixed metaphor," Mathilde said. "I admire it, in a way."

"I take it from your comment that we have come to an accord. Excellent choice. You're not stupid. I shall call my attorney and some boy will bring the papers by in a few hours."

"Oh, wow," Mathilde said softly. "It is going to be so, so wonderful."

"Yes, darling. Sensible of you to take the deal. Good chunk of change, it is."

"No," Mathilde said. "I meant that it will be so wonderful to think up all the ways to keep your son far away from you. It'll be our little game. You'll see. All the holidays, all the birthdays, all the times when you're sick, something urgent will come up and your son will have to stay with me. He'll be with me, not you. He will choose *me*, not *you*. Muvva—Lotto calls you Muvva, so I will, too—until you apologize, until you force yourself to be nice, you won't lay your eyes on him again."

She put the phone gently on the hook and unplugged it and went to take a second bath, her T-shirt having gone transparent with sweat. In a few days, she'd get the first of many notes that Antoinette would send her through the years, spiky with exclamation points. In return, Mathilde would send back photos of Lotto and Mathilde, smiling together; Lotto and Mathilde by the pool; Lotto and Mathilde in San Francisco; Mathilde in Lotto's arms, stepping over every threshold of every new place they'd have. That evening when Lotto came back, she said nothing. They watched a sitcom. They took a shower together. Later, naked, they ate calzones.

5

TIME, AFTER LOTTO DIED, swallowed itself.

Sallie saw it was useless to try to get through; Mathilde was numb still. A force field of fury so thick nobody was going to get in. Sallie went back to Asia, to Japan this time. She'd return in a year, when Mathilde wasn't so angry, she said.

"I'll always be angry," Mathilde said.

Sallie put her dry brown hand on Mathilde's face and barely smiled.

Only Lotto's sister returned again and again. Dear sweet Rachel, pure of heart. "Here's an apple pie," she'd say. "Here's a loaf of bread. Here's a handful of chrysanthemums. Here's my daughter, hold her, salve your sorrow." Everyone else gave her *space*. Gave her *time*.

"Christ, did you have any idea Mathilde could be such a bitch?" friends said, wounded, returning home. "Would you have guessed it when Lotto was alive? Can you believe what she *said* to us?"

"She's possessed by some demon," they said.

"Grief," they all said knowingly, feeling profound. Tacitly agreed: they would return when she was her seemly, elegant, smiling self again. In their own place, they sent gifts. Samuel sent potted bromeliads. Chollie sent towers of Belgian chocolates. Danica sent her personal masseuse, whom Mathilde sent away by ignoring him. Arnie sent a case of wine. Ariel sent a long black dress in cashmere, which Mathilde curled for days within. Strange that this soft gift from an old boss would be the only perfect thing.

———

LATE ONE NIGHT Mathilde found herself on a long straight strip of road. The car a top-of-the-line Mercedes that Lotto had bought just before croaking. His mother had died half a year before her son, and they'd come into an inheritance so vast it was foolish they were driving their fifteen-year-old Honda Civic with the iffy airbags. He'd only ever cared about money when it came to his own comfort; otherwise, he left it for others to worry about.

She put the pedal to the floor. Responsive as fuck. The car shot to eighty, to ninety-five, to one-ten.

She flipped off the lights and the darkness rose to her like a day-dream.

Moonless night. The car slack like a fish brushing along the walls of a cave. After one lifetime, she went stationary, suspended in dark-ness. Calm.

Her car hit the culvert, brushed up the embankment, vaulted a barbed-wire fence, somersaulted. It landed in a herd of sleeping Jerseys.

Mathilde's mouth was bleeding. She'd bitten nearly through her tongue. No matter. She spoke to nobody these days. Otherwise, she was unhurt.

She climbed out of the car, swallowing the gushes of coppery heat. The heifers had moved off, were watching from the shelter of wind-block lindens. But one was still kneeling beside the car. When Mathilde walked around to it, there was a wall of blood where its neck had been.

She watched for a long time as it bled into the grass. There was nothing to be done.

There was nothing to be done and now what? Mathilde was forty-six. She was too young to be finished forever with love. Still in her prime. Fine-looking. Desirable. And uncoupled now, for good.

The story we are told of women is not this one.

The story of women is the story of love, of foundering into another. A slight deviation: longing to founder and being unable to. Being left alone in the foundering, and taking things into one's own hands: rat poison, the wheels of a Russian train. Even the smoother and gentler story is still just a modified version of the above. In the demotic, in the key of bougie, it's the promise of love in old age for all the good girls of the world. Hilarious ancient bodies at bath time, husband's palsied hands soaping wife's withered dugs, erection popping out of the bubbles like a pink periscope. I see you! There would be long, hobbledy walks under the plane trees, stories told by a single sideways glance, one word sufficing. *Anthill,* he'd say; *Martini!* she'd say; and the thick swim of the old joke would return to them. The laughter, the beautiful reverberations. Then the bleary toddling on to an early-bird dinner, snoozing through a movie hand in hand. Their bodies like knobby sticks wrapped in vellum. One laying the other on the deathbed, feeding the overdose, dying the day after, all heart gone out of the world with the beloved breath. Oh, companionship. Oh, romance. Oh, completion. Forgive her if she believed this would be the way it would go. She had been led to this conclusion by forces greater than she.

Conquers all! All you need is! Is a many-splendored thing! Surrender to!

Like corn rammed down goose necks, this shit they'd swallowed since they were barely old enough to dress themselves in tulle.

The way the old story goes, woman needs an other to complete her circuits, to flick her to fullest blazing.

[The refutation would come. During those dusky years of her eighties, in the far-off beyond-the-horizon, she would sit solitary over tea in her London breakfast room and look up to see her own hand like an ancient map and then out the window where a blue budgerigar peered in, naturalized citizen of this unnatural subtropical world.

Suddenly clear, in the small blue shape, she would see her life had not been, at its core, about love. There had been terrific love in it. Heat and magic. Lotto, her husband. Christ, there had been him. Yet—yes!—the sum of her life, she saw, was far greater than its sum of love.]

In the immediacy, though, in stingy moonlight over bruised metal, cow flesh, glass, there was only her bitten tongue and all that blood. The hot rust-tasting flood of it. And the great Now What stretching without end.

6

ONE DAY, the little girl she once was, small Aurélie, found herself
with a blue suitcase in her hand and her hair scraped back from her
face. She must have been five or six.

"You're off to your Paris grandmother's," her tall Breton grandmother said. There had always been something off about the Paris
grandmother, something embarrassing; her own mother had never
spoken of her; they had rarely talked on the phone. Aurélie had never
met her. There were never pretty parcels from that grandmother on
her saint's day.

They were standing in the aisle of a train. The grandmother's
frown stretched to her second chin. "Your mother's mother was the
only relative who would take you," she said.

"I don't care," Aurélie said.

"Of course you don't," the grandmother said. She gave her a packet
of sandwiches and hard-boiled eggs, a jar of warm milk, two *chaussons
aux pommes*, and pinned a note to her coat. "Don't you dare move
from your seat," she said, and gave the girl a bristly kiss on the cheek
and wiped the red rims of her eyes with a starched handkerchief and
left.

The train hooted. All Aurélie knew of the world slid out from
under her feet. The village: black-and-white cows, chickens, huge
Gothic church, bakery. She saw what she was searching for when the
train picked up speed. There. A flash. White hatchback parked under
a yew. Oh, her mother standing cross-armed, pale, in a navy dress,

her hair [yes, white-blond] under a scarf, watching the train go. Her mouth a red slash in the pale. Dress, hair beginning to froth in the train's wind. It was hard to tell what was happening on her face. Then her mother was gone.

Across from Aurélie was a man who stared at her. He had pale shining skin and puffy folds under his eyes. She squeezed hers shut to avoid him, but every time she looked, he was staring. A terrible certainty stole over her. She tried to block it, to squeeze her legs, but it was no use. She pressed both her hands against herself to hold the urine in.

The man leaned forward. "Little girl," he said, "I will escort you to the lavatory."

"No," she said.

He reached forward to touch her and she gave a scream and the fat woman with the dog on her lap in the other corner opened her eyes and glared. "Silence," she snarled.

"Come to the lavatory," the man said. His teeth were many and tiny.

"No," Aurélie said, and let go. The urine was deliciously hot on her thighs. The man said, "Ugh!" and left the carriage, and the pee gradually turned cold. For hours, as the train rocked eastward, the fat woman in the corner gelatined in her sleep, and her lapdog sniffed the air voluptuously, as if tasting it.

All at once, they were at the station.

The grandmother stood before her. She was a woman as pretty as Aurélie's mother, apple cheeks and thick eyebrows, even if this version was wrinkled around the eyes. She was astonishing. Her clothes were both grand and tattered at the same time. The perfume she wore, her elegant hands like pencils in a soft suede case. The grandmother leaned over, took the packet, and looked in. "Ah! Good peasant food," she said. She was missing a lower incisor, which gave her smile some dash. "We shall sup well tonight," she said.

When Aurélie stood, she revealed the wetness of her lap. Over the grandmother's face, like a roller blind flipping upward, the refusal to see.

"Come along," she said airily, and Aurélie took her suitcase and came along. The pee dried as she walked, and chafed her thighs.

On the way home, they bought a single sausage from a butcher who appeared to be seething silently. The grandmother took the suitcase and made the girl hold the white paper package. By the time they reached the heavy blue door of the building, her hands were stained with clammy red grease.

Her grandmother's flat was sparse, if neat. The floors were bare wood, scrubbed skinlike. There had once been pictures on the walls and they'd left dark shadows on the otherwise pale passion-flowered wallpaper. It was no warmer inside, simply less windy. The grandmother saw the girl shivering and said, "Heat costs money." She made her jump fifty times to warm herself. "Jumping's free!" she said. A broom handle from below made a *ratatatat* on the floor.

They ate. Aurélie was shown to her room: a closet with a quilt doubled for a bed on the ground, low-hanging canopy of the grandmother's clothing, smelling powerfully of her skin. "Until I move you to the closet for the night, you will sleep in my bed," the grandmother said. Aurélie said her prayers while the grandmother watched.

Aurélie pretended to sleep as the grandmother washed herself carefully, brushed her teeth with baking soda, put on more makeup and perfume. She left. Aurélie watched the lightbulb's curves on the ceiling. When she woke, she was being carried to her closet. The door was closed. In the bedroom, a man's voice, her grandmother's, the bed squeaking. The next day it was decided that she should just stay in the closet the whole time and was given her mother's old Tintin books and a flashlight. Over time, she would recognize three men's voices: one rich, as if encased in fat like a pâté, one helium giggling, one with rocks in it.

The grandmother kept perishables on the windowsill, where the pigeons and rats sometimes got them. The men came and left. Aurélie dreamt of adventures in strange cartoonish lands, ignored the noises, eventually slept through them. She went off to school and delighted in neatness, the pens with their cartouches, graph paper, the cleanness of orthography. She loved the *goûters* that the school gave out, madeleines filled with chocolate, and milk in pouches. She loved the loudness of the other children, watched them with delight. And so it went for six years or so.

In the spring after her eleventh birthday, Aurélie came home and found her grandmother in déshabille on the bed. She was stiff, skin icy. Tongue protruding. There may have been marks on her neck or maybe they were kisses. [No.] Two of her nails had been ripped off and the fingers ended in blood.

Aurélie went slowly downstairs. The concierge was not in her apartment. Aurélie went down the street and shuddered in the green-grocer's shop at the corner until he finished weighing asparagus for a lady in a fur hat. He was kind to Aurélie, gave her oranges in the winter. When they were alone, he leaned forward, smiling, and she whispered what she'd seen, and his face went stark. He took off running.

Later, she found herself on a plane over the Atlantic. Below, clouds feathered. Water pleated and smoothed itself. The stranger in the seat beside her had a pillowy biceps and a gentle hand, which passed over and over Aurélie's hair until at last the girl slept. When she woke, she was in her new country.

HER FRENCH PROFESSORS at Vassar had marveled: "You have no accent at all," they said.

"Oh, well," she said lightly. "Maybe I was a little French girl in a previous life."

In this one she was American, sounded American. Her mother tongue stayed under the surface. But the way roots push up paving stones from beneath, her French rippled her English. The way she said "forte," as in "Making your life run on rails, Lotto. That's my forte," and in her mouth it was strength, feminine. Lotto looked at her curiously, said, *"For–tay*, you mean?" in the American way.

For–tay: a nonsense word. "Of course," she said.

Or the *faux amis. Actually* for *currently. Abuse* for *mislead.* "I cannot breathe," she said, in the lobby on opening night, the crowd rushing Lotto, "in this affluence." She'd meant *crowd*, but, well, on second thought, the other worked just as well.

Despite her fluency, she would mishear, misinterpret. Her whole adult life she would believe one kept all one's important things— wills, birth certificates, passports, a single photo of a little girl—in a place in the bank called the Safety Posit box. Security, a hypothetical, remaining to be proved.

7

HER TONGUE WAS STILL HEALING from when she flipped the car. Mathilde said very little. The tongue hurt, true, but silence became her. When she spoke, she showed her contempt.

She went out at night and picked men up. The doctor still in his scrubs, smelling of iodine and clove cigarettes. The boy who sold gas at Stewart's, with his downy moustache and ability to pump for hours like a lonely derrick on the dry Texas plains. The mayor of the little village where Mathilde and Lotto had lived so happily; the owner of the bowling alley; a shy divorcé with shockingly floral taste in bed linens. A cowboy with four-hundred-dollar boots, he'd informed her with pride. A black jazz saxophonist in town for a wedding.

By then she'd made a name for herself without saying anything at all. School superintendent; owner of a hunting camp; CrossFit trainer with deltoids like hand grenades; a semi-famous poet she and her husband had known from the city, who'd come up to visit her on an impulsive hajj of Lotto grief. He'd put three fingers up her and she felt the cold of his wedding band.

She picked up a fat balding man who drove school buses. He only wanted to hold her and weep.

"Disgusting," she said. She was in the middle of the motel room, still in her bra. She'd shorn her hair to velveteen that day in the pool. The locks had drifted atop the surface like drowned snakes. "Stop crying," she said.

"I can't," he said. "I'm sorry."

"You *are* sorry," she said.

"You're just so pretty," he said. "And I'm so lonely."

She sat down heavily on the edge of the bed. There was a jungle scene on the comforter.

"Can I put my head in your lap?" he said.

"If you have to," she said. He lowered his cheek to her thighs. She braced herself against the weight of his head. His hair was soft and smelled of unscented soap, and from this vantage, his skin was very sweet, pink and smooth like a piglet's.

"My wife passed away," he said, his mouth tickling her leg. "Six months ago. Breast cancer."

"My husband died four months ago," she said. "Aneurysm." Pause. "I win," she said.

His eyelashes brushed her skin while he thought about this. "So you know?" he said.

"I do," she said.

The flick of the traffic light across the street from the motel filled the room with red and dark and red and dark. "How do you live?" she said.

"Ladies with casseroles. My kids call me every day. I've taken up kite building. It's all so stupid," he said.

"I don't have kids," she said.

"I'm sorry," he said.

"Not me. Best decision I ever made," she said.

"How do *you* live?" he said.

"By fucking the brains out of disgusting men."

"Hey!" he said, then laughed. "How's that working out for you?"

"Awful."

"Then why do you do it?"

Slowly, she said: "My husband was the second man I'd had sex with. I was faithful for twenty-four years. I want to know what I was missing."

"What were you missing?" he said.

"Nothing. Men are all absolutely terrible at sex. Except for my husband."

She thought: Well, there had been one or two surprises, but mostly that was true.

He picked his moon face up off her lap. Pink dent on her thigh, moisture. He looked at her hopefully. "I've been told I'm an excellent lover," he said.

She pulled her dress on over her head and zipped her boots to her knees. "Missed your window there, buddy," she said.

"Oh, come on," he said. "I'll be quick."

"Christ almighty," she said, and put her hand on the doorknob.

His voice went bitter when he said, "Have a good time being a whore."

"You poor sad little man," she said, and went out without turning around.

THERE WAS NOTHING Mathilde could do. Flickering images hurt her head; books left her hollow. She was so tired of the old way of telling stories, all those too-worn narrative paths, the familiar plot thickets, the fat social novels. She needed something messier, something sharper, something like a bomb going off.

She drank a great deal of wine and fell asleep, and when she woke, it was in the middle of the night to a cold bed empty of her husband. That was when she knew, with existential bitterness, that her husband had understood nothing of her.

Somehow, despite her politics and smarts, she had become a wife, and wives, as we all know, are invisible. The midnight elves of marriage. The house in the country, the apartment in the city, the taxes, the dog, all were her concern: he had no idea what she did with her time. It would have been compounded with children; thank goodness for childlessness, then. There was also this: for a number of his plays, at least half, she would silently steal in at night and refine what he had written. [Not rewrite; edit, burnish, make glow.] And she ran the business side of his work; she had horrified visions of all the money he would have let evaporate in his goodwill and indolence.

Once, during the previews of *The House in the Grove*, when, it felt, they were on the brink of a flop, she had been in the office of the theater. Deep afternoon, rain and coffee. She had been reaming out a script supervisor with such softly vicious skill that the poor boy's knees went out from under him and he had to sit on a crimson ottoman to gather himself. When she finished, she said, "You are dismissed."

The boy stood and fled.

She hadn't seen Lotto in the shadows of the hallway, glooming there.

"So," he said. "When directors ask members of the cast to come see you, I gather it's not for a pep talk. I had always thought it was for a pep talk. Magic cookie bars and café au lait, a nice little cry on your bosom."

"Some people just need a different kind of motivation," she said. She stood and stretched her neck, one side, the other.

"If I hadn't seen it," he said, "I wouldn't have believed it."

"Would you like me to stop?" she said. She wouldn't. They'd be in the poorhouse. But she could keep it quieter, make sure he wouldn't know.

He stepped in and locked the door behind him. "In truth, it turned me on," he said. He came close and said, "I see her indeed in the image of a Valkyrie maiden, riding her steed into the circle, amid thunder and lightning, and out again, bearing the body of some dead hero across her saddle." He picked her up and wrapped her legs around his hips, and turned, and pressed her back against the door.

Was he quoting? She didn't care. His voice was full of admiration. She closed her eyes. "Giddyap, steed," she said. He nickered in her ear.

She had a self she didn't devote to him. For one thing, she wrote, and not just invisibly in his manuscripts, which he must have thought magically tidied themselves up in the night. She wrote her own things that she kept to herself: surreptitious, sharp objects part story, part poetry. Published under a pseudonym. She'd begun in despair when she was almost forty and he'd fallen and broken himself, and in the break, she felt him moving away from her.

There was the other thing, the far worse thing. During the same time she began to write, she left him. He was wrapped up in his work. She came back and he never knew she was gone.

SHE'D SEEN THE ARTISTS' COLONY when she dropped Lotto off: they brought you lunch in wicker baskets and gave you your own stone cottage, with these long laughing conversations at night over candlelight. It had seemed a version of heaven. She'd held his face as she moved over him on the small and squeaky bed, but he'd turned her over, and when he shivered and gasped and put his head on her back to catch his breath, she felt a chill. She laughed off the premonition and drove away. For a few weeks, she'd be left alone in the tiny country house with God.

At first, she was sanguine. Her poor husband had had such a bad summer. There had been that spill down the airplane stairs, half of his body broken. He'd drunk too much, worked too little on his new play, been so very sad not to be at his high pitch of activity for so many months with all of the workshops and productions and business. And though she had been happy to have him to attend to in the house with her, to love him with her cupcakes and iced tea and bathing and many tiny kindnesses, she was glad when she took him for his birthday to the Podunk little opera house among the cow fields and watched his face as he sat forward, as he drank it all up. The tears shimmering in his eyes. She watched the contrails at intermission as a woman slunk up to greet him, blushing under the heat of his celebrity. Lotto, body broken, his expression so light, so ecstatic. It had been so long since all his faculties had been engaged.

So she had been fine to drop him off that gray November, to take a few weeks off from the constant care of him. He would be working with a young composer on an opera. Leo Sen.

But even the first week without Lotto, her life, her house, had been so empty. She forgot meals, ate dinners of tuna still in the can, spent too much time streaming films in bed. Time clicked by. The days grew colder, darker. Some days she never turned on the light, waking at eight when the sun rose weakly, sleeping at four-thirty when it bled itself out. She felt ursine. Norwegian. Her husband's calls trickled down from once a day to every few days. In her half sleep, she had fiery nightmares of Lotto telling her he no longer needed her, he was leaving, he loved another woman. In her fever, she imagined some poetess, frail and young, with heifer hips molded for birthing, a girl who was respected in her own rights as an artist, which Mathilde would never be. He would divorce Mathilde, and he and his new whispery paramour would live in the apartment in the city in a glut of sex and parties and babies, endless babies, all with his face in miniature. She imagined the poetess almost into existence. She was so lonely she could choke on it. She called and called, and he never answered the telephone. His calls decreased even more; he called once the last week. He didn't try to get kinky with her, which was so strange for Lotto that he could have been neutered.

He skipped Thanksgiving, though they'd had plans with friends and family in the house in the country; she'd had to cancel, ate the custard out of the pumpkin pie she'd made the day before and tossed the crust out the window for the raccoons. On the phone, Mathilde's voice had wobbled. Lotto's voice went distant. He said he was extending the stay into mid-December. She said something cutting and hung up. He called three times and she didn't pick up. The fourth time, she would, she decided. But though she waited by the phone, he didn't call back.

When he'd talked of Leo, there was a pulse under his words, a thrill. And suddenly, she could taste his infatuation. It left a bitterness on the back of her tongue.

Mathilde dreamt of Leo Sen. She knew he was a young man, from the few bios that existed online. And though Lotto was thoroughly straight—the daily greedy need of his hands told her this—her husband's desire had always been more to chase and capture the gleam of the person inside the body than the body itself. And there was a part of her husband that had always been so hungry for beauty. It was out of the question that Leo Sen's body could steal her husband; it was not out of the question that with his genius Leo could take her place in Lotto's affections. This was worse. In the dream, they were sitting at a table, Mathilde and Leo, and there was a giant pink cake, and though Mathilde was hungry, Leo was eating the cake, delicate bite by delicate bite, and she had to watch him eat it, smiling shyly until it was gone.

SHE SAT FOR A LONG, LONG TIME at the kitchen table, and every moment she sat, the anger took on mass, then darkness, then scales.

"I'll show him," she said aloud to God. God wagged her tail sadly. The dog missed Lotto, too.

It took ten minutes to make the arrangements, another twenty to pack herself and the dog. She drove off through the cherry trees, resolutely not looking at the little white house in the rearview mirror. God had shivered when she handed her over at the kennel. Mathilde had shivered all the way to the airport, on the plane, had taken two Ambien, and stopped shivering to sleep all the way to Thailand, waking with a bleary head and a blossoming urinary tract infection from holding her bladder while she slept.

When she walked out of the airport into the humidity, the human roil, the tropical stink and wind, her legs went weak.

Bangkok flashed by, pink and gold, swarms of bodies beneath the streetlights. Strands of holiday lights snaked up the trees, a kindness to the tourists. Mathilde's skin was thirsty for the moist wind, now blowing rotten with marsh reeds and mud, now blowing eucalyptus. She was too agitated for sleep, the hotel too hygienic, so she wandered back out into the dark. A bent woman swept a sidewalk with a bundle of sticks, a rat perched atop a wall. Mathilde wanted the bitterness of a gin and tonic on her tongue, and followed music blindly under a portico into a nightclub, empty so early in the night. Inside was tiered, balconied, the stage being set up for a band. The bartender patted Mathilde's hand when she delivered the drink, flash of warmth on the skin, then the cold of the glass, and Mathilde wanted to touch the lushness of the woman's black eyelashes. Someone sat beside her, an American man bursting out of his T-shirt, his head fuzzy like a ripe peach. Beside him a plump and laughing Thai woman. His voice oozed with intimacy; he'd already taken possession. Mathilde wanted to seize his words, roll them up in her fist, shove them down his throat. Instead, she left, found the hotel, lay sleepless in bed until dawn.

In the morning, she found herself on a boat to the Phi Phi Islands, salt on her lips from the wind. She had her own bungalow. She'd paid for a month, imagining Lotto coming home to an empty house, no dog, searching all the rooms for her, finding nothing, the terror hatching in his heart. Had someone kidnapped her? Had she run away with the circus? She was so agreeably flexible when it came to Lotto that she could have been a contortionist. Her hotel room was white and full of carved wood; they'd put polished strange fruits in a red bowl on the table and a towel folded in the shape of an elephant on the bed.

She opened the French door to the shushing sea, the call of children down the beach, and stripped the bed of its comforter because she wanted other people's germs nowhere near her skin, and lay back and closed her eyes and felt the old devastation rasp itself away.

When she woke, it was dinnertime, and the devastation was back, sharp-toothed, and it had gnawed a hole inside her.

She cried in the mirror, putting on her dress, her lipstick, cried too much for eye makeup. She sat at her own table alone, among the flowers and shining cutlery, and kind people served her kindly and positioned her facing the sea so she could cry in peace. She ate a bite of her food and drank a whole bottle of wine and walked home to her bungalow in bare feet over the sand.

The only day she had in the sun she wore her white bikini that bagged on her because she'd lost so much weight. The waiters saw the tears sliding out from under her sunglasses and brought her cold glasses of fruit juice without being asked. She burned and stayed in the sun until the skin on her shoulders was blistered.

The next morning, she awoke to an elephant in the window, slowly carrying a little girl up the beach, led by the halter by a slender young woman in a sarong. In the night, the anger had struck at the sadness and chased it off. Mathilde's body ached with yesterday's sun. She sat up and saw her face in the mirror opposite the bed, red and lightning sharp and already resolved.

Here was the Mathilde she'd grown so accustomed to, the one who had never *not* fought. Hers was a quiet, subtle warfare, but she had always been a warrior. That poetess was imaginary, she had to tell herself; that skinny musician named Leo had nothing on her because he was a boy, and he was powerless. Of course she'd prevail. How dare she walk away.

Two days after she arrived, her plane lifted off the ground and she was in the air again. She had spent six days molten on the inside. They handed God to her at the kennel, and the dog was so happy to see her she tried to nose her way into Mathilde's torso. Mathilde came home to the frigid house, stinking of the garbage she hadn't bothered to take out before she left. She put her suitcase in the closet upstairs to deal with later and sat down at the kitchen table with a cup of tea to strategize. The problem wasn't what she would do to go fetch Lotto back to her. It was what she wouldn't do. There were too many choices, there was too much possibility.

In a few moments, she heard a car on the drive. On the gravel came a step with a hitch in it.

Her husband came in the door. She let him wait.

Then she looked at him across the great distance. He was thinner, finer than when he left. As if whittled. On his face there was something she dropped her eyes to keep from seeing.

He sniffed the air, and to prevent him from speaking about the smell of garbage and the coldness of the house, which would have broken something, would have made it impossible to return to him, she crossed the kitchen and locked his mouth to hers. The taste, after so long, was strange, the texture rubbery. A shock of unfamiliarity. There was a slight shifting in him, a sense of bending. He was about to speak, but she pushed her hand hard against his mouth. She would have shoved her hand inside him if she could to keep the words from coming out. He understood. He smiled, dropped his bag, walked her backward into the wall. His great body on hers. The dog whimpering at his feet. She took her husband ferociously by the hips and pulled him ahead of her through the hall and up the stairs.

She pushed him with all she had and he landed very hard on the bed, hissing at residual pain in his bad left side. He looked up at her, a puzzlement moving on his face, and again he tried to talk, but she now cupped his mouth and shook her head and took off her shoes and pants, unbuttoned his shirt, his pants. Oh, those boxer briefs with the hole along the elastic, they broke her heart. His ribs were visible in his pale chest. His was a body having undergone terrific strain. She took four of his ties from the closet, remnants of his prep school boyhood, rarely worn now in his life. He laughed when she tied his wrists to the bed frame, though she felt sickly inside. Deadly. She knotted another tie into a blindfold. He made a strange noise, but she tied the fourth as a gag, and pulled it unnecessarily tight, the blue of the silk digging into his cheeks.

For a long time, she crouched above him, feeling powerful. She left her shirt on to hide her sunburn, the peeling skin; her face she'd explain by a long bike ride. She brushed the tip of him with her pelvis, gently, and at random. He started with every touch. He'd been reduced to this long body, so expectant, the eyes removed, the tongue removed. When he was panting behind his gag, she dropped onto him hard, not caring if it hurt him. She thought of—what? Scissors in fabric. It had been so long. It was so unfamiliar. The taut belly below her like the crisp top of crème brûlée. His face was red under the restraint; he was mouthing his fish mouth as if to free it, and she dug her fingernails into his waist, bringing up crescents of blood. His back arched off the mattress. The veins in his neck raised, blue.

He came before she did, and so she wouldn't. It didn't matter. She'd groped toward something in the dark and had somehow seized it back to her. She thought of the words she'd kept him from speaking, building up, mounting in him until there was unbearable pressure. And though she took the blindfold off, she left the gag, kissing his purple wrists. The way he looked at her now, with the silk darkened in an egg shape by spit, was quizzical. She leaned over and kissed him between the eyebrows. He held her loosely by the waist, and she waited until she knew he wasn't going to say anything about what he had gone through and then untied the last tie on his mouth. He sat up and kissed the pulse under her chin. His warmth, she had missed it so. His body's palette of stinks. He respected the silence. He rose and went to the bathroom to take a shower, and she went downstairs to boil some pasta. Puttanesca. She couldn't resist the dig.

When he came down, he showed her the cuts she'd raised on his sides. "Wildcat woman," he said, and there was a little sadness in the way he watched her now.

This should have been the end; this was not the end. She kept a Google search on Leo Sen. When, the week before Christmas, the terrible news of the boy's drowning in the cold ocean rose on the screen, she'd felt startled. And then victory, hot and terrible, rose in her chest. She looked away from her own face in the reflection of the computer screen.

When Lotto was upstairs, buried in his new play, she went to Stewart's and bought a newspaper. She saved it until the morning of Christmas Eve and put it at the mirror near the front door, where, she knew, Lotto would wait for Rachel and her wife and the children. He loved the holidays, as they matched the hot and jolly center of himself; he would be staring out the window to the country road impatiently and wouldn't fail to see the paper. He would know then what it was that she knew. She heard him whistling and came out of the bedroom at the top of the stairs to watch. He smiled at himself in the mirror, checked his profile, and his hand fell on the paper. He looked more closely and began to read. He went pale, clutched the table beneath him as if he would faint. Rachel and Elizabeth were bickering when the back door opened and they came into the kitchen, and the children were shrieking with excitement, and the dog was screaming with happiness at the prospect of them. She'd saved the paper for right now, because with company he wouldn't argue, he wouldn't make things worse by saying them aloud, and if he didn't say them immediately, he wouldn't say them at all. Lotto looked up into the mirror and saw Mathilde on the stairs behind him.

She looked at him looking at her. A new understanding came into his face and then vanished; he was frightened by this glimpse of what was in her and wouldn't watch it unfurl.

She took a step down the stairs. "Merry Christmas!" she called out. She was clean. Pine-scented. She descended. She was a child; she was as light as air.

WELCH DUNKEL HIER! sings Florestan in Beethoven's *Fidelio*, an opera about a marriage.

Most operas, it is true, are about marriage. Few marriages could be called operatic.

What darkness here! is what Florestan sings.

NEW YEAR'S DAY was the only day in her life she believed in a god. [Ha.] Rachel and Elizabeth and the children still asleep upstairs in the guest room. Mathilde made scones, a frittata. Her life a long and endless round of entertaining.

She turned on the television. Turmoil in black and gold, a fire in the night. A shot of bodies under sheets, neat as tents on a plain; a building with arched windows, blackened and unroofed. Someone's cell phone video just before the conflagration, a band on a stage shouting a countdown to the new year, sparklers spitting out fire, laughing faces. Now, outside, and people being helped to ambulances, lying on the ground. Devastated skin, charred and pink. The thought of meat inescapable. Mathilde felt a slow sickness overcome her. This place she recognized, she had been there just nights before. The press of bodies at the locked doors, the choking smoke, the screams. That juicy girl next to that big American man on the barstool. The bartender with the lush eyelashes, the shock of her cold hand on Mathilde's skin. When she heard Rachel's step on the top stair, she turned off the television, went quickly out into the backyard with God to compose herself in the cold.

That evening over dinner, Rachel and Elizabeth announced that Elizabeth was pregnant.

In bed, when Mathilde wept and wept, in gratitude and guilt and horror for all that she had escaped, Lotto thought it was because his sister was so rich with children and they were so terribly, unfairly poor. Later, he cried, too, into her hair. And the distance between them was bridged, and they were again united.

8

THE AIRPORT DEAFENED. Aurélie, eleven, alone, understood nothing. At last she saw the man holding the sign with her name on it and knew with a rush of relief that this must be her uncle, the much older brother of her mother. The child, the grandmother always said, of her wicked youth; though her old age was wicked as well. The man was jolly, round, red, full of sympathy. Already, she liked him.

"No, *mamzelle*," he said. "*Non oncle*. The driver."

She didn't understand, so he pantomimed driving a car. She swallowed her disappointment.

"No *parlez français*," the driver said. "Except *voulez-vous coucher avec moi*."

She blinked hard, and he said, "No, no, no, no, no. No *vous*. *Excusez-moi*. No *voulez coucher avec vous*." He flushed redder and chuckled all the way to the car.

He stopped off the highway to buy her a strawberry milkshake; it cloyed and made her stomach hurt but she drank it all because it was kind of him. She was frightened of spilling on the leather seats and held the cup carefully all the way to her uncle's house.

They stopped on a gravel drive. The house was a modest place for a man with a driver. Stern old Pennsylvania Dutch farmhouse of impenetrable stone and ancient windows so bubbled they played tricks with the landscape beyond. The driver carried her bag up to her room, which alone was twice the size of her grandmother's Paris apartment. In one wall was her own marble bathroom, with a green shower mat of such thickness it was like new spring grass in the park. She wanted to lie down on it immediately and sleep for days.

In the kitchen, the driver pulled out of the refrigerator a plate with a pale chicken cutlet, potato salad, beans, and a note her uncle had written in French about how he would meet her when he got home. Television, he counseled, was the best way to learn English. Do not leave the house. Make a list of the things she needed and the driver would see to it that she got them tomorrow.

It was hard for her to overlook how many mistakes he made with his spelling.

The driver showed her how to lock the door and put on the alarm. He wore a worried look on his flabby face, but he had to go.

She ate very close to the television, warming herself against its staticky screen, watching some incomprehensible show about leopards. She washed everything and put it all back where she thought it belonged, and tiptoed upstairs. She tried every door, but every one but hers was locked, then washed her hands and face and feet, brushed her teeth, and climbed into the bed, but it was too large and the room too full of shadows. She brought the duvet and a pillow into the empty closet and fell asleep on the carpet that smelled like dust.

In the thick of the night, she woke suddenly to find a thin man peering down at her from the doorway. Something about his large eyes and apple cheeks brought back her grandmother. He had ears like small, pale bat wings. His face brought her mother's, through the smoke of years, to her.

"So," he said in French. "The devil girl." He seemed amused, though he wasn't smiling.

She felt her breath twist. From the first, she understood he was very dangerous, despite his mild aspect. She would have to be careful. She would have to keep to herself.

"I'm not home often," the uncle said. "The driver will take you to buy your necessaries and the groceries you may need. He will drive you to and from the bus stop, which will take you to school. You will hardly see me."

She said a quiet thank-you, because silence would have been worse.

He looked at her for a long moment, and said, "My mother made me sleep in her closet as well. You must try to sleep in your bed."

"I will," she whispered. He closed the door, and she listened to him walking, unlocking, opening, shutting, relocking a series of doors. She kept listening to the silent house until the silence filled her and she slept again.

WITHIN THE FIRST HOUR of American school, the boy sitting in front of Aurélie turned around. He whispered, "Why is six afraid of seven? Because seven eight nine!"

She didn't understand. "You're stupid," he said.

Lunch an incomprehensible slab of bread and cheese. Milk that smelled rotten. She sat on the playground trying to be as small as possible, though she was very big for her age. The boy with the joke came by with three other boys.

"Orally, orally!" they cried, and stuck their tongues in one cheek, mimed a penis going in and out with their hands.

This she understood. She went to the teacher, a babylike worm with sparse white hair who had prided herself on talking to Aurélie all morning in her high school French patois.

Aurélie said as slowly as she could that though Aurélie was her given name, nobody called her that in Paris.

The city's name made the teacher's face light up. *"Non?"* she said. *"Et qu'est-ce que c'est le nom que vous préférez?"*

Aurélie thought. There was a girl in the form above her at school in Paris, a short, strong, and wry girl with flowing black hair. She was mysterious, cool, the one all the other girls courted with *berlingots* and *bandes dessinées*. When she was angry, words came whiplike to her lips. She used her power sparingly. Mathilde was her name.

"Mathilde," Aurélie said.

"Mathilde," the teacher said. *"Bon."*

Like that, all at once, Mathilde grew up over Aurélie's skin. She felt the other girl's stillness come over her, her cool eye, her quickness. When the boy in front of her turned around to mime a blow job, she darted her hand out and pinched his tongue hard through his cheek, and he yelped, and tears rose to his eyes, and the teacher turned to find Mathilde sitting calmly. The boy was punished for making noise. She watched as, over the course of the hour, twin purple grapes developed on his cheek. She wanted to suck them.

AT A PARTY ONCE, in the happy underground years in Greenwich Village, when Lotto and she had been so desperately poor [holes in her socks, lunches of sunshine and water], their Christmas lights making a chain of lemons on the walls, rotgut vodka mixed with juice, she was flipping through the CDs when she heard someone shout out *Aurélie!* and she was immediately eleven again, desperate, lonely, confused. She spun around. But it was her husband, full-bore: *Didn't know it was a suppository, so he took it orally!* Friends hooted; girls danced by with cups in their hands. Mathilde went into the bedroom, feeling robotic, passed the three engrossed bodies on the bed without looking. She hoped when they were done they'd change the duvet cover. She went into the closet that stank of cedar blocks and the dust of her own skin. She nestled among her shoes. Fell asleep. Woke to Lotto hours later opening the door and laughing and picking her up tenderly and putting her into bed. She was glad of the mattress stripped of its sheets, she and her husband alone at last, his hot, avid hand on her neck, her upper thigh. "Yes," she said. She didn't want to, really, but it didn't matter. The weight of his body was pressing her into the present. Mathilde was slowly coming back. [And Aurélie, that sad, lost girl, vanished again.]

AURÉLIE WAS MEEK AND MILD; Mathilde boiled underneath a placid skin.

Once, she was playing tetherball and a boy in her class was winning and she deliberately hit the ball so hard into his face that he was knocked down and his head bounced on the asphalt and he had a concussion. Once, she heard her name from a pocket of girls who then laughed. She waited. At lunch a week later, she sat next to the most popular of those girls and waited until she took a big bite of her sandwich and, underneath the table, stabbed her fork into the girl's thigh. The girl spat out the bite before screaming, and Mathilde had had time to hide the fork under a table buttress. She blinked her huge eyes at the teacher and was believed.

The other children regarded her now with fear in their faces. Mathilde floated through her days coolly, as if she were in the clouds, watching dispassionately down. Her uncle's in Pennsylvania was only a place to stay, chill and dim, not a home. She imagined for herself a separate life, a chaotic mess with six sisters, loud pop on the radio, nail polish stink and bobby pins on the vanity. Game nights with popcorn and screaming fights. Voice from the other bed in the night. The sole welcome in her uncle's house was the warm buzz of the television. She mocked a soap opera, *The Starrs in Your Eyes*, in the characters' own voices, until she lost her accent. Her uncle was never home. Did she burn to see what was behind those locked doors? She did. But she didn't pick the locks. [Already, a miracle of self-possession.] On Sundays, the driver took her to the grocery store, and if she was fast and they still had time, he'd drive her to a little park near a river to feed sheets of white bread to the ducks.

Her loneliness was so huge it took the form of the upstairs hall-way, dark and lined with locked doors.

Once, even, swimming in the river, a leech attached to her inner thigh, so close to what mattered that it thrilled her and she left it there, thought of it throughout her days, her invisible friend. When it fell off in the shower and she accidentally stepped on it, she wept.

To stay away from the house, she joined the time-intensive clubs at school that didn't require her to speak. She swam and joined the chess team and learned the flute for the band, a thoroughly demean-ing instrument, she felt, but easy to master.

In the height of her happiness many years later, she would think of that solitary little girl, face downturned like a demure fucking bell-flower, while inside there was the maelstrom. She'd want to smack that kid hard. Or pick her up in her arms and cover her eyes and run somewhere safe with her.

Instead, her uncle adopted her when she was twelve. She wasn't aware he was going to until the day before the court hearing. The driver told her.

He'd gained so much weight over the year that his stomach had grown a little stomach. When he was lifting her groceries to the trunk, she had the urge to bury her face in the many pillows of him.

"Adopted! Isn't that nice?" the driver said. "Now you needn't worry, *mamzelle*, about having to go somewhere else. You belong here now."

When he saw her expression, he touched her—was it the first time he'd touched her?—on the crown of the head, and said, "Oh, girl pie. Don't take it so hard."

On the ride home, her silence was like the fields they were pass-ing. Ice-wracked, weary with blackbirds.

Inside the car, the driver said, "I'm supposed to call you Miss Yoder now."

"Yoder?" she said. "But that wasn't my grandmother's name."

The driver's eyes in the rearview grew merry. "They say your uncle changed his name to the first thing he saw when he got to Philly. Reading Terminal Market, it was. Yoder's pies."

Then a flash of alarm in his face, and he said, "You won't tell I said so."

"Who would I tell? I don't talk to anybody but you," she said.

"Sweet thing," he said. "You break my heart. You do."

The day Mathilde turned thirteen, she found one door downstairs unlocked and open a crack. Her uncle must have left it for her just so. For a moment, the hunger in her tipped over and she couldn't suppress her curiosity. She entered. It was a library, with leather couches and Tiffany lights, and save for a glass cabinet that held what Mathilde would later find out to be antique Japanese erotica, she could reach all of the books in the room without stretching. They were strange things, ancient hardcovers that seemed, despite their similar deckled edges and cloth bindings, to be gathered randomly. In her sophisticated years, she'd understand that these were books sold by the yard, mostly for decorative purposes. But in those bad years, in her early teens, they were volleys from a kinder Victorian world. She read them all. She was so versed in Ian Maclaren and Anthony Hope, Booth Tarkington and Winston Churchill [the American], Mary Augusta Ward and Frances Hodgson Burnett, that the sentences in her English papers became ever more ornate and elaborate. American education being what it is, her teachers took her rococo sentences to be evidence of a prodigious facility with language that she didn't actually have. She won all the English awards her last year in middle school. She won them all in high school, also. On her thirteenth birthday, she thought, closing the library door behind her, that at this rate she would know what was in every room of the house by the time she was thirty.

Except that, one month later, her uncle left a door unlocked unintentionally.

She wasn't supposed to be home. She had walked back from school because of the half day called—there was a brutal snowstorm on the horizon—and the chauffeur couldn't be reached on the office phone, and she missed the bus anyway. She walked in the freezing cold, her bare knees numbed after five minutes. She pushed the last two miles in a sideways wind with her fingers making blinders to keep the snow out.

When she came back to the stone house, she had to crouch on the doorstep with her hands under her bra to warm them enough to work the key. She heard voices inside, at the end of the hall where the library was. She took off her shoes, feet blocks of ice, and crept to the kitchen, where there were half-eaten sandwiches on the counter. A bag of chips splayed its barbecue guts. Someone's cigarette burned in a teacup, quarter inch of ash. In the windows, the storm was almost black.

She tried to go toward the staircase noiselessly but stopped short: under the stairway there was a small room, and she'd never seen the door open until now. She heard footsteps and stepped inside, quietly shutting the door. The overhead light was on. She flicked it off. She crouched behind a strange statue of a horse head and breathed into her hand. The footsteps passed. There were loud male voices and more steps. In the dark, her warming skin was full of chewing ants.

The great front door slammed, and she waited and waited, but she could feel that the house was empty and that she was alone.

She turned the light on and saw what she'd only vaguely seen before. Along the wall there were canvases with their faces turned away and little pieces of statuary. She picked up a painted board. It was heavy, solid. She turned it around and almost dropped it. Never in her life had she seen a more perfect thing. At the bottom, in the foreground, there was a curvy white horse with a man in blue robes riding it, the fabric so lush she touched it to make sure it wasn't real. Behind him were other men, other horses, a jagged rock face. Up against the blue sky was a soft, pale city so perfect it seemed made of bones.

She memorized it. At last she put it back down and took off her sweater to wipe up the snowmelt that had dripped onto the floor from her hair and clothes. She closed the door behind her and felt a keen loss when she heard the lock fall into place.

She went up the stairs and lay in the dark with her eyes closed to resee the panel. When the chauffeur came in, calling worriedly for her, she reached out her window, gathered two handfuls of snow, put both on her hair, and ran to the kitchen.

"Oh, girl," he said, sitting heavily down. "I thought we lost you in that storm." She didn't mind that his concern had been for both of them, that if he had, indeed, lost her he would have been in danger himself.

"I got in a few minutes ago," she said, still shivering, and he took her hand and felt how cold it was and made her sit and made cocoa from scratch, then chocolate chip cookies, too.

FOR HER FOURTEENTH BIRTHDAY, Mathilde's uncle took her out to dinner. In three years, they had never shared a meal. She'd opened her bedroom door to see the red dress he'd laid on her bed like a skinny girl thrown backward. Beside it was her first pair of high heels, three inches tall and black. She dressed slowly.

The restaurant was warm, a converted farmhouse not unlike her uncle's, but with a fire burning in the hearth. Her uncle looked ill in the golden light, as if his skin were candle tallow, half melted. She steeled herself to look at him while he ordered for both of them. Caesar salad. Steak tartare with a quail's egg atop, followed by filet mignon. Side of roasted potatoes and asparagus. Côtes du Rhône. Mathilde had been a vegetarian since she saw an exposé on television about industrial husbandry, cows hung on hooks and flayed alive, chickens squeezed into cages that broke their legs and living out their days caked in their own shit.

When the salads came, the uncle twirled a brown anchovy on his fork and congratulated her, in French, for being so poised and self-sufficient. He swallowed without chewing; like a shark, she knew from television.

"I have no choice. I've been left entirely alone," Mathilde said. She hated herself for allowing her mouth to twitch and betray her.

He put his fork down and looked at her. "Oh, please, Aurélie. You weren't beaten. You weren't starved. You go to school and the dentist and the doctor. I had none of those things. You are being melodramatic. This isn't *Oliver Twist*, you are not some child in a coal mine. I have been kind to you."

"Blacking factory. Dickens worked in a blacking factory," she said. She switched to English. "No, I wouldn't say you have never been unkind."

He sensed the insult better than he understood it. "No matter. I am all you ever would have had. *Diablesse*, they called you. I must say, I have seen no evidence of your devil, to my disappointment. Either it's not there, or you have learned to dissimulate as all good devils do."

"Perhaps living in fear can drive all devils out of a person," she said. "Exorcism by terror." She drank her water and poured wine to the top of the glass and drank it down.

"You have witnessed nothing you should fear," he said. He leaned forward and smiled. "I could change that if you prefer."

For a moment, she stopped breathing. Perhaps it was the wine that made her vision swim. "No, thank you," she said.

"You are welcome," he said. He finished the salad, wiped his mouth, and said, "Nobody has told you that your parents have new babies. New, well. Relatively. One is three and one is five. Little boys.

Your brothers, I suppose. I'd show you the photo my sister sent, but I seem to have lost it."

[Strange how things are associated with their particular pains: Caesar salad forever a suffocating sadness.]

She smiled at a spot above her uncle's head, where the firelight reflected off an antique barometer. It also shined through his pointed ears. She said nothing.

He said, when the filet came, "You are very tall. Skinny. Odd-looking, which seems fashionable. You could be a model, perhaps. Even put yourself through college."

She drank her water in slow and even sips.

"Ah," he said. "You thought I was going to send you to college. But my obligation ends at eighteen."

"You could afford it," she said.

"I could," he said. "But I'm interested in watching what you'll do. Struggle forms character. No struggle, no character. Nobody gave me a thing in my life," he said. "Not one thing. I earned it all."

"And look at you now," she said.

He smiled at her and the resemblance to her grandmother, her long-ago mother, absent all warmth, made her skin prickle. "Be careful," he said.

The untouched meat on her plate became fuzzy and slowly cleared. "Why do you hate me?" she said.

"Oh, child. I have no feelings about you whatsoever," he said; this was the kindest thing he would ever say to her.

He slurped down a *panna cotta*. There was cream in the folds of his mouth.

The check arrived and a man came up to her uncle and shook his hand, murmuring in his ear, and Mathilde gratefully turned away because, from the corner of her eye, she caught a slight movement in the doorway. A white cat had inserted its head into the room and was pulling its taut body on its forepaws, staring fixedly into the woodpile. Tiny tiger, hunting. For some time, she was lulled by the cat's immobility, only the tiny twitch at the end of the tail to signal life; and then, without warning, the cat leapt. When it turned, a soft, boneless, gray thing hung in its mouth. A field mouse, Mathilde thought. The cat trotted off, its tail jaunty with pride. When she turned back to her uncle and his friend, they were looking at her, amused.

"Dmitri just said that you are the cat. The cat is you," the uncle said.

No. She had always hated cats. They seemed so full of rage. She put her napkin on the table and smiled with all her teeth.

9

THE ONLY ONE WHO RETURNED and returned and returned was Rachel.

Rachel made soup and focaccia, which Mathilde fed to the dog.

Rachel returned alone, with Elizabeth, with the children, who ran in the fields with God until the dog collapsed, and then combed all the tufts and brambles out of her fur and left her lax and panting for hours afterward.

"I don't want to see you," Mathilde shouted at Rachel when she came alone one morning with cheese danishes and fresh juice. "Go away."

"Abuse me all you want," Rachel said. She put the pastries down on the mat and stood again, fierce in the dim morning light. That god-awful tattoo up her arm, all spiderweb and mermaid and a little turnip, some sort of bondage fantasia or, at the very least, a mixed metaphor. The family had a talent for figurative knots. Rachel said: "I won't go away. I'll come back again and again and again until you're well."

"I'm warning you," Mathilde said, through the glass door. "I'm the worst person you know."

"That is untrue," Rachel said. "You are one of the kindest, most generous people I've ever met. You're my sister and I love you."

"Ha. You don't know me," Mathilde said.

"But I do," Rachel said. She laughed, and though all her life Mathilde had felt a sort of sorrow that Rachel was nothing like her brother, so great and shining, now she saw Lotto in his little sister's face, the same semi-dimple in the cheek, the strong teeth. Mathilde shut her eyes and locked the door. Even still, with her endless nervous energy, Rachel came back and she came back and she came back.

SHE'D FALLEN ASLEEP in the pool house. Six months after Lotto died, grim heat of August. Their old friend Samuel had come that morning to remonstrate, nostrils flaring, and she'd waited him out in the pool house while he circled the house, bellowing her name.

Oh, little Samuel! she thought, listening. Kind son of a corrupt senator father. It had become a joke, unbelievable, the trials of Samuel, the DUIs, the divorces, the cancer, the house he'd burned down in his thirties. The racist a year ago who'd found Sam walking home at night from a movie and beat him to concussion. Not the smartest or the bravest, but he'd been born with preternatural confidence. Job was just a whiner compared with him.

Samuel was gone when she woke. Her skin was glazed in sweat. Her mouth was sandpaper and tar and she thought of the berries waiting on the countertop for her, the pie she could already taste. Butter, zest, essence of summer, salt. She heard another car turn onto the gravel. God was barking in the kitchen. She came across the too-bright grass and into the house and up the stairs to see from her bedroom who had arrived. Even the tiger lilies Mathilde had cut for herself seemed to be sweating.

A young person stepped out of an inexpensive little car: some kind of Hyundai or Kia. Rental. City boy. Boy, well. Thirty or thereabouts. Alone so long, Mathilde had taken to thinking of herself as wizened, ancient. To see herself in the mirror was to see the shock of unexpected youth.

There was something about this person's loose-limbed walk across the drive that held her. He was medium-sized, dark-haired, handsome with his long eyelashes and defined jaw. Something whirred in her chest uncomfortably, which she had come to recognize in the past months as a strange chimera of rage and lust. Well! Only one way to exorcise it! She sniffed her armpits. They'd do.

She startled when she saw that the boy was looking up at her in the window as he came up to the door: she had taken to wearing Lotto's white T-shirts and had sweated through this one so it was transparent, her nipples saying a double hello. She pulled on a tunic and descended and opened the door to the boy. God snuffled at his shoes, and he knelt and petted her. When he stood to shake Mathilde's hand, his palm was covered with a fine layer of dog down and was clammy beneath. When he touched her, he burst into tears.

"Well," she said. "Another of my husband's mourners, I see."

Her husband, patron saint of failed actors. Because it was clear now that this boy was an actor. He had that cocksure carriage, the observant brightness. So many of them had shown up to touch the great man's hem, but there was no hem left, Mathilde having given away or burned nearly everything, save the books and manuscripts. Only Mathilde was left, his homelier husk. The old wifey-wife.

"I never knew him. But you can say I'm a mourner, I guess," the boy said, turning away to wipe his face. When he turned back, he was red, embarrassed. "I'm so sorry," he said.

"I've made iced tea," Mathilde heard herself say. "Wait here in the rocker and I'll bring some."

By the time she came back, the boy had calmed. Sweat curled the hair at his temples. She put on the overhead porch fan and set the tray down on the little table, taking a lemon bar for herself. She'd survived on wine and sugar for months because, fuck it, she never really got a childhood, and what was grief but an extended tantrum to be salved by sex and candy?

The boy-man picked up his tea and touched the tray, which she'd gotten in some rag-and-bone shop in London. He touched the herald and read aloud, *"Non sanz droict."* He bolted up in his chair, spill-ing iced tea on his lap, and said, "Oh my god, that's Shakespeare's family—"

"Calm down," she said. "It's Victorian, a fake. He reacted exactly the way you did. He thought we had something that passed through old Willie's hands and almost wet himself."

"For so many years, I dreamt of driving up here," the boy said. "Just to say hello. I dreamt that he'd invite me in and we'd have a nice dinner and talk and talk. I always knew we'd get along famously, he and I. Lancelot. And me."

"His friends called him Lotto," she said. "I'm Mathilde."

"I know. The Dragon Wife," he said. "I'm Land."

With extreme slowness, she said, "Did you just call me the Dragon Wife?"

"Oh. Sorry. That's what all the actors in the company called you when I was in *Grimoire* and *One-Eyed King*. Revival, not first-run. Of course, you'd know that. Because you protected him. You made sure he was paid on time, and kept people away, and you did it all while seeming so nice. I thought it was an honorific. Like, a joke you were in on."

"No," she said. "I was not in on this particular joke."

"Whoops," he said.

"It's true," Mathilde said, after some time. "I could breathe fire."

She thought of how Lotto, in later years, had been called the Lion. With his dander up, he could roar. He looked leonine, too: his corona of white-shot gold, the fine, sharp cheekbones. He'd leap onstage, offended by some actor flubbing his precious lines, and there he'd pace, sleek and swift with his long lovely body, growling. He could be deadly. Fierce. The name was not inapt. But please, Mathilde knew lions. The male lolled beautifully, lazy in the sun. The female, less lovely by miles, was the one who brought back the kill.

The boy was sweating. His blue oxford shirt was hooped wetly under the arms. He was emitting a smell that was not unpleasant, exactly. It was a clean stink. Funny, she thought, looking over the banks of snapdragons to the river. Her mother had smelled of cold and scales, her father of stone dust and dog. She imagined her husband's mother, whom she had never met, had a whiff of rotting apples, although her stationery had stunk of baby powder and rose perfume. Sallie was starch, cedar. Her dead grandmother, sandalwood. Her uncle, Swiss cheese. People told her that she smelled like garlic, like chalk, like nothing at all. Lotto, clean as camphor at his neck and belly, like electrified pennies at the armpit, like chlorine at the groin.

She swallowed. Such things, details noticed only on the edges of thought, would not return.

"Land," Mathilde said. "Odd name for a guy like you."

"Short for Roland," the boy said.

Where the August sun had been steaming over the river, a green cloud was forming. It was still terrifically hot, but the birds had stopped singing. A feral cat scooted up the road on swift paws. It would rain soon.

"All right, Roland," Mathilde said, suppressing a sigh. "Sing your song."

Land told her what she already knew: actor. Had a recurring role on this soap opera, minor, but it paid the bills. *The Starrs in Your Eyes?* he said. "Heard of it?" He looked at her hopefully then grimaced. "I see," he said. "Soaps aren't your thing. Mine, either. It's hackwork. But I got the job as soon as I got to the city. Fifteen years ago, literally the first audition I walked into. And it's good money. And I can do plays in the summer when we don't film." He shrugged. "I'm not a superstar, but I work all the time. That's a kind of success, I guess."

"You don't need to argue for the benefits of a steady gig," she said. She felt reckless, disloyal. "Lotto never got one when he was an actor. It would have been an immense relief to have some pay coming in all those years. I worked my ass off and he made, maximum, seven thousand dollars a year until he started writing."

"Thank god he started writing," Land said. He told her that every birthday he took the day off to drive out to the beach and read *The Springs*. Lancelot never got his fair shakes as the genius he was.

"He would have agreed," Mathilde said drily.

"But I love that about him. That arrogance," Land said.

"I did, too," Mathilde said.

The clouds like blackberry jam in the sky, faint double-boiler thunder from the north. All the things she could do, other than sit here, were gathering in the cool shadows of the house behind her, watching through the window. She was nailed to the chair.

She liked this boy, liked him enormously, more than anyone she'd met since Lotto died. She could just open her mouth and eat him he was so sweet; there was something easy about him, a gentleness she'd always loved in manly men.

"To tell you the truth, I wanted to meet you almost as much as I wanted to meet him," Land said.

"Why?" she said. She was blushing. Flirting? It wasn't impossible.

"You're the untold story," he said. "The mystery."

"What mystery?" she said.

"The woman he chose to spend his life with," Land said. "He's easy to know. There are billions of interviews, and his plays come from him and give you a little window in. But you're back in the shadows, hiding there. You're the interesting one."

It took a very long moment as they sat there on the porch, sweating in silence, for Mathilde to say to the boy, "I am not the interesting one."

She knew she was the interesting one.

"You're a bad liar," he said.

She looked at him and imagined him in bed, those lovely fingers with the buffed nail beds, the neck with the visible cords, the strong jaw, that good body clear under his clothes, that sensitive face, and knew he'd be very good at fucking.

"Let's go inside," she said, and stood.

He blinked, startled. Then he stood and opened the door for her, following her in.

He was attentive, soft where he should be, strong under her arms. But there was something off. It wasn't that she was so much older than he was; she estimated ten years. Fifteen, max. And it wasn't that she didn't know him, really. She hadn't really known anybody she'd taken to bed with her the past six months. The absence of story was what she liked about them. But they were in the bathroom and she was watching his high-boned face behind her, his hand gripping her short hair, the other on her shoulder, and though it felt marvelous, she couldn't focus.

"I can't hold out any longer," he said. He was shining with sweat.

"Don't," she said, and he was a gentleman and pulled out and groaned, and there was a heat on her back just above the coccyx.

"Nice," she said. "Supersexy porn move."

He laughed and dabbed her off with a warm washcloth. In the window, the bushes by the river were being flattened by wind and the hard, sparse rain that had begun to fall. "Sorry," he said. "I didn't know what else to do. Didn't want to, you know. Get you in the family way."

She stood and stretched her arms above her head. "Don't worry," she said. "I'm old."

"You are not," he said.

"Well. I'm barren," she said. She didn't say *by choice*. He nodded and went a little inward, then said, suddenly, "Is that why you didn't have any kids?" Then he blushed and crossed his arms over his chest, and said, "I'm so sorry. That was rude. I was just wondering why you and he didn't. Have kids, I mean."

"That's why," she said.

"Something medical?" he said. "I'm prying. Don't answer if it's annoying."

"I was sterilized when I was younger." His silence was pointed, and she said, "He didn't know. He thought I was just plain barren. It made him feel noble to suffer in silence."

Why was she telling this boy all of this? Because there were no stakes. Lotto was gone. The secret would hurt nobody. Plus, she liked the boy, wanted to give him something; the previous pilgrims had carried off almost everything else. She suspected he had ulterior motives. An article, a book, an exposé at some point. If he wrote about the sex, the rainstorm, she would come off as desperate or sad or desperately sad. It was all accurate. So be it.

"But why wouldn't you tell him?" he said. Oh, the puppy, he sounded wounded on her husband's behalf.

"Because nobody needs my genes in the world," she said.

Land said, "But his genes. I mean, the kid might have been a genius, too."

Mathilde pulled on the bathrobe and swept her hand through her short hair. She looked at herself in the mirror and admired the rosy flush. The rain pounded harder on the roof; she liked the sound, the sense of coziness of the gray and falling day outside.

"Lotto would have been a terrific father," she said. "But the kids of geniuses are never geniuses."

"True," Land said.

She touched his face and he flinched, then leaned forward to rest his cheek in her hand. Little pet, she thought. "I want to make you dinner," she said.

"I'd love dinner," he said.

"And then I want you to fuck me again," she said.

"I'd love to fuck you again," he said, laughing.

At dawn, when she woke, the house had gone quiet and she knew that Land had left.

A shame. I could have kept him around for a little while, she thought. Used him as a pool boy. As human cardio machine. God grumbled at the door, having been banished. When Mathilde went out, the dog came in and flounced herself down on the bed.

In the kitchen, there was a fruit salad macerating in its juices. He'd made a pot of coffee, which was lukewarm now. In the blue bowl with the slowly ripening green tomatoes from the garden, the sweet boy had left a note in an envelope. Mathilde would leave it there for weeks before she opened it. Seeing it there, the white in the red in the blue, made her feel for the first time since her husband left her as if she had kind and gentle company in the house with her. Something hot in her began to cool and, in cooling, began to anneal.

MAKE ME HAPPY, Frankenstein's monster pleaded with its maker, *and I shall again be virtuous.*

10

MATHILDE WAS SIXTEEN. She woke to find her uncle swaying over her; she had learned to sleep in a bed. He was saying, "Aurélie, this is important. Do not go downstairs," and in the hollow after his words, she could hear men's voices below, shouting, music. His face was expressionless but the color in his cheeks was high. Without anyone's saying a thing, she'd begun to understand that her uncle was some kind of manager in a bad organization. He was often in Philadelphia. He hissed orders into a huge, clunky early version of a mobile phone, was inexplicably gone for weeks, and came back if not tan, then tanner. [Still apparent in him, the tiny boy, mewling in cold and hunger. It's less delicious, this badness bred from survival.] He left, and she lay frozen for some time. The shouting now did not seem so joyous. She heard anger, fear. When she could move, she pulled the couch out from where it rested against the wall and brought the duvet and pillow behind it and in that place, the exact shape of her body, she fell asleep swiftly, as if held there. Nobody, as far as she knew, had come to her room in the night. Still, the air felt disturbed, as if she'd narrowly avoided something.

She crept like a mouse through her teenaged years. Flute and swimming and books, all the wordless arts. She made herself so small her uncle would forget her.

———

HER SENIOR YEAR, she opened the letter telling her she'd been accepted to the one school she'd applied to, early, for no other reason than that she'd loved the oddball essay questions in the application. How such small things can decide one's fate. But the whistling conflagration of joy had ebbed to embers days later, when she understood she couldn't pay. If she couldn't pay, she couldn't go. Simple as that.

She took a train to the city. Her life, she would later understand, would be scarred with them.

A Saturday express. Her heart sang with desperation in her rib cage. A newspaper spun slowly on the platform in the wind.

She wore the red dress her uncle had bought for her fourteenth birthday and the high heels that pinched savagely. She made a crown of her blond braids. In the mirror, she'd seen no beauty in her angles and strange lashes, in her grossly fat lips, but hoped others might. She would burn, later, with what she didn't know. That she should have worn her bra, trimmed her pubic hair back to prepubescence, brought photographs. That such things as headshots even existed in the world.

A man had watched her climb into the car from his seat in the rear. He smiled at the way she moved her body as if it were new out of the box, at the dangerous jut to her chin. After some time, he came up the corridor and sat across from her, though the car was otherwise empty. She felt him looking at her and ignored him as long as she could, and when she looked up, he was there.

He laughed. He had an ugly mastiff's face, all bulging eyes and jowl. He had the eyebrows of a jokester, peaked high, giving him an air of intimate mischief, as if he were about to whisper a punch line in her ear. Despite herself, she leaned forward. This would be his effect, a pleasant mirroring, a swiftly established accord. He was the quiet hit of every party; he never said a word, but everyone believed he was simpatico.

He looked at her, and she pretended to read her book, her head on fire. He leaned forward. He put his hands on her knees, the thumbs gentle on the skin of her inside thighs. He smelled delicious, like verbena and cordovan.

She looked up. "I'm only eighteen," she said.

"All the better," he said.

She stood and went shakily to the bathroom and sat there through the pulses of the train, holding herself with her arms, until the conductor said Penn Station. When she got off, she felt liberated—she was in the city!—and she wanted to run and laugh. But as she walked swiftly toward what she knew was her future, she looked up into the mirrored glass by a doughnut store and saw the man from the train ten feet behind her. He was unhurried. She felt the back of her heel go hot then blister and, on the street, a warm wash of relief when the blister burst, then the sting. She was too proud to stop.

She didn't pause until she reached the building where the agency was. The guards, used to pretty, wobbly, underage girls, parted to let her in.

She was inside for hours. For hours, he sat in the café opposite, with a hardcover book and a lemonade, waiting.

When she came out, she felt deboned, her bottom lids red. Her braids had frizzed in the unseasonable heat. He followed her down the street, a plastic bag and the book in his hand, until her stride became a limp and he stepped in front of her and offered a coffee. She'd eaten nothing since dinner the night before. She put her hands on her hips, staring, then right-faced into a sandwich shop and ordered a cappuccino and a mozzarella panini. *"Porca madonna,"* he said. *"Panino.* It's singular."

She turned to the girl at the counter and said, "I'd like two. *Panini.* Two *cappuccini."*

He chuckled and paid. She ate the sandwiches slowly, chewing thirty times with each bite. She looked everywhere but at him. She'd never had caffeine before and it filled her fingers with a kind of elation. She decided to drive the man off with her exigency and ordered an éclair and another cappuccino, but he paid without comment and watched her eat.

"You don't eat?" she said.

"Not much," he said. "I used to be a fat boy."

Now she could see the sad, fat child in the mismatched jowls and thin shoulders, and felt something heavy in her shifting toward him.

"They said I needed to lose ten pounds," she said.

"You're perfect," he said. "They can jump off a bridge. They said no?"

"They said I need to lose ten pounds and send them pictures and they'd start me out with catalog work. Build my way up."

He considered her with a straw in the corner of his mouth. "But you were unhappy with that. Because you're not a girl who starts small," he said. "You are a young queen."

"No," she said. She fought the emotion rising to her face and mastered it. It had begun to rain outside, hard, thick spatters on the hot pavement. A low miasma rose from the ground, and the air shifted toward coolness.

She listened to the pounding of the rain as he leaned forward and took her foot in his hand and took off the shoe. He looked at the bleeding, jagged blister. He dabbed it with a paper napkin dipped in ice water and took from his plastic bag from the drugstore, which he'd visited while she was at the agency, a big box of bandages and a tube of ointment. When he was finished administering to her feet, he took out a pair of plastic shower sandals with massaging nubs.

"You see," he said, lowering her feet to the ground. She could weep for the relief. "I take care of things," he said. He took a wet wipe from his pockets and fastidiously cleaned his hands.

"I see," she said.

"We can be friends, you and I. I'm unmarried," he said. "I'm kind to girls. I don't hurt anybody. I'll make sure you're looked after. And I'm clean."

Of course he was clean; his nails were pearly; his skin had the sheen of a soap bubble. Later, she'd hear of AIDS and understand.

She closed her eyes and pulled the long-ago Mathilde, the one from the Parisian schoolyard, tighter to her body. She opened her eyes and put on her lipstick by feel. She blotted her lips on a napkin, crossed her legs, and said, "So."

He said, in a low voice, "So. Come to my apartment. I'll make you dinner. We can"—and his eyebrows shot skyward—"talk."

"Not dinner, no," she said. He looked at her, calculating.

"We can make a deal, then. Negotiate. Stay the night," he said. "If you can convince your parents. Say you met a school friend in town. I can do a passable imitation of a schoolgirl's father."

"Parents aren't an obstacle," she said. "I only have an uncle. He doesn't care."

"Then what is the obstacle?" he said.

"I'm not cheap," she said.

"All right." He leaned back. She wanted to crush the latent joke he never quite delivered, flatten it under her knuckles. "Tell me. What is it that you most want in the world, young queen."

She took a deep breath and pressed her knees together to stop them from shaking. "College tuition," she said. "For all four years."

He put both hands flat on the table and gave a sharp laugh. "I was thinking a handbag. But you were thinking indentured servitude?" he said.

She thought: Oh. [So young! So capable of surprise.] Then she thought: Oh, no, he had laughed at her. Her face was on fire, she felt, striding out. He was behind her at the door; he put his suit coat over her head and gestured for a cab from the awning. Maybe he was made of spun sugar, would melt in the wet.

She slid in, and he stood bent in the door, but she wouldn't move over to let him in. "We can talk about this," he said. "I'm sorry. You astonished me. That's all."

"Forget it," she said.

"How can I?" he said. He touched her gently under the chin and she had to fight the urge to close her eyes and rest her head in his palm.

"Call me on Wednesday," he said, putting a card in her hand, and though she wanted to say no again, she didn't, and she didn't crumple it up. He tossed a bill over the seat to the driver and shut the door gently behind her. Later, in the window of the train, her face was pale and floating over a green spin of Pennsylvania. She was thinking so hard she noticed neither face nor landscape.

SHE CAME INTO THE CITY again the next Saturday. There had been a phone call, trial gently proposed. Same red dress, heels, hair. A trial? She thought of her grandmother in Paris, her rumpled elegance, the rat-gnawed cheese on the windowsill, the blaze of her crazed dignity. Mathilde had listened from her closet and thought: Never. Never for me. I'd die first.

Never's a liar. She had nothing better, and time was running out. The man was waiting outside the train station, but he didn't touch her as she sat on the leather seat of the town car. He ate a throat lozenge and the air smelled of it. Her eyes were dry, yet the world had gone misty. A lump in her throat bigger than the neck could contain.

She registered the doorman as hairy, squat, Mediterranean, though she didn't look directly at him. All inside was smooth marble.

"What's your name?" the silvery man said in the elevator.

"Mathilde," she said. "Yours?"

"Ariel," he said.

She looked at herself in the reflective brass doors, a smear of red and white and gold, and said in a very low voice, "I'm a virgin."

He took a handkerchief from his breast pocket and dabbed at his forehead. "I would never have expected less of you," he said, and bowed elaborately as if for a joke and held the door for her as she went in.

He handed her a glass of cold sparkling water. The apartment was enormous, or at least appeared so, walled on two sides with glass. The other walls were white, with huge paintings that registered as shimmers of color. He took off his suit jacket and hung it up and sat down, and said, "Make yourself at home."

She nodded and went to the window and looked out onto the city.

After some time, he said, "By make yourself at home, what I really meant was for you to please undress."

She turned away from him. She took off the shoes and unzipped the dress and let it pool at her feet. Her underwear was black cotton, a little girl's cut, which had made the people at the agency smile the week before. She didn't wear a bra; she didn't need one. She turned back, her arms behind her, and looked at him gravely.

"All of it," he said, and she slowly took off her underwear. He made her wait while he looked at her. "Please turn around," he said, and she did. Outside, the buildings were obscured in the fog and dim, so that when the lights in the buildings opposite came on they were squares floating in space.

She was shuddering by the time he stood and came toward her. He touched her between the legs and smiled at the moisture he found on his fingertips.

His body seemed too bony for his fleshy face and was almost hairless, save for brown coronas around his nipples and a darker arrow from navel to groin. He lay on the white couch and made her crouch above him until her thighs burned and shook. Then he seized her hips and pulled her suddenly down, smiling at the pain on her face.

"Easier to dive than wade in, my dear," he said. "Lesson one."

She didn't know what kept her from standing, dressing, escaping. The pain felt like hate. She bore the pressure by counting, staring fixedly at a golden square of window in the dark. He took her face and forced it to his. "No," he said, "please look at me." She looked. There was a technological glow from the corner of the room, some digital clock, which turned the side of his head slightly green in pulses. He seemed waiting for her to flinch, but she wouldn't; she willed her features into stone, and there was a pressure that built and burst and the relief, removal, and she stood, feeling knots in her legs and an internal burn.

He cut a banana into slices and laid them on her body and slowly ate them off her, which was his dinner. "More than that," he said, "I inflate." For her, he ordered a grilled cheese sandwich and fries from the diner across the street and watched her mouth closely as she ate every bite. "More ketchup," he said. "Lick that cheese off your finger."

In the morning, he washed her very carefully and instructed her how to trim herself and watched from a hot bath as she put her leg on a teak chair and did so.

And then he had her lie on her back in the huge white bed and point her knees upward. On the television embedded in the wall, he put on a tape with two women, redheaded and dark-haired, licking each other. "Nobody likes what I'm about to do to you at first," he said. "You need to fantasize to make it work. Stay with it. A few times from now, you'll understand."

It was terrifying, his unlovely face there. The heat of his mouth and the scrape of the stubble. The way he watched her in her shame. It was the closest anyone had ever come to her. She'd never been kissed on the lips. She put a pillow on her face and breathed and thought of a young man without a face, just a muscular, shining body. She felt a long, slow wave building in her until it turned huge and dark and crashed down on her, and she shouted into the pillow.

He pulled away from her, sudden flood of white light. "You surprising little thing," he said, laughing.

She didn't know she hated Chinese food until he ordered it and asked her to eat it all on the rug, moo shu tofu to steamed shrimp and broccoli to the last grain of rice. He had nothing; he watched. "If you need to go home, I'll take you back to the station after you shower again." There was a kindness in him despite his gargoyle's face.

Mathilde nodded; she'd already bathed three times in his marble shower, always after eating. She had begun to understand him. "I just need to be back in time to go to school tomorrow," she said.

"Do you wear a uniform?" he said.

"Yes," she said, lying.

"Oh god," he groaned. "Wear it next weekend."

She put down the chopsticks. "You've decided."

"Depends on where you're going to college."

She told him. "You're smart," he said. "I'm glad to hear that."

"Maybe not," she said, motioning at the apartment around her, her own naked body with a grain of rice on her breast. She smiled, then took the smile off her face. He didn't get to know she had a sense of humor.

He stood and moved to the door. "All right. We have a deal," he said. "Come to me from Friday afternoon to Sunday evening. I'll call you my goddaughter to avoid unnecessary questions. Four years. Starting now. Intern with me at the gallery during the summers. I am eager to see how well I can teach you what you'll need to know. Do your catalog modeling if you think you need to explain your money. We'll get you on birth control. While we're together, to avoid diseases, among other horrors, please do not touch or look at another boy or girl. If I hear you even kissed someone else, our deal is off."

"I won't even think a lewd thought," she said, deliberately thinking: black cock. "Where are you going?" she asked.

"Buying you underwear and a bra. It's disgraceful, your going around like that underneath. You shower and take a nap, and I'll be back in a few hours."

He went toward the door, then stopped. He turned around. "Mathilde," he said kindly. "No matter what, you need to understand that this is only business. I can't have you thinking that it's more than that."

She smiled broadly for the first time. "Business," she said. "Not a single emotion will occur. We will be as robots."

"Excellent," he said, and closed the door.

Alone, she felt sick, dizzy. She looked at herself reflected in the window, the city slowly moving beyond. She touched her stomach, her chest, her neck. She looked at her hands and saw they were shaking. She was no more rotten than she'd been as the girl on the train, but still she turned away from the Mathilde in the glass.

Two MONTHS. High school finished and she moved into Ariel's apartment. She had so little to take from her uncle's house. A few books, the red dress, glasses, a dog-eared photograph of herself—fat-cheeked, pretty, French—before she went bad. It all fit into her school knapsack. She left a note under the chauffeur's seat when he was using the bathroom; she couldn't see his many stomachs and chins one last time without bursting into tears. She knocked for the first time on her uncle's study door, and without waiting for him to speak, she went in. He looked up over the top of his glasses. A wedge of light from the window fell on the papers on his desk.

"Thank you for the shelter you've given me these past few years," she said.

"You're leaving?" he said, in French. He took his glasses off and sat back, looking at her. "Where are you going?"

"A friend's," she said.

"Liar," he said.

"Correct," she said. "I have no friends. Call him a protector."

He smiled. "An efficacious solution to all of your problems," he said. "If, however, a more carnal one than I'd hoped. But I shouldn't be surprised. You grew up with my mother, after all."

"Good-bye," she said, and turned toward the door.

"Frankly," he said, and she stopped, her hand on the doorknob. "I had thought better of you, Aurélie. I had believed you'd work for a few years, head off to Oxford or something. I had thought you would fight harder. That you were more like me. I must admit that I find myself disappointed."

She said nothing.

"Know that if you have nothing else, you can find food and a bed here. And do visit, from time to time. I am curious to see how you change. I predict either something ferocious or something thoroughly bourgeois. You will be a world-eater or a mother of eight."

"I won't be a mother of eight," she said. She wouldn't visit, either. There was nothing of her uncle's that she wanted. She took a last look at him, the lovely winglike ears and round cheeks that made a liar of his face, and one side of her mouth curled up, and she bid a silent good-bye to the house as she went through, the secret masterpiece under the stairwell that she yearned to see again and the long dark hallways with locked doors and the huge oak front door. Then she was in the air. She began to run down the packed dirt lane in its blaze of white sun, her legs swinging good-bye, good-bye, to the ruminants in the Mennonite fields, the June breeze, the wild blue phlox on the bank. This sweat she worked up was a glorious one.

THE LONG SUMMER of her nineteenth year. The things one can do with a tongue, a breath. The taste of latex, smell of oiled leather. Box seats at Tanglewood. Her blood thrilled. His voice warm in her ear before a Jackson Pollock spatter, and suddenly, she saw the brilliance. Sultry heat, pisco sours on the terrace, an ice cube's painful slow melt on her nipples as he watched from the door. He taught her. This is how you cut your food, order your wine. This is how you make people believe you agree with their opinions without saying anything at all.

Something softened around his eyes, but she pretended not to see it. "Business," she said to herself, her knees burning on the tile in the shower. He put his hands in her hair. He brought her presents: bracelets, videos that made her face hot, underwear no more than three strings and a patch of lace.

And then college. It went far faster than she thought it would. Classes like flashes of light, blips of dark weekends, light again. She drank her classes in. She did not make friends; Ariel took up so much time, and the rest was taken by studying, and she knew that if she made one friend, she'd be too hungry to stop. On soft spring days, forsythia sunbursts in the corners of her eyes, her heart was rebellious; she would easily have fucked the first boy who walked by, but she had so much more to lose than the thrill she'd gain. She watched, longingly, chewing her fingernails to blood, as the others hugged, laughed, passed inside jokes. On Friday afternoons, on the trains down the dusk-sparked Hudson, she hollowed herself out. When she modeled, she pretended to be the kind of girl who felt insouciant in bikinis, who was glad to show her new lace brassiere to the gaping world. Her best shots were those where she thought of doing physical violence to the photographers. In the apartment: rug burn, lips bitten. He ran a hand down her back, cleaved her buttocks: Business, she thought. The train back to college, each mile an expansion. One year, two. Summers in the apartment and the gallery, like a fish in an aquarium. She learned. Three years, four.

Senior spring. Her whole life ahead of her. Almost too much brightness to look at directly. Something in Ariel had grown frantic. He took her to four-hour dinners, told her to meet him in the bathroom. She woke Sunday mornings to find him watching her. "Come work for me," he said, thickly, once when she, on his cocaine, unspooled a full essay out of her brain about the genius of Rothko. "Work for me at the gallery and I'll train you and we can take over New York." "Maybe," she said agreeably, thinking, Never. Thinking, Business. Soon, she promised herself. Soon she would be free at last.

11

SHE WAS ALONE for an afternoon. She came downstairs to find that God had chewed the kitchen rug, had left a mess of urine on the floor, was looking at her with a bellicose light in her eye. Mathilde showered, put on a white dress, let her hair drip the fabric wet. She put the dog into her crate, her toys and food in a plastic bag, put it all in the car. The dog screamed in the back, then settled.

She stood outside the general store in town until she saw a family she vaguely knew. The father was the man they'd hired to plow their driveway in winter, with a steer rustler's face, maybe a little slow. The mother was the dental receptionist, a big woman with small ivory teeth. The children had gorgeous fawn eyes. Mathilde knelt to their level, and said, "I want to give you my dog."

The boy sucked three fingers, looked at God, nodded. The girl whispered, "I can see your boobies."

"Mrs. Satterwhite?" the mother said. Her eyes flicked over Mathilde; and by this, Mathilde knew she was dressed inappropriately. Ivory dress, designer. She hadn't been thinking. Mathilde put the dog in the husband's arms. "Her name is God," she said. The woman gasped, then said, "Mrs. Satterwhite!" but Mathilde was walking to her car. "Hush, Donna," she heard the man say. "Let the poor lady be." She drove home. The house echoed, empty. Mathilde had been liberated. She had nothing to worry about now.

SO LONG AGO, it was. That day the light had fallen from the sky as if through green blown glass.

Her hair had been long then, sun-shot blond. Skinny legs crossed, reading *The Moonstone*. She bit her cuticle to blood and thought of her boyfriend, a love one week tender, and the world was made bright with him. Lotto, said the train as it came: *Lotto-Lotto-Lotto.*

The short, greasy boy watching her from the bench was invisible to her because she had her book; she had her joy. To be fair, she hadn't met Chollie yet. Since Mathilde and Lotto had found each other, Lotto had spent every spare moment with her; had ceded his dorm room to his childhood friend, who was illegally auditing classes, not an actual student at the school. Lotto had time for nothing but Mathilde, rowing, and classes.

But Chollie knew of her. He was there at the party when Lotto looked up and saw Mathilde and she saw him; when Lotto crushed a crowd of people to get to her. It had been only a week. It couldn't be serious yet, Chollie had believed. She was pretty, if you were into stick figures, but he figured Lotto would never tie himself to one pussy at twenty-two, with his whole life of glorious fuckery ahead of him. Chollie was sure that if Lotto had been perfectly handsome he would never have the success he did. His bad skin, his big forehead, the slightly bulbous nose moderated what was an almost girlishly pretty face into something sexy.

And then, just the day before, he'd caught sight of Lotto and Mathilde together under the confetti of an overblown cherry tree, and he felt the air knocked out of his chest. Look at them together. The height of them, the shine on them. Her pale and wounded face, a face that had watched and never smiled now never stopped smiling. It was as if she'd lived all her life in the chilly shadows and someone had led her out into the sun. And look at him. All his restless energy focused tightly on her. She sharpened something that threatened to go diffuse in him. He watched her lips as she spoke, and took her chin gently between his fingers and kissed her with his long lashes closed, even while she was speaking, so that her mouth moved and she laughed into his kiss. Chollie knew immediately that it was correct, that they were in very deep. Whatever was between them was explosive, made even the professors gape as they passed by. The threat of Mathilde, Chollie had understood then, was real. He, striver, knew another striver when he saw one. He who'd had no home had found a home in Lotto; and she had usurped even this.

[The Saturday after this one in the train station, Chollie would be napping in Lotto's bed, hidden under a heap of clothes, and Lotto would come in, smiling so broadly that Chollie would stay silent when he could have spoken and made his presence known. Lotto, ecstatic, would pick up the phone and call his fat hog of a mother in Florida, who had once threatened to castrate Chollie years ago. There would be banter. Weird relationship, that one. And then Lotto would tell his mother he was married. Married! But they were babies. Chollie was shocked cold, missing much of the conversation, until Lotto left again. It couldn't be true. He knew it was true. After some time had passed, he had wept bitterly, poor Chollie, under his heap of clothes.]

But on this day, before they were married, there was still time to save his Lotto from this girl. So here he was. He climbed onto the train behind Mathilde, sat behind her. A lock of her hair escaped the crevasse between seat backs, and he sniffed it. Rosemary.

She got off at Penn Station and he followed. Up from the underground stink to heat and light. She went toward a black town car, and the chauffeur opened the door and she was swallowed up. Midday in crowded Midtown, Chollie kept up on foot, though he was quickly sweating and his breastlets were heaving with effort. When the car paused before an Art Deco building, she got out and went in.

The doorman was a silverback gorilla in a costume, some kind of

Staten Island accent: bluntness would be key. Chollie said, "Who was that blond?" The doorman shrugged. Chollie took out a ten and gave it to him. The doorman said, "Girlfriend of 4-B." Chollie looked at him but the doorman put out his hand and Chollie gave him all he had, which was a joint. The man grinned and said, "She been coming for too many years for a girl so young, you dig me? He's some kind of art dealer. Name's Ariel English." Chollie waited, but the man said mildly, "That's all you get for a little bud, little bud."

Later, Chollie sat waiting in the window of the diner across the street. He watched. His sweaty shirt dried, and the waitress grew tired of asking if he wanted to order and just slopped coffee into his mug and went away.

When the shadows engulfed the building across the street, he almost gave up, headed back to his squat in academia. There were options. He'd look in the phone book for galleries. He'd research. But then the doorman straightened and opened the door crisply, and out came a chimera, a man with a jowly face and a body like a wisp of smoke poured into a suit. Wealth in the way he moved, his sleek grooming. Behind him, there was an animated mannequin. It took Chollie a moment to recognize Mathilde. Her heels were tall, her schoolgirl's skirt cut nearly to the crotch, her hair swept high, far too much makeup. [She had refused to extend the terms of the arrangement beyond four years; in pique, Ariel had dressed her, knowing her, knowing how to cut.] Her face was bare of that constant low-level smile that she wore, both shield and magnet. Blank, it was something like an abandoned building. She walked as if unaware of the world around her, that her nipples were visible under her gauzy shirt.

They crossed the street, and there was dread in Chollie when he saw that they were coming into the diner toward him.

They sat in a corner booth. The man ordered for both—egg-white Greek omelet, him, chocolate milkshake, her. He watched their upside-down bodies in the chrome napkin dispenser. She ate nothing, gazed at air. Chollie saw the man whispering in her ear, saw his hand disappear in the darkness between her legs. She let it, passive. [On the surface; beneath, the controlled burn.]

Chollie was overwhelmed. He felt a swift spinning in him. Fury for Lotto; fear of losing what he, Chollie, had worked so hard to keep. He stood in agitation and went back on the train drawn through the dusk and pressed his burning face against the cool glass and, at last home at Vassar, collapsed for a brief nap into Lotto's bed to plan how to tell him about his new girl, who she secretly was. A whore. But he fell asleep. He woke to laughter in the common room, the sound of a television. Past midnight on the flashing clock.

He came out and almost fell down with astonishment. The only explanation: Mathilde must have a twin. He'd followed the wrong girl to the city. There was a girl in Lotto's lap in sweatpants and a messy ponytail, laughing at something he was whispering in her ear. She was so different from what he'd seen that he knew he was wrong in having seen it. A dream? A half-eaten popover with apple butter was on the table, and Chollie almost lurched for it, he was so hungry.

"Hey," Lotto bellowed. "Chollie! You haven't met my"—he laughed—"my Mathilde. My girl I'm madly in love with. Mathilde, this is Chollie, my oldest friend."

"Oh!" she said, and leapt up and moved toward Chollie, towering over him. "I'm so happy to meet you," she said. "I've heard all the stories." She paused then hugged him, and she smelled of plain Ivory soap and, aha, rosemary shampoo.

Many years later, when the gardener would try to grow rosemary on the patio of the penthouse, Chollie would toss the plants thirty stories to the sidewalk below and watch them explode in mushroom clouds of dirt.

"You," he said. "I've seen you before."

"Hard to miss. Six feet of perfect, legs to the moon," Lotto said.

"No," Chollie said. "Today. On a train to the city. I'm sure it was you."

The slightest of hesitations, then Lotto said, "Must've been some other stunner. She was writing her French final in the computer room all day. Right, M.?"

How narrow Mathilde's eyes had gone when she laughed. Chollie felt their coldness on him. "All morning, yeah," she said. "But I was done fast. It was only a ten-pager. When you were at your rowing lunch, I went off to the city to the Met. We have to do an ekphrastic poem for my writing class and I didn't want to do the same dumb Monet water lily from the campus museum that everyone else is doing. I just got back, actually. Thank you for reminding me!" she said to Chollie. "I bought Lotto something at the gift shop."

She went to her overlarge purse and pulled out a book. It had a Chagall painting on the cover, Chollie would see later, when he stole it. Mathilde had also stolen it, just as she left Ariel's apartment for the very last time. She'd gotten her last check. Now she was free to sleep with Lotto.

"*Winged Cupid Painted Blind,*" Lotto read. "*Art Inspired by Shakespeare.* Oh," he said, kissing her chin. "It's perfect."

She looked at Chollie. Another glimmer through the dark. This time, perhaps not so benign.

Fine, Chollie thought. You'll see how well I can wait. When you're least expecting it, I will explode your life. [Only fair; she had exploded his.] A plan began to itch at the back of his brain. He smiled at her and saw himself reflected in the darkened window. He liked how he looked so different in reflection: so much thinner, paler, so much more blurred than he was in life.

12

HER HUSBAND HADN'T WOKEN HER with a mug of coffee. Every day they had lived under the same roof, he had woken her with a cup of milky coffee. Something was wrong. She opened her eyes to full morning. Inside her, an abyss. She couldn't see all the way to its black bottom.

She dawdled. Washed her face. Talked to the dog, who ran from Mathilde to the door frantically. Opened the curtains to find the world deep in midwinter gloom. Stared down the stairwell for a long time.

Barrel of a gun, she thought.

He's left me, she thought. I knew from the moment I saw him that this day would come.

She came down the dim steps and he wasn't in the kitchen. She whispered to calm herself as she climbed up to his study in the attic. A crumble of relief when she came in the door and saw him sitting at his desk. His head was down. He must have worked all night and fallen asleep. She looked at him, the leonine hair with the gray temples, the magnificent forehead, the soft full lips.

But when she touched him, his skin was lukewarm. His eyes were open, empty as mirrors. He was not resting there, not at all.

She slid behind him in the chair and pressed herself to him, tailbone to nape. She put her hands up his shirt, feeling the thin rubber of his belly flab. Her finger went into his navel to the second knuckle. She put her hands down his pajama pants and his boxer briefs, where it was still warm. The wool of pubic hair. The satin head of him, humble in her palm.

For a long time, she held him. She felt the heat of him leave. She stood only when she could no longer recognize his body, like a word repeated until it has lost all meaning.

13

MATHILDE WAS AMBUSHED in the pool by Chollie. She had been six months and one week without her husband.

Chollie left his car a mile up the road and hoofed it so she couldn't hear him and flee to the pool house and hide.

She had eschewed a bikini that morning for a full-body browning. Who was she going to scandalize, the crows? Her sere, unloved body of a widow. But here Chollie was at the edge of the pool, groaning. She peered at him through her sunglasses and wiped her cheeks with her palms.

Little goblin-man. Once he'd tried to push her into a bathroom at a party and she'd had to knee him in the nads to get him away from her.

"Fuck, Chollie," she said. She paddled to the side of the pool and climbed out. "I can't have a little solitude? Hand me that towel," she said. He did, if with excruciating slowness.

"There's solitude and then there's suicide," he said. "You look like a chemo patient with that hair. Or lack thereof."

"Why are you here?" she said.

"Everyone's worried. I've gotten ten calls in the past week alone. Danica thinks you're going to do yourself in."

"Well, now you can go home and report that I'm alive," she said.

"So I see," he said, grinning. "Vividly. In the flesh. I'm too hungry to drive. Feed me."

She sighed. "The only thing I have is ice cream," she said. "And it's pistachio."

He followed her into the kitchen, and while she scooped the ice cream for him, he reached for the letter perched in its blue bowl of tomatoes. He was always grabby, looking at things that didn't concern him. She once found him in her office, reading the strange, spiky pieces of fiction she wrote on scraps.

"Hands off," she said now. "Not for you."

They went out to sit on the warm stones of the veranda while Chollie ate.

"It appears that I have a long history of sneaking up on you," Chollie said. He belched and drove the spoon into the ground.

She thought of his hands on her forearms at some long-ago party, the need in his face. The tongue he'd once shoved into her ear. "Yes. We all know you're a pervert," she said.

"No. I mean, yes, but no, I'm thinking of something else. Did you know I followed you once? Back at Vassar. I hadn't met you yet. You and Lotto had just gotten together and I knew there was something sketchy about you. So I followed you to the city."

Mathilde went still.

"Strange to see the new girlfriend of my best friend getting into some limo. Don't know if you remember, but I was fit back then, and I kept up. You got out and went into an apartment. So I sat in a diner across the way. You remember that diner."

"Couldn't forget," she said. "And you were fat back then. You've never been fit, Choll."

"Ha. Anyway, you came out in this awful outfit. See-through shirt, miniskirt like a Band-Aid. And you're with this weird flabby-faced man who put his hands up your skirt. And I think, Huh. My buddy Lotto is the best person on the planet. Loyal as shit and kind, and lets me crash with him and is more my family than my family, just brilliant, this real fucking genius, though I don't really think anybody knew that back then, but there was something in him. Charisma. Gentleness, a kind of acceptance of people for who they are. That's rare, you know? Someone who never, never judges. Most people have a nasty interior monologue going on at all times, not Lotto. He'd rather think kindly of you. Easier that way. And he was so good to me. My family was a bunch of sadistic assholes, and I quit high school halfway through senior year so I could get away, and the only person on the planet who showed me consistent kindness was Lotto. From the time I was seventeen, Lotto was my home. So, anyway, here's this astounding person, best person I ever knew, and his girlfriend is sneaking off to New York to fuck some old dude? So I go home, all ready to tell my best friend his girl is sleeping around, because what kind of person would lead Lotto on like that? I mean, the kind of person who'd hang a puppy for fun. The kind of girl who'd marry him for the money. But somehow you beat me back to the dorm. Or I fell asleep. I don't remember. But I came out, and then I saw the way you and he were together and I knew I couldn't tell him. Not yet. Because I saw then that he was cooked. He was so deep into you that if I said anything it'd be me to get the boot, not you."

She was squinting at a troop of ants on the hot gray stone.

He waited, but she wouldn't say anything, so he said, "So I thought I'd sit back and wait my time and then drive the knife in when nobody was expecting it."

"Twenty-four years. And he died before you could," she said softly. "Too bad. Tragedy."

"Wrong," he said.

She looked at him, sweating, pink. The last month before Lotto died returned to her. His sullenness, his monosyllables. The way he looked flinchingly in her direction. She searched for the last time they had seen Chollie together before Lotto died. And suddenly she saw the night in Ariel's gallery, where he'd dragged her for Natalie's posthumous opening, huge metallic sculptures with screaming faces in them, the place turned into a fairy-tale forest, all shadowy and dark. Perhaps, she had told herself, it had been so long, perhaps there was no more danger in Ariel. But some pretty little waiter-boy spilled red wine all over her silk dress and she hurried off to blot it away, and when she came back, her husband had been replaced by a robot that looked like him, a man who didn't smile when he looked at her, who spoke to her glancingly, who, later, seethed. Somewhere between the moment he kissed her gently on the forehead, before the wineglass tipped off the tray and, with terrible slowness, spilled on her skirt, and the moment she returned, Chollie had told him about her arrangement with Ariel. The world flickered before her.

He saw the understanding and laughed, and said, "My dick's on the table, baby. I play a long game."

"Why?" she said.

"You took him," he said, and his voice came out too raspy, too quick. He shuffled his glasses on his nose, folded his hands. "He was the only person I had and you took him. But also you're a bad person who never deserved him."

"I meant," she said, "why now? Why not ten years ago? Why not twenty years from now?"

"We both know how much our old friend loved vagina. Any and all. And frankly, dear, I always knew that someday yours would be getting pretty old. All flabby and loose. Menopause setting in soon. And poor Lotto had always longed for a kid of his own. With you out of the way, he could have had the kid he wanted. And we all wanted to give him what he wanted. Didn't we."

She did not trust herself not to kill him with the spoon. She stood and came inside and locked the door behind her.

For hours after she'd watched Chollie walk down the gravel drive, Mathilde sat in the kitchen. Night fell and she didn't turn on the lights. For dinner, she opened a bottle of gift wine from some producer of Lotto's play years ago, wildly expensive and smoky and lingering on her tongue. When the bottle was finished, she stood and went all the way up to her husband's studio at the top of the house. His jade plant, so long neglected, had blackened. His books were splayed, wide-winged around the room, his papers were still spread on the desk.

She sat on the leather chair and sank into the divot made by long years under her husband's weight. She rested her head on the wall behind her, where it was shiny from his head. She looked at the window where he'd dreamt for so many hours, lost in his imaginings, and was filled with a kind of dark tingle. She felt enormous, the size of the house, crowned with the moon, wind in her ears.

[Grief is pain internalized, abscess of the soul. Anger is pain as energy, sudden explosion.]

This one would be for Lotto. "This will be fun," she said aloud to the empty house.

14

GRADUATION DAY. Hills purple, sun astringent. The processional went too fast, so everyone was out of breath and laughing. Swift glimpse of Chollie's fat face squeezed among the bystanders, unsmiling. Mathilde hadn't bothered to tell her uncle she was graduating. She would have liked to see the driver, but she didn't know his real name. She hadn't spoken to Ariel since the last trip to the city, just after her final rent check went through, the contract fulfilled. Nobody was here to see her. Well. She hadn't expected anyone.

They poured into the quad and endured the long speeches and some comedian she couldn't listen to because Lotto was in the row ahead of her and she stared at the pink curl of his ear, wanting to put it in her mouth and suck. She walked across the stage to polite applause. He walked across the stage to a roar. "Terrible to be so popular," she said, later, after the confetti of caps and they found each other, kissed.

The quickie in his dorm room, before he packed up. Her tailbone on the hard oak desk, the shushing laughter when there was a knock on the door. "Just about to take a shower!" he called out. "Be out in a sex."

"What?" It was his baby sister, Rachel, her voice at knob level in the hall.

"Oh, shoot," he whispered. "Just a second," he shouted, blushing, and Mathilde bit his shoulder to keep from laughing.

When Rachel came in, Lotto was whooping at the cold water in the shower, and Mathilde was on her knees, packing his shoes into a cardboard box. "Hello!" she said to the little girl, who was, poor thing, nothing close to as stunning as her brother. Long skinny nose, tiny jaw, close eyes, dun-colored hair, taut as a guitar string. How old? Nine or so. She stood in her pretty, frilly dress, goggling, and said with a gasp, "Oh! You're so pretty."

"I like you already," Mathilde said, and she stood and walked over and bent and gave the girl a kiss on the cheek. And then Rachel saw her brother coming out of the bathroom, steam rolling off his shoulders, in a towel, and ran over to hug him around the waist, and he hooted, and said, "Rachel! Rachey-ray!"

Behind Rachel came Aunt Sallie, ferret-faced, of the same gene pool as the little girl. "Oh, my," Sallie said, stopping short on beholding Mathilde. A blush rose out of her high lace neckline. "You must be my nephew's girl. We were wondering who'd be special enough to pin him down, and now I see. Nice to meet you, you can call me Sallie."

Lotto was looking at the door, his face darkening. "Is Muvva in the restroom?" he said. "She still making her way up the steps?" Clear as a windowpane: get his mother and wife in the same room, and they'd fall in love, he was thinking. Oh, sweet boy.

Mathilde shored her shoulders, jutted her chin, waiting for Antoinette to enter, the glance exchanged, the situating. She had gotten a note that morning in her campus mailbox. *Don't think*, it said, *that I don't see you*. Unsigned, but smelling of Antoinette's roses. Mathilde had saved it in a shoe box that, one day, would be full of such notes.

But Sallie said, "Nope. Sorry, baby boy. She sent her regards. She gave me this to give you," and she handed over an envelope, the check in it visible against the light of the window, the handwriting Sallie's, not his mother's.

"Oh," Lotto said.

"She loves you," Sallie said.

"Sure," Lotto said, and turned away.

What Lotto couldn't pack into his station wagon, he put out for the scavengers to pluck. He owned so little; Mathilde would always love his indifference to things. After he'd carried everything up to her apartment to keep there the last week of her lease, they went off to an early dinner with Sallie and Rachel.

Mathilde sipped her wine to hide her emotion. She couldn't remember the last time she had sat as a part of a family, let alone in such a peaceful and decorous place as this quiet, fern-lined room, with its white cloths and brass chandeliers, the happy graduates and their boozing parents. On their side of the table, Lotto and Sallie were outstorytelling each other, cackling.

"You thought I didn't know what you were up to with that caretaker's whelp in the old henhouse when you were little?" she was saying, and his face was pink and shining with pleasure. "All that poking and prodding and guilty sweaty pumpkin heads when you came out? Oh, sweetmeat, you forget I can see clear through walls." Then she made a face as if remembering Rachel, but Rachel was paying her no mind. She was staring at Mathilde, blinking so rapidly Mathilde worried for her eyelids.

"I like your necklace," the girl whispered.

Mathilde put her hand up to her neck, touched it. It was gold, with a large emerald, which Ariel had given her last Christmas. The green was meant to go with her eyes; but her eyes were changeable. She took it off her neck and put it on Rachel's. "It's yours," she said.

Later, she would think of this gift, so impulsive, the ten-thousand-dollar necklace to a little girl, and feel warmed by it, even during their decade in the underground apartment in Greenwich Village, even when Mathilde didn't eat lunch so they could pay for phone service. It was cheap to buy a lifetime of friendship.

The little girl's eyes went wide, and she took the emerald in her fist and nestled her head into Mathilde's side.

When Mathilde looked up, she went still. At the next table sat Ariel. He was looking at her over his untouched salad, his mouth smiling but his eyes as cold as scales.

She wouldn't look away. She let her face go slack and stared back until Ariel motioned to the waiter. He murmured something and the waiter hurried off.

"You've got goose bumps," Rachel said, touching Mathilde's arm; and then the waiter was standing too close to Mathilde and opening up a bottle of extremely nice champagne, to which Sallie snapped, "I didn't order this," and the waiter said placatingly, "I know, I know. It's a gift from an admirer. May I?"

"How nice! Please do. Lotto has a ton of admirers," Mathilde said. "His Hamlet made him a celebrity in these parts. He's brilliant."

"Oh, I know," said Sallie. And Lotto beamed with pleasure, preening, eyes darting around to see which kind soul in the room could have sent along the champagne, the force of his delight such that wherever his eyes landed, the recipients of the gaze would look up out of their food and conversation, and a startled expression would come over their face, a flush, and nearly everyone began grinning back, so that, on this spangled early evening with the sun shining through the windows in gold streams and the treetops rustling in the wind and the streets full of congregating relieved people, Lotto sparked upwellings of inexplicable glee in dozens of chests, lightening the already buoyant mood of the room in one swift wave. Animal magnetism is real; it spreads through bodily convection. Even Ariel smiled back. The stunned grins stayed on the faces of some of the people, an expression of speculation growing, hoping he would look at them again or wondering who he was, because on this day and in this world, he was Someone.

"While we have champagne," Mathilde said, watching the tiny

bubbles flea-jump out the top of her glass, "Lotto and I have an announcement to make."

Lotto looked across the table at Mathilde, blinked, then grinned and turned to his aunt and his sister. "I'm sorry Muvva isn't here to witness this. But I guess we can't hold it in any longer. We're married," he said. And he kissed Mathilde's hand. She looked at him. Waves of heat built in her, one atop another. She would do anything in the world for this man.

In the ensuing flutter and exclamations, the tables closest breaking out into applause, eavesdroppers all, Rachel bursting into happy tears, Sallie fluttering her hands near her face though it was evident she'd already known the news, Mathilde looked for a long moment at Ariel. But he had stood and left the dining room, his slim navy back winking out the door. She was shed of him. For good, she thought. There was a relief like a cold wind blowing through her. She downed her glass and sneezed.

A WEEK AFTER GRADUATION, Mathilde was looking up through the casement windows into the courtyard garden where the Japanese maple waggled its leaves in the wind like tiny hands.

Already she knew it. This apartment would be her first real harbor in so many years adrift. She was twenty-two. She was so terribly tired. Here, at last, she could rest.

She could feel Lotto to her right behind her shoulder, emanating Lottoness. In a moment, she knew, he'd turn and crack a joke and the realtor would laugh and a warmth would come into her voice for the first time; despite herself, despite knowing better than to invest in such young and penniless people, she would take an interest in them. She would deliver a quiche on the day they moved in; she would stop by when she was in the neighborhood and bring them gifts of candy. Oh, Lotto, Mathilde thought with loving despair. Like most deadly attractive people, he had a hollow at the center of him. What people loved most about her husband was how mellifluous their own voices sounded when they echoed back.

Mathilde smelled the beeswax on the floor. She heard the neighbor's cat mewling in the hallway. The soft scrape of leaf against sky. It filled her, the kindness of this place.

She had to push down the tiny loud thing in her that willed her to say no, to walk away. She deserved none of this. She could still explode it all by shaking her head sadly, saying they should continue to look. But then the problem of Lotto would remain. He had become, after all, her home.

On cue: the joke, the laugh. Mathilde turned. Her husband—god, my god, hers, for life—was smiling. He lifted his hands and cupped her jaw and traced her eyebrows with his thumbs. "I think she likes it," he said, and Mathilde nodded, unable to speak.

They could have lived on happiness alone, in their glamorous poverty, in their apartment. They were as slender as fauns with lack; their apartment was spacious with it. Rachel's gift—the girl's saved-up allowance—was gone in three parties and as many months' rent and groceries. Happiness feeds but doesn't nourish. She tried bartending, canvassing for the Sierra Club, failing at both. The lights went out; they lit candles she'd stolen from a restaurant's alfresco tables and went to bed at eight PM. They held potlucks with their friends so they could eat as much as they wanted, and nobody minded if they kept the leftovers. In October, they had thirty-four cents in their checking account and Mathilde walked into Ariel's gallery.

He was looking at a vast green painting on the wall at the end of the room. He looked at her when she said, "Ariel," but he didn't move.

The receptionist was new, skinny, brunette, bored. Harvard, for sure. That gleam of entitlement, the length and gloss of hair. This would end up being Luanne. "Have an appointment?" she said.

"No," Mathilde said.

Ariel folded his arms, waiting.

"I need a job," she called to him across the expanse.

"There are no openings," the receptionist said. "Sorry!"

For a long moment, Mathilde looked at Ariel, until the receptionist said very sharply, "Excuse me. This is a private business. You need to leave. *Excuse* me."

"You are excused," Mathilde said.

"Luanne, please go get three cappuccini," Ariel said.

Mathilde sighed: *cappuccini*. The girl slammed the door when she went out.

"Come here," Ariel said. Mathilde's fight with herself was not visible as she neared. "Mathilde," he said softly, "in what world could I possibly owe you a job?"

"You owe me nothing at all," she said. "I agree."

"How can you ask me for anything after your behavior?"

"Behavior?" she said.

"Ingratitude, then," he said.

"Ariel, I was never ungrateful. I'd fulfilled the contract. As you always say, it was business."

"Business," he said. His face had grown red. His eyebrows were spiked high. "You married this Lancelot person two weeks before you graduated. I can only assume a conjugal relation. That's not fulfilling the contract."

"I met you in April of my senior year in high school," she said. "If you're counting, I extended the contract by two weeks."

They smiled at each other. He closed his eyes and sighed. When he opened them, they were moist. "I know it was business. But you hurt my feelings very much," he said. "I was not unkind to you. To walk away without keeping in touch, that surprised me, Mathilde."

"Business," she said again.

He looked her up and down. He'd bought these beautiful shoes she was wearing, worn at the toe. He'd bought the black suit. Her hair had not been cut since summer. He narrowed his eyes, cocked his head to the side. "You're skinny. You need the money. I understand. All you have to do is beg," he said softly.

"I don't beg," she said.

He laughed and the sullen receptionist clanged back in with a tray of cappuccinos in her hand and Ariel said, sotto voce, "You are lucky I feel fondness for you, Mathilde." Louder, he said, "Luanne, meet Mathilde. She'll be joining us here tomorrow morning."

"Oh. Goody," Luanne said, and fell back into her seat. She watched them carefully, sensing something.

"The gallery's employee," Mathilde said, as they walked slowly up to the front. "Not yours. I'm off-limits."

Ariel looked at her, and she, who'd been with him so long, could see him thinking, We'll see.

"Touch me," she said, "I walk. That's a promise."

LATER, WHEN SHE WAS SIXTY and Ariel seventy-three, she'd hear he was sick. From where the news came, she couldn't say. The sky would speak it in her ear, maybe. The air itself. She'd know only that he had pancreatic cancer. Swift and ferocious. For two weeks she perseverated, and at last she went to see him.

He was on a hospital bed on the deck outside his apartment. All copper and topiary and view. She held her eyes wide open and breathed. He was a droop of flesh with bones in it.

"I like," he rasped, "to see the birds." She looked up. No birds.

"Hold my hand," he said. She considered the hand but did not. He moved his head toward her. The flesh slid on the jaw.

She waited. She smiled at him. Buildings were sun-shocked in the corners of her eyes.

"Ah," he said. A warmth moved into his face. The almost joke in it had returned. "She won't be forced."

"Correct," she said. But she thought, Oh, you murderous girl, hello. I haven't seen you for so long.

"Please," he said. "Mathilde. Take the cold hand of a dying man."

And then she took his hand and pressed it to her chest with both of hers and held it there. What didn't need to be said stayed unspoken. He fell asleep and the nurse came out on angry tiptoes. Mathilde went into the apartment, sterile and tasteful, and didn't linger at the pictures she once knew too well for the ferocity with which she stared at them, counting the minutes until she could leave. Later, she walked through the cold shadows and blaze of concentrated afternoon light that poured between the buildings, and she couldn't stop; she could barely breathe; it felt too good to be on those coltish terrified legs once more, not to know, once more, where she was going.

15

THE PRIVATE INVESTIGATOR her attorney had hired was not what Mathilde had expected. Not the weary hard-boiled whiskey-barrel type. Not the soft-haired British-grandmother type. Reading had infected Mathilde, she saw of herself, amused. Too much Miss Marple and Philip Marlowe. This girl was young, nose like a hatchet, shaggy peroxided hair. An ample display of bosoms, with a dolphin over the top curve of a breast, as if it were leaping into her décolletage. Huge earrings. She was all abubble on the surface with a watchfulness beneath.

"Ugh," Mathilde had said out loud, when they shook hands. She hadn't meant to. She'd been left too long alone, had neglected the upkeep of niceties. It was two days after Chollie ambushed her naked in the pool. They were meeting in the courtyard of a Brooklyn coffee roastery and the wind was in the trees overhead.

But the girl hadn't taken offense; she laughed. Now she opened the folder with Chollie's photograph, address, phone number, all the details Mathilde could think of to tell her on the phone.

"I don't know how far you've gotten in your research," Mathilde said. "He was the one who started the Charles Watson Fund. You know, the investment brokerage firm. I don't know if you know that yet. About twenty years ago, he started it when he was just a kid. Total Ponzi scheme, I'm pretty sure."

The girl looked up, spark of interest in her face. "You invest?" she said. "Is that what this is?"

"I'm not a fucking moron," Mathilde said.

The girl blinked and sat back. Mathilde said, "Anyway. Ponzi scheme is the way to go, and I need proof of it, but I also need more. Personal stuff. The worst you can get. You meet the guy for three seconds, and you know he has a closet full of skeletons. Possibly literal ones. He's a fat shithead puckered-asshole sniffer and I want to flay him alive." She smiled sunnily.

The girl considered Mathilde. She said, "I'm good enough that I can pick and choose my cases, you know."

"Glad to hear it," Mathilde said. "I don't hire ninnies."

"My only hesitation about yours is that it seems like a personal vendetta," the girl said. "And those get sticky."

"Oh, well. Murder's too easy," Mathilde said.

The girl smiled, and said, "I like a bit of spunk in a lady."

"But I'm no lady," Mathilde said, already tired of this strange flirtation, drinking her coffee down so that she could go.

Mathilde stood, and the girl said, "Wait." She pulled the arms of her shirt through the sleeves and turned it around so the low collar was in the back, now crisp-looking, professional. She pulled off her shaggy wig to show brown hair, cut boyishly short. She took off the earrings, the false eyelashes. She was a different person, severe and sharp. She looked like the only female grad student at a math department mixer.

"That was some Bond-level disguisecraft," Mathilde said. "Hilarious. I bet it usually seals the deal for you."

"Usually," the investigator said. She seemed abashed.

"And the boob dolphin?" Mathilde said.

"I had a stupid youth," the girl said.

"We have all had stupid youths," said Mathilde. "I find them delicious." They smiled at each other across the table freckled with pollen. "All right. You'll do," Mathilde said.

"Honey, I'll more than *do*," the girl said, and leaned forward and touched Mathilde's hand just long enough to make her meaning clear.

Anger's my meat; I sup upon myself,
And so shall starve with feeding.

Volumnia says this in Shakespeare's *Coriolanus*. She—steely, controlling—is far more interesting than Coriolanus.

Alas, nobody would go to see a play called *Volumnia*.

16

THE CLOUDS HAD DESCENDED, though the day through the window gleamed with sunlight.

She was new to her Internet company. It was a dating site that would later be sold for a billion. She'd been at the gallery for three years; every morning she would take a breath on the sidewalk, shut her eyes, steel herself to walk in. All day, she'd feel Ariel looking at her. She did her job. She took care of the artists, calming them, sending them birthday gifts. "My prodigy," Ariel would say, introducing her. "One day Mathilde will run the show." Luanne's face pinched every time he said so. And the day came when a jittery artist flew in from Santa Fe, and Ariel and he went out for a long dinner, and when they came back, Mathilde was still in the dark in the back office, writing catalog copy for an exhibit. She looked up, froze. Ariel was in the door, watching her. He came close, closer. He put his hands on her shoulders and began massaging. He pressed himself to her back. After so long waiting for the end, she was obscurely disappointed in his lapse of taste: an unexpectedly gross gesture, frottage. She stood, and said, "I'm done," and walked past Luanne, who'd been watching from the front, and took all her sick leave at once and found a new job in days without ever telling Ariel she was leaving the gallery for good.

But this morning, Mathilde could not keep her eyes on her work. She begged off in her boss's office, and he watched her go with his eyes narrowed behind his glasses, his mouth in a sour twist.

In the park, the maple leaves had a sheen to them, as if gilded at the vein. She walked so far, was so lost, that when she came home her knees felt jellied. There was a bitterness on the back of her tongue. She took a stick from the twenty-pack she kept, in her terror, beneath the towels. Pissed on it. Waited. Drank an entire Nalgene of water. Did it again and again and again, and every time the patient stick told her *yes*. Plus sign. You're cooked! She shoved the wands into a bag, put the bag as deep in the trashcan as she could.

She heard Lotto come in and ran her eyes under cold water. "Hey, baby," she called out. "How was your day?" He clattered around, talking about an audition, some mean little bit in a commercial, he didn't even want it, it was humiliating, but he saw that boy from that television show in the late seventies, the one with the cowlick and weird ears, remember? She dried her face, finger-brushed her hair, practiced her smile until it wasn't so ferocious. She came out, still in her coat, and said, "I'm just off to pick up a pizza," and he said, "Mediterranean?" And she said, "Yup," and he said, "I adore you with all the marrow in my bones." "Me, too," she said, with her back turned.

She closed their front door and sank down on the steps that led to the lady upstairs, lay back, her arms crossed above her eyes because what was she going to do, what was she going to do?

Mathilde became aware of a strong smell of feet. She saw on the steps beside her face a pair of battered embroidered slippers held together with string.

Bette, the upstairs neighbor, gloomed down at Mathilde. "Come along," she said, in her prim British way.

Numb, Mathilde followed the old woman up the stairs. A cat pounced at her like a tiny clown. Apartment painstakingly clean, midcentury modern, Mathilde saw with surprise. Walls a high-gloss white. Bouquet of magnolia leaves on a table, deep green shine with a luscious brown underneath. On the mantel, three burgundy chrysanthemums burned. None of this was expected.

"Sit," Bette said. Mathilde sat. Bette shuffled away.

Presently, the old lady came back. A cup of hot chamomile, a LU Petit Écolier Chocolat Noir. Mathilde tasted it, returning to a schoolyard, light through leaves on the dust, snap of a new cartouche in her pen.

"I can't blame you. I never wanted a child, either," the old woman said, looking at Mathilde down her long nose. There were crumbs on her lips.

Mathilde blinked.

"In my day, we didn't know anything. Didn't live in a time when there was any choice. I douched with Lysol, you see. Such ignorance. When it was my time, there was a lady over the stationery store with a thin-bladed knife. Terrible. I wanted to die. Could have, easy. Instead, I got the gift of barrenness."

"Christ," Mathilde said. "Have I been speaking aloud to myself?"

"No," Bette said.

"But how did you know?" Mathilde said. "I barely know myself."

"It's my superpower," Bette said. "I see it in the way a woman carries herself. Many times I have gotten myself in trouble by mentioning it when it was an unpleasant surprise. Been clear to me in your case for about two weeks."

They sat there in the long afternoon. Mathilde watched the chrysanthemums and remembered to drink her tea only when it was lukewarm.

"Forgive me," Bette said. "It must be said that from my viewpoint, at least, a child wouldn't be the worst thing. You have a husband who adores you, a job, a place to live. You seem to be almost thirty, old enough. A child in this house wouldn't be the worst thing. I should like to watch over a baby once in a while, teach it the nursery rhymes of my Scottish granny. *Eenity feenity, fickety feg*. Or, no, *As eh gaed up a field o neeps*, eh? Spoil it rotten with biscuits. When it could eat biscuits, of course. Not the worst thing."

"It *would* be the worst thing," Mathilde said. "It wouldn't be fair to the world. Or to the child. Also, I'm only twenty-six."

"Twenty-six!" Bette said. "Your womb is practically antique. Your eggs are getting all wonky up in there. And what, you think you'd bear a monster? A Hitler? Please. Look at you. You've won the genetic lottery."

"You laugh," Mathilde said. "But my children would come out with fangs and claws."

Bette looked at her. "I hide mine well," Mathilde said.

"I am not one to judge," Bette said.

"You're not," Mathilde said.

"I'll help," Bette said. "Don't get your hackles up. I will help you. You won't be alone in this."

"SHOOT, THAT TOOK A BILLION YEARS," Lotto said, when she entered with the pizza. He was too hungry to see her until he'd eaten four slices. By then she had recomposed herself.

In the night, she dreamt of things that lived in the dark. Writhing blind worms with a pearly gleam, flurries of blue-veined parchment. Slick and drip.

She'd always hated pregnant ladies. The original Trojan horses, they.

Horrible to think that inside a human being there could be a human being. A separate brain thinking its separate thoughts. Much later, at the grocery store, Mathilde would watch a woman swollen to bursting, reaching up for the popsicles on the high shelf, and she'd imagine what it was like to have a person inside one that one hadn't swallowed whole. One that wasn't doomed from the start. The woman looked irritably over at Mathilde, who was gigantic, tall enough to reach; then her face changed back to the thing that Mathilde most disliked about pregnant ladies, the reflexive saintliness. "Can I help you?" the woman said, all treacle. Mathilde turned abruptly away.

Now she rose from the bed where Lotto lay breathing sweetly in his sleep, and took a bottle of rum up to Bette's apartment. She stood outside the door, not knocking, but still Bette opened it in a slattern's nightgown, her hair a gray swirl.

"In you go," she said. She put Mathilde on the couch, covered her with a woolen blanket, plunked the cat onto her lap. By Mathilde's right hand, hot chocolate with a glory of rum. On the television, Marilyn Monroe in black-and-white. Bette lay back on the ottoman and snored. Mathilde tiptoed home before Lotto woke, and got dressed as if going in to work and then called in sick. Bette, face up against the steering wheel, sitting on pillows from her sofa, drove her to the clinic.

[MATHILDE'S PRAYER: Let me be the wave. And if I cannot be the wave, let me be the rupture at the bottom. Let me be that terrible first rift in the dark.]

FOR A LONG TIME AFTERWARD, Mathilde was clammy on the inside. A grayish clay crumbling on its surface. It wasn't that she regretted a thing; it was that the call had been so close. Lotto was distant from her, on the peak of some hill she was too tired to climb. She moved through her life, letting the days drag her after them.

But there were tiny miracles to rouse her. A rosewater macaroon in the brass mailbox, in a waxed paper envelope. One blue hydrangea like a head of cabbage on the doorstep. Cold, wrinkled hands pressed to her cheeks, passing on the stairs. Bette's small gifts. Bright lights in the dark.

"A difficult thing," Bette had said in the waiting room. "But right. What you're feeling will slowly lessen." It would.

When Mathilde was twenty-eight, her husband left for Los Angeles for a week for a small speaking role in a cop drama, and she scheduled the sterilization.

"Are you sure?" the doctor said. "You're young enough that you might change your mind. You never know when the clock will start ticking."

"My clock is broken," she said. And he looked at her, high boots to blond crown, the eyeliner she wore those days curved on the outside to make cat's eyes. He thought he saw her, and he believed her vain. He nodded, turned curtly away. He planted the tiny coils in her tubes; she ate Jell-O and watched cartoons and let the nurses change her catheter. It was a very pleasant afternoon, in fact.

She would do it again if she had to. To save the horror. To save herself. She would do it again and again and again and again and again and again and again, if she had to.

17

MATHILDE DIDN'T RECOGNIZE the private investigator on the steps of the Met. She was looking for the girl from the coffee roastery in Brooklyn from two weeks earlier, either incarnation, frizzled and dolphined or sleek and sharp. There was a family of heavyset tourists, a cashmere-skinned young man whom Mathilde looked at carefully, and a scowling blond schoolgirl in a kilt and blazer with an overflowing backpack. She chose to sit next to the schoolgirl, and the girl turned to wink at her.

"Holy god," Mathilde said. "Body language and all. Gangly legs and attitude. I thought I was looking at my own doppelgänger from thirty years ago."

"I had a stakeout earlier," the investigator said. "I love my job."

"You were that little girl with a costume box, huh," Mathilde said.

The investigator smiled and there was a sadness there. She looked her age briefly. "Well, I was an actress," she said. "A younger Meryl Streep, that's what I wanted to be."

Mathilde said nothing and the investigator said, "And yes. Of course, I knew of your husband. Knew him, in fact. I was in one of his plays in my youth. The workshop for *Grimoire* at ACT in San Francisco. Everyone was in love with him. I always thought of him in terms of a duck, you know? Lancelot Satterwhite is to adoration as a duck is to water. He only wanted to be swimming around in a great pool of it, but it never soaked in to touch him, just always rolled off."

"Sounds about right," Mathilde said. "I see that you did know him."

"Maybe I shouldn't say this," the girl said. "But I don't see the harm, now that he's gone. You of all people knew the way he was. But the cast and crew had a sort of bet. Whenever anybody flubbed something in rehearsal, they had to put a quarter in the pot, and whoever was able to seduce Lancelot first got to keep the cash. Guys and girls both. All twelve of us."

"Who won?" Mathilde said. There was a twitch at the corner of her lip.

"Don't fret," the girl said. "Nobody. Opening night, we gave the cash to our stage manager because he had a new baby at home." She took a file from her backpack and handed it to Mathilde. "I'm still working the personal angle. There's definitely something there, but I just have to find it. In the meantime, I've bought us an informant at Charles Watson. Senior VP. Sees himself as a noble whistle-blower, but only after he amassed a fortune, a house in the Hamptons, ad nauseam. This file right here is the skim off the surface. And boy, does it go deep."

Mathilde read, and by the time she looked up, the street had gone bright with sun. "Holy of holies," she said.

"There's more," the investigator said. "It's pretty dire. There's going to be lots of pissed-off rich people. Whatever the motivation, we're doing the world a good thing."

"Ah, well. I've always been suspicious of self-congratulation," Mathilde said. "We'll celebrate properly when you hand me the personal stuff."

"Celebrate? You and me and champagne and a suite at the St. Regis?" the investigator said, standing.

Mathilde looked at her strong bare legs, the narrow hips, her watchful face buried under all that blond. She smiled, felt the rusty mechanism of flirting begin to move. She'd never been with a woman.

It would probably be softer, less muscular, like sexual yoga. It'd at least be novel. She said, "Maybe so. Depends on what you give me."

The investigator gave a low whistle, and said, "Off to work I go."

FOUR YEARS AFTER LOTTO DIED, when Mathilde was fifty, she bought a ticket to Paris.

Everything was so bright off the plane that she had to wear sunglasses. Even then, the brightness got in, bounced around her brain like a Spaldeen. Also, she wanted nobody to see how the smell of the place she was returning to ravaged her, made her eyes leak.

She had become tiny again here. In this language, she was again unable to be seen. She gathered herself at a café outside the gate. When the waiter in the airport brought her the espresso and *pain au chocolat* in a plastic pouch, he spoke to her in crisp French even though he turned and spoke uninflected English to the sophisticates at the table beside her. When it came time to pay, she didn't understand this euro business. She searched her purse for francs.

In the grainy gray day, Paris overwhelmed her with the scents. Exhaust and piss and bread and pigeon shit and dust and shedding plane trees and wind.

The cabdriver, his nose besponged by pores, looked at her for a long while in the rearview mirror and asked her if she was all right. When she didn't answer, he said soothingly, "You may cry here, cabbage. Cry as much as you wish. It is no hardship to watch a pretty woman cry."

She showered and changed in the hotel, then rented a white Mercedes and drove out of the city. The roaring river of traffic comforted the American in her.

The roundabouts became tighter. The roads smaller. Eventually, they were dirt. There were cows, tractors, semi-abandoned villages of a sooty gray stone.

What had been so huge in her mind was, in fact, terribly small. The house's stucco had been refreshed, painted white under the climbing ivy. The stones on the driveway were new, creamy, soft-edged gravel. The yews had grown, were neatly shaved across their tops like boys on the first day of school. The wine grapes in the back twined green as far as she could see, deep into her grandmother's old cow fields.

A man a little younger than Mathilde was fixing a motorcycle's wheel in the drive. He had a cycling jacket on and a swoop of gelled bangs cresting over his forehead. Mathilde recognized her own long fingers in his. Her own long neck. The same folded tip of the left ear.

"Papa," she said aloud, but no, this man was far too young.

Into the bay window came a woman. Stout, bleary-eyed, elderly, though her hair was dyed a squid-ink black. She was wearing a thickness of eyeliner below her lower lids. She peered at Mathilde in the car and her puckered mouth moved, as if she were chewing something. The hand clutching the curtain was red, ragged, as if it had spent a lifetime among the cold guts of fish.

Mathilde remembered a cabinet full of ripening cheeses, the overwhelming smell. Blind at first, she drove away.

In the little village, the cathedral was embarrassing. A Romanesque pebble, when she remembered it grand, shocking, Gothic. The *tabac* sold eggs still crotted with chicken shit. It was barely noon and the *boulangerie* was closing. She went into a salon that was also a pizza takeout and the *mairie*.

When the mayor sat down and Mathilde told her what she wanted, the mayor blinked so furiously she left streaks of black mascara on the insides of her glasses. "But you are absolutely sure?" she said. "That house, well. It has been in their family for hundreds of years."

"It is the only house in the world for me," Mathilde said. The Breton accent came back easily to her tongue. Sturdy as heifers, as the rocks in the fields.

"It will cost you," the mayor said. "They are very cheap, that family, very close with their money." She puckered her mouth, made a rubbing motion with her fingertips close to her chest.

"I can see myself being happy there," Mathilde said. "And only there. I long to come to this town in the summer. Maybe even open up a little antique shop with a tea place, draw the tourists." The mayor's face loosed with this. Mathilde pulled out the creamy card of her attorney and pushed it across the table. "Please conduct all business through this man. Of course, you'll get a five percent commission."

"Six," said the mayor.

"Seven. I don't care. Whatever it takes," Mathilde said, and the mayor nodded, and Mathilde stood and in leaving said, "Do your magic."

She returned to Paris feeling as if someone else were steering the car. It had been twenty-four hours since she'd last eaten when Mathilde sat down at her own table at La Closerie des Lilas. Not the best food in Paris. The most literary of restaurants, though. She'd dressed in a silver silk sheath, her hair back, her face flushed prettily.

When the waiter came over, Mathilde said only, "It has been a long time since I've been in France. I miss the food like a phantom limb."

His brown eyes sparkled. His moustache gave a leap like a goosed mouse. "I shall bring you our best dishes," he promised.

"And the wine to pair with them," she said.

He feigned exasperation. "But of course," he said. "Would I blaspheme?"

When he set the champagne before her, and the langoustine in its herbed mayonnaise, she said, "Thank you." She ate, her eyes half closed.

All along, she'd known Lotto was with her, across the table, enjoying her food with her. He would have loved this night, her dress, the food, the wine. The lust welled in her until it was almost unbearable. If she looked up, she knew, she would see only an empty chair. She would not look up.

After the cheese, the waiter brought her a plate of tiny pastel marzipan fruit, and Mathilde smiled up at him. *"À la victoire,"* she said.

"À l'amour," he said, twinkling.

She walked slowly back to her hotel over the cobblestones steaming from the swift summer storm that had passed lightly over the city while she ate. Her shadow paced beside her. She was able to make it to the bathroom, sitting calmly on the yellow travertine tub before she leaned over and vomited.

She flew home to the little white house in the cherry orchard. The purchase of the house in France took months. On the day the sale was finalized—for a fraction of what Mathilde would have paid, but, apparently, a great deal more than the house was worth—her lawyer sent her a bottle of Château d'Yquem.

She called him. "Excellent work, Klaus," she said.

"Thank you, Mrs. Satterwhite," he said. "They were . . . exigent."

"Oh, but they're exigent people," she said lightly. "Sorry to say it, but I'm afraid I have more work for you."

"Of course. That is why I am here," he said.

"Now, if you please, have the house torn down. Roof to joists. The vines in the back ripped from the ground. All of it. I know it is ancient and against all sorts of laws, but do it so fast nobody has time to know what you're doing. And do it as soon as possible."

Only the slightest hesitation. She adored this discreet man. "As you wish," he said. In the photographs he sent a week later, there was sky where there had been chimney, a clear view to the orchard where the four-hundred-year-old stone walls had been. The ground was a smoothly spread cloak of dirt.

It was less, she thought, like looking at a corpse than like looking at the place where a corpse had been buried.

Her heart cracked open and leaked. This one had been for her.

She sent Klaus a car much nicer than her own. His voice was amused this time when she called him. "The work is done," he said, "but not without much screaming and much, much rage. Many tears. I am afraid you cannot show your face in that town at any time soon."

"Ah, well," she said. "What else is new."

She said it lightly, yes. Still, she felt the old beast stirring in her.

18

"You're a pathological truth-teller," Lotto once said to her, and she laughed and conceded that she was. She wasn't sure just then if she was telling the truth or if she was lying.

Great swaths of her life were white space to her husband. What she did not tell him balanced neatly with what she did. Still, there are untruths made of words and untruths made of silences, and Mathilde had only ever lied to Lotto in what she never said.

She didn't tell him that she never minded being the breadwinner during the long span of their twenties, even the poverty, even the skipped lunches and the suppers of rice and beans, even the shifting of money from one tiny account to pay off the most pressing bills, even accepting money from Lotto's little sister, who gave it because she was one of the few people in the world who were truly good. His gratitude for what he thought was Mathilde's sacrifice indebted him to her.

She did mind something she never said aloud: she'd wished her husband were better at what he chose to do.

All of that standing in line in the rain. Going in only to perform a monologue. Home again to wait by the phone that rang with no job. Sulking, drinking, throwing parties. Growing fat, losing his hair, losing his charm. Year after year after year.

The very last winter in the underground apartment, she painted the ceiling gold to simulate sunshine, to cheer herself up, to give herself courage to sit Lotto down and tell him, gently, the truth: that though she believed in him, he might want to find a career he believed in as well. This acting pursuit was not going to work out.

Before she could gather the courage, New Year's Eve came around. He got drunk as usual, but instead of drifting to sleep, he stayed up and at a white heat wrote what had been sitting on his heart for decades. When she woke in the very early morning, she saw the computer and thought, first, of her jealousy, so assiduously suppressed, of him chatting on Instant Messenger with some pretty, blond avatar of a sad sixteen-year-old outcast. She picked the laptop up to read what he'd written. And she saw with wonder that it was a play and that it had the bones of a marvel in it.

She took it into the closet in the bedroom and worked feverishly. She edited, condensed, cleaned up the dialogue, and reshaped the scenes. He didn't remember what he'd written when he woke. She easily passed it off as entirely his.

In a few months, *The Springs* was finished. Polished. Mathilde read it over and over at night in the closet while Lotto slept, and knew it was good.

But though it was a wonderful play, a play that would later change their lives, nobody wanted to read it. Lotto took it around to producers, theater directors. They took the copies he'd had bound, and nobody returned his call. And Mathilde watched her husband's reborn twinkle dwindle again. It felt like a slow death of debridement, tiny constant bleeds.

An idea came in the form of one of Antoinette's notes, a short article ripped out of a magazine on Han van Meegeren, the art forger who had convinced the world his own wan paintings were Vermeers, though every Jesus he painted had the forger's own face. Antoinette had circled an X-ray of a fake, where, through the ghostly round face of a girl, you could see the uninspired seventeenth-century canvas Meegeren painted on: a farmyard scene, ducks, watering cans. *Fake layer atop bad base. Reminds me of someone,* Antoinette wrote.

Mathilde went to the library one weekend when Lotto was up in the Adirondacks camping with Samuel and Chollie, a vacation that she had planned, to get him out of the way. She found the plate she wanted in a heavy book. Gorgeous white horse carrying a blue-robed man in the foreground, a confusion of heads on other horses, a stunning building on a hill against the sky. Jan van Eyck, she'd discovered many years ago, in college. When she saw the slide during the class, her heart had gone still.

And to think she had held it in her hands in the tiny room under the stairway in her uncle's house. She had smelled it: old wood, linseed oil, time.

"Stolen in 1934," the professor had said. "One panel of a larger altarpiece. It is assumed that it was destroyed many years ago." He clicked to the next example of disappeared art, but she could see nothing but brilliant fuzz.

At the library, she paid for a color photocopy and typed up a letter. No salutation. *Mon oncle*, it began.

She sent both letter and photocopy in the mail.

A week later, she was cooking spaghetti, blending up pesto, and Lotto was on the couch, staring at a copy of *A Lover's Discourse*, his eyes unfocused, breathing through his mouth.

He answered the telephone when it rang. He listened. "Oh my gracious," he said, standing. "Yes, sir. Yes, sir. Yes, sir. Of course. I couldn't be happier. Tomorrow at nine it is. Oh, thank you. Thank you."

She turned, a spoon steaming in her hand. "What was that?" she said.

He was pale, rubbing his head. "I don't even," he said. He sat heavily.

She came over and put herself between his legs, touching his shoulder. "Baby?" she said. "Is something wrong?"

"That was Playwrights Horizons. They're putting on *The Springs.*

A private financier went crazy for it and is funding the whole thing."

He put his forehead on her chest and burst into tears. She kissed him on the cowlick at the back of his head to hide her expression, which she knew would be ferocious, grim.

WHEN, A FEW YEARS LATER, an attorney contacted her on her phone at the theater where Lotto was helping to cast his new play, she listened intently. Her uncle, the attorney said, had died [carjacking; crowbar]. He'd left his money to a home for indigent mothers. There was, however, a collection of antique Japanese erotica he'd left to her, Aurélie. She said, "But I'm not the person you're looking for. My name is Mathilde," and hung up. When the books were delivered to the apartment anyway, she took them to the Strand, and with what she earned, she bought Lotto a watch that would stay watertight to four hundred feet deep.

ON THE OPENING NIGHT of *The Springs*, Mathilde stood with Lotto in the dark.

Broadway! To begin so grandly! He'd been dazzled by the luck; she smiled, knowing that luck was not real.

The workshops had gone brilliantly; they'd attracted a Tony winner for the role of Miriam: undulant, lazy, simmering, the mother. The actors playing Manfred and Hans, the father and son, were barely known now but would be, a decade later, marquee names in feature films.

There was a smattering of strangers, some intrepid avant-gardists. But, confronted by the director in a whispered tête-à-tête with the dismal advance sales the afternoon before, Mathilde had spent all morning and afternoon on the telephone, and had filled the empty seats with their friends. The audience was boisterous, and the mood of the theater giddy and friendly before the houselights dimmed. Only Lotto could draw three hundred loyalists at the last minute out of goodwill alone. He was beloved, uniquely, deeply.

Now, in the dark, she watched the subtle transformation as her husband lost himself. So anxious these past months he'd become again the thin, too-tall boy she'd married. The curtain parted. And she watched with amusement at first and then with a warmth that bordered on awe as he mouthed the lines, made faces for each character as the actors came on and off. It became a sort of one-man show in the shadows.

In the scene where Manfred died, Lotto's face was slick and shining. Sweat, not tears, at least she believed. Hard to tell. [Tears.]

There were standing ovations, eight of them, the performers coming back again and again and again, not merely because of the audience's great love for Lotto, but because the play came together, like magic, congealed at the moment of airing. And when Lotto walked out from the wings, the roar from the audience could be heard in the little bar up the block, to which the friends who had been begged to attend and who had arrived to find the show sold-out had decamped to start their own impromptu party.

The glow lasted through the night, beyond the bar's closing, when there were no cabs on the street, and so Mathilde and Lotto decided to walk home, her arm in his, chatting about nothing, about everything, the unpleasant hot breath of the subway belching up from the grates. "Chthonic," he said, booze letting loose the pretension at his core, which she still found sweet, an allowance for the glory. It was so late there were few other people out, and it felt, just for this moment, that they had the city to themselves.

She thought of all the life just underfoot, the teem of it that they were passing over, unknowing. She said, "Did you know that the total weight of all the ants on earth is the same as the total weight of all the humans on earth?"

She, who never drank to excess, was a little bit drunk, it was true; there was so much relief in the evening. When the curtains closed against the backdrop, an enormous boulder blocking their future had rolled itself away.

"They'll still be here when we're gone," he said. He was drinking from a flask. By the time they were home, he'd be sozzled. "The ants and the jellyfish and the cockroaches. They will be the kings of the earth." He was amused by her; he, who was so often drunk. His poor liver. She pictured it inside him, a singed rat, pink and scarred.

"They deserve this place more than we do," she said. "We've been reckless with our gifts."

He smiled and looked up. There were no stars; there was too much smog for them. "Did you know," he said, "they found out just a little while ago that there are billions of worlds that can support life in our galaxy alone." He did his best Carl Sagan: "Billions and billions!"

She felt a sting behind her eyes, but couldn't say why this thought touched her.

He saw clear through and understood. [He knew her; the things he didn't know about her would sink an ocean liner; he knew her.] "We're lonely down here," he said. "It's true. But we're not alone."

IN THE HAZY SPACE after he died, when she lived in a sort of time-less underground grief, she saw on the Internet a video about what would happen to our galaxy in billions of years. We are in an immensely slow tango with the Andromeda galaxy, both galaxies shaped as spi-rals with outstretched arms, and we are moving toward each other like spinning bodies. The galaxies will gain speed as they near, casting off blue sparks, new stars, until they spin past each other. And then the long arms of both galaxies will reach longingly out and grasp hands at the last moment, and they will come spinning back in the opposite direction, their legs entwined but never hitting, until the second swirl becomes a clutch, a dip, a kiss. And then, at the very center of things, when they are at their closest, there will open a supermassive black hole.

THE NEXT MORNING, after the glorious first night, when everything was good and the light was sweet and possible, she went out for the paper and a whole box of patisserie, *pains au chocolat* and *chaussons aux pommes* and croissants, and ate a brilliant almond *viennoiserie* in four bites as she walked back. Once home in their cozy gold-ceilinged burrow, she poured a glass of water while Lotto rifled through the paper with his hair a bed-head wilderness, and when she turned back around, his great lovely face had blanched. He made a curious grimace, drawing down his lower lip until he showed his bottom teeth, for once, perhaps the first time ever, wordless.

"Uh-oh," she said, and came swiftly to him and read over his shoulder.

When she was finished, she said, "That critic can eat a bowl of dicks."

"Language, love," he said, but it came out automatically.

"No, seriously," Mathilde said. "Whatsername, Phoebe Delmar. She hates everything. She hated Stoppard's last play. She called it self-indulgent. She actually said that Suzan-Lori Parks was failing at being Chekhovian, which is insane because of course Suzan-Lori Parks isn't trying to be Chekhov, duh. It's hard enough to be Suzan-Lori Parks. That's like the simplest criterion for being a critic, right, evaluating a work on its own terms. She's like a bitch-face failed poet who knows nothing and is trying to make a name for herself by tearing people down. She only does pans. Don't even pay any attention at all."

"Yeah," he said, but too softly. He stood and turned around haplessly for a moment like a great tall dog about to sink down into the grass for a nap, then went to the bedroom and crawled under his covers and stayed there, unresponsive, even though Mathilde crept naked into the room on her hands and knees, and dug the sheet out from under the mattress and slithered up the length of his body from the toes up, her head popping out of the duvet at his neck; but his body was lax and his eyes were closed and he wouldn't respond, and even when she placed both of his hands on her bum, they slid off bonelessly in his misery.

Nuclear option it was, then. She laughed to herself; oh, she loved this hapless man. Mathilde went into the garden, overgrown now that poor Bette had passed away, and made a few phone calls, and at four in the afternoon, Chollie rang the doorbell with Danica on his arm—"Kiss kiss," Danica shouted in each of Mathilde's ears, and then, "Fuck you, I hate you, you're so pretty"—and Rachel and Elizabeth came in, hand in hand, sporting matching tattoos of turnips on their wrists, the meaning of which they gigglingly refused to divulge, and Arnie came and made sloe gin fizzes, and Samuel came in wearing his baby on his chest. When Mathilde succeeded in putting Lotto in a nice blue button-up and khakis, and dragged him out to his friends, and with every hug, every person who came up and told him earnestly how wonderful the play was, she saw an inch of spine returning to him; she saw the color coming back to his face. The man swallowed praise the way runners swallow electrolytes.

By the time the pizza came, Mathilde opened the door, and though she was in leggings and a semitransparent top, the delivery man's eyes were sucked to Lotto in the middle of the room, turning his arms into monster arms and bugging his eyes, telling a story of when he was mugged in the subway, pistol-whipped on the back of the head. He was emitting his usual light. He mimed a stagger then fell to his knees, and the pizza man leaned in to watch, ignoring the cash Mathilde was trying to hand him.

When she closed the door, Chollie was standing at her side. "Pig to man in a single hour," he said. "You're a reverse Circe."

She laughed silently; he'd pronounced it *Chir-chee*, as if Circe had been a modern Italian. "Oh, you dirty autodidact," she said. "It's pronounced *Ser-see*."

He looked wounded, but shrugged and said, "I never thought I'd say it, but you're good for him. Well, hell!" he said, now in a vicious Florida accent. "Empty-head friendless blond model gold digger actually turning out good. Who'd a thunk? At first, I done figgered you was going to take the money and run. But no. Lotto got hisself lucky." In his normal voice, Chollie said, "If he turns out to do something big with himself, it'll be because of you."

Despite the hot pizzas in her hands, the room felt cold. Mathilde held Chollie's eye. "He would have been great without me," she said. The others still on the couch, laughing up at Lotto, though Rachel was looking at Mathilde from the counter in the kitchen, clutching her own elbows.

"Even you couldn't have magicked that into being, witch," Chollie said, and he took a pizza box from her, opened it, folded three slices together, and put the box back on the stack to eat the mass in his hands, grinning at her through a mouthful of grease.

DURING THE YEARS when Lotto felt as if he were getting to be good enough and secure enough, even when he was working constantly, his plays all being published, productions all over the country steadily increasing so that they alone provided a comfortable living, even then he was gadflied by this Phoebe Delmar.

When *Telegony* appeared, Lotto was forty-four, and the acclaim was instant and near universal. Mathilde had seeded the idea in his head; it had been seeded in hers by Chollie years earlier with his Circe comment. It was the story of Circe and Odysseus's son Telegonus, who, after Odysseus had abandoned them, was raised by his mother in a mansion in the deep woods on Aeaea, protected by the enchanted tigers and pigs. When he left home, as all heroes must, Telegonus's witch mother gave him a poisoned stingray spear; he floated to Ithaca on his little ship, started stealing Odysseus's cattle and ended up in a terrible battle with the man he didn't know was his father, finally killing him.

[Telegonus married Penelope, Odysseus's long-suffering wife; Penelope's own son with Odysseus, Telemachus, ended up marrying Circe; half brothers became stepfathers. As Mathilde always read the myth, it was a roar in support of the sexiness of older women.]

Lotto's play was also a sly nod to the nineteenth-century idea of the term *telegony*: that offspring could inherit the genetic traits of their mother's previous lovers. Telegonus, in Lotto's version, bore the pig's snout, the wolf's ears, and the tiger's stripes of the lovers Circe had turned into animals. This character was always played in a terrifying mask, the fixity of which made the soft-spoken character all the more powerful. As a joke, Telemachus was also played in a mask in the round, with twenty different eyes and ten different mouths and noses for all of Penelope's suitors when Odysseus was off on his little meander over the Mediterranean.

The whole thing was set in Telluride in the modern day. It was an indictment of a democratic society that somehow was able to contain billionaires.

"Didn't Lancelot Satterwhite come from money? Isn't this hypocritical of him?" a man could be heard wondering at intermission in the foyer. "Oh, no, he was disinherited for getting married to his wife. It's such a tragic story, actually," a woman said, in passing. From mouth to mouth it spread, viral. The story of Mathilde and Lotto, the epic romance; he was unfamilied, cast out, not allowed to go home to Florida again. All for Mathilde. For his love for Mathilde.

Oh, god, thought Mathilde. The piety! It was enough to make her sick. But, for him, she let the story stand.

And then, perhaps a week after the opening, when the advance orders for the tickets were extended out to two months and Lotto was drowning in all of the congratulatory e-mails and calls, he came to bed in the middle of the night, and she woke instantly, and said, "Are you crying?"

"Crying!" he said. "Never. I'm a manly man. I splashed bourbon in my eyes."

"Lotto," she said.

"I mean, I was cutting onions in the kitchen. Who doesn't love to chop Vidalias in the dark?"

She sat up. "Tell me."

"Phoebe Delmar," he said, and handed over the laptop. In its dim gleam, his face was stricken.

Mathilde read and let out a whistle. "That woman better watch her back," she said darkly.

"She's entitled to her opinion."

"Her? Nope. This is the only hatchet job you got for *Telegony*. She's insane."

"Calm down," he said, but he seemed comforted by her anger. "Maybe she has a point. Maybe I am overrated."

Poor Lotto. He couldn't stand a dissenter.

"I know every part of you," Mathilde said. "I know every full stop and ellipsis in your work, and I was there when you wrote them. I can tell you better than anyone in the world, much more than this bombastic self-petard-hoisting leech of a critic, that you are not overrated. You are not overrated one single whit. She is overrated. They should cut off her fingers to keep her from writing anything more."

"Thank you for not cursing," Lotto said.

"*And* she can fuck herself lingeringly with a white-hot pitchfork. In her dark shit-star of an asshole," Mathilde said.

"Aha," he said. "Thy wit is a very bitter sweeting, it is a most sharp sauce."

"Try to sleep," Mathilde said. She kissed him. "Just write another one. Write a better one. Your success is like wormwood to her. It galls."

"She's the only one in the world," he said sadly, "who hates me."

What was this mania for universal adoration? Mathilde knew herself unworthy of the love of a single soul, and he wanted the love of everyone. She stifled a sigh. "Write another play, and she'll come around," she said, as she always did. And he wrote another one, as he always did.

19

MATHILDE BEGAN GOING for much longer runs in the hills. Two hours, three hours.

Sometimes, when Lotto was alive and he was in full steam up in his study in the attic and she could hear even in the garden outside as he cracked himself up, doing his characters' lines in their own voices, she had to put on her running shoes and set off down the road to prevent herself from going up the stairs and warming herself against his happiness; she had to run and run as a reminder that having her own strong body was a privilege in itself.

But after Lotto left, her grief had begun to radiate into her body, and there was a run after she had been several months a widow when Mathilde had to stop a dozen miles from the house and sit on a bank for a very long time because, it appeared, her body had stopped working the way it should. When she stood, she could only hobble like an old woman. It began to rain and her clothes were soaked, her hair stuck to her forehead and ears. She came slowly home.

But the private investigator was in Mathilde's kitchen, the light on over the sink. The dim brown dusk of October was falling outside.

"I let myself in," the investigator said. "About a minute ago." She was wearing a tight black dress, makeup. Like so, she looked German, elegant without being pretty. She wore figure eights in her ears, infinity swinging every time she moved her head.

"Huh," said Mathilde. She took off her running shoes, her socks, her wet shirt, and dried her hair with God's towel. "I wasn't aware that you knew where I lived," Mathilde said.

The investigator waved that away, said, "I'm good at what I do. Hope you don't mind that I've poured us a glass of wine. You're going to want it when you see what I found about your old friend Chollie Watson." She laughed at her own pleasure.

Mathilde took the manila envelope she held out, and they went out to the stone veranda where the watery sun was going down over the cold blue hills. They stood watching it in silence until Mathilde began to shiver.

"You're upset with me," the investigator said.

Mathilde said, very gently, "This is my space. I don't let anyone in. Finding you here felt like an assault."

"I'm sorry," the investigator said. "I don't know what I was thinking. I thought we had chemistry. I sometimes come on too strong."

"You? Really?" Mathilde said, relenting, taking a sip of her wine.

The investigator smiled, and her teeth gleamed. "You'll be less mad at me in a few minutes. I found some interesting stuff. Let's just say your buddy's got lots of friends. All at the same time." She gestured at the envelope she'd given Mathilde and turned her face away.

Mathilde pulled out the photographs inside. How strange to see someone she had known for so long entangled like that. After she'd seen four pictures, she was shuddering, and it wasn't from the cold. She went through all of them, resolute. "Excellent work," she said. "This is repulsive."

"Also expensive," the investigator said. "I took you at your word when you said money was no object."

"It isn't," Mathilde said.

The investigator came closer, touching Mathilde. "You know, your house surprised me. It's perfect. Every detail. But so tiny for someone who has so much. It's all light and planes and white walls. Shaker, almost."

"I live monastically," Mathilde said, meaning, of course, more. Her arms were crossed, wine in one hand, photographs in the other, but it didn't stop the investigator, who leaned over the arm of the chair to kiss Mathilde. Her mouth was soft, searching, and when Mathilde smiled but didn't kiss back, the woman went back down in her seat, and said, "Oh, okay. Sorry. Worth a shot."

"You don't have to be sorry," Mathilde said, squeezing the other woman's forearm. "Just don't be a creep."

YOU COULD STRING TOGETHER the parties Lotto and Mathilde had been to like a necklace, and you would have their marriage in miniature. She smiled at her husband down on the beach where the men were racing model cars. He was a redwood among pines, the light in his thinning hair, his laugh carrying past the waves, the music emanating mysteriously from the ceiling, the conversations among the women on the shaded veranda, drinking mojitos and watching the men. It was winter, freezing; they were all wearing fleeces. They pretended not to mind.

This party was near the end, though neither Mathilde nor Lotto knew it.

Just a lunch to celebrate Chollie and Danica's upgrade in the Hamptons. Ten thousand square feet, live-in housekeeper, chef, and gardener. Stupid, Mathilde thought, their friends were idiots. With Antoinette gone, Lotto and she could buy this place many times over. Except that later, in the car, Lotto and she would laugh at their friends for this kind of idiotic waste, the kind he was raised within before his father kicked the bucket, the kind they both knew meant nothing but loud pride. Mathilde still cleaned both the country house and the apartment, she took out the garbage, she fixed the toilet, she squeegeed the windows, she paid the bills. She still cooked and washed up from the cooking and ate the leftovers for lunch the next day.

Unplug from the humble needs of the body and a person becomes no more than a ghost.

These women around her were phantom people. Skin taut on their faces. Taking three nibbles of the chef's fine food and declaring themselves full. Jangling with platinum and diamonds. Abscesses of self.

But there was one woman there whom Mathilde didn't know, and this woman was blessedly normal. She was brunette and freckled but wasn't wearing makeup. Her dress was nice, but not fine. She had a wry expression on her face. Mathilde angled herself toward her.

Mathilde said, sotto voce, "One more word about Pilates, I'll pop."

The woman laughed silently, and said, "We're all doing planks while the great American ship goes down."

They talked about books, the bondage manual disguised as a novel for teenagers, the novel painstakingly pieced out of photos of street graffiti. The woman agreed that the new vegetarian restaurant in Tribeca that was all the rage was interesting, but said that a whole meal that revolved around the sunchoke had a certain sameness, plate to plate.

"They may want to consider other chokes. For instance, the arti," Mathilde said.

"I think they've put too much consideration into the arty," the woman said.

They kept taking tiny steps away from the others until they were alone by the steps. "I'm sorry," Mathilde said. "I'm not sure I know your name."

The woman sucked in her breath. She sighed. She shook Mathilde's hand. "Phoebe Delmar," she said.

"Phoebe Delmar," Mathilde repeated. "Hoo boy. The critic."

"The same," she said.

"I'm Mathilde Satterwhite. My husband is Lancelot Satterwhite. The playwright. Right there. That big lunk with the superloud laugh whose plays you have eviscerated over the past fifteen years."

"I was aware. Occupational hazard," Phoebe Delmar said. "I tend
to pop up at parties like a scolding aunt. My boyfriend brought me. I
didn't know you'd be here. I would never have ruined your fun with
my presence." She seemed sad.

"I always thought I'd deck you if I met you," Mathilde said.

"Thank you for not doing so," Phoebe said.

"Well. I haven't decided definitively against it," Mathilde said.

Phoebe put her hand on Mathilde's shoulder. "I never mean to
cause pain. It's my job. I take your husband seriously. I want him to
be better than he is." Her voice was earnest, sweet.

"Oh, please. You say that as if he's sick," Mathilde said.

"He is. Great American Artistitis," Phoebe Delmar said. "Ever
bigger. Ever louder. Jostling for the highest perch in the hegemony.
You don't think that's some sort of sickness that befalls men when
they try to do art in this country? Tell me, why did Lotto write a war
play? Because works about war always trump works about emotions,
even if the smaller, more domestic plays are better written, smarter,
more interesting. The war stories are the ones that get the prizes. But
your husband's voice is strongest when he speaks most quietly and
clearly."

She looked at Mathilde's face and took a step back, and said,
"Whoa."

"Lunch!" Danica called, ringing a great brass bell on the porch.
The men picked up the model cars, ground out the cigars, came
trudging up the dune, their khakis rolled to their knees and their skin
pink with cold wind. They sat at a long table with their plates heaped
from the buffet. Space heaters disguised as shrubbery exhaled warmth.
Mathilde sat between Lotto and Samuel's wife, who was showing her
photos of their new baby—Samuel's fifth child—on her cell phone.
"Lost a tooth on the playground, that monkey," she said. "She's only
three."

Down at the end of the table, Phoebe Delmar was listening wordlessly to some man whose voice was so loud, bits of his conversation were audible all the way to Mathilde. "Problem with Broadway these days is that it's for *tourists* . . . only great playwright America has produced is August Wilson . . . don't go to theater. It's only for snobs or people from Boise, Idaho." Phoebe caught her eye, and Mathilde laughed at her salmon steak. God, she wished she didn't like the woman. It would make things so much easier.

"Who's that lady you were talking to?" Lotto said in the car.

She smiled at him, kissed his knuckles. "I never caught her name," she said.

When *Eschatology* was performed for the first time, Phoebe Delmar loved it.

In six weeks, Lotto would be dead.

I HAD OFTEN SAID *that I would write, The Wives of Geniuses I Have Sat With. I have sat with so many. I have sat with wives who were not wives, of geniuses who were real geniuses. I have sat with real wives of geniuses who were not real geniuses. . . . In short I have sat very often and very long with many wives and wives of many geniuses.* Gertrude Stein wrote this in the voice of her partner, Alice B. Toklas. Stein being, apparently, the genius: Alice apparently the wife.

"I AM NOTHING," Alice said, after Gertrude died, "but a memory of her."

AFTER MATHILDE flipped the Mercedes, the policeman came. She opened her lips and let the blood run out, for the sake of drama.

LAUREN GROFF

The flashing blues and reds made him look ill, then well, then ill again. She saw herself as if his face were a mirror. She was pale and skinny with a shorn head, with a chin full of blood, blood down her neck, blood on her hands and down her arms.

She held up her palms, which she'd cut on the barbed-wire fence, climbing over it to the road.

"Stigmata," she said as tonguelessly as possible, and laughed.

20

SHE HAD ALMOST DONE the right thing. At first, that bright April morning after *Hamlet* at Vassar, after the full and heady flight into Lotto, the love in her blood already humming like a beehive.

She'd woken to the flick of dark when the path lights out the window extinguished themselves. Her clothes still on, no telltale soreness below. Her promise to Ariel kept, then; she hadn't had sex with Lotto. She'd broken no commitments. She'd only slept beside this charming boy. She looked below the sheet. He was naked. And how.

Lotto's fists were balled up beneath his chin, and even in sleep, absent that waking wit, he was plain. The scarred skin on the cheeks. The hair still thick and swirling around his ears, the lashes, that carved jaw. She had never in her life met such an innocent. In nearly everyone who had ever lived there was at least one small splinter of evil. There was none in him: she knew it when she saw him up on that windowsill the night before, the lightning shocking the world behind him. His eagerness, his deep kindness, these were the benefits of his privilege. This peaceful sleep of being born male and rich and white and American and at this prosperous time, when the wars that were happening were far from home. This boy, told from the first moment he was born that he could do what he wanted. All he needed was to try. Mess up over and over, and everyone would wait until he got it right.

She should be resentful. But she could not find resentment toward him anywhere inside her. She wanted to press herself against him until his beautiful innocence had stamped itself on her.

In her ear, the voice she tried to block out all these years told her sternly to go. To not inflict herself on him. She had never been made to be obedient, but she thought of him waking to find her there, how irreparable the damage would be, and she obeyed; she dressed and fled.

She pulled the collar of her jacket over her cheeks so nobody would see her distress even though it was still dark outside.

There was a diner in town, deep into the grayer, less gleaming streets, a place most Vassar students would never go near. This is why she loved it. Also: the grease and smell and the homicidal cook who smashed the hash browns like he hated them and the waitress who seemed to be neurologically lopsided, her ponytail pulled unintentionally toward an ear, an eye floating off toward the ceiling as she took the order. On one hand, her nails were long; on the other, they were short and polished red.

Mathilde took her usual booth and hid her face behind the menu and let her smile fall off her face, and the waitress didn't say a word, just put the black coffee and rye toast and a small linen handkerchief with blue embroidery before Mathilde, as if she knew that tears would come. Well. Perhaps they would, though Mathilde hadn't cried since she was Aurélie. One side of the waitress's face winked and she went back to the radio that was fuzzily playing some shock jock, all brimstone and perdition.

Mathilde knew how her life would go if she let it. Already, she knew that she and Lotto would be married if she seeded the thought in his brain. The question was if she could let him off the hook. Practically anyone would be better for him than she would be.

She watched the waitress swaying behind the homicidal cook to grab a mug from the rack under the counter. She saw how she put her hands on his hips, how he bumped back against her with his rear, a little slapstick in-joke, kiss of hips.

Mathilde let the coffee and the toast go cold. She paid, tipped far too much. And then she stood and walked into town, and stopped at the Caffè Aurora for cannoli and coffee, and was at Lotto's room with two aspirin and a glass of water and the food when his eyelashes gave a little flutter and he looked up from whatever dream—unicorns, leprechauns, merry forest bacchanals—to see her sitting beside him.

"Oh," he said. "I thought you couldn't be real. I thought you were the best dream I ever had."

"No dream," she said. "I'm real. I'm here."

He put her hand on his cheek and rested there against her. "I think I'm dying," he whispered.

"You're severely hungover. And we're born dying," she said, and he laughed, and she held his warm, rough cheek, having committed to him in perpetuity.

She shouldn't have. She knew it. But her love for him was new, and her love for herself was old, and she was all she'd had for so very, very long. She was weary of facing the world alone. He had presented himself at the exact right time, her lifeline, although it would be better for him if he had married the kind of soft, godly woman she'd know soon enough his own mother wanted for him. That Bridget girl would have made everyone happy. Mathilde was neither soft nor godly. But she made a promise that he would never know the scope of her darkness, that she would never show him the evil that lived in her, that he would know of her only a great love and light. And she wanted to believe that their whole life together he did.

"MAYBE, AFTER GRADUATION, we could go visit Florida," Lotto said, into the back of her neck.

This was just after they were married. Days, maybe. She thought of Lotto's mother on the telephone, the bribe Antoinette had dangled. A million dollars. Please. For a moment, she considered telling him all about the call, then thought of how he'd be wounded, and knew she couldn't. She'd protect him. Better for him to believe his mother punitive than just plain cruel. Mathilde's apartment above the mission-style antique shop was bizarrely elongated in the streetlight filtering up. "I haven't been home since I was fifteen. I want to show you off. I want to show you all the places I juvenile delinquented," he said, his voice deepening.

"That's not a word," she murmured. And she kissed him so long, she made him forget.

Then: "Baby," he said, cleaning up with his bare foot and a paper towel a glass of water he'd spilled on the oak floor in their new, sub-rosa apartment in Greenwich Village, gleaming as it was, still sans furniture. "I was thinking that maybe we could take a weekend and visit Sallie and my mom on the beach. I'd love to see your bod kicking it with tan lines."

"Definitely," Mathilde said. "But let's wait until you get your first big role. You want to come back the conquering hero. Besides, thanks to your mother, we don't have any money." When he looked doubtful, she stepped closer, slid her hand down the waistband of his jeans, and whispered, "If you come back with a role under your belt, you can return the cock of the walk." He looked down at her. He crowed.

Then: "I think I have seasonal affective disorder," he groused, watching sleet turn the street pewter, shivering from the draft coming from the windows that touched the sidewalk. "Let's go home for Christmas and get a little sun."

"Oh, Lotto," Mathilde said. "With what? I just bought our weekly groceries with thirty-three dollars and a handful of quarters." Her eyes went damp with frustration.

He shrugged. "Sallie will pay. Three seconds on the phone, and it's done."

"I'm sure," she said. "But we are too proud to take handouts from anyone. Right?" She neglected to say she'd called Sallie just last week; that Sallie had paid two months' rent, plus the phone bill.

He shivered. "Right," he said sadly. Staring at his darkening face in the window. "We are very proud, too proud, aren't we?"

Then: "I can't believe," Lotto said, coming out of the bedroom, still carrying the telephone on which he'd had his weekly update from his mother and Sallie, "that we've been married for two years and you've never met my mother. That's insane."

"Completely," Mathilde said. She was still smarting from a note Antoinette had sent to the gallery. No words this time. Only a painting ripped from a glossy magazine, Andrea Celesti's *Queen Jezebel Being Punished by Jehu*, the lady defenestrated and being gobbled by dogs. Mathilde had opened the envelope and laughed in surprise; Ariel, peering over her shoulder, had said, "That. Oh. Not our kind of thing." She thought of this note and touched the handkerchief she wore on her hair, cut recently in a wedge, dyed a strange bright orange. She was repositioning a painting on the wall that she'd salvaged from the dumpster at the gallery; a moving blue that she'd hold on to for the rest of her life, long past the loves, the bodily hungers. She looked at Lotto, and said, "But I'm not so sure she'd want to meet me, love. She's still so mad you married me that she hasn't come to visit us once."

He picked her up and leaned her against the door. She put her legs around his waist. "She'll relent. Give it time." So transparent, her husband, how he believed that if only he could show his mother how right his choice was to marry Mathilde, everything would be all right. God, they needed the money.

"I've never had a mom," she said. "It breaks my heart, too, that she doesn't want to know me, her new daughter. When was the last time you saw her? Sophomore year of college? Why can't she come visit you? Xenophobia is a bitch."

"Agoraphobia," he said. "It's a real disease, Mathilde."

"That's what I meant," she said. [She, who always said what she meant.]

Then: "My mom said that she'd be glad to send us tickets for Fourth of July this year if we want to go celebrate."

"Oh, Lotto, I wish," Mathilde said, putting her paintbrush down, frowning at the wall, which was a strange greenish navy. "But remember, there's that huge show we're doing at the gallery that's going to be taking up all the time I have. But you can go. Go ahead! Don't worry about me."

"Without you?" he said. "But the whole purpose is to make her love you."

"Next time," she said. She picked up the brush, and dabbed his nose gently with the paint, and laughed when he smushed his face up against her bare belly, leaving fading stamps against the white.

And so it went. There was never the money, and when there was the money, he had a gig, and when he didn't have a gig, she had to work really hard on this huge project, and no, his sister's coming to stay that weekend, and they had that party they've already committed to going to, and, well, maybe it would be easier if Antoinette came to visit them? I mean, she's loaded and doesn't have a job, and if she wants to see them so desperately, she can just hop a plane, can't she? They are so busy, every moment jam-packed, and weekends are *their* time, the precious little time that they get to spend remembering why they got married! And it's not like the woman ever made the slightest effort, seriously, she didn't even come to Lotto's college graduation. Any of his performances; any of the first-runs of his own plays. That. He. Wrote. Himself. For fuck's sake. Not to mention that she never saw their wee first apartment down in that basement in Greenwich Village, that she never came to see even this slightly better walk-up, that she never in her life has come to the country house among the cherries, Mathilde's joy, which she crafted from a wreck with her own hands. Yes, of course, agoraphobia is a terrible thing, but Antoinette's also the woman who has never once wanted to talk to Mathilde on the phone. Whose gifts every birthday and Christmas clearly come from Sallie. Does Lotto not know how much that hurts? Mathilde, motherless, familyless, to be discarded so; how painful it is to her to know that the love of her life has a mother who rejects her.

Lotto could have gone by himself. Absolutely. But she was the one who always ordered their lives; he'd never once bought a plane ticket, rented a car. Of course, there was also the worse reason, a darker one that he turned from quickly every time he brushed up against it, a tarry fury that he ignored so long that, by now, it had become too enormous to contemplate.

The urgency abated when they bought Antoinette a computer and the Sunday chats migrated to video. Antoinette didn't have to leave her house to send her white face floating in the darkened room like a balloon. For a decade, every Sunday, Lotto's voice transitioned into the bright, overarticulate child he must have been. Mathilde had to leave the house when the call came in.

One time, he left the video chat to fetch something, a review, an article, to share with his mother, and unsuspecting Mathilde came in from a run shining with sweat in her sports bra, shoving her wet hair back from her cheeks, and she pulled out the foam roller, and lay on her side with her back to the computer, and levered herself back and forth across it until her IT band had loosened. It was only when she turned over for the other side that she saw Antoinette watching from the screen, so close to the camera that her forehead was enormous, her chin arrowed to a point, red slash of lipstick, hands in her hair, gazing with such intensity that Mathilde could not move. A tractor drew up their dirt road and went away with a lower tone. Only when she heard Lotto's steps coming down the stairs could she get up, get away. From the hall she heard him say, "Muvva. Lipstick! You've made yourself

pretty for me," and she said in a sweet, soft voice, "Ah, you're imply-
ing that I'm not always pretty," and Lotto laughed, and Mathilde fled
outside, into the garden, feeling loose around the knees.

Then: Oh, honey, don't cry, absolutely, they should visit Antoinette, as sick as she is these days, at least four hundred pounds now,
diabetic, too heavy to do more than totter from bed to couch. They
must. They absolutely must. They will. [This time Mathilde meant it.]

Before she could make plans, though, Antoinette, ailing, called
Mathilde at the house in the middle of the night, her voice almost too
soft to hear.

She said, "Please. Let me see my son. Let Lancelot fly down to me."

Capitulation. Mathilde waited, savoring. Antoinette sighed, and
in the sigh there was irritation, superiority, and Mathilde hung up
without speaking. Lotto called down from his study upstairs, where
he was working, "Who was that?" And Mathilde called up the stairs,
"Wrong number."

"At this hour of the night?" he said. "People are the worst."

Wrong number. She served herself a bourbon. She drank it in the
bathroom mirror, watching the flush fade from her face, her eyes sizzling, all pupil.

But then a curious feeling came over her, as if a hand had reached
in and seized her lungs. Squeezed. "What am I doing?" she said aloud.
Tomorrow. She would call Antoinette and say, Well, of course Lotto
could come down. He was Antoinette's only son, after all. It was
too late now; first thing in the morning, she'd call. First thing, well,
after her eighty-mile bike ride. He wouldn't even be awake until she
got back. She slept well and went out in the night bluing into dawn.
Morning fog, swift swim up the glorious hills, the cooling drizzle,
the sun burning off the damp. She'd forgotten her water; she returned
after only twenty miles. The glide down the country road to her little
white house.

When she clipped back into the house, Lotto was in the doorway, his head in his hands. He looked up at her, pale and distraught. "My mother's dead," he said. He wouldn't be able to cry for another hour or so.

"Oh, no," Mathilde said. She hadn't thought death possible when it came to Antoinette. [So immense, what was between them, immortal.] She walked over to her husband, and he put his face against her sweaty side, and she held his head there in her hands. And then her own grief rose, a surprising sharp bolt in the temples. Now who did she have to fight? This was not the way it was supposed to go.

IN COLLEGE, Mathilde went once with Ariel to Milwaukee.

He had business there and she was his on the weekend, to do with what he liked. She spent most of her time shivering at the bay window of her room in the bed-and-breakfast. Downstairs: polished brass, plates of scones, walls thick with oils painted by Victorian spinsters, a woman whose flared nostrils told her what she thought of Mathilde.

Outside, snow had fallen thigh-deep in the night. The plows had swept the street snow into mountains bordering the sidewalk. Something was deeply soothing about so much untouched white.

Mathilde watched as down the street came a little girl in a red snowsuit with purple racing stripes. Mittens, a cap too big for her head. Disoriented, the girl turned around and around and around. She began to climb the snow mountain that blocked her from the street. But she was so weak. Halfway up, she'd slip back down. She'd try again, digging her feet deeper into the drift. Mathilde held her breath each time, let it out when the girl fell. She thought of a cockroach in a wineglass, trying to climb up the smooth sides.

When Mathilde looked across the street at a long brick apartment complex taking up the whole block, ornate in its 1920s style, she saw, in scattered windows, three women watching the little girl's struggles.

Mathilde watched the women as they watched the girl. One was laughing over her bare shoulder at someone in the room, flushed with sex. One was elderly, drinking her tea. The third, sallow and pinched, had crossed her skinny arms and was pursing her lips.

At last, the girl, exhausted, slid down and rested, her face against the snow. Mathilde was sure she was crying.

When Mathilde looked up again, the woman with crossed arms was staring angrily through all the glass and cold and snow directly at her. Mathilde startled, sure she'd been invisible. The woman disappeared. She reappeared on the sidewalk in inside clothes, tweedy and thin. She chucked her body into the snowdrift in front of the apartment building, crossed the street, grabbed the girl by the mittens and swung her over the mountain. Carried her across the street and did it again. Both mother and daughter were powdered with white when they went inside.

Long after they were gone, Mathilde thought of the woman. What she was imagining when she saw her little girl fall and fall and fall. She wondered at the kind of anger that would crumple your heart up so hard that you could watch a child struggle and fail and weep for so long, without moving to help. Mothers, Mathilde had always known, were people who abandoned you to struggle alone.

It occurred to her then that life was conical in shape, the past broadening beyond the sharp point of the lived moment. The more life you had, the more the base expanded, so that the wounds and treasons that were nearly imperceptible when they happened stretched like tiny dots on a balloon slowly blown up. A speck on the slender child grows into a gross deformity in the adult, inescapable, ragged at the edges.

A light went on in the mother and daughter's window. In it the girl sat down with a notebook. Her small head bent. After some time, the mother put a steaming cup beside the girl, and the girl picked it up and cradled it in both hands. In Mathilde's mouth came the forgotten sweet-salty taste of hot milk.

Perhaps, Mathilde thought, watching flakes fall into dark and the empty street, I've been wrong. Perhaps the mother had watched her daughter fail and fail and didn't move to help out of something unfathomable, something Mathilde struggled to understand, a thing that was like an immense kind of love.

AT MIDNIGHT ON THE DAY Mathilde shoved the dog away from her into a new life with the little family, she woke to find herself outside in the overcast night, no glim of moon, the pool a tar pit. Still wearing the floor-length ivory sheath, she found herself screaming for the dog.

"God!" she was shouting. "God!" But the dog was not skittering back to her. There was no noise, all still and lightless and watchful. Her heart began to pound. She went in, calling, "God? God?" She looked in all the closets, under all the beds; she looked in the kitchen, and it wasn't until she saw the crate missing that she remembered what she'd done.

Handed the creature to strangers, as if the dog weren't a piece of her.

She barely made it to dawn. Day was one orange scratch against the dark when she knocked on the door of the split-level out in the fields. The husband answered, pressing his finger to his lips, and came out in his bare feet. He leaned inside, whistled once, and God bounded out the door, a purple ribbon around her neck, squealing and moaning and scrabbling at Mathilde's feet. She crouched to press the dog against her face for a long while, then looked up at the man.

"I'm sorry," Mathilde said. "Tell your kids I'm sorry."

"No apologies," he said. "You're sorrowing. If my wife died, honey, I'd burn the house down."

"That's next on the list," she said, and he chuckled once without smiling.

He fetched the crate, the toys, put it all in her car. When he came out again, his wife came with him, tiptoeing in the frosted grass, something steaming in her hands. She wasn't smiling or unsmiling; she just looked tired, her hair mussed. She handed blueberry muffins through the window, leaned in, and said, "Don't know whether to smack you or kiss you."

"Story of my life," Mathilde said.

The woman pivoted and marched off. Mathilde watched, burning her hands on the pan.

She looked in the mirror at God's foxy face in the backseat, the almondine eyes. "Everyone leaves me. Don't you dare," she said.

The dog yawned, showing her sharp teeth, her wet tongue.

DURING THEIR LAST YEAR, though she said nothing, Ariel must have felt her strengthening. Their contract ending. The world opening to her, almost painful in its possibility. She was so young still.

She had an idea of her life after college, after Ariel. She would live in one high-ceilinged room painted a soft ivory, the floors a pale wash. She would wear all black and have a job with people and come to make friends. She had never, really, had friends. She didn't know what friends could possibly have to talk about. She would go out to dinner every night. She would spend all weekend alone in the bathtub with a book and a bottle of wine. She could be happy growing old, moving among people when she wanted, but alone.

At the very least, she wanted to fuck someone her own age. Someone who'd look her in the face.

In March, just before she met Lotto and he put color into her world, she came into Ariel's apartment to find him already there waiting for her. She put her bag down warily. He was on the couch, very still.

"What would you like to eat?" he said. She hadn't eaten since the night before. She was hungry.

"Sushi," she said, unwisely. She could never eat sushi again.

When the delivery boy came, Ariel made her open the door naked to pay. The delivery boy could barely breathe, looking at her.

Ariel took the styrofoam package, opened it, stirred the soy sauce and wasabi, and took a piece of nigiri and dabbed it into the mix. He set the single piece on the tile in the kitchen. The floor was scrupulously clean, as was everything about him.

"Down on your hands and knees," he said, smiling with all his teeth. "Crawl."

"Don't use your hands," he said. "Pick it up with your teeth."

"Now lick up the mess you made," he said.

The parquet pressing into her palms and knees. She hated the part of her, small and hot, that enflamed itself being here, on hands and knees. Dirty girl. She burned. She made a vow: she would never crawl for another man. [The gods love to fuck with us, Mathilde would say later; she became a wife.]

"Another?" Ariel said. He dipped it, put it at the end of the hallway, twenty yards away. "Crawl," he said. He laughed.

THE WORD *wife* comes from the Proto-Indo-European *weip*.

Weip means *to turn, twist, or wrap.*

In an alternative etymology, the word *wife* comes from Proto-etc., *ghwibh.*

Ghwibh means *pudenda.* Or *shame.*

21

THE INVESTIGATOR SHOWED UP at the grocery store. Mathilde put the groceries in the trunk and slid into the front seat, and there the girl was waiting with a document box on her knees. Her makeup was all smoky eyes and red lips, sexy.

"God!" Mathilde said, startling. "I said not to be creepy."

The girl laughed. "I guess it's my signature." She motioned toward the box. "Ta-da. I've got it all. This dude will never get out of federal prison. When are you blowing this sucker up? I want to be there with popcorn when it's all over cable news."

"Phase one is the private photos. That starts in a few days," Mathilde said. "There's a party I have to go to. I'm going to make him suffer a little before phase two." She started up the car and drove the investigator to the house.

It was neither as strange as Mathilde had expected nor as sexy. She felt sad, staring at the chandelier and feeling the familiar warmth building in her; one would expect a lesbian to have expertise, but really, Lotto had been better. Oh, Christ, he'd been better at every-thing than anyone. He'd ruined her for sex. What, really, was the point of this? There could be no second act in this little bed play of theirs, just a reprisal of act one, with the characters reversed, no thrilling, messy denouement, and frankly, she wasn't at all sure what she felt about sticking her face in some other lady's bits. She let the orgasm spark in her forehead and smiled at the private investigator when she came up out of the sheets.

"That was," Mathilde began, but the investigator said, "No, I get it. Loud and clear. You're not into chicks."

"I wasn't *not* into it," Mathilde said.

"Liar," the girl said. She shook out her dark hair and it puffed out like a mushroom. "But it's better. Now we can be friends."

Mathilde sat up, looking at the girl, who was putting her bra back on. "Other than my sister-in-law, I don't think I've ever had a real female friend," she said.

"Your friends are all guys?" the girl said.

It took a very long time before Mathilde could say, "No." The girl looked at her for a moment and leaned forward and gave her a long motherly kiss on the forehead.

LOTTO'S AGENT CALLED HER. It was time, he intimated with a quaver in his voice, that she begin to take over business matters again. A few times he had been the recipient of her soft venom.

She paused for so long that he said, "Hello? Hello?"

There was a large part of her that wanted to put the plays behind her. To face forward into the unknown.

But she held the phone to her ear. She looked around. Lotto wasn't in this house, not on his side of the bed, not in his study in the attic. Not in the clothes in the closets. Not in their first little underground apartment, where, a few weeks ago, she'd found herself looking through the casement windows, seeing only a stranger's purple couch and a pug dog leaping at the doorknob. Her husband wasn't about to pull up the drive, though she was always on alert, listening. There were no children; his face wouldn't shine up out of a smaller one. There was no heaven, no hell; she wouldn't find him on a cloud or in a pit of fire or in a meadow of asphodel after her body quit her. The only place that Lotto could be seen anymore was in his work. A miracle, the ability to take a soul and implant it, whole, in another person for even a few hours at a time. All those plays were fragments of Lotto that, together, formed a kind of whole.

So she told the agent to send her what needed to be done. Nobody would forget Lancelot Satterwhite. Not his plays. Not the tiny fragments of him in his work.

EIGHT MONTHS AFTER she'd been made a widow, almost to the day, Mathilde was still feeling the shocks in the ground where she stepped. She climbed out of the cab into the dark city street. In her silvery dress, in her new boniness, in the hair she'd bleached white in its boy's cut, she was Amazonian. She wore bells on her wrists. She wanted them to hear her coming.

"Oh my god," Danica cried out when Mathilde opened the door and walked into the apartment, handing her coat to a servant girl. "Widowhood sure as shit becomes you. Christ, look at you."

Danica had never been pretty, but she hid it now with skin orange and pumped with botulism, sinewy yoga muscles underneath. Her flesh was so thin one could see the delicate ribs where they met in the center of her chest. The necklace she wore cost a middle manager's yearly salary. Mathilde always hated rubies. Dried corpuscles polished to a gloss, she thought.

"Oh," said Mathilde. "Thanks." She let the other woman air-kiss her.

Danica said, "God. If there was a guarantee that I'd look like you when I'm a widow, I'd let Chollie eat bacon for every meal."

"That's a terrible thing to say," Mathilde said. And Danica said, her black eyes moistening, "Oh, I'm so sorry. I was trying to make a joke. God, I'm the worst. Always putting a foot in it. I've had too many martinis, haven't eaten a thing, trying to fit into this dress. Mathilde, I'm sorry. I'm a jerk. Don't cry."

"I'm not crying," Mathilde said, and went over and took the glass from Chollie's hand and drank the gin down. On the piano, she put Danica's present, the Hermès scarf that Antoinette—well, really, it was Sallie—had sent her a few birthdays ago, still in its ostentatious orange box. "Oh, so generous!" said Danica, and she kissed Mathilde on the cheek.

Danica went to the door to greet other friends, a former candidate for mayor and his shellacked wife.

"Forgive her. She's drunk," Chollie said. He had slid up unnoticed. As usual.

"Yes, well, when is she not?" Mathilde said.

"Touché. She deserves that," he said. "Life is hard for her. She feels so insignificant, trying to keep up with all those purebred social-ites. Do you want to head to the powder room to compose yourself?"

"I am never not composed," Mathilde said.

"True," Chollie said. "But your face, it looks. I don't know, strange."

"Oh. That's because I've stopped smiling," Mathilde said. "For so many years, I never let anyone see me without smiling. I don't know why I didn't stop earlier. It's enormously relaxing."

He looked pained. He held his own hands and flushed, and said, darting a look at her face, "I was surprised you RSVP'd, Mathilde. It shows maturity after our talk. After what I revealed. Forgiveness. Kindness. I didn't think you had it in you."

"You know, Chollie, I was so angry," she said. "I wanted to garrote you with my shoelaces. I almost killed you with that ice cream spoon. But then I realized that you were full of shit. Lotto would never have left me. I know this as deep as my bones. No matter what you did, you couldn't have hurt us. What we had was so far beyond anything you could ever do to ruin it. You're just a little mosquito, Chollie. All itch, no poison. You are less than nothing."

Chollie was about to say something, but only looked weary and sighed.

"Anyway. Despite it all, we are old friends," she said, squeezing his forearm. "One doesn't get many old friends in life. I missed you. Both of you. Even Danica."

He stood still for a long time, looking at her. At last, he said, "You always were too kind, Mathilde. We are all undeserving of you." He was sweating. He turned away, either annoyed or moved. For some time, she flipped through a lavish book on the coffee table called *Winged Cupid Painted Blind* that seemed strangely familiar to her, but the panels all blended together and she saw nothing at all.

Later, as everyone was moving through the living room on the way into dinner, Mathilde stayed a few seconds behind, ostensibly looking at the small Rembrandt that Chollie had just bought. If a Rembrandt could be boring, this was. Classical composition, three bodies in a dark room, one pouring some unguent from a vase, one sitting, one speaking. Well, nobody had ever accused Chollie of having taste. She went back toward the piano. She pulled a second gift out of her handbag, this one in light blue paper. It was thin. The size of an envelope, wrapped. There was no card on this one, but she was sure it was the best gift of the bunch. Almost artistic, strobe-lit naked Chollie among all that stranger flesh.

At noon the next day after Danica's birthday party, Mathilde was waiting. She sat reading the paper in the breakfast room, luxuriating in her pajamas. She picked up the phone on the first ring, already grinning.

"She left me," Chollie spat. "You hell-dog monster bitch-face cunt."

Mathilde took off her reading glasses and propped them on her head. She fed God a rind of her pancake. "Would you look at that. My dick's on the table," she said. "Seems my game's longer than yours. Just wait until you see what's coming for you next."

"I'll kill you," he said.

"Can't. I died eight months ago," she said. She gently hung up.

SHE SAT IN THE KITCHEN, SAVORING. The dog on her bed, the moon in the window. In the beautiful blue bowl, the tomatoes from her summer garden had gone wrinkled and were emitting a powerful earthy sweetness, just before rot. For two months, she had left the letter from Land there, for what she imagined was in it. What? Gratitude? Sexy words? An invitation for her to visit him in the city? She'd liked him immensely. Something in him was balm to her. She would have gone, spent the night in his surely overpriced exposed-brick loft in a trendy riverfront area, and would have driven home at dawn feeling ridiculous. Also, she would have felt smooth and fine, loudly singing to thirty-year-old pop. Sexy. Young again.

She had just come back from her penultimate meeting with the FBI detective. He had salivated for what she told him she had. The filthy photographs of Chollie had done their magic. [In three months, Danica would be a divorcée rich beyond measure.] The box of files that, tomorrow, she would give to the sweaty small agent with the sideburns was her footrest in the kitchen tonight. She kept looking down through the dark where the box was as lunar pale as a toadstool.

On her laptop there was a French movie. In her hand, a globe of malbec. There was something satiated in her; something calmed. She was imagining Chollie's headlong fall. She pictured his fat face on the television as he was squeezed into the cop car; how childlike he would look, how at a loss.

The doorbell rang. She opened the door to Rachel and Sallie. On the porch, doubled, her husband briefly shining out.

Mathilde let herself lean for a few breaths into the buttress of their arms, felt the weight of her own body relieved for the first time in so long.

She opened cold champagne for them. [Why the hell not.]

"Celebrating?" Rachel said.

"You tell me," Mathilde said. She'd noted Sallie's collar askew, the ring twisted wrong around Rachel's finger. Nerves. Something was up. But they didn't tell her, not yet. They sat drinking. With her long and bony face, Rachel in the twilight looked molded of resin; Sallie polished in a silk jacket, chic haircut. Mathilde thought of Sallie on her world tour, imagined lushness, fruit in the shape of swans, lovers in damp sheets. The word *spinster* hid behind it a blazing freedom; and how hadn't Mathilde seen this before?

Rachel put the glass down and leaned forward. The emerald tapped three slowing swings against her clavicle, dully gleamed when it came to rest in the air.

Mathilde closed her eyes, said, "Say it."

From her pocketbook, Sallie pulled a thick kraft file and put it on Mathilde's knees, and Mathilde lifted a corner with her index finger and opened it. From most recent to least, a gallery of vice. Most were not even hers. From freshest to oldest; all before Lotto died. Grainy photo of Mathilde in a bikini on a beach in Thailand, the failed separation. Mathilde kissing Arnie's cheek on a street corner. [Ludicrous, even if she were canted toward infidelity, he was too slimy.] Mathilde, drawn, a skeleton, young, walking into the abortion clinic. Her uncle, strange shiny pages smuggled from some sort of secret file delineating his purported offenses as of 1991—she would read it like a novel much later. Finally, her Paris grandmother and her rap sheet in French, smiling wickedly at the camera, *prostituée* like flyspecks across the page.

Great gaps here: a lacework of her life's tissue. Thank god that the worst of it remained holes. Ariel. The sterilization, the baseless hope for children she'd let live in Lotto. What Aurélie had done all those years ago. All the deficits of goodness that added up to a shadow Mathilde.

Mathilde reminded herself to breathe, looked up. "You researched me?"

"No. Antoinette did," Sallie said, clicking her teeth against her glass. "From the first."

"All this time?" Mathilde said. "She was committed." A pang. All this time, and Mathilde had been vibrantly alive in Antoinette's head.

"Muvva was a patient woman," Rachel said.

Mathilde closed the file and tapped the papers neatly back. She poured the rest of the champagne equally into the glasses. When she looked up, Sallie and Rachel were both making grotesque puffed-up faces that startled her. Together, they began laughing.

"Mathilde thinks we're about to hurt her," Sallie said.

"Sweet M.," Rachel said. "We wouldn't."

Sallie sighed, wiped her face. "Don't fret. We kept you from harm. Twice Antoinette tried to send packets to Lotto, once with your uncle and then the abortion, and again when you left him. She overlooked that I was the one to walk mail down to the box at the end of the drive and back."

Rachel laughed. "The will she sent me to have notarized was lost. Donating Lotto's share of the trust to a chimp rescue. Poor needy monkeys are going to go without their bananas," she said. She shrugged. "It was Muvva's fault. She never expected gross perfidy from the meek and mild."

Mathilde saw her own face reflected in the window, but no, it was a barn owl on a low branch in the cherry trees.

She could barely master herself. She had never expected this. These women. Such kindness. Their eyes shining in the dim room. They saw her. She didn't know why, but they saw her and they loved her even still.

"There's one more thing," Rachel said, so quickly Mathilde had to concentrate to understand. "You don't know this. We didn't until my mother died. I mean, it was a total shock. We had to process it before we did anything. And then we were going to tell Lotto after we put things in order. But he." She left the sentence unfinished. Mathilde watched as her face, as if in slow motion, collapsed. She handed over a photo album in inexpensive cordovan. Mathilde opened it.

Inside: a confusion. A face startlingly familiar. Handsome, dark-haired, smiling. With each successive page, the face grew younger until it was a red, wrinkled baby asleep in hospital blankets.

An adoption certificate.

A birth certificate. Satterwhite, Roland, born July 9, 1984. Mother: Watson, Gwendolyn, aged 17. Father: Satterwhite, Lancelot, aged 15.

Mathilde dropped the book.

[A puzzle she'd thought she'd solved revealed itself to go endlessly on.]

22

MATHILDE HAD ALWAYS BEEN a fist, in truth. Only with Lotto had she been an open hand.

SAME NIGHT; ROTTING TOMATOES. Sallie's perfume lingered, though she and Rachel were dreaming drunkly in the guest rooms above. In the window, a paring of moon. Bottle of wine, kitchen table, dog snoring. Before Mathilde, an expanse of white paper, easy as a child's cheeks. [Write it, Mathilde. Understand.]

Florida, she wrote. Summer. 1980s. Outside, sun blaze unbearable over the ocean. Inside, carpets in beige. Popcorn ceilings. Potholders in the olive kitchen silkscreened with the lewd shape of Florida, mermaids on the left, rockets on the right. Naugahyde recliners; a bestiary of modern American life flashing on the television. Floating alone in the hot cave of the house: a boy and a girl. Twins, barely fifteen. Charles, called Chollie; Gwendolyn, called Gwennie.

[Odd, how easy it all is to summon. Like a pain from a dream. A life you'd imagined so long that it had almost become a memory; this middle-class American childhood of the eighties that you'd never had.]

In her room, the girl rubbed Vaseline on her lips, face blooming white breath in the mirror.

She would emerge in pink pajamas when the father came home, her wild curly hair in two braids, and warm up the dinner she'd saved for him, some chicken and a boiled vegetable. She'd yawn and pretend sleep. Keeping their father company in the kitchen, her brother would imagine the metamorphosis inside his sister's bedroom: legs peeled, pale in the miniskirt, eyes darkened with makeup. A strange creature, so different from the sister he knew, breaching into the night through the window.

Her nighttime changes were not despite the fear; they were about it. Small even for a fifteen-year-old, she could have been held down by any passing boy. A refutation of the girl who had already studied calculus, who had won science fairs by building her own robots. She went shivering down the dark streets, toward the convenience store, feeling acutely the untouched place under her skirt. She walked it down the aisles. Burt Bacharach; the cashier watching her with open mouth, skin piebald with vitiligo. Man in a white jumpsuit, watching her in the soda section, jangling the change in his pocket. *Get me one a those,* he ordered, but about the greasy spinning hot dog. Under the angry moth light outside, three or four kids were flipping their skate-boards. She didn't know them. They were older, college-aged though she doubted—greasy hair, baja hoodies—they were in college. She stood by the pay phone, dipping her finger in and out of the coin slot. No change, no change, no change. Slowly, one came closer. Bright blue eyes under a monobrow.

Debatable how long the seduction took. The smarter the girl, the swifter these things go. Physical forwardness as intellectual high-wire act: the pleasure not of pleasure but of performance and revenge against the retainer, the flute, the stack of expectations. Sex as rebellion against the way things should be. [Sounds familiar? It is. No story on earth more common.]

For nearly a year, a besotment of fingers and tongues. Out the window in the dark she went, again and again; and school came and debate team and band practice. Slow solidification beneath the ribs like rubber cement exposed to air. The body knows what the brain refutes. She wasn't dumb. That year she was lucky in fashion: sweatshirts worn huge, to the knees. The mother came home late on Christmas Eve. The girl came out on Christmas morning in her flannel nightgown and the mother turned, singing. She saw her daughter, the bulge at the waist, and dropped the monkey bread she'd been making.

The girl was taken to a cool place. Nobody was unkind. Her insides were scrubbed. Voices soft. She left, not the same girl as she'd been when she went in.

[The lives of others come together in fragments. A light shining off a separate story can illuminate what had remained dark. Brains are miraculous; humans storytelling creatures. The shards draw themselves together and make something whole.]

The twins turned sixteen in the spring. There were the new locks outside her door, on the windows. Her brother suddenly three inches taller than she. He began to follow her around, a goofy-looking shadow. "Play Monopoly?" he'd say, as she crossed through the room one of the dull Saturday nights. "Don't worry about me," she said. She was grounded, she had to murmur to the skateboarding boys who hung around the school gates waiting, to the girls she'd known since kindergarten, who'd wanted her to join them watching *The Dark Crystal* and eating Jiffy Pop and crimping their hair. She was always more popular than her twin, but soon a whiff of sex sullied her. She had only her brother. Then Michael.

MICHAEL WAS BEAUTIFUL, half Japanese, tall and dreamy with a fashionable slab of black hair over one eye. In class, Gwennie had spent weeks surreptitiously imagining her tongue licking the pale skin of his inner wrist. He dreamt of boys; Gwennie dreamt of him. Chollie liked him grudgingly; her brother required absolutes: loyalty, generosity, things Michael couldn't give. But the marijuana he shared relaxed Chollie enough to make him begin to crack jokes, to smile. So it passed until the end of school. Her mother in San Diego, Milwaukee, Binghamton; she was a traveling nurse who took care of babies almost too tender to survive.

They met Lotto. Painfully tall, face blitzed with acne, his sweet boy's heart. Summer stretched out before them: different drugs, beer, huffing glue, all fair game as long as the twins were home for dinner. Gwennie was the center of this circle; the boys spun around her, satellites.

[Such a brief time, this ménage à quatre. Only all summer tipping into October, but it changed everything.]

On the crenellations of the old Spanish fort, they did whippets with stolen cans. St. Augustine with its herds of tourists shining below. Michael sunbathed, twitching to the music from the tape deck, the glorious smoothness of that body. Lotto and Chollie were in deep conversation as usual. The sea below winking light. She needed them to look at her. She stood on her hands at the edge of the fort, a forty-foot drop into death. She'd done gymnastics until her body turned traitor with boobs; she held the pose. From upside down, their faces against the blue, her brother standing up in fear. She came down and almost passed out from blood to the brain, but sat. The pulse so loud in her ears she didn't hear what he was saying, just waved her hand, and said, "Chill the fuck out, Choll. I know what I'm doing."

Lotto laughed. Michael's abs flexing to look at Lotto. Gwennie looking at the abs.

In early October, they spent a Saturday on the beach. Their father had begun trusting her again, or trusting Chollie to keep her in line, and had flown off to Sacramento to be with their mother for the weekend. Two free days like an open mouth. They drank beer all day in the sun and passed out, and when she woke, she was burnt all over and it was sunset and Lotto had started building something enormous with sand, already four feet high and ten feet long and pointing toward the sea. Woozy, standing, she asked what it was. He said,

"Spiral jetty." She said, "In sand?" He smiled and said, "That's its beauty." A moment in her bursting open, expanding. She looked at him. She hadn't seen it before, but there was something special here. She wanted to tunnel inside him to understand what it was. There was a light under the shyness and youth. A sweetness. A sudden surge of the old hunger in her to take a part of him into her and make him briefly hers.

Instead, she bent and helped, they all did, and deep into the morning when it was done, they sat in silence, huddled against the cold wind, and watched the tide swallow it whole. Everything had changed, somehow. They went home.

The next day, Sunday. Sunrise sandwiches eaten over the sink, bleed of yolk. Bed until three in the afternoon. When she came out to eat, Chollie had sunburn blisters on his face, but he smiled. "I scored some acid," he said, the only way to bear the party at the abandoned house beside the swamp that night. She felt a pang of fear. "Great," she said coolly. They took burgers to the beach again. Where the lifeguard's chair had been buried at the end of their spiral jetty, it was dug out, set upright, like a raised middle finger. She abstained from the drug, but the boys partook. The strange thing between Lotto and her sharpened. He stood close to her. Chollie climbed atop the lifeguard chair and stood against the stars, shouting, holding up a handle of rum. "We are gods!" he said. Tonight, she believed it. Her future was one of those stars, cold and brilliant and sure. She would do something world-bending. She knew it. She laughed at her brother, shining in the bonfire and starlight, and then Chollie gave a shriek and jumped, hovering for a long time like a pelican, with his flabby neck, his awkward limbs, in midair. He landed with a crack. And then her brother's screams, and she held his head, and Lotto sprinted off to get his aunt's car, and when he drove up the beach, Michael picked Chollie up in his arms and threw him into the backseat and jumped into the driver's side and took off without Gwennie or Lotto.

Desolate, they watched the taillights go up the ramp to the road. With Chollie's screams removed, the wind was too loud.

She asked Lotto to come with her to tell her dad, and he said of course. [Lo, that sweet young heart.]

At home, she washed off her makeup, took out the piercings, braided her hair in two tails, put on a pink sweatsuit. He'd never seen her plain but he held in his laugh, kindly. The father's flight came in at seven, and at seven-twenty, his car pulled under the porte cochere. He walked in the door with discontent pouring off him: it must have been a bad weekend with the twins' mother, their marriage as thin as a thread. Lotto was already inches taller than the older man, but her father filled the room and Lotto took a step back.

Her father's face, so furious. "Gwennie, I told you, no boys in the house. Get him out of here."

"Daddy, this is Lotto, he's Chollie's friend, Chollie jumped off something and broke his leg, he's in the hospital, Lotto just came a second ago to tell you because we couldn't get in touch with you. I'm sorry," she said.

Her father looked at Lotto. "Charles broke his leg?" he said.

"Yes, sir," Lotto said.

"Was alcohol involved? Drugs?" the father said.

"No, sir," Lotto lied.

"Was Gwennie present?" the father said.

She held her breath. "No, sir," he said smoothly. "I only know her from school. She hangs out with the smart kids."

The father looked at them. Nodded, and the space he took up in the room was suddenly smaller.

"Gwendolyn," the father said, "you call your mother. I'll go to the hospital. Thank you for telling me, boy. Now out."

She shot a look at Lotto, and the father's car pulled out fast, and when Gwennie came out the front door, she'd put on her miniest skirt, the shirt cropped below the boobs, makeup slashed on her face.

Lotto was waiting in the azaleas. "Fuck him," Gwennie said. "We're going to the party."

"You're trouble," he said with admiration.

"You have no idea," she said.

They rode Chollie's bike. She sat on the handlebars and Lotto pedaled. Down the tunnel of the black road, frogs singing mournfully, the rot of marsh rising. He stopped the bike and put his sweatshirt over her. It smelled nice, like fabric softener. Someone at home loved him. Lotto stood on the pedals when they got to coasting, and rested his head on her shoulder, and she leaned back into him. She smelled the astringent on his ravaged cheeks. The house was lit by bonfires, headlights left burning. Already hundreds here, the music deafening. They stood, backs to the splintery siding, drinking beer that was mostly foam. She felt Lotto looking at her. She pretended not to notice. He came close to her ear as if to whisper, but he was, what? Licking her? A separate shock went through her and she marched toward the fire. "What the fuck," she said, and punched a shoulder very hard. The head rose, the mouth smeary, Michael. He had pulled his face away from the blond head of some girl.

"Oh, hey, Gwennie," Michael said. "Lotto, my man."

"What the fuck?" Gwennie said again. "You're supposed to be with my brother. With Chollie."

"Oh, no," Michael said. "I booked it when your dad got there. He's one scary-ass dude. This chick gave me a ride," he said.

"I'm Lizzie. I'm a candy striper on the weekends?" she said. She nuzzled her face into Michael's chest.

"Whoa," Lotto whispered. "That's a girl."

Gwennie seized Lotto's hand and pulled him into the house. Candles on the windowsills and flashlights that cupped light on the wall and bodies on mattresses someone had dragged in here for the purpose, bare asses and backs and limbs shining. Knot of music from separate rooms. She took him up the stairs to the window that led out to the porch roof. They sat in the cool night, hearing the party thump, able to see only a glare of firelight. They shared a cigarette in silence, and she wiped her face and kissed him. Their teeth knocked. He'd spoken of makeout parties wherever he'd come from in the boonies, but she hadn't really expected he'd know what to do with his mouth and tongue. Indeed he did. She felt the old swoon in the joints. She took his hand and pressed it against her, let him slide his fingers beneath the elastic to feel how wet she'd gotten. She pushed him on his back. She straddled his legs, took his penis out into the air, watched it grow, put him in. And he gasped up, astonished, then grabbed her hips and really went for it. She closed her eyes. Lotto's hands pushed her shirt up and bra cup down so that her boobs pinched out like rockets. There was a new thing, a terrific heat, heat like the center of the sun. She didn't remember such heat from all the other times. He lurched into her and she felt him leaving and she opened her eyes to see him rolling, face full of terror, over the side of the porch, and falling down. She looked around and saw in the window a curtain of fire. She jumped, her skirt flipping up, what he'd left in her leaking as she fell.

[Something wrong in getting turned on, summoning this dead girl, this dead boy, so they can fuck.]

At the jail, she shivered all night. Her mother and father were grim, set, when she came home.

Lotto was gone for a week, then two, then a month, and Chollie found a letter on his nightstand saying that Lotto's mother had sent him off to an all-boys' boarding school, poor sucker. He told Gwennie but she'd stopped caring. The entire party, the firemen, and the police officer had all seen the way Gwennie and Lotto had monkeyed themselves. The whole school knew she was a slut. End-stop. Pariahed. Michael didn't know what to say; he drifted away, found other friends. Gwennie stopped talking.

In spring, when her condition became impossible to ignore again, the twins stole the neighbor's car. His fault for keeping the keys in the ignition. They came up the drive, pondering the sago palms and grasses, the tiny pink box on stilts. Chollie made a sound of disappointment; he'd hoped that Lotto's family was insanely rich, but it didn't appear so. [One never can tell.] Sea oxeye daisies taunted, nipplelike in the grass. They knocked on the door. A tiny and severe-looking woman opened it, her mouth pressed thin. "Lancelot's not here," she said. "You should know that."

"We're here to see Antoinette," Chollie said. He felt his sister's hand on his arm.

"I was heading out for groceries. Well, you might as well come in," she said. "I'm Sallie. Lancelot's aunt."

They had been sitting for ten minutes, drinking the iced tea and picking at the sable cookies when a door opened and a woman came out. She was tall, grand, plump, her hair heaped elaborately atop her head. There was something feathery about her, the gauze of her clothes, the way she moved her hands, something disarmingly soft. "How pleasant," she murmured. "We weren't expecting guests."

Chollie smirked in his chair, reading her, hating what he read.

Gwennie found Antoinette's eyes on her and made a twisting motion with her hands to show her stomach.

On Antoinette's face, an expression like a paper blazing into fire. Then she smiled brightly. "I suppose my son had something to do with that. He does love girls. Oh, dear."

Chollie sat forward to say something, but out of her bedroom waddled a baby in a diaper, her hair in twin puffs. He closed his mouth. Antoinette put the baby on her knee and sang, "Say hello, Rachel!" and wagged the baby's fat hand at the twins. Rachel chewed on her fist, watching the visitors with her anxious brown eyes.

"So what is it you want of me?" Antoinette said. "Ending a pregnancy sends a girl directly to hell, you know. I will not pay for one."

"We want justice," Chollie said.

"Justice?" Antoinette said mildly. "We all want justice. And world peace. Frolicking unicorns. What do you mean precisely, little boy?"

"You call me little boy again, you fat hog, and I'll punch you in the fucking mouth," he said.

"You only show spiritual poverty when you swear, little boy," she said. "My son, bless his pure heart, would never be so vulgar."

"Fuck you, cunt-face hag," he said.

"Darling," Antoinette said very softly, putting her hand on Chollie's, stopping him short with her touch. "It does you credit to fight for your sister. But unless you would like me to take a cleaver to your manhood, I suggest you wait in the car. Your sister and I will come to an agreement without you."

Chollie paled, opened his mouth, opened his hands, closed them, and then walked out the door and sat in the car with the window open, listening to sixties pop on the radio for an hour.

Alone, Antoinette and Gwennie smiled politely at Rachel until the baby waddled back into the bedroom again. "Here's what we'll do," Antoinette said, leaning forward. Gwennie would tell her brother and parents that she'd had an abortion. One week later, she would run away, although, in fact, she would go to an apartment in St. Augustine. It would all be arranged through Antoinette's lawyers. She would be cared for as long as she stayed inside. Also arranged would be the adoption. After the birth, Gwennie would leave the baby in the hospital and walk back into her own life. She would never breathe a word to anybody or else the monthly allowances would cease.

[Echoes everywhere. Painful, the backstage manipulations, how money trumps heart. Good. Press the finger into the wound; bear down.]

The girl listened to the ocean, muted through the window. Rachel came in again and pressed the button for the television and sat, sucking her thumb, on the carpet. Gwennie watched her, wanting to hurt this woman who reeked of roses, baby powder. At last, Gwennie looked at Antoinette without smiling. "You won't acknowledge your own grandchild?" she said.

"Lancelot will have a brilliant future," she said. "Less brilliant if this happens. A mother's job is to prop open all possible doors for her children. Besides, there will be likelier candidates to bear his children." She paused, smiled sweetly. "Likelier children as a result."

Inside Gwennie's stomach, a snake was twisting. "Fine," she said.

[How much of this is supposition, projection? All. None. You hadn't been there. But you knew Antoinette, how her lazy sweetness belied ferocity. She would say this speech again, though the dart would miss its target the second time. Oh, yes. You knew Antoinette in your bones.]

In the car again. Chollie drove and felt queasy, watching his sister cry into her elbow. "You tell her to go to hell?" he said. He would sue that warthog for everything she had, screw the fact that she was Lotto's mother. He'd take her for all she was worth and live in that beach house for the rest of his life, exulting, rich.

Gwennie took away her arm, and said, "Money for silence. Don't fight me. I signed the contract."

He tried to say with his own wordlessness what he wouldn't say aloud, but she was having none of it. "I liked her," she said, though this was terribly untrue.

They showed up at their parents' house because there was nowhere else they wanted to be. Okra and chicken and cornbread from a box, their mother dropping her spatula, coming over with open arms. Gwennie announced both the pregnancy and the termination over butterscotch pudding. It was for Chollie, so he wouldn't meddle. Her father put his forehead on the edge of the kitchen table, wept there. Her mother stood without speaking and flew the next morning to El Paso for work. It was easy for Gwennie to pretend to run away. She packed a small duffel and climbed into the car that came for her when she should have been at school, and was installed in a two-room apartment, all oatmeal carpet and plastic mugs, and was visited by a nurse every week and had groceries show up at the door and as much television as she could process, which was perfectly welcome, since she couldn't have read a book if there had been one anywhere around, which there probably wasn't, not in this entire sad condo complex with its turquoise fountains, dyed red cypress mulch.

The baby took. It took from her bones and took from her youth day by day. Gwennie ate little, watched talk shows all day. *Dear Lotto,* she wrote once to the boy banished to cold northern misery, but half the words were already a lie so she tore up the letter and put it below the coffee filter in the trashcan. Only floating in the bathtub gave relief.

Her life had paused; but in fast-forward the baby was born. Gwennie had an epidural; it was a dream. Her personal nurse came to the hospital and did everything. She put the baby in Gwennie's arms, but when she left the room, Gwennie put the baby back in the bassinet. They wheeled him away and kept bringing him back even though she told them not to. Her body healed. Her breasts hardened. Two days, three days. Green Jell-O in cups and American cheese on bread. One day, she signed a paper and the baby was gone. There was an envelope full of cash in her backpack. She came out of the hospital to blazing July heat. She was beyond empty.

She walked all the way home, more than ten miles. She came in the house to find Chollie in the kitchen, drinking Kool-Aid. He dropped his cup. He turned red in the face and screamed at her, that their parents had filed a police report, that their dad spent all night every night casing the streets, that Chollie had nightmares of her being raped. She shrugged and put her backpack down and went into the rec room to turn on the television. After some time, he brought her scrambled eggs and toast and sat beside her, watching the light move on her face. Weeks passed. Her body worked independently of her brain, which was elsewhere, in another hemisphere. There was something dragging at her, an anchor snagged on something invisible below. It took great effort to move.

Her parents were gentle. They let her skip school, took her to a therapist. It didn't matter. She lay in bed. "Gwennie," her brother said, "you need to get help." There was no point. Her brother, without looking at her, took her hand. So gently, so tenderly, that she wasn't embarrassed. Weeks passed since she'd showered. She was too tired to eat. "You stink," Chollie said angrily. You always stink, she thought but didn't say. Chollie was worried, gone now only during school hours. Her father only during work. The overlap when she was alone was three hours, short. On a day when she had more energy than usual, she called Michael's neighbor who sold drugs. He came, looked at her matted hair, her little girl's nightgown, seemed reluctant to hand over the paper bag. She thrust money into his hands, slammed the door in his face. She put the bag between her mattress and box spring. Day after day, all the same. Sticky fringe of dust on the blade edge of the overhead fans. Enough.

Chollie had showed her his stash of Ecstasy and slyly said, "This is how my quest for world dominance begins." Said he'd be out all night selling at a rave, would she be okay? "Go," she said, "make your money." He went. Their father was in his room, sleeping. Now she put the envelope of Antoinette's cash under her brother's pillow and considered it; then she changed his smelly sheets and placed the money under the pillow again. She took the bag of drugs from under her own mattress and swallowed one pill and waited for it to seize her, then shook the whole bottle in her mouth and swallowed the pills with milk from the carton. The ache began in her stomach.

Already woozy. The air had turned muddy. She collapsed into bed. Vaguely, she heard her father leave for work. Sleep stole over her like waves. In the waves, a sweetness, a peace.

[Go ahead and weep into your wine, angry woman, half a life away. What do you hope will follow you out of the dark? Morning coming into the window as every day it does, the dog waking on her bed out of dreams of chipmunks; but there is no such thing as resurrection. Still, you did it anyway, didn't you, brought the poor girl back. Now what are you going to do? Here she is before you, as alive as she'll ever be, and your apology would never have meant a thing.]

Chollie came home to a heavy silence and knew something was wrong. The father away at work, Chollie overdue because of the concert. He stood in the door, hearing nothing, then he ran. Found what he found. Everything in him flipped over. He waited for the ambulance, and as he waited, the plan emerged, what he would do, the years it would take. He slid his sister's head on his lap and held it there. From a mile away, the sound. The sirens.

IT WAS DAWN, a thin pale spreading over the distance. Mathilde was shaking, but not from cold. She pitied them, the cowardly ones. Because she, too, despaired; she, too, was blinded by the dark, but to turn your back is too easy. Cheating. The handful, the cold glass, the swallow. The chair kicked back, the burn on the skin of the throat. A minute of pain, then stillness. Despicable, such lack of pride. Better to feel it all. Better the long, slow burn.

Mathilde's heart was a bitter one, vengeful and quick. [True.]

Mathilde's heart was a kindly one. [True.]

Mathilde thought of Land's gorgeous back, muscled and long, the spine a delicate splitting serration. It had been Lotto's back as well. The lips, the cheekbones, the eyelashes, all the same. The ghost manifest in the living flesh. She could give the boy this gift. If not father or mother, still blood, an uncle. Chollie had known Lotto second best, after all; he could tell Land about Lotto, summon a person out of what, to Land, had just been details, gleanings: interviews, plays, a brief moment with the widow, but Mathilde knew how closed off she was, how she'd shown him only her body, nothing real. Chollie could bring Gwennie to him, a mother. Mathilde could leave Land with something living. She could give Land and his uncle time.

She stood. The thing that had given her lightness these past months had fled, and her bones felt made of granite, her skin stretched like an old tarp over them. She hefted the box, feeling all the weight of Chollie's evil in her arms, and set it in the sink.

She lit a match and watched its blue edge suck down the stick, and for a moment, the lightness returned, the breath to blow out the flame just behind her lips—fuck it, Chollie deserved the worst for what he'd done to Lotto in his last days, the doubt he'd created—but something stopped her breath. [Internal; not us.] Just before the flame singed her skin, she dropped the match onto the box. She watched the papers burn, bereft, her curse on Chollie going up in a tongue of smoke. She would send a letter in her own hand, later, to both men. Land could call his newfound uncle every day of his life. He would. Chollie would host Land's wedding at his palace by the sea. Chollie would be at Land's children's graduations, would drive up in the Porsches he'd give them. Land would be loved.

"That's not nothing," she said aloud.

The dog woke, screaming at the smoke. When Mathilde looked up from the charred mess, the small, dark girl she'd summoned had gone.

23

DECADES LATER, the nursemaid would come into the tea room in Mathilde's house. [Blue canvas on the wall; a cool, twilit sense of being young and lovelorn.] She would carry a platter of the cakes that were the only thing Mathilde would eat anymore. She would talk, this woman, talk and talk, because there was a smile on Mathilde's lips. But when she touched her, the nursemaid would find the old woman gone. No breath. Skin cooling. The last spark in Mathilde's brain was pulling her toward the sea, the raspy beach, a fiery love like a torch in the night almost imperceptible down the shoreline.

Chollie, who heard the news an hour later, took a flight. In the middle of the morning, he outsmarted the locks of Mathilde's flat in London and came in with his halting, panting steps. He was as fat and antique these days as a potbellied stove. Through everything, he survived, like the rats, the jellyfish, the cockroaches would. He took the three slender books that Mathilde had written to an echoing lack of acclaim and put them in his bag. [*Alazon, Eiron, Bomolochos*; she was sly but unsubtle in this. In a room in his house the rest of the print runs sat in cardboard boxes, being eaten by cockroaches.] Though he was old, he was as sharp as ever. He poured bourbon, then neglected the glass and took the bottle to the attic with him. He spent a night paging through the valuable first drafts of Lancelot Satterwhite's plays in their careful archival boxes, searching for the first ludicrously yellowed printed-out draft of *The Springs*. It would be worth more than this entire house. He wouldn't find it. It was no longer kin of the other plays, having left Mathilde decades earlier one dawn, filched by the hand of a young man who had woken in shame and fury in an alien house, who had let the dog out in the dark to pee and made fruit salad and coffee without turning on the light. He had slid the papers under his shirt, had warmed them with his skin as he drove back to the city. In the end, it didn't matter. Land had had a claim as strong as any, it is true; a boy who had explained the theft in a letter he'd tucked in a great blue bowl full of ripening tomatoes, a boy who had felt in his bones what only one other person had truly known.

Two years a widow, Mathilde went to see Land in New Jersey. A production of *The Tempest*. He'd been Caliban. He acquitted himself well, but alas, there was no spark. The children of geniuses rarely being geniuses, et cetera. His greatest talent was the gorgeous face he hid behind the latex.

After the curtain call, she walked into the dusk. She hadn't disguised herself, thinking there would have been no need; she was a healthy weight, her hair had returned, and it was a natural soft brown. But there he was in front of the theater, smoking a cigarette in his lumpy makeup, the hump on his back, the rags. "What did you think, Mathilde?" he called across the eddy of people leaving for dinner, for the babysitter, for a drink.

The look he gave her. Christ. It was as if he could see into her dark heart and was sickened to death by what he saw.

Well, it's true, Lotto had the same moral rigidity. Had he known— all that she had done, all that she was, the anger sparking like lightning under her skin, the times when she would hear him boast at some party, jovially drunk, and hate the words coming out of that beautiful mouth, how she wanted to incinerate the shoes he kicked off everywhere, the lazy way he had with people's swift and delicate feelings, the ego heavier than the granite slab their house was hitched to, how she was sometimes sick of his body that had once been hers, the smell of the body, the flab on the waist, the unsightly hairs of that body that was now bones—would he have forgiven her? Oh, Christ, of course he would.

She stopped still. Stand straight, she told herself. She gave poor Land her largest smile. "Don't lose heart. Onward!" she said.

She saw his face again and again as she drove back fast through the night to get home to her house, her dog. How ugly a handsome man can sometimes be. Perhaps Land was a far better actor than she'd ever believed him to be; better, for sure, than Lotto had been. Well, she knew what that was like.

EMPTY THEATERS ARE MORE SILENT than other empty places. When theaters sleep, they dream of noise and light and motion. She found only one door unlocked to the street and stepped out of the freezing wind. Even now, bird-bone Danica and pretty Susannah were exhausting their small talk, waving off the waiter, almost ready to start badmouthing Mathilde for standing them up. So be it. All day at work she'd felt a ratcheting of anxiety, and when Lancelot wouldn't answer her texts, when he didn't come home, she went to find him. *Gacy* on the marquee. Play about evil, corroding him internally. She followed the faint traces of his voice through the backstage, hands out, shuffling, to feel her way in the dark; she wouldn't turn on a light and warn him she was there. At last she was in the wings, and there he was onstage, of course, in dim light, saying:

> *Poor honest lord, brought low by his own heart,*
> *Undone by goodness! Strange, unusual blood,*
> *When man's worst sin is, he does too much good!*
> *Who, then, dares to be half so kind again?*
> *For bounty, that makes gods, does still mar men.*

It took her to the end of the scene to identify it: *Timon of Athens*. Her least favorite Shakespeare. He started the next scene. Oh. He was doing the whole play. Alone. To nobody.

She was safe in the darkness, and there allowed herself to smile at him—ludicrous, sweet man—and the smile expanded alarmingly in her diaphragm so that she had to breathe deep, stern breaths to keep from laughing. Because look at him, too tall, stalking the stage. Keeping the old dream moribund with these infusions of acting; the old self she thought dead still secretly alive. But stagy, too loud. Not the actor he thought he was.

She stood in the black folds of the curtain, and he finished and bowed and bowed; then he caught his breath and came back down into his body again. He flicked off the lights. He had a light on his cell, and he guided himself out with it, but she was careful to stay away from its dim circle. He passed close by her and she caught a whiff of him: sweat and coffee and his own human smell, and maybe bourbon to loosen him. She waited until the door echoed closed, and then she came more swiftly through the dark by feel, outside into the icy street, and jumped into a cab and raced him home. When he came in, it was only minutes after her, but she'd smelled the winter in his hair when he leaned his head against her neck. She held his head gently, feeling his secret happiness moving in him.

LATER, UNDER HER NOM DE PLUME, she wrote a play called *Volumnia*. It played in a fifty-seat theater. She gave it her all.

[She shouldn't have been surprised when nobody came.]

24

So long ago, and she had been so little then. There was a long darkness between what she remembered and the results. There was something ajar here. A four-year-old is still an infant. It seemed too harsh to hate a baby for being a baby, for making a baby's mistake.

Perhaps it was always there; perhaps it was made in explanation, but all along she had held within her a second story underneath the first, waging a terrible and silent battle with her certainty. She had to believe of herself that the better story was the true one, even if the worse was insistent.

She was four years old, and she heard her brother playing upstairs in her grandmother's house when the rest of the family was eating pheasants her father had shot that morning. In the window, the family was gathered under the tree, baguettes and cassoulet on the table, wine. Her mother's rosy face was tipped back, sun full on her skin. Her father was feeding Bibiche a morsel. Her grandmother's mouth was more dash than *n*, signaling happiness. The wind was rising, the leaves shushing. There was a smell of good manure on the air and a delicious *far Breton* waiting clammy on the countertop for dessert. She was on the potty, trying to go, but her brother was more interesting with his songs and thumps above. He was supposed to be sleeping. Bad boy, he would not.

The girl went up the stairs, gathering dust with her fingertip.

She opened the door to the room. Her baby brother saw her and crowed with happiness. *Come on,* she said. He tottered out. She followed him to the stairs, golden old oak shining from the slippers that buffed it up and down, day after day.

Her brother stood at the top of the steps, wobbly, his hands reaching for hers, sure she would help him. He pressed up against her. But instead of taking his hand in hers, she moved her leg where it was touching him. She didn't mean to, not really, well, maybe some of her meant it, perhaps she did. He tottered. And then she watched the baby tumble slowly down the stairs, his head like a coconut, *thump-a-bump* all the way down.

The still knot of him at the bottom. Thrown laundry.

When she looked up, she saw the ten-year-old cousin where she hadn't seen her before, standing in the door of the upstairs bathroom, gaping.

This was the bad version. This version was what later events told her had happened. It was as real as the other. They played simultaneously in a loop.

Yet Mathilde could never quite believe it. That twitch of a leg a later insertion, surely. She could not believe and yet something in her did believe, and this contradiction that she held within her became the source of everything.

All that remained were the facts. Before it all happened, she had been so beloved. Afterward, love had been withdrawn. And she had pushed or she hadn't; the result was all the same. There had been no forgiveness for her. But she'd been so very young. And how was it possible, how could parents do this, how could she not have been forgiven?

25

IT WAS MATHEMATICAL, marriage. Not, as one might expect, additional. It was exponential.

This one man nervous in a suit a size too small for his long, lean self. This woman in a green lace dress cut to the upper thigh with a white rose behind her ear. Christ, so young.

The woman before them was a Unitarian minister and on her buzzed scalp the gray hairs shone in the swab of sun through the lace in the window. Outside, Poughkeepsie was waking. Behind them, a man in a custodian's uniform cried softly beside a man in pajamas with a dachshund: their witnesses. A shine in everyone's eye. One could taste the love on the air. Or maybe that was sex. Or maybe it was all the same then.

"I do," she said. "I do," he said. They did; they would.

Our children will be so fucking beautiful, he thought, looking at her.

Home, she thought, looking at him.

"You may kiss," said the officiant. They did; would.

Now they thanked everyone and laughed, and papers were signed, and congratulations offered, and all stood for a moment unwilling to leave this genteel living room where there was such softness. The newlyweds thanked everyone again shyly and went out the door into the cool morning. They laughed, rosy. In they'd come, integers; out they came, squared.

———

HER LIFE. In the window the parakeet. Scrap of blue midday in the London dusk. Ages away from what had been most deeply lived. Day on a rocky beach, creatures in the tide pool. All those ordinary afternoons, listening to footsteps in the beams of the house and knowing the feeling behind them.

Because it's true: more than the highlights, the bright events, it was in the small and the daily where she'd found life. The hundreds of times she'd dug in the soil of her garden, each time the satisfying chew of spade through soil, so often that this action, the pressure and release and rich dirt smell, delineated the warmth she'd found in that house in the cherry orchard. Or this: every day they woke in the same place, her husband waking her up with a cup of coffee, the cream still swirling into the black. Almost unremarked upon, this kindness. He would kiss her on the crown of her head before leaving, and she'd feel something in her rising through her body to meet him. These silent intimacies made their marriage, not the ceremonies or parties or opening nights or occasions or spectacular fucks.

Anyway, that part was finished. A pity. Her hands warming on tea looked like clumps of knitting a child had felted in grubby palms. Enough decades and a body slowly twists into one great cramp. But there was a time, once, when she had been sexy, and if not sexy, at least odd-looking enough to compel. Through this clear window, she could see how good it all had been. She had no regrets.

[That's not true, Mathilde; the whisper in the ear.]

Oh. Christ. Yes, there was one. Solitary, gleaming. A regret.

It was that, all her life, she had said *no*. From the beginning, she had let so few people in. That first night, his young face glowing up at hers in the black light, bodies beating the air around them, and inside her there was the unexpected sharp recognition; oh, *this*, a sudden peace arriving for her, she who hadn't been at peace since she was so little. Out of nowhere. Out of this surprising night with its shatters of lightning in the stormy black campus outside, with the heat and song and sex and animal fear inside. He had seen her and made the leap and swum through the crowd and had taken her hand, this bright boy who was giving her a place to rest. He offered not only his whole laughing self, the past that built him and the warm beating body that moved her with its beauty and the future she felt compressed and waiting, but also the torch he carried before him in the dark, his understanding, dazzling, instant, that there was goodness at her core. With the gift came the bitter seed of regret, the unbridgeable gap between the Mathilde she was and the Mathilde he had seen her to be. A question, in the end, of vision.

She wished she'd been the kind Mathilde, the good one. His idea of her. She would have looked smiling down at him; she would have heard beyond *Marry me* to the world that spun behind the words. There would have been no pause, no hesitation. She would have laughed, touched his face for the first time. Felt his warmth in the palm of her hand. *Yes,* she would have said. *Sure.*

ACKNOWLEDGMENTS

My gratitude begins with Clay, whom I saw for the first time in 1997 when he exited the crew room at Amherst College with his long black ponytail, and I turned, stunned, to my friend and said I'd marry him, even though I didn't believe in marriage. The book began its life on the page at the MacDowell Colony, with the help of the work of Anne Carson, Evan S. Connell, Jane Gardam, Thomas Mann, William Shakespeare, and too many others to list; it was made immeasurably better as it traveled through the hands of my agent, Bill Clegg, and brilliant friends Jami Attenberg, Kevin A. González, Elliott Holt, Dana Spiotta, Laura van den Berg, and Ashley Warlick. Riverhead provided it (and me) a warm new home, and I'm grateful to everyone there, especially Jynne Martin and Sarah McGrath, who awes me with her unflappable calm and astonishingly bull's-eye edits. Bless the fact-checkers and copy editors of the world, all of them. Bless, too, the readers of this book. While we're at it, bless the readers of all books. Beckett and Heath are my purest joys, my stays against despair, but so are the people who take care of them so I can work. And if this book begins with Clay, it also ends with him: the ponytail has been shaved off and we're older and slower, and though I am still ambivalent about marriage, I can't believe my luck in ours.